THE IMAGE OF OUR LORD

THE IMAGE OF OUR LORD

Edward Burman

St. Martin's Press
New York

Library of Congress Cataloging-in-Publication Data
Burman, Edward.
    The image of Our Lord / Edward Burman.
        p.   cm.
    ISBN 0-312-05876-4
        1. Templars—History—Fiction.   2. Inquisition—Fiction.
    I. Title.
PR6052.U654I4   1991
823'.914—dc20   90-28770
                                                                        CIP

First published in Great Britain by Barrie & Jenkins Limited.

First U.S. Edition: May 1991
10   9   8   7   6   5   4   3   2   1

For Nadia and Nicholas

·——— Prologue ———·

'It's now ten years since the decease of your father, I believe.'

'Decease? That's a fine word, typical of you churchmen. Murder is more like it.' The young man instantly regretted the sharp edge to his voice, but hours of discussion and diplomatic compliments had worn down his usual veneer of deference.

His host smiled, and ran his forefinger inside his finely starched ecclesiastical collar. 'Come, you know full well I loved your father as no man but yourself.' He shifted his bulk across the broad leather chair, and mopped perspiration from his brow. 'Then the wound still runs deep?'

'Noble blood never ceases to run, my lord, even after death. It is perpetuated in name and honour.'

'Sire Nicolas de Lirey. It sounds well. Even without lands,' the older man agreed.

Nicolas rose to his feet. He had not ridden as far as Avignon simply to have his father's memory denigrated. 'The lands are ours in God's eye, my lord. The bastard King of France is a mere trespasser, both on this earth and on my land.'

This reaction seemed to delight the host, whose eyes flickered with pleasure. 'There is no need to inform a man of the Church of God's opinion,' he admonished the young man. His chubby fingers fondled a bronze crucifix set with a single giant ruby.

Nicolas needed little reminding. It was a strong-willed and powerful man who could walk through the corridors of the headquarters of the Inquisition lightly. In spite of Lord Bernard de Caen's affection for his late father, and the warm and sincere welcome, it was hard to forget that this man was one of the most ruthless in the Holy Roman Church, the Inquisitor-General for Provence and reputed head of the most secret organization in the Church, the feared *Opus Christi*. It was said there were no limits its members would not go to to preserve the power of the Church. The austere vaulted room, the vast oak table which served as desk, the piled bundles of trial transcripts on another table,

1

the scene of St Sebastian's violent death painted vividly on wooden panels behind Bernard as if to intimidate his visitors, the very air which seemed heavy as though it bore the weight of the damned souls who had passed through it to their eternal penance, all served to inculcate respect and fear. It was hard to reconcile this accumulation of palpable terror with the jolly man he could remember holding him as a child.

Bernard waited, almost as though he desired his guest to reflect upon these things. Then, after a long pause, he spoke again: 'The question is, what are you prepared to do about it? I knew and loved your father, and would hope to find the same blood flowing in your veins.'

'You will, Lord Abbot. I will do anything to avenge him and regain the lands at Lirey for my family.'

'Anything?'

Nicolas regarded him closely. The corpulent body seemed throttled inside its tight black habit, with pearl buttons resisting but tearing the fine cloth. Such constriction increased the ruddiness of the abbot's face, the colour of morning sun through thick ground mist. He looked liked nothing more than an aged putto, curly locks long since gone and represented only by wisps of reddish hair which fell at random over the bald crown. Boys would laugh at this rotund, perspiring figure like a perambulating turnip were it not for the eyes, small piercing eyes with large irises the colour of spring grass, that drilled into a man's soul like a dagger in sand. His father had told him that Bernard's arrival in a tribunal had once been enough to drive an innocent man to confess the most heretical depravations. That was twenty years ago, before his hair was lost and his body bloated. But Nicolas knew from his own experience that even now boys never laughed, but shrank back on the Inquisitor-General's rare walks through the city. Now he heard the keen edge to Bernard's voice and knew he was in earnest. Whatever Bernard had in mind, it might be the chance for which he had been waiting so many years. The summons had certainly been urgent enough.

'Yes, anything,' Nicolas said, with an assurance that was spoken from his heart.

'Good.' Bernard clasped his hands in pleasure, then leaned forward onto the table which separated them. 'So you will accept the delicate task I have outlined to you? It requires someone I can trust totally, as if with my own life. And after your poor dead father there is no better person than you.'

Again the compliments. Nicolas bowed his head.

2

'But of course you will need a trained inquisitor.' Bernard raised his right hand, palm forwards, in an attempt to silence the protest he saw coming. Beads of perspiration glistened in a spiralling shaft of sunlight.

'Me? Work with an inquisitor? Isn't that tantamount to acting as a delator?' Nicolas asked disdainfully.

Bernard sighed. 'When the future of the Christian world is at stake such words have no meaning. This inquisitor is a young man I've been watching for some time, and perhaps the most brilliant theologian I know.'

'But he doesn't know the full story?'

'There are certain things he would not understand yet. And any hint at what he must search for might put him off track. It's his intuition I wish to exploit.'

This made little sense to Nicolas. 'Why not provide him with more background, such as you gave me earlier?'

'Because he's brilliant and persistent. A dangerous combination.'

Nicolas thought this over, trying to conjure up an image of this man. 'Is he ambitious?'

'Not yet, but that will come when he begins to taste power. You must watch him carefully then.'

Nicolas nodded. There was raw power in these words, he thought, and no inquisitor would ever be a match for the Inquisitor-General. Bernard too was a brilliant man, and dangerous, he knew. But there was love as well as power in his gaze. Nothing for *him* to fear. 'Well, let's see this inquisitor then,' he suggested.

Bernard rapped his table with a tiny hammer. An usher appeared in the doorway. 'Bring the inquisitor,' he ordered.

Nicolas rose, and walked to a niche in the wall beneath a large window. There he sat down, leaning back onto large purple cushions. Then the inquisitor entered. From his position in the sun Nicolas knew himself to be invisible, and allowed his eyes to run quickly over his prospective companion. A very ordinary-looking man, neither tall nor short, neither thin nor fat. His face was pale, dough-like rather than of an aristocratic pallor; in strange contrast to this his stance was rustic, like a farmer in his field looking out in search of rain clouds, with feet slightly larger than they ought to be for his height.

Nicolas fancied that under the perfect white habit of the Cistercian Order would be an ill-shaped body, bent and scarred by labour. Yet the man, with high forehead and angular hairline, held his head well

3

and wore his mousy hair cropped short at the front and straight across the back at the level of his chin, like a fashionable Parisian. A protruding upper lip suggested conceit that must surely have been overcome with his vows. The face was taut, the eyes darting here and there nervously, but that was normal in the presence of Bernard de Caen. The same eyes, with a slight downward slant which gave a melancholy appearance to the face, could be intelligent. Last of all Nicolas saw the hands as the inquisitor brought them forward: fine, bone-white, with thin long figers like those of Christ in a crucifixion in the Byzantine style, with no sign of manual labour. The man was a curious admixture.

Bernard beckoned the inquisitor forward. 'I was just telling Sire Nicolas here about your success in Caen . . .'

'Most interesting . . .' Nicolas said with as much enthusiasm as he could muster.

The voice seemed to come from a niche in the wall. The inquisitor had to squint to make out the figure basking like a lizard in bright sunshine. He was curious to see the man who had been called simply 'Sire Nicolas'. It was unlike his Superior to be so informal.

'Come forward, Brother Jacques.' The voice of the Inquisitor-General for Provence commanded legs to move without the consent of their owner's mind. Jacques approached the table, head bowed. The long series of ever richer rooms and ever better-armed guards enhanced his normal subservience.

'Be seated.'

Again, as if in a dream, the body obeyed. It was a great honour to be seated in Lord Bernard's presence. This was the man rumoured to be second only to the pope in real power. The puppeteer who pulled the strings in the Church's darkest and most secret affairs.

Bernard waved him forward. 'Brother Jacques, this is Nicolas de Lirey, dispossessed knight of France and a man I would trust with my own life.'

This puzzled Jacques. He looked askance at the young man lolling on silk cushions in the window niche. It sounded a wild compliment for such an effeminate individual, who looked the epitome of the fashionable young aristocrats he depised. Yet Bernard rarely used such words of praise, so there must be something behind them.

'There is a mission, most secret and of vital importance for the survival of the church . . . and I wish you to accept Nicolas as your *socius* . . .'

4

'Is Sire Nicolas an expert in uncovering heresy?' Jacques asked. He was quite happy with the companion with whom he had worked for the past two years, and had no desire to make an exchange with this lolling aristocrat.

Bernard ignored the sarcasm. 'This is as much a matter of politics as heresy. Nicolas will inform you.'

At first this seemed like a slight. But Jacques could not help being impressed by the knight's height and bearing as he loomed up from the window, with a slight stoop which meant that his fine face seemed to arrive before the rest of his body. The eyes were dark and placid, the skin as soft as his blue silk doublet with embroidered cuffs. A shock of black hair had fallen forward over his forehead, and as he stopped he pushed it back again. 'There is a knight of the Temple we must visit . . . who you must interrogate . . .'

Brother Jacques felt the man's breath on him, and looked at his Superior for guidance.

Bernard de Caen pushed himself to his feet, and walked to the window. 'There is the Rhône,' he announced portentously, although each man knew perfectly well which river flowed through the city. 'The other bank is within the royal domains. But we are outside France . . . only just, but outside. And we wish to remain so. Now, Brother Jacques, I must impress upon you the utter secrecy of this mission, which will aid us in this matter.' Bernard paused for breath and came closer so that Jacques found himself gazing upon the glistening crown of his head. When the words came, they had a prophetic ring as if from an oracle: 'Failure may mean not only the total control of the Church by King Philip the Fair, but the end of Christendom as we know it.'

The urgency in Bernard's voice left no doubt. The audience was over. Nicolas de Lirey and Brother Jacques looked askance at one another, like tomcats staking their ground and preparing for battle.

Each man bowed reverentially to Bernard de Caen, and turned away without regarding the other. Then they walked out of the study in uneasy unison.

5

1

Aigues-Mortes

The thud of the prison door behind him followed the last chime of vespers at a perfect interval, shutting him off from his favourite moment of the day. Sudden absence of light and warmth induced a faint sense of dizziness. He shivered. Then a blazing torch appeared in the darkness. Wavering from side to side, it began to advance towards him through the arches of the vaulted passageway. Heavy treading paces followed it, echoing ominously over the vaults. He glanced around, searching the gloom for his unwanted companion.

When he turned back, the faces of two guards hung like moons in the torch-glow: one was young and gaunt, with the bulging innocent eyes of a squirrel; the other world-weary and wise, hare-lipped with a curious twisted smile which seemed to emanate from hell itself.

'This way please, Brother Jacques,' the elder man intoned, with reverence worthy of the Magnificat. He bowed low. Then he motioned to the figure standing in the dark behind Jacques, this time without bowing. 'This way,' he repeated flatly.

But something in the second friar's bearing as he emerged into torch-light appeared to disturb him. He made an attempt at reparation, bowing awkwardly: 'Sire Nicolas,' he said nervously. Then he indicated the way down the rough-hewn staircase behind the younger guard, whose swaying torch spiralled constantly away from them like a rabbit disappearing into its burrow.

As Brother Jacques felt his way through the first turn he gathered his habit, swearing softly to himself as it caught on a nail. A sprinkling of dust from above told him that his companion had made a sharp halt to avoid falling on him. He sensed the disdain on that aristocratic face cutting through the darkness like a prayer through evil.

It was then that he noticed the stench: first, stagnant sea water, then the more pungent odour of decomposing flesh. It must have risen with the tide, he thought. The sound of lapping water reverberated up the steps. But they were dry. He hoped the stench would go when the tide turned. There was no choice but to continue down.

He wondered what could be so vital about the ageing knight he was supposed to question. The order had been sudden, his departure urgent; as if the fate of Christendom hung on the words of this prisoner. For days he had read and re-read records of interrogations done years before. The transcripts were good and complete, covering every conceivable aspect of the charges. He was to seek the slightest anomaly, a hook to penetrate the man's inner soul; yet the prisoner's answers were never more than confused assemblages of stock phrases. There seemed to be no sense in it. Instead of a day's work in the cool of his study, he had ridden under the scorching sun to this damned hell-hole of a prison. 'Curse him,' he muttered as he slipped on a broken flag.

'What did you say?' The resonant voice bounced mockingly off the walls.

'Nothing!'

'You never were keen to come here.' There was a hint of sarcasm in the voice now.

Had the man read his thoughts, or was he merely guessing his state of mind? 'We could have done without this journey. It's like closing the stable door when the horse has bolted.'

'I'm sure our Lord Bernard of Caen had good reason to send us here.'

The face was invisible, but the very breath of that voice was upon him. Jacques spoke cautiously. 'I've yet to meet a Templar with anything interesting to say.'

'But this one was a preceptor. Even a Templar needed a certain ability to reach that rank.' At least the sarcasm was not directed against him, this time.

The preceptor! Now he remembered. When he had been summoned to his Superior's presence, and introduced to this young aristocrat, they had been talking about a preceptor: 'the preceptor is the only man living who knows'. Those were the words he heard. And then they'd been sent here. It began to fit together: messengers had arrived in a flurry just the day before, and had gone straight to Bernard. Since then he'd been in a state of heightened anxiety. The message had been about the man they were going to see; and his companion believed it was useless, even though he was here. 'Do you know anything about him?' he asked.

The reply emerged from darkness. Had there been light Jacques would not have caught the slight hesitation which to an expert ear was like a fanfare to the lie: 'No more than you.'

'Has our Lord Bernard interrogated him before?' Jacques asked, acting on a hunch. He wished he'd thought of it before leaving.

'I've no idea. I'm not an inquisitor.' Sarcasm failed to disguise the new lie.

Jacques continued down. It might be something Bernard had missed during the questioning of the Templar knights years ago. For he was assigned here at the time, and must have interrogated half the men in this prison. Something Bernard missed which had now become vitally important.

Just then they reached a crescent-shaped landing. The guard was turning a key in a studded door. As his torch swung away Jacques glimpsed another staircase. 'What's down there?'

The hare-lipped guard laughed; a throaty gurgle that echoed round the curving walls. 'The clean-out room.'

'What do you mean?'

'It's where we throw the dead and dying about this time of year . . . Autumn tides get rid of them for us.'

'Your superiors know of this?'

' 'Course they do. Saves carrying the stiffs across the lagoon to the heretics' burial ground, doesn't it?'

'I suppose it would.' Rats scuttled away as they entered a new corridor. Jacques felt his bowels loosen, and was glad for the darkness that covered a quick shiver of fear. His habit snagged again on a rough nail, and brought him to a sharp halt as though he should not continue. But the voice seemed to entice him forwards.

'Part of the job, sire. You gets used to it after a while.' The guard chuckled to himself, then turned and pushed the door ajar. 'Follow me!'

A dozen paces into a steeply sloping corridor, light slanting diagonally across the earthen floor drew them into a barrel-vaulted chamber at least sixty paces in length and nearly as high.

As he looked in, Brother Jacques repeated the guard's words to himself: 'you gets used to it'. The inquisitor's nose, they called it. And now it was telling him that Bernard himself did not know exactly what to search for. 'Listen for anomalies,' he had said, 'check your memory against the transcripts made six years ago. Everything. The slightest error or ambiguity. Pander to him, do whatever you need to. He's sharp enough and it won't be easy. And let me know at once – the future of the Church might depend upon it,' he had concluded in a whisper. Those astonishing words now echoed obsessively in Jacques' mind like an oncoming migraine. They had an absurd ring to them here: with the gloom, the stench, these evil, lamp-lit faces, and the strange young knight in place of his regular *socius*. He shivered again, this time with cold fear; he wanted to climb back into the sun, yet at the same time something drew him in.

You gets used to it.

2

The chamber was lighted by a series of barred windows near the vault, at ground level. Benches, chairs and tables were scattered around the room in no apparent order. Here and there, again in disarray, were piles of rope and chains. Half-way along the outer wall was a broad chimney-breast which rose vertically through the vault, breaking its symmetry. A slow fire smouldered in the fireplace, in front of which was a bed-like wooden frame and a metal screen. On the far side of the fireplace a scribe sat writing at a trestle-table while two black-robed Dominicans conversed quietly behind him. Beyond them, uncouth guards in brown tunics held a prisoner firm against the wall with what appeared to Jacques an excess of zeal. The prisoner was naked save for a loincloth, and could barely stand. Nearer to them, a frayed rope dangled loosely just above head height from a small pulley wheel cemented into the brick vault. It traced a lazy arc like a festoon across the room to a simple wooden winch bolted to the wall. Evening sunshine threw a thin looping shadow from the rope that seemed to lead across the floor towards the high-backed chairs prepared for them opposite the fireplace a few paces from the doorway where he was standing.

Jacques moved towards them. The chamber had recently been brushed with herbs to clean the air, but an acrid stench clung to the limestone walls as if it were part of them. The odour of burnt rope; and perhaps flesh. He tried breathing through his mouth to avoid the stench. 'Bring our prisoner!' he ordered the hare-lipped guard.

As he spoke, a heavy crash of wood on metal reverberated around the chamber.

'No! Idiot!' someone shouted.

Jacques spun sharply to see one of the Dominicans by the fireplace across the chamber strike the bald prisoner viciously with a staff. 'Like this!'

He watched while the admonished guard bowed before the inquisitor as if to a potentate of the Church.

But above all, the violence unleashed by the figure in the black habit surprised him. Turning slowly away, expecting his shock to diminish, he found instead that his stomach thrust upwards against his ribs with such force that he had to choke back vomit. Before him stood a gaunt and decrepit old man with the wild eyes of a starving wolf and feet encased in dried mud. The whole was barely covered by a rat-ravaged tunic. He gripped his abdomen. 'My God,' he muttered. He drew a handkerchief from a pocket and lifted it to his nose, uncomfortably aware of a cynical smile on his companion's face. Instinctively, he moved away towards the chairs prepared for them.

Even at ten paces the fetor emanating from the prisoner was intolerable. Jacques was glad they were near the door. Throughout the journey he had dreaded a battle of wits with a proud and haughty knight, and had been haunted by fear that his inexperience would reveal itself immediately. Instead, here was a cowering, filthy old man. Nothing more. His trepidation vanished. 'Open the manacles, and bring him closer,' he ordered with new confidence, and without seeking Nicolas' agreement.

He sensed the guards' shock and dismay at this departure from normal practice. The hare-lipped guard in particular shook his head as if he had never heard anything like it.

Jacques sat down, ignoring the criticism implicit in the grim faces of the guards, and made himself comfortable. He folded his handkerchief and placed it back in his pocket. Then he beckoned to his companion to take the other chair. But the tall, thin figure stood ostentatiously behind it, unused to being summoned in such a fashion by social inferiors.

The prisoner stood with his back to the wall, massaging his newly freed wrists. Close up, it was the Templar's deep-lined face which drew Jacques' attention: the dull, empty expression of a man who was tired of looking out at the world and had turned in on himself. He must have been about sixty-five; a man who'd seen much in his Order if he'd been in it since his youth. A knight now bent by age and fatigue but once broad-shouldered and tall, perhaps a little over six feet. As good as dead, Jacques was thinking when, quite unexpectedly, the old Templar caught his eye and broke into a slight smile. The hint of irony and superiority in the expression was disturbing.

Jacques beckoned to one of the scribes to sit on a bench near him. Light faded as the sun began to drop. The rope shadow disappeared as if it no longer served.

He was about to speak when the sharp clipping of well-shod hoofs on the drawbridge outside drowned them out. At first he relaxed, and waited, for it was a common enough noise. It would last a few seconds,

11

he thought. But it continued. He concentrated, staring at the floor to block out visual stimuli, worried because such heavy, regular steps implied that this was no ordinary party. As he did so he heard men's voices: shouted commands and farewells; other indistinguishable noises. The metallic clash of shields and armour punctuated the monotonous hoof-clip as the party crossed. Then the clatter was followed by an eerie stillness as the horsemen reached the road beyond the moat. Inquisitors, scribes and prisoner alike leaned expectantly towards the silence, as if each were convinced that this was a pause and not the end.

The new sound came. Jacques recognized it as that of battle chargers being led by pages behind the knights. Their stately walk and heavier shoes were clearly distinguishable; for they never galloped or even trotted except when going into battle. He heard the pages shout at them as they passed the bridge, and imagined them tugging and pushing the chargers back from the brink. They in turn were followed by the steady rolling sound of supply carts, most likely laden with armour for the knights and their mounts. Last of all were some smaller animals, probably pack-horses or mules.

Jacques was perturbed, since he knew that these were not sounds of peace. If these were troops of King Philip the Fair, it augured little good for the Church; if not, the presence of a foreign power – which might be just as bad. Yet France had been firmly in the hands of King Philip for quarter of a century now, and there had been no external threat since the war with Navarre ended. At the same time he was certain at least fifty knights had passed: an entire squadron. And he fancied that such a noisy and confident exit from the walled city suggested urgency in their mission.

An urgency that seemed to surround him since he had been summoned to Bernard de Caen's study a few days earlier. It was after that meeting when his secular companion had been assigned to him, he now realized with a shock, that he had heard similar sounds outside the convent in Avignon, just as they were preparing to start out on their journey here. And more than once during the journey the guards had remarked on the strange absence of bandits and wayside thieves. The intensified military presence had scared them deep into the forests. He recalled how a band of knights had arrived noisily at one of their hostels long after most travellers were snug in the big, ten-men beds. The noises of war seemed to follow him, even though France was at peace. Could it be true that King Philip was planning to march

12

on Italy? Strange rumours had abounded in Avignon before they left for this hell-hole: that the King wanted to, but couldn't. They made no sense, since he was powerful enough to do as he wished. What could possibly hold him back?

And Bernard had implied that this mission was part of an attempt to prevent such an invasion. Secret and urgent. The first time a secular *socius* had been used to make up a pair of inquisitors, everybody said. A haughty young knight and aristocrat! He wondered whether they knew in Paris. Then, what could it have to do with this wrecked preceptor of the Temple? And him? Jacques shook his head in disbelief. His mind was reeling when he needed lucidity and concentration.

Then he realized with embarrassment that the guards and his prisoner were all staring at him.

'In the name of Our Lord, amen,' he began with feigned enthusiasm. He was half-consciously listening for the distant rumble of the squadron across the earthen dyke which led to the mainland.

He glanced at the first scribe, and nodded, indicating by wagging his forefinger that he was speaking off the record. Pen in hand, the man, a thin, grey-faced spectre who looked as if he had been sitting there since the chamber was built, stared back as if in admonition for this new irregularity.

Jacques ignored him. He addressed the prisoner slowly, with carefully chosen words: 'We, I and my colleague, are here to ask you some questions. You may answer, or you may choose not to answer . . . but I believe it will be better for you if you do answer our questions.' He closed his eyes and made the sign of the cross on his breast. 'May God be with you.'

Then he nodded again for the scribe to begin his record. *'In Christi nomine, amen.* On this day, the fourteen of August in the Year of Our Lord One Thousand Three Hundred and Thirteen, we, Brother Jacques Fournier of the Cistercian Order and Nicolas de Lirey, Knight of France in the service of the Church, do here at Aigues-Mortes examine the prisoner . . . ' He looked up slowly, trying to push away with his tongue the unpleasant taste of the name of his newly imposed companion. 'Your name?'

'Pietro of Ocre.' The man spoke automatically in a weary voice.

'Family!' Jacques snapped.

'The counts of Ocre, a branch of the counts of Marsica . . .'

'In Italy?'

'Yes.'

'Rank?'

'In the Order of the Temple? Preceptor.'

'Province?'

'Apulia.'

The seated scribe recorded each word meticulously while the other one listened, ready to take over if the session developed into a long one.

'His Holiness the Pope and his Royal Highness King Philip of France have been informed by reliable witnesses of the errors and abominations of your Order. But in view of the past honours of the Order, I am instructed to inform you that in the event of a full and spontaneous confession of the truth you will be given a full pardon and allowed to return within the bosom of the Holy Roman Church.' It was all carefully rehearsed, a formality to be done with.

Not even a monosyllable issued from Pietro's mouth this time. But his attitude spoke volumes: he had heard it many times over the years.

Nicolas watched in silence. Bernard de Caen had sworn to him that if any man could draw the secret from this prisoner then Jacques Fournier was the man; and his own father had told him years ago before his death, that there was no shrewder judge of character than Bernard himself. But Nicolas had yet to see any evidence of such acumen. The questions asked were routine; the answers empty of significance. The stocky inquisitor would have been more suited to work in the fields or even in the forge. It was true that the supposedly brilliant Cistercian on loan to the Inquisition could not be given fuller information without endangering Bernard's plan. But surely he ought to be trying harder? There was no trace of brilliance in those dull grey eyes, Nicolas thought. Could wisdom come from that low forehead with its thick eyebrows, and the angular wind-chiselled face of the kind that could be seen in every French village?

Jacques sensed the criticism in his companion's passive participation. He moved his body aslant in the chair, and lifted his habit almost sensuously as if consciously to contradict his companion's perceptions. Then he addressed the prisoner once more. 'You will commence by explaining the ceremony by which you were, let us say, *received* into the Order of the Temple.'

Again, Pietro said nothing.

'We already possess a record of your previous interrogations and are well aware of your depravities,' Jacques continued in his most

14

persuasive voice. 'It is for the good of your own soul that we suggest this new confession.'

Nicolas could not resist a smile.

Jacques glanced towards the fireplace. Guards had begun to strap the bald prisoner to the wooden frame. 'You need not describe the formal ceremony in all its detail, since we possess excellent descriptions in our archives and it was after all approved by His Holiness Innocent III. But, for the sake of your soul and your eternal salvation, it would be wise for you to confess yourself of the black sins that followed this ceremony. Those sins of which the *Canon Episcopi* and Burchard of Worms write with such eloquence but which I am loth to pronounce even in this dungeon.'

The Templar indulged in the luxury of looking straight into his inquisitor's face. But Jacques outstared him. He continued to watch as the prisoner's gaze turned towards Nicolas, as though the aristocrat appeared to him to be less of a threat.

Then the prisoner turned back with provocation in his eyes. 'And if I refuse to confess? Will you torture me, like the poor soul over there?'

'It was not my intention. I am here to question you.'

'By what right do you plan to torture an innocent knight of the Order of the Temple?'

The inquisitor was surprised by this irrelevance, which showed the prisoner's state of mind after years in prison: he was replying by rote, responding to statements he expected rather than those actually spoken to him. Jacques decided that he must humour him for a while, and play the role of savage inquisitor which was expected. 'By order of the Inquisitor-General for Provence, who has instructed us to examine the truth "*avec la torture s'il en est besoin . . .*" You do speak French, don't you?'

The Templar said nothing. But a slight tightening at the corner of his eyes said he had learned the language well during his years of imprisonment, and would prefer it to scholastic Latin.

'I myself do not believe such practices are efficacious,' Jacques continued. He paused for effect, and looked deep into his prisoner's eyes. He was convinced that only a subtle interrogation would work with this man: the preceptor would have no fear of torture. It would be important to reassure him, provide him with some small luxury, and then extract whatever secrets he held in the deep recesses of his mind. Other inquisitors had gained nothing in weeks of questioning, so he did not expect to achieve fast results. He recalled the unusual urgency implicit in his Superior's order to come here, and resolved to find out how much time he had.

Again the Templar used all his energy to rebuff the inquisitor's stare. But the point was won.

'Shall we go on?'

'As you wish.' The voice was now flat and resigned. 'If you have time to waste.'

But he used French. That was encouraging.

Nicolas noticed too. Blood was beginning to ooze from the stone.

'Let us come to the matter of the charges against you,' Jacques went on, 'which I see here have been brought to your attention on no less than seven separate occasions without positive results. That is to say, with no spontaneous confession on your part.' He was matter-of-fact once again.

'You can't seriously accuse me of such ridiculous charges. I deny, for now and for ever, so God help me, participation in any activity not expressly permitted by our Rule.' Genuine anger flickered in his eyes. A disgust which years of imprisonment had not placated. Suddenly he was no longer old and weary.

Jacques watched the transformation with interest. 'Then you obeyed the precepts of your Rule?'

'Certainly. What kind of a Templar would I have been otherwise? You inquisitors seem to think every brother was either a pervert or disloyal. You have much to learn!'

He had thrown down the gauntlet. Privately, Jacques was inclined to agree with him, since the idea that thousands of men indulged in homosexual and heretical practices *secretly* had always appeared absurd to him. A notion that could only have come from a mind like that of the Inquisitor-General in Paris.

But nonetheless this confidence unsettled him. He was following the line of questioning of the trial transcripts in Avignon. There was nowhere else to start. At this point most of the Templars denied this accusation vehemently because they knew well that the Rule itself was tainted with heresy, and that such an admission was therefore tantamount to a confession of heresy – and could earn perpetual imprisonment. Pietro di Ocre *was* different; at least in this.

Jacques needed to gain time to think, and turned to one of the scribes. 'Bring the manuscript,' he ordered.

There was a pause as they waited. Jacques fancied he heard a scuffing sound like that of leather against stone in the direction of the doorway. He moved silently towards the door. The noise ceased. He assumed it had been made by rats. But he stayed close to the door. Crashing chains across the chamber smothered whatever sound might have been heard. Then manacles were thrown against the limestone walls, briefly echoed, and fell on the chains. The bald prisoner let out a hideous shout as he was lifted from his place towards the rack. A further pause was followed by gruff, incomprehensible commands and another scream. Then silence.

Again the scuffing from outside, too casual for rats. More like an impatient man. Inquisitorial intuition told Jacques they were being spied on. He glanced at Nicolas and saw that he had heard too. Nicolas stood up quietly, motioned silently to the hare-lipped guard and stepped towards the doorway. Reaching into the darkness he seized a cloth garment and jerked it into the chamber. 'Hold him!' he ordered the guard as a black-robed friar appeared abruptly in the light.

In his surprise the guard obeyed. But embarrassment soon replaced confusion, and it was obvious from the fear etched across his face that he was used to taking orders from his new prisoner.

'What does this mean?' the captured Dominican demanded in an attempt to regain the initiative.

'Ah! Brother Jean!' Jacques remarked as if greeting a boon companion. They had first met in the governor's office on arrival. Jean was a short, stocky man of the sort common in Jacques' own village. But there had been no shared feeling. Jacques had felt that sinister half-closed right eye studying his every movement. Even then he had sensed a simmering distrust beneath Jean's apparent friendliness.

'Indeed, and bringing a message to you when you so rudely dragged me in here.' The guard loosened his grip warily.

'I'm so sorry. We must be careful in our job, you know.' Jacques relished this exchange of lies and false courtesies. 'The message?'

Fear and uncertainty flickered in Brother Jean's eyes for an instant. 'Our Superior would like to see you,' he said blandly. Sunlight flashed on his tanned bald crown as he spoke.

'Ah! That is good. Thank you.' Jacques' tone entailed dismissal, and Brother Jean was quick to take the opportunity to depart.

Jacques turned to his companion. 'He *was* listening. Who do you think sent him?'

'He was in the governor's office when we presented . . .'

'. . . but left before we had finished,' Jacques said. As soon as he had learned the overt purpose of our mission, he reflected.

17

'You noticed too?'

Brother Jacques regarded Nicolas suspiciously. He regretted giving himself away. 'Perhaps it was just natural curiosity.'

'I don't think so.'

'No?'

'I saw Brother Jean talking to our guide in the stables when we arrived. Now there's another man I'd never trust. A spy as like as not.' This time Nicolas allowed himself a satisfied smirk. 'Our Jean was clearly agitated by what he heard. Perhaps some information from Avignon. Then he almost ran back into the keep.' He plainly enjoyed his moment of supremacy over the young inquisitor.

Jacques barely noticed. The news was stunning. 'You think he could already have received information about our mission? Can it be that important?' More to the point, he realized as he spoke, was the matter of the guide. If he had brought a message, then who had sent it? Surely Lord Bernard would not use such a man with Nicolas present.

'More so than you would believe,' Nicolas said quietly. He was curious to see that the inquisitor's stocky frame had drawn itself almost to his own height.

Jacques froze. 'Do you . . .?'

His words were smothered by a spine-chilling scream which seemed to echo from the bowels of hell.

He closed his eyes tightly, as if that would make the sound disappear, and stared at the earthen floor. His mind was in turmoil, uncertain whether it was Nicolas' quiet statment or the hellish cry of terror which disconcerted him most. Jacques looked up again, and watched Pietro di Ocre slowly massaging his wrists carefully. Who was he to merit such urgency? What had he done? What did he know?

His thoughts were broken when the scribe returned with a well-bound volume of manuscript held tight to his breast.

'Come,' Jacques said, reaching for the volume. There was work to be done and time for thought later. He resolved to question their guide as soon as he had finished. 'Stand by the door,' he ordered the hare-lipped guard. He opened the volume carefully at a leather bookmark, made sure his prisoner was watching, and then stabbed at it with his forefinger. 'Your Rule, Preceptor,' he began. 'It states here without possible equivocation that members of your Order are "to go where excommunicated knights are gathered". Is that not to act against the dictates of the Holy Roman Church? And were not

18

your chapters carried out in secret, in darkness and to the exclusion of all potential witnesses?'

Pietro shook his wrists, then threw a curious gaze as if he were admonishing his interrogator: 'Certainly. There was no reason why laymen should take part in the chapters of a Holy Order, and if our chapters took place in darkness it was the darkness of dawn, after lauds. And our Rule does not require that lauds begin "when a man may recognize a man" according to the Rule of St Benedict. There is no evil in that!' He seemed pleased to score a point by demonstrating his knowledge of the religious orders.

Jacques pressed: 'Did you not build your own churches, and bury in them the bodies of those who had died without the blessing of the Holy Roman Church?' He felt Nicolas' cold stare on him as he spoke.

'Of that I know nothing.'

'And did you not deny Christ in your weekly chapter meetings, and spit on His cross, and practise the obscene kiss?' He himself had always found these charges to be preposterous, although he had never dared to state his opinion of them in the presence of his fellow inquisitors. He closed the manuscript volume now the interrogation had gained momentum again.

'You may criticize the terms of our Rule, and perhaps I was wrong to say I followed every paragraph to the letter.' Now Pietro was backtracking. But before Jacques had time to savour this small success, the Templar drew himself up on the bench and addressed him with a new and confident tone: 'But I can assure you, Sire Inquisitor, that my most Christian conscience is clear, that I have never denied my God or his Son, Our Lord and Saviour, any more than you have done, and if you are expecting me to confess these accusations then you may as well send me back to prison at once and save your breath.'

It was a rehearsed answer, but the prisoner was gaining in audacity. Jacques was pleased. He dreaded stubborn silence more than anything: once a prisoner began to play the game it was usually only a matter of time until he confessed his sins. Yet this was no ordinary prisoner, he reminded himself, and he would have to tread cautiously. Within the apparent sincerity of this declaration he had sensed something else: beneath the smooth delivery learned by rote many years before was an almost indiscernible hesitancy that an untrained man would not have noticed. He sensed for the first time that there was indeed something behind the accusations of heresy.

Jacques glanced at Nicolas, recalling the affirmation that his own Superior would not have sent them here for nothing. Again the questions came. What could this decrepit knight possibly know that demanded such urgency? What knowledge could lead to his *socius'* substitution by this haughty young man? He fought to avoid looking straight at Nicolas, and turned his eyes full upon the prisoner instead. 'Come,' he continued, 'we are reasonable and educated men. Let us sit and discuss this matter thoroughly.' Then, to a guard, 'Bring a stool for the preceptor. Quickly now.'

Then he followed Nicolas' gaze across the chamber towards the bald prisoner near the fireplace. They had now strapped him horizontally to the wooden frame with his legs tied tightly just below his knees, so that it was impossible for him to move them. The lower part of the frame ended at mid-calf, so that his feet extended beyond the frame. At a sign from one of the friars, two guards pushed the frame so that it stood at right angles to the fireplace. A screen protected the prisoner's naked soles.

Beyond the screen, embers were being raked out of the fire onto a metal shelf.

Earlier, Jacques had briefly considered passing the interrogation over to Nicolas, even though that would be against the specific order of his Superior. Now his interest was engaged, and he knew that he would follow it through to the end. He banged his clenched fist on the arm of the chair in a gesture of determination, at the same time becoming uneasily aware of the scribe watching him from the corner of his eye. The man could easily be there to spy on him, he realized. To break this irksome moment, he leaned forward to watch the activity across the chamber. The scribe's field of vision was then blocked by Nicolas.

Lard was being applied to the prisoner's naked feet.

He turned back to the preceptor. 'Well? Shall we go on?'

'You'll wait,' Pietro said quietly. The gentle provocation was a brave attempt to ignore what was happening across the chamber. But it sliced through that musty air with the steeliness of prophecy.

The tension precluded further questions for the present. Jacques forced himself to sit back in his chair, willing himself to appear indifferent to the activity around him.

At a signal from one of the Dominicans, the screen was removed. An uneasy hush fell over the chamber. In that silence he seemed to hear in his mind's eye a quiet sizzling sound, like the first sealing of a suckling pig over the spit. They all waited, as if by common consent between inquisitors, guards and prisoners, for the first screams of pain. Jacques examined the frayed cuffs of his habit.

Then it came. At first a strange, eerie, almost squeaking sound that seemed to rise up and spiral towards the vault of the chamber. As if the scream could not quite believe itself. Then a full-blooded howl like that of a speared boar filled the whole space.

Jacques felt his stomach turn and gasped for breath, forcing himself to watch his prisoner's reaction. At first he saw anger rise to the old knight's face: for an instant it showed fear of a violent death with no chance of defence. But just as it must once have done in war, this intense fear suddenly transformed itself into the mad impulse which leads to heroism. Jacques watched fascinated as the whole body of the man hardened as if ready for battle. The energy of present and past was channelled into fierce defiance through those wide-opened eyes and the frantically moving Adam's apple. Then the Templar turned towards Nicolas, fearing him but at the same time obviously recognizing the fellow soldier in him. 'Torture will gain you nothing!' he shouted above the bald prisoner's screams.

So there was something after all. Jacques spoke quietly: 'But if what you say is true, why do you not answer my questions?'

Again, no response.

Nicolas watched in fascination. He was indifferent to the pain and suffering of the preceptor, but nevertheless charged with a common pride in the man's resistance. He was a true knight indeed, and Nicolas found himself hoping that he would react in similar fashion if such torture were ever applied to him. Pain was for women and men of the Church. He studied Jacques as this thought came to him: he looked as strong as an ox, as befitting his humble birth, and he had suffered the hot ride from Avignon without complaint. Nicolas wondered how the inquisitor would react to his own medicine, yet at the same time did not openly criticize him since he know the mission required all possible means to succeed. Lord Bernard would be worse. To be tortured by him would strike fear into any knight, Nicolas thought wryly, since he could penetrate the mind.

That consideration made him shudder. For what would his and Brother Jacques' fate be in the event of failure? For an instant a sense of their shared destiny caused him to regard the inquisitor with a certain sympathy. Then it passed.

21

Jacques felt his gaze, and sensed the distant companionship between Nicolas and Pietro, but chose to ignore them. The Templar's obstinacy, and the challenge implicit in his words, had at first angered him. But now he realized that he could hardly expect more, for whatever Pietro di Ocre knew must lie very deep, both in time and in importance. Deeper than torture. Now Jacques was beginning to warm to the task. There was something unique in this strange prisoner's attitude which forced him to recall the odd circumstances of this interrogation – for which he rather than men of greater experience had been chosen. The problem must be theological, he reflected, and Bernard de Caen had chosen him to tease out something which required theological acumen beyond mere inquisitorial skill. A profound sense of pleasure suffused his being as this realization came. But why involve Nicolas de Lirey?

Just then a fresh scream echoed round the chamber as the prisoner's feet were once more bared to the coals.

Pleasure was knocked from Jacques' mind. He was barely able to force back rising vomit in his throat. He stood abruptly in order to hide his discomfort, wishing to give the impression of an important decision. This was the wrong place for his task. He beckoned the guards. 'Manacle him again, and take him to your Governor's office.' He then walked quickly towards the door with his face averted so that scribes, guards and Nicolas following him could not see it.

He was glad of the darkness on the stairs now, for it allowed him time to regain composure and push the scene below from his mind.

Outside, a horse neighed as if in answer to the tortured man's desperate pleas. It reminded Jacques of the earlier horsemen. As they emerged from the dungeon he stopped one of the guards, and drew him close.

'Who was it we heard riding across the drawbridge before?'

'German knights.'

'German?'

'The Emperor Henry's knights, Brother.'

'Henry of Luxembourg? Here?'

'No, sire, his knights.' The guard spoke with the condescension usually reserved for inquisitive children.

'But why here?'

'Travelling to Italy, sire, to join the Emperor. They were in Aquitane, sire, and are taking ship here, from St Louis' crusader port. They say the Emperor will have Rome before the new wine's ready.' He began to move away.

'Ah!' Brother Jacques murmured, unaware that his audience was now several paces away. Italy again, he thought; why was it that in the past few days all roads seemed to lead to Italy?

He felt Nicolas de Lirey's presence behind him. 'Everyone seems to want Rome,' Jacques observed sardonically, without bothering to face his companion. 'There are knights of every shape and colour roaming around, and they all seem to be going to Italy.'

'They always have,' Nicolas replied as casually as though he was talking about the weather, 'and here we're in a no-man's-land between France and Germany. Moreover, word says that Prince Henry is in league with King Philip . . .'

Jacques turned quickly. Now what was coming?

'. . . so it is King Philip who wants Rome. And more. And it is our duty to stop him.'

There was a strange vehemence in these last words. Jacques studied his firm, thin lips. '*Our* duty?'

'Yes, Brother. You don't imagine I'm here to catch a petty heretic out, do you? This is a political matter of the greater importance.'

Jacques was still staring at Nicholas. Now his mouth dropped open.

'We must stop him. *Absolutely*.' Again, that vehemence.

The inquisitor's mind reeled. 'Of course,' he said vacantly. A shiver of fear ran through him as he began for the first time to see the importance of his mission.

As he entered the new interrogation room a presentiment that the answer lay with the Counts of Ocre began to form in Jacques' mind, like the distant drone of a mosquito which insinuates itself in the mind and prevents sleep although it does not attack. The ride here had been tedious. There was no better place in the world than his own cell, no greater sense of spiritual security and well-being. Yet Jacques realized, with a start, that part of his mind was already beginning to relish the prospect of a journey to Ocre. It was implicit in Bernard de Caen's instructions, and seemed both inevitable and exciting.

He dismissed the thought before it took root.

The new room was plain and rectangular, and ran parallel to the main prison wing. It was freshly whitewashed and sparsely furnished. A window gave onto the courtyard, and when Jacques looked out briefly he observed two friars standing casually in the corner of the courtyard.

Too casually, it seemed to Jacques. It was as if the friars were there to observe them, and perhaps move apparently just as casually towards the window to eavesdrop like Brother Jean. Had they been near the Governor's office when they arrived there? A sinister sense of being followed took root in Jacques' mind. An intuition, nothing more; but it was firmly placed. When he looked back, Pietro di Ocre had been taken to the far end of the room and seated on a bench beneath a crucifix on which Christ's head could just be made out in a pale ochre colour. Legs and body had been weathered to the wood.

The younger guard sat with him at the far end of the bench where a jug of water and a clay mug had been placed on the floor within Pietro's reach. Two high-backed chairs upholstered with thick leather had been placed in front of him ready for the inquisitors. Jacques indicated scribes and door to Nicolas with no more than a lifted eyebrow. Then waited as Nicolas ordered the scribes to wait outside and closed the door on faces tense with curiosity and disappointment. A single guard, notorious for a partial deafness which allowed him to disobey orders when it suited him, remained. He could hear nothing beyond six paces.

'What do you think?' Jacques asked when they were alone.

The young aristocrat could not resist a hint of superiority. 'If you would like my opinion . . .' he ventured, seeking confirmation, 'it seems to me that the secret we're here to unravel may have something to do with his *family*.' The measure of every man was in his family history and, in such a man as Pietro di Ocre, whatever interested Bernard de Caen must be in his past.

This talk of families irked Brother Jacques. During their journey together Nicolas had been full of stories of his ancestors. But this time Jacques ignored the tone, sensing that he might well be right. He contemplated Pietro di Ocre.

Presently he walked to the other end of the room. Nicolas followed him. They sat down on the leather chairs. As the prisoner waited, Jacques opened the ledger containing transcripts of previous interrogations. He searched for several minutes, disregarding the quizzical gaze which was fixed on him, quickly reading through the relevant sections until he found what he was searching for. Then he looked up with a satisfied expression which disconcerted the prisoner. He leaned forward. 'Your family claims descent from Charlemagne, I believe,' he began casually, as if he were conversing with a new acquaintance at the papal court.

Pietro looked up warily.

'Is that not the case?'

'It is true.'

'You claim royal blood?' Nicolas de Lirey had not read the transcripts, and his voice registered his incredulity. '*French* royal blood?'

Jacques relished his shock. Even in the heat of pride for his father, the distinguished knight Jean de Charny, lord of Lirey and Montfort, Nicolas had never made such claims. Then he returned his attention to Pietro. 'Well?' he said softly.

'The first count of the Marsica was Berardo, who married Princess Matilda, daughter of Pippin the Younger.' Pietro spoke with quiet dignity. 'Berardo held a hundred castles from Perugia to Apulia.' He paused, and seemed to invest the silence with a sense of immense family pride. 'My grandfather was also Berardo, Count of Ocre. His son Tommaso was known as Thomas Berard by the English.'

'The Grand Master of the Temple?' Jacques was unable to conceal his surprise. Nicolas' hunch was already proving a goldmine. 'Was he not English?'

'He was born within the walls of the castle of Ocre, as I was myself,' Pietro replied firmly. 'His correct name was Tommaso di Berardo dei Conti di Ocre.'

Jacques glanced at Nicolas and saw the same astonishment that he felt. But he also noticed disdain mellowing into what seemed like an innate sympathy for the aged Italian.

The Master of the Temple appeared nowhere in the transcripts. Was it not strange that a team of experienced investigators had worked for weeks with Pietro and had no idea of his relationship to the Grand Master? The aged preceptor immediately assumed fresh importance in Jacques' eyes.

'But, my Lord Preceptor . . .' Nicolas continued after a brief pause. He too was surprised by this new information. He wondered for a moment whether Bernard de Caen knew of this: he was pleased to observe that the inquisitor did not know.

At first Jacques wanted to interrupt, but then saw how this false courtesy might work. He nodded to Nicolas.

'. . . your family has lost its lands, unless I am mistaken. You were, let us say, *forced* to become a Templar, having no lands of your own.' An almost imperceptible pause allowed the full weight of Nicolas' arrogant tone to fall on the verb.

Jacques watched as the sympathy which had appeared on Nicolas' face such a short time ago was replaced by a more familiar contempt, as if the knight who had appeared noble to him a few moments before was again a pathetic old man.

The preceptor rose to his full height, showing something of the immense force he must once have used in battle. 'You young whipster!' he hissed. 'How dare you?'

Jacques stared in fascination while the Templar's cheeks flushed as if he had swallowed a consignment of Tyrian purple. Thick veins stood out on his neck. His outstretched hand for an instant menaced Nicolas, but then seemed to hang emptily like that of a Roman statue whose wooden sword has long since rotted away. The guard moved hastily towards him, dagger in hand, but Jacques waved him back.

Pietro di Ocre spoke to Nicolas as if Jacques did not exist. 'You are too young to understand. It is true that we have lost our lands. But we have not lost everything. No, young man, you would be surprised . . .'

'And how would that be?' The question was gentle, probing. The tone in Pietro's voice told Nicolas there was indeed something important to be drawn out of this Templar. That an Italian from some remote castle in the south should claim even indirect descent from Charlemagne with such plausibility intrigued him. He would like to question him further sometime; alone. 'Well? How would that be?' he repeated.

But there was no reply. The prisoner sank back onto the bench, his cheeks suddenly sunken and losing their colour as quickly as it had come – as if he knew he had gone too far.

Jacques also regarded him with interest, his intuitions confirmed by this extraordinary outburst. 'Why don't we begin from the moment of your arrest?' he asked softly.

The prisoner began grudgingly, as if he had been asked to give his own blood. 'The arrest?'

'When did it take place? And where?'

'Six years ago.'

'Be more precise!'

'Friday 13th October, at dawn. The same morning that all the Templars in France were arrested. We'd heard the rumours, but the castle was strong and we felt safe.'

'Where?'

'The commanderie at Greoux. You know it?'

'Yes, we know the castle well. But why were you there?'

Nicolas glared at Jacques over the pronoun, but let it pass, since the preceptor seemed willing to talk.

'My old friend and comrade-in-arms, Ancelin de Gizy, was the commander. We'd fought together often in the old days, in Egypt and at the fall of Acre. A good soldier and loyal friend – who now lies rotting in your prisons at Paris. He left a sergeant in charge, a certain Bertrand, but he was a local man and had never fought in the Holy Land. He didn't have the courage to resist the King's seneschal, and allowed him to walk into the castle and do as he wished.' Contempt tinged Pietro's voice.

'You have not answered my question. Why were you travelling through France?'

'We were on our way to Paris on business of the Order,' Pietro said tersely, the flow broken.

'We?'

'I and two sergeant brothers who are still down there,' he said, pointing across the floor towards the dungeon, 'and our retinue of guards, grooms and cook.'

27

'From Ocre?'

'Yes.'

'Where is Ocre, exactly?'

'Three days' ride north-east of Rome, in the mountains.'

Jacques registered this information. In his mind's eye he saw a road winding from the sea up through the mountains. Though he had never been to Rome, he seemed to know the city; and to recognize the villages and castles as his party wound its way towards Ocre. Then he snapped this foolish delusion from his mind, and forced himself to concentrate on the man in front of him. 'And who was the seneschal? Do you remember?'

He was astonished by the reaction to his simple question.

Blood rose again to the prisoner's face and the veins in his forearms seemed to stand up. The scar was deep, and unhealed. 'That bastard? I shall never forget him as long as I live! Him and his bawdy soldiers. Ponsard de Boyzol was his name, the commander at Aix, an arrogant churl if ever I saw one. If Ancelin had been there, he would never have taken us. He tricked a young guard, a peasant with no experience of battle. Archers, tunnelling and all the other tricks of the Turks would never have let him in. As it was, his men stormed into the dortoir while I was still sleeping. I barely had time to brush the dust and straw of a night's rest from my tunic and put on my mantle before they dragged me down into the courtyard. There he read the royal arrest order, accusing us of the most abominable crimes under the sun . . . and the bastard said he had come all the way from Aix, as though it were a special honour for us. I shall never forget that.'

Jacques encouraged him, and felt Nicolas' approval as he pressed on. 'What did you think when you had time to consider it afterwards?'

The old Templar almost laughed with disbelief, as if it had never really happened. The anger released by memories of his arrest had loosened both memory and tongue. 'It seemed absurd, and I was sure it wouldn't last. After all, the arrest order was for the *French* Templars, so what did it have to do with me? It wasn't until we reached the beginning of this God-forsaken, putrid marshland that I began to worry. This place is enough to bring on an attack of melancholy to the brightest soul.'

Jacques was willing to concede that.

'Nothing but bullrushes, saltwort and flat sky. Whistling teal and croaking heron – like a nightmare. And the guards who never stopped insulting and taunting me.' He spat on the floor.

'What did they say?'

'Vulgar jokes, mostly. But one of them never stopped taunting me. I'd like to meet him again. "You're Italian, are you?" he shouted, "are all Italians cock-suckers, or just the Templars?" I remember as clearly as if he were here now. Odoard, his name was, a surly character. His humour knew no depths.'

Now six years of prison had tempered the pain, and there was no anger in the Templar's voice. 'It didn't stop until we got to this damned place,' he observed; 'then at least I was left alone.'

Jacques nodded, glancing at the accumulated notes on the table in front of him. He was aware of Nicolas' curious stare turned on him, and tried to sound reasonable. He wished he could have been left alone with his regular *socius*. But there was no chance of that. 'I understand it was this Odoard who caused your limp?'

'Hobbled me, you mean? Yes. When we got to this scum-heap of a prison he shoved me off my mount as if my hands were free. Even the bastard seneschal called him to order. But it was too late. I wrenched my thigh, and have never been able to walk without pain since. The damp in this hell-hole doesn't help much either.'

'I don't suppose it does.' It was Nicolas who spoke this time. 'Neither can it be easy for a man of your birth to be stuck here . . .' He thought a show of sympathy might produce results.

Pietro looked up, unconvinced.

'. . . and yet you continue to deny all the charges so readily confessed by your comrades-in-arms, when confession would free you from this place. You should accept my companion's advice.'

The preceptor laughed at the old trick. He turned towards Jacques again. 'I bet you'd like to know what really happened in our chapters,' he taunted.

'Devil worship? Games?' Jacques threw the provocation back.

'The devil with you, you don't know the half of it. There were real secrets and real power in there. Things you would never dream of . . .'

Jacques waited, willing the prisoner to substantiate his statements.

'It was only a matter of getting it back,' Pietro muttered as he collapsed in on himself again. His face bore the wistful, noble yet slightly sad expression of a man who had known a kind of greatness.

Jacques sat absolutely still.

Pietro di Ocre's voice diminished to a hesitant, hoarse whisper, as if he were seeking to express his inner ideas but could not find the words.

29

'We would have had the Church, but for . . .' The last words passed over them incomprehensibly. Then, as if in profound repentance, Pietro settled back into the chair. His next words came clearly, with the same defiance he had shown before: 'Yes, we had the key.'

They sliced the air like a dagger through snow.

An obstinate silence followed. It was obvious they would get nothing more from him that day, and Jacques realized that he must regain the initiative quickly. He recalled the scuffing in the cellar and the prying friars outside and turned to Nicolas confidentially: 'We must move him out of this place.' Then he dismissed the deaf guard who had been allowed to remain, and stepped briefly outside to dismiss the scribes as well. Finally, he turned back to Pietro di Ocre. 'Preceptor, perhaps you would like to avail yourself of the chance of some private prayer?'

Darkness had fallen, and a breeze aired the courtyard. It was just warm enough to drive away the prison chill, but cool enough to refresh after the daytime heat. In the chapel, altar candles seemed to flicker towards them around the slender columns which divided the nave into three sections. Pietro walked ahead, and knelt quietly on the bare stone flags in front of the altar. Jacques held back. He had been struck by the genuine piety of his prisoner, and was glad to give him this opportunity to pray for his soul. It was an unusual practice; but this was an unusual assignment.

Then, as the friars watched, Pietro spoke once more. As quietly as before, but audibly in the death-still chapel. 'The Pope was ready,' he seemed to say, gazing at the crucifix, 'and we could have saved the Church from its disgrace. And our dear Order . . .'

Jacques scarcely believed what he had heard. The very silence seemed to bespeak conspiracy. His mind was already confused by this unorthodox mission, and now these mysterious phrases: 'the Pope was ready' and 'save the Church from disgrace'. His first impulse was to challenge Pietro di Ocre immediately, but as soon as it came to him he knew it was wrong. Whatever the preceptor's secret might be, it would take time to draw it out; even though it was vital for the survival of the Church, Bernard de Caen himself had not been able to draw it out. But Jacques did not wish to remain in this prison under constant observation, something that had never happened to him before but was was already unnerving. In the austere calm of the chapel, with candles flickering around him and his prisoner there on his knees, he pondered his options. The earlier suspicion that this 'short mission', as Brother Bernard had described it, would become his task for many months ahead continued to grow within him.

He prayed.

When he stood again, he had made his decision. He needed to use carrot and stick. Make the prisoner feel comfortable, and then hit him hard. There was no need to consult Nicolas. It was an inquisitorial matter. 'Come on, Preceptor; we need a good rest before the journey which awaits us tomorrow.'

'Journey?'

'We are taking you to Avignon. This dungeon is unsuitable for a man of your rank.' He noticed Nicolas' gentle nod of assent, then took Pietro's arm and led him through the chapel door. 'Guards,' he shouted, 'take this man back to his cell until dawn.'

The prisoner muttered to himself as he was led away. But then the name of their destination seemed to sink in. 'Avignon? In the lands of Anjou?' he asked suspiciously, with a touch of what sounded like venom – as if the name touched a now deep but once exposed nerve.

Jacques turned to Nicolas. 'Would you mind going to find our guide? Bring him here as soon as you can.'

Then he shut the door and sat down.

But Nicolas was back before he had time to gather his thoughts. 'He's gone, Brother,' the knight announced.

'Gone? Where?'

'To Avignon.'

'Shouldn't he have come back with us?'

Nicolas nodded. 'We'll find another.'

Jacques agreed. A guide would hardly be necessary now, he thought. Then another question formed in his mind. 'Did he leave alone?' he asked.

'No, with a party of royal officials.'

'Royal?' Jacques spoke aloud. His thoughts were more sinister, for this meant that the guide could have brought messages to Aigues-Mortes from the King's men.

An intensely physical reaction, churning his innards, again informed his rational mind that he was entering a political quagmire.

31

4

A ghost-like shroud enveloped the swamps the next morning as if expressly laid to conceal the enemies Pietro seemed to fear. They left after matins in order to escape the Camargue before summer sunshine sucked up the humidity and made riding acutely uncomfortable. Distant bells summoning monks to Prime whispered through the shroud in the absence of wind. Travelling north towards Nîmes as fast as Pietro's rough mount would allow, they reached the main road from Montpellier by late afternoon and stopped at a small hospice at the junction. Brother Jacques reckoned that it would take them two further days to Avignon.

As they rode, he was amused to see that Pietro's eyes were bright and eager, feasting on the sight of things he had not seen for years. Manacles were no handicap to his eyes. His head jerked from side to side like an excited country boy in a big city for the first time. He absorbed the sight of peasant women carrying fodder and bunches of faggots on their heads with such intensity that some of them shrank back. He must have appeared as a madman to them. Only once did he pale, when they came across the garrotted corpses of highwayman victims: unreal, white and swollen like pig's bladders against the dark sodden bullrushes into which they had been thrown.

At regular intervals they drank the cool water drawn from underground cisterns, lacing it with salt; at midday they stopped to rest the mules for an hour and to eat bread and olives they had carried with them. Beside the road, peasants harvested wheat and rye. The only other traffic until they reached the main road consisted of four-wheeled ox-wagons laden with grain on their way to the water mills of the lower Rhône for grinding. When they stopped for the second night Jacques watched village women collecting the season's first honey. Children were hanging bunches of lavender and herbs to dry under the eaves of their wayside hostel.

Sweat-salt had rubbed into Jacques' chafed thighs as he rode and the sun burned into his skull, so he was pleased to dismount, dunk his head in a barrel of cool water and sit, legs apart, in a corner of the ground-floor room of the hostel. Nicolas had taken Pietro and their two guards to the barn behind, away from the road through a thicket of thorns swaying like protective soldiers.

But his fellow guests' faces were far from reassuring. In the opposite corner sat a toothless man who seemed at first sight aged but who had the quick gestures and ready laugh of a younger man. He was protected and perfumed by an aura of garlic so strong that he must have bathed in it; Jacques' nostrils twitched as he thought of his favourite dish of haricot beans and garlic as his mother made it. Beside this rogue sat his companion, a sweet-faced boy with one eye slightly askew, who might have passed for the village simpleton had it not been for the vicious and well-kept dagger thrust into his belt, ready for action as only an expert would carry it. His hand hovered near it between gulps of the soup he was drinking noisily. Jacques wondered for a moment whether these were the men who had robbed and murdered the travellers whose corpses they had passed. They had the air of men capable of murdering their own mothers and then going to Mass without the slightest twinge of conscience. A pair of guards would not be enough to thwart such beast-men.

To obviate these thoughts he turned to watch the host's wife, who was chopping chunks of rancid fat and throwing them into the cauldron which simmered over a low fire even at the height of summer. She was an attractive, well-formed woman of good temper, who responded to the coarse comments of those who passed her with honest laughter. She reminded Jacques of the widow Ida, the subject of his previous interrogation.

Hers was a more conventional and theologically interesting case as he now recalled it. The thought of her, 'Ful of Love' as she was known from Milan to Avignon, warmed him now. He wondered if her cheerful laugh would have survived this place.

She had made a fine change from the usual run of witches, having been arrested while trying to seduce two Dominicans out in the fields during last autumn's harvest. An honest, intelligent and warm woman who had outraged the tribunal as she answered the president's questions. Jacques had warned him, but the senior inquisitor was loth to follow a young man's advice. Titters had rippled around the room as she had mimicked the pompous voices of the two Dominicans: 'Go away, woman, leave us alone. We are looking for grain,' they had apparently insisted. She was a natural storyteller. Then she had returned to her own rich voice: 'Ah, but I know what kind of grain you're looking for. You want to screw with me, that's your grain,'

33

she had repeated to the court. 'And they wouldn't listen to me, sire. There was nothing wrong in what I asked.' This had again sent barely suppressed laughter around the courtroom. When the president of the court had called her to order again, she had replied with a logic which privately amused Jacques even then: 'Why is it a sin?' she had shouted, now furious. 'It's not a sin at all, because God himself ordered it, for friars and priests are men as much as other men, and God endowed them too. Yes, they are well-endowed and serve women well. And if it were a sin and God didn't want it, he would not have allowed this to happen.' Brother Jacques had been glad that his responsibility ended as they entered the court.

The thought of Ida's beckoning gesture brought a half smile to his lips. There was something undeniably attractive about her. No wonder so many brothers had succumbed.

A sudden cacophony of shouts, crashing doors and horses leaping to the gallop blasted the privacy of his thoughts.

'Wait! Back here! Guards!' It was the shrill voice of Nicolas de Lirey. Jacques rushed to the door, thinking there might have been another murder. He glanced at the corner of the room, but the villainous-looking pair were still seated there greedily stuffing bread into their mouths.

Outside, all was pandemonium.

'What is it?' Jacques shouted at his companion. Nicolas and the guards were engaged in combat with a group of ruffians on the narrow path which led behind the hostel to the barn.

'Get the boy. The boy!' Nicolas' rising, pointing arm was struck backwards violently as he spoke. He spun round, grasping his opponent's throat with his other arm and drawing him across his thigh to the ground. The man was strong enough, but knew nothing better than to thwack a stick across an undefended skull. In an instant he would be able to deal with the others, Nicolas thought.

Jacques looked over at where Nicolas had been trying to point. There was a boy standing with the reins of four horses – the escape route. But Jacques could not understand the reason for this attack. He was about to run towards the boy when a mighty roaring curse stopped him in his tracks.

Nicolas had been struck to the ground by a horseman who had appeared suddenly from the barn. He was a huge, ruddy-faced man with an evil smile like a gargoyle, and he rode through the startled guards as if they didn't exist, his staff swatting them aside like flies.

To his horror, Jacques saw that on the saddle behind this giant of a man Pietro di Ocre was bound and gagged like hunting prey. Now he understood the reason for the attack.

He was also reassured to see his companion stagger to his feet. Then the unmistakable supercilious voice swore loudly: 'Damn! Had we knights rather than priests!'

The words sliced though a break in the din, and cut Jacques to the quick. Instinct prevailed over good sense. He leapt forward almost into the path of the oncoming horse on the rider's undefended left side. Slipping his arm under the rider's thigh with his elbow against the horse's shank, he took a strong grip on the leg, dug his elbow in, and with one mighty heave pulled the man straight out of the saddle onto the ground. By this time the prison guards had joined them and caught the horse by the reins as its rider fell. 'Hold it, whatever you do,' Jacques commanded, 'and free our prisoner.'

As they obeyed, the man got up and, disposing of the guards' feeble efforts to detain him, limped as fast as he could towards the boy and waiting horses. In what seemed to Jacques a matter of seconds since he came out of the hostel, the mounts were disappearing beyond a bend in the road.

Pietro di Ocre had been carried inside when Nicolas approached them, his face lightly scarred and scratched, yet he seemed almost cheerful. He regarded Jacques with genuine admiration. 'Not bad for a baker's son,' he smiled.

'Instinct,' Jacques muttered. It was only now that the terror of the situation broke through to him. He began to shudder in fear. He prayed, then smiled with new confidence and turned full-face towards Nicolas. 'I had an uncle who fought bulls in Arles. We would listen to his tales by the fireside and dream of emulating him. My first ambition was to be a bullfighter. But the nearest I got was the calves in a field behind the village, with my brothers and sisters. Dopey animals, those calves, but I learned to bring them down. And horses as well as calves have four legs .' He burst into laughter fuelled by the energy of fear.

'I never imagined you were so strong,' Nicolas observed as he took in this surprising insight into his new companion's youth. It had always seemed as though Brother Jacques had been born a scholar and inquisitor – a monk without childhood.

'Knights are not the only strong men. My grandfather was as good with a poleaxe as any knight. Kneading dough before dawn is as good as fencing or jousting practice with ponies.'

'I suppose it would be.' Nicolas had no idea how bread was made, but a twinge of conscience spurred his interest. 'Was your grandfather a baker too?' It had never occurred to him before that peasants had ancestors as well. 'In the Pays de Foix, wasn't it?' What was the village called? He'd been told just the day before.

Again, Jacques' fright erupted in nervous laughter. 'Saverdun.'

'Ah.' Nicolas seemed to consider this carefully. Then looked up sharply as if a new thought had occurred to him. 'And your mother?'

'She helped too, and she taught me a good deal that helped me today.'

'What on earth could a woman have taught you about battle?' Nicolas drew a kerchief from his tunic and began to dab warm blood which ran from cuts on his cheeks. From the corner of his eye he watched a thin smile which softened the inquisitor's face. His eyes turned upwards, and he looked as happy as a small boy who has just received his first riding lesson.

'Perseverance. That was her favourite word. When I went rabbit-trapping with my brothers she always used to say "Persevere, you're the only one who can. And just as you'll always catch a rabbit in the sandpit if you are patient, so you will equal the great men. Make your traps strong, be patient and persevere."'

'Sounds like a fable,' Nicolas laughed. It was all right for boys; but useless for knights. But he looked at Jacques with grudging interest. There was a new force in the monk's replies, a pride which must derive from his own person since it could not be hereditary. Jacques' drab grey eyes suddenly appeared as strong as his hands: they cleared and took on a hint of azure as he spoke of his mother. The stocky body stood rock still, feet too wide apart and angled for the Court; but firmly placed. It would take several men to move the inquisitor against his will. His head was lifted proudly, his hair falling back in thick curls like that of a sculpted gargoyle. Nicolas was struck for a moment by the other person who seemed to emerge from the peasant priest.

Jacques felt the gaze, but sought to ignore it. 'It's true,' he went on. 'And she was right. Patience, perseverance and strength. That's what you need.'

'And will it catch us that villain?' Nicolas indicated the road with his thumb. Sarcasm came naturally to him as the peasant in his interlocutor dominated again. Such homespun philosophy was not much use in battle, he reflected. Still, Brother Jacques had proved himself a brave man; so he kept his thoughts to himself.

36

'I doubt it. And I doubt it would be worth catching him. Where did he spring from?'

'He was in the barn with the other rogues. I sent our Pietro in first. Someone grabbed him, and the others set on me and the men. I should have checked. Without the surprise they'd never have taken him.' The confession of error cost him dear, but he knew he ought to have gone into the barn first.

'They didn't,' Jacques observed. 'Who do you think might have sent him? That would be worth knowing.' He wondered if this episode was linked to that of Brother Jean. He looked behind him sharply, as if he expected to find the stocky Dominican there.

Nicolas continued unaware. 'Someone who wants our Pietro. That's clear enough. But why?'

'You should know.'

'*Me?*' Does he think I'm conspiring against him, Nicolas thought. Surely he doesn't think Bernard de Caen would play such a double game? The monk's naïveté was astounding.

Nicolas' surprise seemed genuine, and Jacques was pleased, but his suspicions remained intact. 'Well, the entire mission is unconventional, as you know. Why was the order to be kept a secret? Why were we chosen? You're Lord Bernard's man. Tell me.'

Nicolas turned sharply, shaking his right arm. There was both darkness and hatred in his eyes. 'Has this burst of strength affected your mind, Brother? I am merely here because of the importance attached to your mission. Lord Bernard desired a secular knight to accompany you. It is a matter of politics, not of heresy. And I must say the full details are beyond my knowledge too.' He rose to his full height, and stormed back towards the barn. What right had a peasant, a baker's son – no matter if he is an inquisitor – to address him in such fashion? What was the world coming to? Ancient blood boiled within him.

So that was it. Nicolas de Lirey was simply there to observe, as Jacques had expected. He realized once the knight had disappeared from view that it was this strange sense of having been selected for reasons he did not understand, to carry out an assignment which had not been specified, that created the unease within him. Could it be, he wondered, that he was not supposed to discover the real truth, but to uncover a group of ideas from which Brother Bernard would recognize the right one? What was Nicolas hiding from him? He would have to keep his own counsel for a while, trusting neither Nicolas nor even Bernard de Caen. The bungled kidnap attempt indicated that this truth was something of great importance. But Jacques felt a slight start within himself as he realized that he was doubting his own Superior. It was something which had never happened before, and made him look around at the others with the astonishment a man might feel on suddenly finding himself in a new world.

He feared this empty swamp, and knew that he would not rest easy until they reached Avignon.

5

The new bridge across the Rhône appeared to Brother Jacques like an arching forefinger leading to haven. But he noticed that the first steps off the bridge into the city wrought the opposite effect on their prisoner: his face was taut and his eyes anxiously darted about as if seeking some enemy in the streets. Jacques watched the crowd carefully, but saw nothing. 'Something wrong?' he asked.

Pietro rode ahead in silence.

'What is it?' he insisted.

Again, there was no reply, so Jacques threw his cowl forward over his face and covered mouth and nose with a large handkerchief. At this time of year there was little of the proverbial wind of Avignon to drive away the lingering smell of sun-dried sewage, and the handkerchief also protected his throat from the dust thrown up by cartwheels and hoofs. After the noble stone of Aigues-Mortes, the low, pounded-earth houses and dusty streets seemed squalid to his eyes. Soon, he knew, the city would be transformed, with cobbled roads and stone palaces; but for the moment he yearned for autumn winds and rain which would carry away the stench. The muddy lanes he so often despised in winter did not stink like this.

For Jacques, unlike Pietro, Avignon was the new city of Pope Clement V and his own home for six years – with no taint of Anjou to stain it. He glanced at Nicolas, wondering what it might be for him. All he really knew about this young knight was that he was the son of a man who Bernard de Caen had once known well in Italy. And what little had transpired from a week in the saddle together.

It was more than he was used to. Jacques smiled to himself as he shifted himself in search of virgin flesh to sore. He was beginning to savour the comforts of his cell in advance when his horse suddenly reared up, neighing nervously and tossing its head from side to side. It took all Jacques' strength to pull it down, and it was only when he had succeeded that he noticed a strange tension pervading the air. He peered forwards through the dust his own mount had kicked up, but saw nothing, for there was a sharp bend ahead of them. Then he looked about anxiously, keeping one eye on the prisoner. Women who sat sewing in doorways took up their stools as one and went inside; children playing in the streets abruptly vanished; even trees lining the road seemed to stiffen as though they knew what was beyond the bend. He glanced at Pietro, wondering whether the preceptor might have sensed it earlier.

Then he too heard the deep, rhythmic thud of horses and men marching on clay.

First a herald appeared. A warm, smiling young man whose carefree gait and tossing long black hair belied the threat of the gathering rumble behind him, which approached with the profound menace of a growling summer thunderclap positioning itself above the spectator for its final burst of energy. He wore tight yellow hose and a crimson doublet with a curious wimple cut squarely like crenellations around his neck. Such bright colours were in gaudy contrast to the stark mud walls and dusty road. In his hand he bore a mock sceptre, which suggested the rank of his liege. He shook it at walls and onlookers like a priest swinging the censer of incense. Court fool as much as a herald, Jacques realized with a grin.

Then, as he watched the herald meander through the street, his small party was thrust aside by a wall of advancing knights like the Red Sea by Moses' rod. Jacques' grin disappeared. He stepped back aghast and stood in fear with his back pressed to a stone doorpost. The others followed him, one guard and their pack-mules being forced to the opposite side of the street by this tidal wave before he could gain the same building. A score of knights on chargers, armed with lances and swords, thrust their way through the narrow street regardless of bystanders. Jacques covered his mouth and nose against gusting grains of sand and dust. It was as if those knights rode through his party with disdain, their brightly-painted shields strapped carelessly across their backs. Each man wore fine, pointed shoes and silk hose, and richly-coloured silk or satin doublets. Jacques noticed that some were wearing the latest basinet-style helmets with projecting aventails to guard eyes and nose. Such devices were superfluous in Avignon, merely a sign of wealth and arrogance. The air rang – as they probably intended it to – with clattering armour and weapons, the quieter rattle and creak of loose harnesses, and what sounded like mocking laughter. It was only as the dust subsided and he was gazing on the horses' finely decorated rumps that he noticed the long blond hair which predominated amongst those knights who went helmless. He turned to Nicolas, who was two paces away along the wall, holding Pietro by the arms. 'Germans?' he shouted, lowering his arm from his face for an instant.

40

Nicolas nodded without uncovering his face. It would necessitate freeing his prisoner.

On their way to Rome for the Emperor Henry, Jacques reflected.

But there was no respite. For these knights were followed by at least fifty squires, on lighter horses and wearing less elaborate armour, and the same number of mounted archers with wooden crossbows and the new stirrup for easy loading ostentatiously on display. They rode with less style, but equal swagger. Pack-horses bearing armour for the chargers brought up the rear. Now the street disappeared entirely in a thick cloud.

War noises again, Jacques thought. Yet there was no war at hand, and they were in the full heat of summer. He assumed it was a display of strength designed to intimidate the people of Avignon; and the papal court, like a German foreboding of what was to happen in Rome.

As soon as the pack-horses were out of sight he shook the dust from his habit. 'Let's move now,' he ordered the vague figures in the dust-cloud. 'We're only a stone's throw from our destination.' He was relieved when the cloud passed and the abbey came into sight, lowering his arm again at last. For a moment he studied the crenellated walls that rose up just beyond, and the square tower which housed the few prison cells available. They had reached the main gate of the Black Friars' headquarters, and he was pleased that the passing knights had cleared the street of onlookers and they could approach the gate unobserved. The sewing-women had not reappeared yet, and no casually placed friar awaited them. He glanced at Pietro, who would be housed in the tower, reluctant to allow the preceptor out of his sight. But he needed time to meditate.

He wiped settled dust from his lips with the back of his hand, licked away what little remained and then cleared his throat. He looked up at his secular companion, who had remounted. 'Nicolas? Would you mind consigning our prisoner to the guards of the House? I have much to do.'

Nicolas jerked his horse to a halt before the sentence was ended. 'What?' he shouted. 'How dare you address me thus?' There was no limit to the inquisitor's audacity. '*Sire* Nicolas, if you please.' Then he recalled Lord Bernard's instructions and was sorry for his anger in front of the others, though nothing would alter his private sentiment.

Brother Jacques chose to ignore this outburst. He needed the knight's help, and the road was long yet. 'And make sure he's given a separate cell, sire,' he added almost absentmindedly.

'Orders now?' Nicolas said sarcastically. A polite request was reasonable, and would give him a few minutes alone with the prisoner. But this baker's son must be reminded of his rank, even though he was in fact playing into Nicolas' hands. 'Very well,' he agreed. The upstart's time would come, but not today.

Jacques felt embarrassment warm his cheeks as Nicolas left. He handed the reins of his hackney to an abbey groom, and escaped from that gaze through a wicket-gate.

For a moment he regretted his treatment of Nicolas, yet a feeling that he was in the right soon overwhelmed his regret and he allowed himself to break another rule. Instead of reporting his arrival to the Provincial he walked painfully through the main cloister to the infirmary, where he obtained a jar of ointment for his saddle-sores. Then he went to the small courtyard where his own cell was to be found.

Cool darkness drew him inside and soothed him. Even the stone niche beneath his window seemed soft after days in the saddle. He sat there with his habit drawn up, softly massaging the salve into his inner thighs.

Each chap and sore seemed to represent a road, and each road was fraught with danger: highwaymen, thieves, kidnappers, the Emperor's soldiers, German knights, Pietro di Ocre and the road to Italy. Beyond them all, linking and co-ordinating this pattern of violence and heresy in some mysterious way was the person of Bernard de Caen. The idea struck terror in him, for to question the rectitude of such a powerful man – even in one's mind – was courting danger. Yet the vague notion of a link persisted.

The salve was now spread evenly over his thighs, which had taken on a pale yellow colour. Like ochre. Or *ocre* in French, Jacques realized.

The vagueness suddenly came into focus.

From the beginning he had known that the name Ocre was not new to him. Now he knew why: it was Bernard himself who had told him many years ago that he was once prior of a house in Italy, Santa Maria di Casanova. And amongst the dependencies of Casanova, if his memory did not fail him now, was a Santa Maria or Santa Something of Ocre . . . He leapt to his feet and leaned on the windowsill, looking onto vegetable gardens behind the convent. The pain from his chaps retreated as his excitement grew.

So Bernard knew the whole story.

6

On an impulse Brother Jacques left his cell, and strode quickly through the convent. He knew he would not be expected until the morning for his new Superior never received visitors so late in the day. But he wished to see Bernard de Caen immediately. He ignored friars who greeted him, plunging though the tunnel of the main cloister with a single thought in his mind. A faint sense of being a man apart insinuated itself as he realized that such impulsiveness was something new. This bee in his bonnet was already driving him as it always did when he was fully engaged in an inquiry.

Two guards stood to attention as he entered the slightly curving corridor which led a dozen paces in from the cloister to Bernard's study. It was as if they expected him. He hesitated, and looked at each in turn. He had never seen guards at the beginning of the corridor in the past; furthermore, he had never before known guards to stand to attention as he passed. The landmarks of the world which he had come to know in his years in the convent were changing with disconcerting speed. Nothing remained as it had been. What on earth could be the reason for this new security?

His momentary hesitation alerted him to the voices in Bernard's study. They seemed to spiral towards him through the corridor. The door was slightly ajar, the occupants clearly safe in the knowledge that their lair was well protected. Jacques looked back, and realized that the guards could no longer see him.

Instinct overcame training. For the first time in his life something within him told him to challenge authority and eavesdrop. He asked forgiveness of the Lord, crossed himself, and moved forwards quietly, straining his ears to pick up something of the conversation within; quickly enough not to rouse the suspicion of the guards. He was glad for his soft convent shoes; the heavy open sandals he had worn on the journey could have been heard a hundred paces away. At the half-way point the words suddenly became clear, as if the voices were hovering above him. He glanced up at the vaulted ceiling, wondering what strange effect it had caused.

Jacques concentrated.

'. . . an image . . . something of extraordinary beauty and power. They said it was once in Ocre.' The unmistakeable thin voice of Bernard de Caen was agitated. He was certain.

'What do you say about that?' It sounded like Nicolas de Lirey this time. But what could he be doing there?

There was a brief silence. Jacques froze. Cold sweat dripped from his neck.

Then the reply came. 'I've heard of it. But you will never find it now.' At first he did not recognize the voice. It was certainly familiar, but at the same time odd. 'No one will!' the voice went on.

That finality gave the game away. It was Pietro di Ocre. Jacques wished he could be a fly on the wall. He was deliberately excluded from this interview as he had been the first time. And yet Nicolas was there. He continued to move silently forward, almost within touching distance of the door now. He reached out to knock. Then, as another voice started he allowed his clenched fist to open and his fingertips to run slowly down the rough wood of the door.

'Is that what King Philip is searching for in Italy?' It was Bernard de Caen talking again.

Pietro laughed, with an ease which Jacques had never heard in their three days together. It was a remarkable transformation. 'How should I know? I've been in his wretched prison these last years. Ask him. Or find it for yourselves.'

Jacques began to feel the guards' eyes drilling into his back, even though he was sure they could not see him. But he did not dare to turn round. He hunched his shoulders and twisted his perspiring neck inside his collar. But it was impossible to wait there any longer. He rapped the door with his knuckles.

'Enter!' Bernard's squeaky voice replied. 'Ah! Brother Jacques,' he continued as the door swung open, without the slightest trace of surprise, 'we were expecting you.' It was the most blatant falsehood Jacques had ever heard from those ambiguous lips. Then his Superior shouted into the corridor: 'Guards! At once!'

Jacques stood dumbfounded in the doorway. Here were the three men sitting as if at an informal dinner with a bottle of wine on the table beside them. Pietro di Ocre had been washed and brushed, and given a new tunic. He looked quite human.

Jacques stepped aside as the guards came running, took Pietro by his arms, and led him away. Then he stepped inside and closed the door behind him. 'I thought I asked you to deliver the preceptor to his cell?' he asked as soon as Pietro di Ocre was led away.

Nicolas stared angrily at him. Orders; and now reprimands. 'You must remember that Lord Bernard is . . .'

'Your Superior, Brother Jacques. Yes, it was my responsibility. News came to me that you had returned, and I at once asked for the prisoner to be brought here.' He pause, and smiled. 'Come and sit down.'

Nicolas thanked him silently for the lie with a smile which barely lifted his upper lip.

Jacques looked about the study for comfort. Bare stone walls, a heavy wooden table, piled papers and candlesticks – all seemed linked by a common force against him. The study had always appeared to him homely in comparison with his own and other cells; this evening the usual warmth had vanished into chill hostility. Even Christ on his cross above the fireplace seemed to look down on him mockingly with his half-closed eyes.

There was nothing to be done. Rank had been established, and as he had suspected Bernard clearly knew more than he was letting Jacques know. 'Did you discover anything new?' Jacques asked. He tried to make the question as innocent as possible. He was uncomfortably aware that Bernard had asked nothing about *his* interrogation.

'We couldn't do in ten minutes what you and Sire Nicolas failed to in an entire day,' Bernard answered smoothly. 'I just wanted to meet the man. Now he's all yours.'

Yet he had questioned him. About an image. Something which had once been in Ocre. How much more had there been? The meeting could have lasted as much as two hours if Nicolas had taken Pietro di Ocre there immediately, after a quick wash. Suppose he had not come here now on an impulse? Would Bernard have interrogated the Templar all evening? There was no way of knowing. There was only an order. And feigned gratitude. 'Thank you. I will see what we can do,' Jacques said.

But the suspicion was lodged in his mind.

7

What could it all mean? What was Bernard de Caen's game? Had Nicolas already received the order to deliver the prisoner directly to Bernard before they left Avignon? What was his own role in an inquiry in which he was not being given full information?

He clenched his fists and swore gently to himself, for he was being asked to draw out something without sufficient information. Hardly a clue whatsoever. Moreover, *he* had been excluded while his Superior took the chance to ask his own questions. It was true that it was Lord Bernard's right, and that he must defer to power; but at the same time Jacques recalled his previous exclusion, and the sense that both Bernard and Nicolas possessed information which was withheld from him rankled. And he was supposed to find the relic. Yet at the same time it dawned on him that Bernard himself could not be much better informed. Perhaps it was ignorance he was concealing, not knowledge.

This recognition assuaged his mounting anger. It was essential to think rationally. An image. That could be anything. Yet it was an image of incredible importance, which both Bernard de Caen and King Philip craved. Even though Bernard might not know exactly what it was, he certainly knew what he wanted to do with it. The purpose was incised on his features as he spoke about it. But Jacques could not interpret it yet.

In the solace of his own cell, with pain freshly stabbing his thighs, Brother Jacques thought of Bernard's earlier summonings each of which had represented a turning-point in his life. And they had each been odd.

The first time had been when Jacques came to the end of his novitiate at Mirepoix. He remembered as clearly as though it had been the day before. There had never been any question about his faith, but months previously he been plagued by doubt about his vocation. The routine at Mirepoix was dampening his enthusiasm for the monastic life. His only real pleasure, the cold, quiet solitude of the vaulted scriptorium where he spent days copying manuscripts, was soon denied him. For he had been unable to prevent himself stopping to comment on the texts, and as a punishment was assigned to the abbey forge. He was beginning to despair of ever finding sufficient stimulus when he had been summoned by Abbot Guibert.

'Enter,' the white-haired abbot had said simply. Jacques guessed that he knew of his faltering vocation and was on the point of announcing his decision to leave the abbey.

But another presence had distracted him and seemed to draw him into the room. A short, stubby and middle-aged figure wearing a starched white Cistercian habit, who was seated on the leather chair reserved for important guests. 'Is this the young man?' he had asked in a curiously squeaky voice.

'Yes, sire.' Jacques had never heard his superior speak with such deference, not even to the Countess of Foix when she made her annual visit.

'Let me see you, lad.' The man beckoned Jacques towards him.

Jacques had quailed under such an intense scrutiny, but managed to keep staring back. Small, round, bright-green eyes penetrated his very being, he remembered, and had seemed to explore his conscience. He had turned away when it became too much for him.

As he did so, the guest nodded to the abbot. His heavy lower lip almost broke into a smile. He appeared satisfied.

The abbot took a manuscript volume from his table, then turned to address the novice.

Jacques had then been asked to provide an impromptu commentary on one of Peter Lombard's *Sentences*, 'On knowledge of the Creator through creatures, in whom the trace of the Trinity appears'. It came easily to him, since for months he had been studying the *Sentences* every morning.

He had delivered his commentary to the stranger, with only occasional remarks made towards the abbot. A mixture of fear and fascination possessed him, together with an odd feeling that his words were being sucked out of him. The stranger made no visible attempt to listen, often peering through the window as if he had heard it all before. He probably had. Yet Jacques noticed that whenever he faltered, or made the slightest hesitation, those small round eyes suddenly focused on him. It was uncanny, and disturbing. A cold sweat broke out on his neck and palms even in that chill room. The man was neither attractive nor warm, but possessed a unique, compelling personality. Whoever he was, he must be very sharp, Jacques thought as he spoke. And very powerful.

When he finished, the stranger had sunk back into his chair intent on his tiny, chubby fingers. Again he nodded to the abbot.

'Thank you, Brother Jacques,' Abbot Guibert said.

The guest remained silent.

'You may leave now.'

That night Jacques had barely slept. The bell which called them to vigils brought him a sense of relief he had never known before. Something in the stranger's expression haunted him through the following day and night, until he began to look back on the interview as a nightmare.

Three days later he had been summoned to the abbot's private study again. The abbot regarded him with an expression he could not fathom, a curious blend of disdain and admiration. 'You must make ready for a journey,' he said simply.

'Am I to leave? Where to?'

'Paris.'

'Paris,' Jacques repeated foolishly. It was like a dream.

'You will study for the doctorate in theology at the new College de Sorbon.'

'*Me?*' The brusque delivery of this startling information conferred a ring of implausibility. Yet his throat had tightened with fear of the unknown, for the abbot would never invent such a story.

'You have been recommended by Lord Bernard de Caen. It is a great honour.' There had been no further explanation. It would have been superfluous; an instinct had told him.

When his studies in Paris were completed, and he had passed a year as a *biblicus* lecturing on the scriptures, he had been just as mysteriously assigned to this convent in Avignon and seconded to the Dominican inquisitors. He had assumed that Bernard de Caen was responsible for this move too, although in four years he had seen Bernard no more than a dozen times, and never alone. He had heard rumours of Bernard's frequent absences from the convent, but dismissed the wilder stories which circulated out of a blind and inexpressible loyalty. Then, one day, as unexpectedly as on the first occasion, he was summoned to the Inquisitor-General's office.

Bernard de Caen had not exactly aged, though his face was fatter and his hair thinner. His eyes had lost none of their capacity to freeze men solid at a glance. Jacques had been motioned towards a chair, and then, to his surprise, offered a glass of the finest Saint Pourçain of Auvergne, the wine he knew was drunk only by the noble and wealthy. 'Young man,' the Inquisitor-General had begun, 'we have been pleased with your work. I have read you reports with great interest. You are to be complimented for your perspicacity and comprehension of the more abominable heresies.'

Jacques had wished to thank his Superior, but was struck dumb by cold fear. It was some time before he realized that there were no guards or companions present.

'This is a profession requiring great trust,' Bernard began with carefully measured words. 'As you know. And our most trusted men are often put into situations of extreme delicacy, consorting with heretics and understanding their false beliefs. We have been especially pleased with your discretion.' He emphasized the last word by raising his voice slightly and screwing his eyes into a tighter stare. 'I have a particularly delicate mission for you. Its successful completion will lead to certain promotion. You may have heard of the *Opus Christi*?'

A lump formed in Jacques' throat, causing him to swallow hard. At the same time he felt the muscles beneath his eyes twitching, and hoped they could not be seem. Rumours about this clandestine organization were the stuff of many muffled conversations in the cloister: that it was formed of men willing to commit any deed – even sacrilege – in order to maintain the power of the Church. Jacques trembled as he recalled that Bernard was believed to be the head of this organization, reporting to the Pope himself. According to this view, his role as Inquisitor-General for Provence was merely a cover. Jacques had never fully believed in the existence of the *Opus*, so the implications of Bernard's question unsettled him. 'Yes,' he replied hesitantly.

'There is a problem in the diocese of Caen,' Bernard continued obliquely, staring over his listener's head.

Far beyond your jurisdiction, Jacques thought. But he simply nodded as Bernard then fixed his gaze upon him. It was, after all, his Superior's native city.

'It's a delicate matter, and I need someone I can trust. Someone with considerable theological acumen . . .'

Jacques' body tensed as he sought to imagine what this was leading up to, and what it might have to do with the *Opus Christi*.

'There has been an unfortunate series of delations concerning three women of Caen. Neighbours accuse them of having set up a "church" for the Amis de Dieu, and furthermore of declaring themselves "bishops" of the new diocese they claim to have founded.'

The contempt he placed on the words 'church' and 'bishops' caused him to splatter his table and Jacques' hands with saliva.

Jacques nodded again. *Delatores* were the stuff of all inquisitorial trials; the Amis de Dieu were Cathars. Yet it was odd that Bernard had not strengthened his nouns with the customary adjectives: it should have been the 'abominable Cathar church', 'diabolical bishops', peppered with phrases like 'sunk into heretical depravity'. Curious now, he dared to voice his earlier thought: 'But Caen falls within the jurisdiction of Paris, my lord,' he suggested.

Now the green eyes threatened to transfix him to the door behind. But the words Bernard spoke were gentle, the sign of inhuman self-control. 'I realize that, young man, and did emphasize that it was a delicate matter.' He paused, clasped his hands, and looked vacantly towards the ceiling as if doubting the trust he might be able to place in this inquisitor.

Jacques sat as stiff as a fresh corpse, all senses alert. Sounds from the courtyard outside came to his ears with terrifying clarity. Doors slamming, distant cries, a thrush imitating the song of a lark, murmered conversations as if the walls were alive with the pleas and screams of past generations of victims, the dull squeak of an axe jamming in damp wood. That's it, he reflected ironically at this last sound: awaiting the executioner's axe must be just like this.

Then Bernard spoke. Judgement was made. 'The problem is, young man, that one of these women is my sister Beatrice.'

Contradictory impulses almost overwhelmed Jacques. The implication that he was to be trusted made him want to relax; at the same time he had to fight to prevent his mouth dropping agape. This new fact fully explained Bernard's avoidance of the customary inquisitorial language.

'I should like you to travel to Caen at once. The situation needs a firm hand and all your dialectical gifts. You will find the recompense commensurate with the task.' He looked away.

'My lord,' Jacques bowed, amused by his Superior's attempt to escape embarrassment by expressing himself so pompously. But what in Heaven's name did it mean? Could this be a trial to assess his worthiness for the *Opus Christi*? But training soon shifted his mind from rhetorical questions to immediate practical difficulties. 'Is the evidence against her strong?' he asked.

'The strongest. Moreover, the president of the tribunal is no fool. As I said, it requires theological skill.'

Bargaining skill, more like it, Jacques thought to himself as he glimpsed a solution to the problem. 'What of the other women?'

'It is they who have led her astray,' was the laconic response. 'Here are letters of introduction to men of the Church at Caen.' He passed over a purse containing folded letters, and heavy coins which Jacques could feel through the thin leather. There were also copies of the trial documents.

Brother Jacques had departed at once with his *socius* or companion, preparing his strategy as he rode north through the Kingdom of France. The evidence was stronger than Bernard had intimated, and conviction seemed certain according to the transcripts he was able to read. There was little doubt that she would be invited to place herself in perpetual imprisonment in penance, as the formula had it.

But Bernard de Caen's letters and money aided theological acumen and bargaining. It was eventually agreed that Beatrice and the other women should be taken to Avignon, where the Cathar heresy had been eradicated together with the city walls. There, her case might be compared with that of other Cathar 'bishopesses' held by the Inquisition. As a kind of punishment for his success, Jacques was forced to listen to her constant sermons and attempts to convert passers-by to the Cathar cause as he escorted her and the two friends who, according to her brother, had 'led her astray'. In private, Jacques was inclined to believe the opposite.

The commission which had tried Beatrice in Avignon was carefully chosen and naturally absolved her. She and her friends were placed in the hands of the Superior of the Cistercian nuns at Villeneuve.

'Good,' was all Bernard de Caen had said after hearing a full report. No mention of the *Opus Christi*.

Jacques had believed, or at least hoped, that he had read a hint of satisfaction at his work in the inscrutable expression of his Superior. But he never understood. No more than he had seen reason when that Nicolas de Lirey had been assigned to him as his temporary, secular, *socius*.

Why Nicolas?

8

'Well? What do you think?'

Straight to the point as usual, Nicolas thought. 'Of Brother Jacques?'

Bernard de Caen nodded solemnly.

'A clever man. And courageous too. Whether or not he'll solve your problem is another matter. He's searching for a needle in a haystack without knowing what a needle is.' All pleasure in his adapted proverb was wiped from his face by Bernard's glare. The small body seemed somehow to rise up like spiritual dough and fill the entire space of the study. A single gaze could suffocate a man: heaven knew what it must be like for a prisoner. Or even an inferior, Nicolas mused, thinking of Brother Jacques again. 'Could we not inform him?'

'Of the image? Certainly not. He would not accept your presence, which I deem essential. This is much more than a question of a relic: it is an affair of state.'

It sounded grand. 'Then why use him at all?'

'Because he's the most brilliant theologian we have. It's unusual for a Cistercian to be attached to our Order, you know. The Dominicans don't allow anybody into their private garden, unless they really need them.' He pointed his finger in admonition, just like the de Lirey tutor many years ago. 'And the job needs a theologian.'

'The relic you heard about with my father . . .' Nicolas thought aloud. 'Twenty years ago. Do you think it still exists?'

'I'm certain it does. And I'm certain other people are certain. We must find it now.'

'But you yourself questioned this preceptor when he was arrested. Did nothing come of that?'

'I wasn't sure he knew then.'

'And now?'

'Now I know,' Bernard said simply.

'And Brother Jacques?'

'He knows how to draw a man out. He knows enough. But not enough to endanger us. If he knew the truth now, we would have trouble on our hands; but I trust he will burrow it out in the end.

And you will be there to make sure he does nothing foolish. It will not be long.'

Nicolas looked at him. But Bernard's lips were sealed with his forefinger. So he had received information recently: hence the haste. The knight turned to leave, then stopped. 'It is a great honour to be a small part of the *Opus*, my lord.'

'Nonsense.' Bernard stood up, and walked towards him. 'It's nothing more than you deserve. I'll always trust a de Lirey an inch further than another man.'

Nicolas blushed at the admonishment. When he looked up again, he saw the rotund figure of his father's friend as if for the first time. A body broken by lack of exercise, a face that sweated even in this cool room; it seemed like something that belonged to a fresco of hell rather than to the headquarters of the Inquisition. He nearly shuddered, then recalled Lord Bernard's background. That was enough. His appearance would indeed have been unacceptable in a trader's son . . . or a baker's . . . but Bernard was the youngest son of a knight of Normandy, and destined for high places in the Church. He bowed courteously.

Bernard looked thoughtful for a moment. Then he spoke softly: 'Will you sup with us?'

'Thank you. No. I'm expected at my cousin's across the river.' Nicolas left the study with a swift movement, relieved to be alone again. With no more than a quick glance at prison and convent, he strode towards the stable.

Shortly afterwards, Brother Jacques walked in the great cloister before supper. A few monks were seated between the columns, but none paid attention to him. Water splashed in the fountain at the centre of the cloister, freshening the air. Bees delved deeply into roses and honeysuckle. A solitary thrush sang amidst the shrubbery. He was concentrating so intensely that only at the last moment did he notice the rotund figure of Bernard de Caen approach. He waited, curious to see the man's reaction.

The waddling figure drew so close that Jacques could feel the heat of his Superior's dragon-like breath. He saw the piercing eyes, their pupils shrunk, like a cat's, against bright evening sunshine, open in wonder. Then they dilated as full control returned. 'Come,' Bernard de Caen said casually, 'I am on my way to His Holiness.'

For a few minutes they walked in silence. Jacques had never been so uncomfortably afraid of the Inquisitor-General's unpredictable behaviour, and walked in fear of his wrath like a guilty schoolboy beside his master. But the chubby figure waddled beside him apparently unconcerned. It was only as they approached the far corner of the great cloister that he stopped abruptly and turned towards Jacques. 'Well! What does your prisoner have to say for himself?' he asked sharply.

'Nothing of special interest. He seems a very ordinary Templar, and our records provide a full documentation of his life.' Jacques wanted to say: you've already spoken to him yourself; but dared not. Instead he watched the round face carefully while he spoke, looking for some sign. There was only the slightest tightening of facial muscles and an intensification of that quizzical gaze. 'I've gone through the records very carefully,' Jacques went on nervously, 'and there are no *obvious* places to start . . . digging further.' He allowed the last words to hang between them, again hoping for confirmation. As he did so he realized that Bernard had deliberately waited for Nicolas to leave before asking about the interrogation. He clearly operated on the principle of divide and rule.

'I don't doubt that for a moment,' Bernard de Caen said. He made no attempt to disguise the irony in his voice. He paused and half turned as if to see whether they were being followed, then continued walking. 'Tell me,' he then began softly, as if the potential for anger had passed, 'did he mention any names?'

'Names?' Jacques relaxed, and thought quickly. 'His uncle. Thomas Berard.'

'No others?'

'Not that I recall.'

'Saints? Names of churches or sanctuaries?'

'No.'

'None at all? He didn't mention a San Eusanio, for instance?'

'No, my lord.' Jacques inclined his head towards Brother Bernard. Now what was this? Who in the name of the Lord was San Eusanio? Before he had a chance to find out, they reached the entrance to the new wing which Clement had built in what had once been the vegetable gardens, jutting out from the compact monastery plan like the tail on a setter.

'Wait here,' Bernard said simply. But although the words were spoken gently it was a firm command.

Guards came sharply to attention as Bernard de Caen approached. The clash of heavy mail-coats and swords brought an usher scurrying from a niche. Jacques watched as he stepped between the guards and knocked on the door. A small, severe-faced friar appeared at the door with the same promptitude, smiled, and then genuflected. 'Your Grace,' he said with practised respect. The gesture with which he indicated the passage grew naturally from the movement of rising from his knees. When it was complete he swivelled on the balls of his feet and pushed the door fully open. Then he stepped back, and allowed his eyes to drop ostentatiously to the floor.

Such obsequiousness fascinated Jacques. He retraced his steps as Bernard entered and sat in the cloister. It was the hour between vespers and compline, and the monks were seated on the stone benches between columns awaiting the daily reading from the *Collationes*. He joined them, now painfully aware of his diversity. He wished it could be winter, so that the darkness would disguise him.

As he had feared, when the reading was finished a fellow inquisitor came to sit beside him; a garrulous Gascon renowned as the convent busybody. Jacques knew him well by sight, but had no idea of his name.

'Good evening,' the monk said.

The kindness of his voice and gentleness of manner did much to assuage Jacques' initial aversion to the man. 'Good evening,' he replied without falsity.

'They tell me you've been in the south.'

'That's true enough.' Jacques was caught unprepared by the directness of the statement, but there was no point in denial.

'On a mission for Lord Bernard?'

Jacques hid a grimace. The man was living up to his reputation after all.

'Strange things are afoot,' the monk continued.

'Indeed they are.' Jacques realized that here was a chance to use this curious monk for a change. Give, and you will be given. 'The roads were cluttered with fully armed knights: German, so I understand.'

'Travelling south or north?' His interlocutor looked up with interest.

'South, towards Italy. The Emperor Henry's men. They say he's on the point of taking Rome. I shouldn't be in the least surprised if His Holiness were to move to Rome, out of King Philip's reach. What news from Paris?' He tried to make the question casual.

The Dominican was clearly glad for this titbit of information, and in return responded warmly.

'You don't know?' He sounded surprised. 'That's Lord Bernard's preserve ... at least, that's what they say. King Philip threatens to take over the property of the Templars immediately and, naturally, His Holiness is doing everything to thwart him. The latest word is that the whole matter is coming to a head.'

'What do you think will happen?'

The Gascon rose proudly to his role as valued confidant. 'I fear the King will win. He's ambitious, ruthless and strong. But there have been rumours that Pope Clement has something up his sleeve ... something to do with Lord Bernard. You wouldn't know anything about that, would you?'

'No. Nothing at all.' It was an honest answer, but Brother Jacques failed to conceal his embarrassment. For the words of this garrulous monk had revealed to him an inkling of the truth, and of the motivation behind the order to ride to Aigues-Mortes.

'He wants the Empire,' the monk said abstractly.

Jacques stared at him. Philip as Emperor, and Pope Clement under his thumb while the Church falls apart. It was an abominable idea. So soon after the success of Pope Boniface's Jubilee. But he realized there might be some truth in the monk's words. He shuddered as a new question began to form in his mind.

But the Gascon forestalled him. 'And we all know what Lord Bernard wants, don't we?' he added in a conspiratorial tone.

Jacques leaned forward, curious.

'More variety in womanfolk . . .'

'What do you mean?' Jacques broke in angrily.

'Come on, you know he likes a bit on the side, like many another powerful man. And I dare say you do too,' the monk laughed.

At that moment Bernard de Caen reappeared from the inner sanctum of the Pope. The Gascon faded behind a column as quickly as he had appeared. Jacques thought he perceived a new brightness in the Inquisitor-General's expression; the rotund figure moved in a strange, urgent flurry of robes. He seemed taller, younger. Noble. Surely the Gascon's insinuations were unfounded?

Bernard approached Jacques and made an impatient gesture with his hand. 'Come. There is much to be done. In three days we shall leave for Paris, if you so desire.'

'*We*? Paris?' The unpredictability again. Just like the first time he had been summoned.

Bernard took his arm as they walked through the cloister. 'His Holiness wishes you to accompany me. We have discussed your future,' he went on, choosing each word with care. 'We believe you have proved yourself loyal and perceptive. And at this moment of great danger, with His Holiness pressed on all sides, we need men like you.' He allowed the compliment to sink in, and then turned towards Jacques with a paternalistic expression on his face. 'It seemed to me that it would be a good idea for you to come to Paris. You know the city well and you understand its people. You must watch, listen carefully and remember that you too are under observation. We all are in the *Opus*.'

Jacques halted abruptly as the word jolted him afresh.

Bernard drew him on as if nothing had happened. 'I will not pretend there is no danger, and will not force you to join me. But it is something of vital importance for the Holy Roman Church. *You* must decide whether you will commit yourself to our cause. We leave in three days.'

'But my Lord, we have barely returned from Aigues-Mortes,' Jacques protested.

Bernard smiled. 'If you do decide, then you must be prepared for much travel.'

'And our prisoner? We've brought him all the way here to interrogate him.'

'He'll wait. He's been in prison for years, and he'll be here when you return. And, what's more, there are two big advantages which you might gain.'

'Advantages?' Jacques failed to disguise his scepticism.

'Yes, young man. You have much to learn. First, our Pietro will be in suspense and he will have time to think. In a few weeks he may be ready to talk. Second, and even more important, your journey to Paris may make the questioning easier. There are larger matters of which you are as yet unaware.' He waved his hand abstractly, as if indicating invisible larger matters.

Jacques watched the hand, and then regarded the bland face intently. But no further explanation would be forthcoming. He realized that he would have to commit himself first.

Then another thought came to him. 'And Nicolas de Lirey?'

'Someone must be here to watch over the prisoner.'

'To question him?' Jacques asked suspiciously.

'Just to watch over. Nicolas has other tasks.' He paused, and smiled. 'And you must see something of the world, young man.'

Jacques pursed his lips: if he were with the spymaster, the spy would be superfluous.

'I believe our cause will benefit by your journey to Paris,' Bernard said with the air of a final observation, 'and both Nicolas and Pietro di Ocre will be here when you return.' He paused to let the words sink in: it was a politely formulated command. 'But I will leave it up to you. I bid you good evening.'

Bernard turned without awaiting an answer, and was gone.

The 'cause'. It sounded grand. Jacques began to see that his journey was intended to be an oblique initiation into the *Opus Christi*.

It was then that he noticed the letter, a furled scroll with the papal seal clearly visible under Bernard de Caen's arm as he walked away.

Fear gnawed at his stomach, as it had done when he had first met Bernard. The decision implied drastic changes in his life. But the fear was soon replaced by a new sensation as the self-pride which he had worked for years to suppress suddenly resurfaced.

He had three days, and knew that there was only one place in which he could spend them.

9

'Welcome, Brother Jacques. We are pleased to have you with us again.'

'It's only a brief visit, Lord Abbot.' He was pleased to see Guibert again. The old man's hair was now as pure as snow.

'Our pleasure has no limits of time. You are welcome in your own house for a day or a lifetime. Either at Mirepoix or here.'

Jacques smiled within. There was neither severity nor disappointment in Guibert's face, and his words signalled that he bore no grudge over his one-time protégé's desertion and unorthodox career. Jacques knew he had made the right decision. Apart from the fact that his convent was only half a day's ride from Avignon, he knew no demands would be made upon him to explain what he was doing. Guibert had not changed: he was still slim, with quick hands which sliced through the air as he talked, and the ruddy countenance of a peasant. His gentle and uninquisitive voice was itself a reassurance.

'Do you have news of Father Guilhem?' the abbot continued.

'Not of late. But I'd have heard if he weren't well.' The evasive answer stabbed at Jacques' conscience. For he knew that the village priest's simple conception of Church and World would never encompass the ideas and actions of such as Bernard de Caen. Yet without Father Guilhem he would have remained a baker's apprentice, or gone to tend the flocks in the hills nearby. He wondered now what the priest had perceived in him at such a tender age; how he might have discerned the facility for learning Latin which paved the way to Mirepoix under Guilhem's supervision. The written word had replaced rabbit snares in his boyish enthusiasm; the soul, game.

Long summer evenings in the sacristy when work was done had been his school, and he had often looked back with gratitude from Mirepoix and Paris at the thorough grounding in grammar he had received there. At the same time – although he did not realize it then – Father Guilhem was carefully lodging in his father's mind the idea that his son Jacques would eventually go off to take holy vows. Nothing seemed more natural when the time came, and it was Guilhem's friendship with Abbot Guibert which smoothed the way. Lately, he had slipped from Jacques' mind; but at this moment of decision, a warm feeling of gratitude suffused him. 'I'll write to him,' he resolved aloud as he left the abbot's chamber.

The monastic scansion of the day brought relief, as if the herbalist-brother had been able to prepare a salve which reached the depths of his soul. He derived a feeling of absolute trust from the serenity of the monks, so unlike the ambiguity of association with Nicolas de Lirey and Brother Bernard. The daily office brought rhythm to his thought and prayer, restoring an inner peace he had been lacking for too long. He warmed to the sacristan brother who sounded the hours, as if that simple ancient was personally responsible for this sense of certainty. He slept in the communal dortoir without a screen or any other privilege.

The sounding of the *tabula* calling the monks to hear the division of work brought liberation to him; even the blisters of unaccustomed labour nurtured pleasure within their pain. But he was there to rest and meditate, so the abbot insisted that he did not join the work parties which went out twice a day to the harvest.

Yet Jacques' conscience pressed, for his mind had been opened to new stimuli, and this sanctuary might only represent temporary respite from them. Church and Empire were endangered and the world was changing alarmingly. Would these brothers be allowed to go on with their routine of work and prayer forever? Was there any guarantee that their Order would not go the way of the Templars? As he prayed and observed the monks at work these questions plagued him.

On the second evening Jacques requested an audience with the abbot. 'I knew you would come,' Guibert smiled.

'Then you know?'

'Absolutely not. Your face betrays the depth of your travail. Your nervousness and the way you penetrate our lives with your stares are enough to reveal the severity of your dilemma.'

'Then it is obvious to all and sundry?'

The abbot waved his hand. 'Fear not . . . but tell me, my son, how may we help you?'

'It is restful here,' Brother Jacques began abstractedly.

'And you may stay as long as you wish . . .'

'But at the same time I am restless, I must confess. These past weeks have been confusing.'

'Then take your time. Please sit down.' Abbot Guibert indicated a stool at the end of his table.

'I cannot take time. That is the problem.'

The abbot was clearly taken aback by the decisiveness of tone. He asked the question in his mind by lifting an eyebrow.

'Tomorrow I am called upon to make a decision. To commit myself to undertake something which has not even been made clear to me,' Jacques said slowly. Even as he spoke, he was painfully aware of patterns and undercurrents in his own life which did not tally with the monastic scansion of offices. Had the assuagement of his first day here been an illusion?

'With Lord Bernard de Caen?' It was the closest Abbot Guibert came to direct interrogation, and embarrassment showed clearly on his face. They were well informed here.

There was no point in denying it. 'Yes, with Lord Bernard.' Jacques' body slumped while he spoke, as though an invisible salve had been applied to his tense muscles. 'I must travel to Paris with him on a matter of great urgency, and I'm not sure that I'm ready for such responsibility.'

'Lord Bernard would not have chosen you had he not thought you were ready,' the abbot suggested softly.

'That is all the more worrying. It appears he has been observing and grooming me for years as if for this very task. My studies in Paris and my work in Avignon were his doing. Would that I had been a simple monk in your abbey rather than a doctor of theology.' His head fell into his hands, and he ruffled his hair as he spoke, suddenly exhausted. 'I was summoned to his study, deprived of my regular *socius*, lumped together with an arrogant from Champagne who thinks of little ese but his family name, and dispatched to the swamps of the accursed Camargue on a most improbable search for a mysterious object which Lord Bernard seems to believe will "save the Church" – to use his own words. And now, with barely time to heal my saddle sores, I must leave for Paris. Amidst hushed talk of the *Opus Christi*.'

Abbot Guibert drew his breath sharply and stared at Jacques. When he spoke, it was with the tone of a judge making a carefully considered verdict: 'Well, if it is Lord Bernard then it is for the good of the Church,' he pronounced.

'It is a great honour,' Jacques replied, 'but at the same time I fear the unknown. It is a world I don't know.'

'But you are young and strong. Lord Bernard would not have chosen you if he did not believe you capable of fulfilling whatever task he has in mind for you.'

'The task has not been made explicit. If it had, my decision would be easier.'

The abbot laid his hand upon Brother Jacques' arm.

'There are certain tasks which the Lord deems best left vague. He requires different things of each of us and it is not for us to decide our duty. These things are in the hands of God.'

'Then what should I do, my Lord Abbot?'

'Only you may decide, Brother Jacques, with God's blessing. It is a strange calling, but one which must be obeyed.' The abbot had given his advice.

Jacques woke in the heart of the night. But his body was well rested and his mind alert. He longed for the sound of the bell calling him to vigils, so that he could begin his day. Meanwhile, he lay there watching the single lamp in the dortoir, listening to the bell rope as it flayed against the shaft which led up to the bell-tower, to an owl in the great oak outside, and to the distant millrace. The sense of initiation into greater things, and of opportunity beyond his previous dreams, seemed to make even that static atmosphere tingle with excitement.

The thrill dissolved doubt as the rising sun disperses early morning mist. His conscience sparkled like mountain air. This was a vocation which Father Guilhem would never understand, but he must follow it.

Taking care not to awaken the brothers, he felt his way towards the forked stick where his clothes hung. For although it was summer the night air was chill and he felt the need of his scapular. Then, still in his night-slippers, he felt his way down the stairs to the chapel. At one with himself and with his God, he knelt on the damp earthern floor to pray. His soul was at peace, and his mind resolved.

He would go to Paris.

10

The papal stables in Avignon rang with the shouts, commands and restless scraping of hoofs that mark a great departure. It looked to Jacques as though the entire convent was there, with grooms leading out the horses, papal guards saddling their mounts, and servants loading pack-horses. Behind them, blacksmiths worked noisily at their anvils and cursing stable-boys mucked out the stables. His own mount had been upgraded to a rouncy, which seemed to him to stand well beside Bernard de Caen's palfrey.

As he waited, now impatient to leave, he felt something soft and warm nudging against his back. Turning suspiciously, he saw that it was a huge bay, a strong animal with the haunches and thighs of a horse which could keep up high speed for long distances. It stood a good two hands above any other horse in the stable, save Bernard's palfrey. A white blaze ran from forehead to muzzle, so that it would stand out amongst a hundred others. It was sweating heavily after a recent hard ride.

Then he noticed the rider, the leader of the guards who were to accompany them. He was as distinctive as his mount, wearing a flamboyant sealskin belt with yellow buckle and a large, flat Milanese cap made of black velvet. After his recent adventure, Jacques found it reassuring that such a murderous-looking individual was to escort them.

He watched as Bernard de Caen spurred his palfrey away from two white-haired cardinals towards this guard. In the saddle, that rotund figure gained a certain grace. Then he realized that this guard was not, after all, going to accompany them. As they left, one of the others turned in his saddle and shouted, 'Briac!'

'Ho!' the sealskin-belted guard replied.

'Chambéry in two months?'

'By the wounds of St Sebastian, I'll be there.' He saluted his friend with a flourish of a huge axe such as Jacques had never seen before, with a head as long as a man's arm. Then he galloped off with two other guards. His shoulders were twice as broad as those of the men who rode with him. Jacques noticed that he did not only use the *langue d'oc*, but spoke with a familar heavy accent, like that of Saverdun. The voice brought to his inner eye an image of the little church of St Sebastian in the next village.

As they moved northwards towards Chalon and on to Paris he saw men in the fields threshing wheat with wooden flails, monks pickling and preserving fruit and vegetables, and country folk collecting acorns as winter fodder for their pigs. Everywhere, men, women and children were gathering dead wood, making faggots, and then stacking them under the external staircases of their simple dwellings. It was the season of labour; but even as they toiled, their peasant curiosity was at its zenith; behind each simple gesture or greeting lurked distrust. Cider presses and cauldrons boiling fruit exuded a sticky fear, and the peasants seemed unusually reluctant to complete their task – as though instinct told them they would never enjoy its fruits. Jacques felt that the world was suddenly alive to the uncertainty of its future.

In the forest of Fontainebleau the dimness of paths burrowed through a heavy cover of oak and chestnut exercised a similar effect on Bernard de Caen. He became nervous and irritable in the endless mossy tunnels which drove through the forest. He would suddenly call a halt and order broad ferns to be lifted back. But they discovered nothing. One morning he appeared in Dominican robes, smiling benevolently at Brother Jacques' astonishment. 'The Black Friars in this Province are under direct command of Guillaume de Paris,' he said by way of explanation. 'They would do anything for the King.'

'But why dress as a Dominican if you do not trust them?' Jacques asked.

Bernard smiled. 'I am many things to many men. The times are strange, and strange remedies must be found. You must not be surprised. Like this I will pass unnoticed.'

Jacques was acutely aware that he was being drawn into a world which repelled him and attracted him equally. But he remembered the words of Abbot Guibert, and prayed to God to give him strength.

From the last ridge, the streets and houses of Paris clustered beneath them around the royal palace and cathedral like anxious crowds pressing forwards to watch a tournament. Bernard de Caen ordered the guards to take their horses around the city walls to the Cistercian house. He and Jacques remained on foot, seeking to enter the city unobtrusively, although he would not say why.

Jacques was struck by how much it had expanded. The new royal palace that had been started in his student days was now complete, and seemed to grow from the island itself into endless crenellated walls. Beyond the twin towers of Notre Dame he could see the more functional and less decorative walls and tower of the Temple, now void of the red and white banner that once fluttered there.

They entered a postern gate near the College de Sorbon. Inside, they walked through fruit orchards and vineyards to a simple stone house set half-way between the crest of the hill and the river below.

Although the door was ajar, Jacques could see nobody inside.

'My lord Bernard.' The faceless voice was like that of a ventriloquist.

'Gilles. You received my message.'

Jacques started, then understood why the guard called Briac had ridden ahead of them.

'Brother Jacques, I would like you to meet Abbot Gilles of our house in Paris.' Abbot Gilles bowed courteously, and indicated to Jacques that he should enter the building.

Jacques stared in astonishment as he crossed the threshold. 'My lord,' he stammered, without managing to hide the shock in his voice. He knew of Abbot Gilles, who was renowned as one of the most learned scholars of the day. Yet here he was in the simple habit of a novice, with no guards or servants. 'I am honoured, my lord,' he said as he regained composure.

'Would you do me the honour of avoiding both the use of my title, and the courtesies of rank, Brother Jacques? We are here on matters of great urgency and secrecy.'

Jacques bowed again. Was Abbot Gilles also part of the *Opus*? That kindly face seemed to him an open book of honesty and goodness, with none of the secrets of Bernard de Caen hidden in the corners of his eyes. The abbot was about the same age as Bernard, much taller and lean-faced with an ascetic spirituality in his expression. He could have been Nicolas' father, Jacques thought irreverently.

He found the air inside musty. The fireplace had clearly not been used in months, but the sparse furniture had recently been dusted. Something in the foetid atmosphere reminded him of the underground chamber at Aigues-Mortes. On a small table in front of the empty fireplace was a table with bread, eggs, a shoulder of ham, and jugs of mead and water.

But they did not eat. As soon as they were seated Bernard de Caen spoke: 'Brother Jacques, you realize that these are exceptional circumstances in which to meet, and I can assure you there is good reason. Even our own convents have eager walls. You understand the need for absolute secrecy?'

'It is part of our Rule, my lord.' The words came woodenly. He shivered as the bright green eyes screwed into him.

Bernard seemed satisfied. He turned to Abbot Gilles. 'Well?' he asked, in a voice which betrayed his anxiety.

'Events are precipitating, my lord. Yesterday at this very hour fifty-four Templar brothers were burned near the convent of Saint-Antoine.' He spoke quickly and confidently.

Bernard sat forward at this news. 'On whose orders?'

'The King's.'

'Directly?'

'No. It was the Archbishop of Sens, brother to the royal Chamberlain. The Templar lawyers have been organizing a good defence, and it seems the episcopal inquiries would only be able to punish certain individual knights within their jurisdiction. The diplomacy of His Holiness the Pope seems to be succeeding, my lord.' He looked straight into Bernard's eyes as he made the compliment.

'Was there no resistance?'

'None, officially, for they all made "free" confessions. My informants report quite the opposite. King Philip has lost his patience and is using all the means at his disposal. He has been sick lately, and fears that his long-term plans for the Capetian line will never be brought to fruition if he doesn't move fast.' The abbot hesitated, glancing first at Jacques, then regarding Bernard plaintively as if asking whether he should continue.

'Go on,' Bernard ordered sharply.

'My source in the office of the Keeper of the Seals has provided some astounding information.' Again he paused, glancing in turn at his listeners. 'That is why I asked His Holiness to send a personal messenger,' the abbot continued. 'It is something that could never be put into writing, even with the most trusted of bearers.'

Bernard de Caen shifted to the edge of his bench as though he were willing himself into the abbot's mind.

Jacques grimaced involuntarily as he felt a strange tautness in his abdomen. His palms exuded cold sweat.

'For many years now,' Abbot Gilles went on, 'it has been obvious that King Philip wished to destroy the Order of the Temple and appropriate its wealth . . .'

66

'Go on!' There was an irritated impatience in Bernard's voice.

'... and we assumed that he desired their wealth to pay his debts. That is to say, to pay finally for the wars with Navarre.'

'You are suggesting this is not so?'

'Indeed. King Philip's plan is quite different. What's more, it's known to a mere handful of advisers. I have been able to discover its nature only in the past month, although it must have been in his mind for years.' Now the abbot was visibly enjoying his moment of ascendancy, playing his listener longer than prudence might counsel.

Bernard de Caen failed to disguise his impatience this time. He thumped the bench beside him with a clenched fist. 'Well,' he shouted, 'what is this plan?'

'To control Christendom.' The abbot spoke the words simply, as if he were telling them it was time for supper.

'That's preposterous!' It was uncanny how Bernard managed to charge each syllable of the adjective with venom while not allowing the whole word to become angry. Such fine-tuned restraint bespoke frightening mental powers. 'Control ... How dare he contemplate such a project?'

'He is a Capetian,' the abbot replied coolly. 'Nothing is too grandiose for a Capetian King of France to contemplate.'

Bernard seemed not to hear. 'It's preposterous,' he repeated.

'I am afraid it is not as preposterous as it may seem at first sight, my lord. The plan will be put into action as soon as he lays his hands on the Templar treasure. Already Henry of Luxembourg is preparing the way in Italy ...'

Goose-pimples rose on Jacques' forearms as he recalled the knights in Aigues-Mortes and Avignon. The rumours were true. He watched his Superior with trepidation.

'But Henry *is* Emperor!' Bernard observed.

'Emperor in name,' Abbot Giles conceded, 'but not in fact. King Philip supported him, gave him men and supplies, but such generosity was the means to *his* end. If we do not stop him, King Philip will dispose of Henry and become Emperor himself.' He paused to let his words take effect. 'First he will have himself crowned as Holy Roman Emperor by Pope Clement in the fashion of Charlemagne, but the ceremony will be here in Paris. Souls to the Pope; bodies to the Emperor: that's how the theory goes. But Philip would have both ...'

'Facts, without your glosses and prophecies!' Bernard's voice had become harsher.

Jacques was amazed at the tone Lord Bernard dared to use with such a distinguished man as Abbot Gilles. It was a clear indication of his real power.

'Through his sons he will control the world: Louis will be made King of Jerusalem and lead a united passage to the Holy Land with a single Crusading Order: young Philip will be made King of Italy and Spain; Charles will become the King of England. Then Pope Clement will be forced to come to Paris, and build a palace within the royal precinct.' He paused, and watched for a reaction on his listeners' faces.

None came. Jacques was flabbergasted into stony stillness. Bernard's eyes were fixed on the earthen floor in desperation.

Gilles continued. 'Then, my lord, His Highness the King of France would control Christendom. He would go down in history as the equal of Hugh Capet and Charlemagne.' Again there was no reaction, so he went on. 'The frightening thing is that this plan seems almost feasible. If nothing is done, then King Philip will have his way. And we know what that would mean for the Church.'

Bernard de Caen looked up slowly. 'It's preposterous,' he said yet again. But this time his voice was softer than Jacques had ever heard it, as if his mind were disengaged from the present, absorbing the implications of this intelligence; planning countermeasures.

Time was scarce, Jacques knew, since they were to present Pope Clement's letter to the King at the first opportunity.

11

Gold, silver and precious stones in quantities beyond his wildest imagination glittered in morning sunlight, bedazzling Brother Jacques. The instinct honed in years of digging remorselessly into people's past lives enabled him to feel the raw power behind this panoply of refinement. It struck fear into his heart. As he anxiously sought a quiet corner of the royal audience hall he found himself pressed into a group of ushers, friars and minor courtiers near the entrance. A sullen Franciscan was regarding him with curiosity. 'Lost, are you?' he asked in a friendly voice.

'Not at all!' Jacques snapped unnecessarily.

'Quite normal here,' the friar continued unperturbed. 'As soon as our superiors get within striking range of His Majesty we underlings are forgotten.'

Jacques scrutinized his new acquaintance, who had evidently seen him enter with Bernard de Caen. For a moment he suspected the old Franciscan might be another of Bernard's spies. But the wizened face was too open, the man's concern too genuine. He relaxed, and smiled. Then looked round the hall again.

He had entered at one end of a rectangular hall the size of a good basilica. On the wall to his left was a series of high windows giving onto a courtyard, with tall, narrow tapestries in each of the interstices between them; on that to his right much larger tapestries of hunting scenes which disappeared into the painted and gilded wooden barrel vault. At the mid-point was a dais surmounted by a richly canopied throne which formed the centrepiece of the hall, exactly opposite huge double doors as high as three of the king's guards. Between throne and doors a double cordon of these royal guards in livery created a broad passage, beyond which Jacques could make out the figure of Bernard de Caen accompanied by the falconer who bore the papal gift for His Majesty.

As he absorbed the wealth of detail a fanfare was sounded by six heralds with straight metal hunting horns twice as long as any he had ever seen. They were standing in a precise arc in front of the royal dais, like that of an apse behind an altar. The ringing clarion seemed to rise up from the bell-shaped lips of the horns, fill the air, and then be sucked into the tapestries lining the walls. When it had died away the players stepped aside. Then the double doors were thrown open by crimson-robed ushers holding what seemed to be like golden sceptres. To Jacques, they looked as tall as the doors themselves.

The King of France entered, stepping elegantly over floral-patterned carpets towards his throne. Such extravagance of colour, like spring flower-flecked meadows, only served to emphasize King Philip's pallid features and the pale golden hair which fell almost to his shoulders and covered his ears. He was dressed in a Tyrian purple gown so long that it trailed across the carpets behind him, made of a cloth which shimmered like silk. A border of gold and silver thread encircled his neck and then fell to the ground with the vertical hem of his gown. In his right hand he bore a golden staff which culminated in a massive fleur-de-lis as a column flows naturally into its capital. Huge loose cuffs were studded with pearls and precious stones of every colour.

The throne itself was draped, Jacques noticed as the king moved towards it, with a thick purple cloth also studded with pearls, and placed under a silk canopy shaped like the open tents at tournaments. Its velvet border, of the same imperial purple, was embroidered at intervals the length of a man's arm with the escutcheon of the royal house of Capet. Beneath this border was a delicate fringe of shimmering gold thread which danced in the turbulent air.

Jacques had seen the king before when he was a student in Paris, but never at such close quarters. He watched entranced as Philip the Fair took his place on the throne. It was lower than he would have imagined, seemingly made of solid gold, with claw-feet and armrests which curved away from the royal forearms into gilded lion's heads with flowing manes. Around the throne men exchange views on the king's demeanour and dress, seeking to gauge his mood. A quiet murmur arose after the silence of the royal entrance. Jacques fancied that a faint smile came to the thin lips of the king as he sat: he passed the staff to a courtier and rested his arms on the lions' shoulders. Now it was possible to see purple slippers under the royal gown. Jacques pushed himself forwards to gain a good view of the crown, which consisted of a simple golden band which reposed on the king's high forehead. In the band were square, diamond shaped and circular apertures clearly designed to lighten the weight, while above it beaten gold rose into shapes that looked from such a distance like oak leaves and more fleurs-de-lis. Jacques was enthralled by this display of riches.

But all comment around him was for the king's attire.

'So much for your sumptuary laws,' a shrill voice stated with daring contempt above the hubbub.

Jacques turned, curious. 'What do you mean?' he asked the liveried servant behind him.

The old man pushed forward, pleased to have a sympathetic audience. 'In the old days, when Queen Joan was alive, His Majesty would never have worn robes studded with precious stones and pearls. As if the King of France needed to impress his people!'

The wizened Franciscan now joined them furtively. 'Yes,' he agreed, 'there was none of this gold and silk, let alone carpets. The floors were strewn with fresh straw and herbs. Now it's more like a lady's boudoir.'

'A bordello, more like it,' the old retainer said, 'and look at the wallflowers around him. Nothing but the latest fashions, each one of them with breeches to mid-calf and points to their shoes which would make the Polacks themselves cringe that they'd invented them.'

Jacques studied the strutting courtiers, now seeing breeches and stockings of more colours than he had imagined possible. Some of them were even wearing velvet and brocade slippers, again with the curling Polish point. They all wore loose scarlet or royal blue blouses of cloth with tight sleeves and slits down the side to reveal fashionable fur and satin linings in pink or azure. 'Yes, you're quite right,' he agreed. He tried to imagine Pietro di Ocre dressed in this finery.

'Would I have lied to you?' The man opened his palms and lifted his shoulders in a gesture of innocence. 'Just look at the hoods and caps . . . good Brother . . .?' He lifted his right eyebrow as his voice modulated into a question.

'Jacques. Brother Jacques.'

'. . . good Brother Jacques. And I am Jorge of Navarre, come to Paris in the train of Queen Joan nigh thirty year since.' He smiled a broad toothless smile and slapped the friar's back. Then he stared emptily, as if recalling where he was. 'Hoods and caps,' he suddenly continued, 'that's where you see the difference in rank. These young men don't know how to wear them. Look at 'em! Flat caps with a short hood barely touching the shoulders. And the more fashionable ones with those caps flaring behind them like a cockscomb. No idea at all!'

'Disgusting display, like peacocks,' the Franciscan agreed.

71

'But nothing to that of their elders,' Jorge went on, warming to his theme. His breath stank as he drew close to Jacques. 'The entire court consists of upstarts. Look at those other hoods! Some of them fall to the waist. And hoods ruffed and embroidered, stitched in dainty folds like the finest noblewoman's gown.' Men nearby laughed as he imitated an exaggeratedly feminine gait, tossing his long tunic behind him. 'Some of 'em are even studded with pearls. What is the world coming to?'

'Like peacocks,' the Franciscan muttered again. 'We need the old sumptuary laws again if you ask me.'

Fortunately his words were drowned out by a new fanfare. Jacques pushed forwards again and watched as Bernard de Caen stepped up with the falconer to present Pope Clement's gift. His simple black habit was incongruous in such a luxuriant setting. Silence fell as Bernard bowed deeply and knelt before the king. 'Your Majesty,' Jacques heard that resonant voice say as clearly as though he were standing next to his Superior, 'His Holiness Pope Clement wishes you to accept this Scottish falcon, which has been reared by the monks of Fountains Abbey, as a token of his goodwill towards your most royal person.' He lowered his head and motioned the falconer forward.

King Philip studied the bird with the minute care of a true fancier, oblivious of the crowded courtiers as though the cares of the throne were another man's burden. He caressed its neck with the back of his right forefinger. 'An excellent bird, excellent bird,' he commented softly. But his clear metallic voice carried through the hall. 'His Holiness' gift is most welcome, as is his goodwill.'

Bernard de Caen then reached into his habit. 'There is also a letter, Your Majesty,' he added in what seemed to Jacques well-feigned humility.

King Philip nodded, then proffered his own arm to the falconer to accept his gift. He fondled its neck again as its claws sank into the royal purple.

'That'll please His Majesty,' the old man behind Jacques said as a ripple of applause ran through the hall. 'The King leaves for Fontainebleau this very week.'

Jacques observed that the king's delight with the falcon was genuine. Then his concentration was broken by strange shouts coming from a distant courtyard somewhere outside. He listened attentively. Short, sharp calls at regular intervals. But no sound of men, or horses, or arms. It was odd.

72

He leaned forward as the king eventually accepted the papal scroll, coldly, with no trace of emotion. A shaft of sunlight played in his blond hair, and emphasized his reddish cheeks. But he sat rock still, more like a Roman statue than a living king.

Then Philip the Fair came to business. He summoned one of his own falconers, who came to take away the gift, then unrolled the papal letter, held it at arm's length and read it slowly. When he had finished, he passed it to the adviser standing to his right. He waited, motionless as stone, for the second man to finish the letter.

'That's Guillaume de Nogaret, Keeper of the Seals. The King's lawyer,' the old man said.

Jacques nodded. De Nogaret's enormous head, with almost fanatical eyes, large hooked nose and long curly hair made him easily recognizable. He remembered lectures in his student days, and how the thick lower lip agitated as de Nogaret developed enthusiasm – until it took on a rhetorical life of its own. The students had nicknamed him 'Floppylips'. 'Who's the cleric beside him?' he asked.

This time it was the Franciscan who replied. The liveried retainer, embarrassed by his ignorance, looked away, pretending he had not heard the question. The friar spoke with reverence, as if he were presenting the man to the court. 'Guillaume de Paris. Inquisitor-General for the Province of Paris, Rouen, Troyes and Reims.'

And instigator of the Templar trial, Brother Jacques thought to himself. He could not help but read evil against his own Order in that grey, bland and seemingly featureless face. As head of the Parisian Dominicans this man represented the enemy, for no other religious Order had subjected itself so totally to the royal will. Yet he was a man who could pass unnoticed in the street.

De Nogaret passed the letter to the Inquisitor-General, who in turn read slowly through it and then returned it to the king.

Jacques strained his ears to catch fragments of discussion.

'. . . a matter of organization . . .'

'I believe there will be no real problem,' de Nogaret said, then turned away so that his words were absorbed by tapestries.

'. . . treasures . . .' floated across the hall, as if the word had been given special emphasis.

'When?' Guillaume de Paris asked forcefully. That chill, authoritative voice would be recognizable in the middle of the summer fair at Toulouse.

The main dialogue was between Bernard de Caen and Guillaume de Nogaret. There, Jacques sensed, was the real tussle. He thought again of the *Opus Christi*, and his own role. A pattern was beginning to emerge in his deepest consciousness. He strained his ears to listen.

On the dais, de Nogaret had called forward a scribe who unrolled a large vellum and held it before them in such a way that Bernard could not read it.

Words were replaced by figures, punctuated by words like 'gold', 'silver', 'besants', 'tons', 'Temple', 'treasury' as de Nogaret emphasized them. He pointed excitedly at the manuscript as he spoke.

King Philip sat impassively. For long intervals he remained silent. Then, '. . . for the love of God . . .' his cold voice would repeat. He would sit forward on his throne, then turn to question his counsellors, and turn back again to the Pope's envoy.

'. . . that is impossible . . .'

'. . . but under the supervision of His Holiness . . .'

'Impossible,' de Nogaret asserted angrily.

Jacques wondered why Bernard had wished him to be present at this audience. The only connection between that trial and his own assignment was Pietro di Ocre, but it was difficult to link the ragged prisoner with such power and talk of treasures. He moved forward into the hall as far as he dared, leaving behind the distractions of ushers and guards.

'Ten thousand!' de Nogaret shouted suddenly, his body trembling with excitement and his shock of black hair falling forwards over his forehead. But try as he might, Jacques could not understand the words that followed this outburst.

He knew now that they were discussing how the Templar wealth should be distributed. He also knew that Pope Clement wished it to be given to the other religious Orders, especially the crusading Order of the Hospital. Anything to keep it from Philip's grasp.

'. . . to Avignon,' he heard Bernard's voice suggest.

'No difference whatsoever. Our inquisitors . . .' The voice faded as Jacques finished the sentence in his own mind: 'will do the job as well as any papal commissioner'.

'. . . to bring them back within the jurisdiction of the Church,' Bernard de Caen continued.

At this, Jacques saw the Inquisitor-General for Paris move quickly to his sovereign's ear. Silence enveloped the hall. It was easy enough to guess what he was saying: that legally the Templar trials were within

74

the jurisdiction of the Diocese of Paris, since he, Guillaume de Paris, was responsible for the arrest order.

Again Jacques heard shouts somewhere outside. In that moment of lull he thought he heard the word 'miss'. He looked at the old man, who had moved up beside him.

'Archers.' For him it was a sufficient explanation.

'Archers? Here?'

'New men. Gascon crossbowmen. They've been here less than a week. They're the best.' The last words were spoken with pride.

Just then Philip the Fair waved the Inquisitor-General aside. Momentarily, Jacques felt sympathy for him.

De Nogaret's voice was clearer, and sometimes came through with a full sentence. 'However, there is no question that the trials will end soon.'

Bernard de Caen's next remark was lost as he addressed the King. Only a few words filtered through when he half-turned to speak to de Nogaret: '... but His Holiness wishes ... trials throughout the Kingdom of France ... some guarantee ...'

'Never!' King Philip said emphatically. This affirmation ended the discussion. Both de Nogaret and de Paris stepped back from the dais. Bernard bowed his head in respect for the royal will.

Then, to Jacques' amusement, Philip the Fair did something which caught his advisers by surprise. He stood, motioned to Bernard de Caen to follow him, and walked away from the dais towards the wall. There, with their voices stifled by thick tapestries, the two men stood huddled in conversation. Finally, King Philip turned away with what seemed from the doorway to be a flash of anger on his pallid face and returned to his throne. 'There is little time,' he said clearly. 'The campaign must be under way by next summer!'

No one dared to move as he stared out into the hall. The courtly hubbub ceased. Silence was broken only by the sporadic shouts of soldiers somewhere in an inner courtyard.

Then he sat forward again. 'We shall provide you with an answer for His Holiness at Matins,' he announced in a clear, strong voice so that all could hear. 'Today there will be a banquet in honour of the ambassadors from King Jaime of Aragon. You and your suite will be pleased to attend.'

12

'You will come too,' Bernard de Caen said brusquely as they left the royal palace together; 'it will be a valuable experience for you.' His eyes flickered as he spoke, darting here and there as if he were afraid of missing something. 'Tomorrow we'll leave for Avignon. We must deliver the King's reply, and there's much else to do besides.'

There was no time for Jacques to ask questions. On his last word, Bernard bustled off on unexplained 'official business'.

After a moment's disappointment at being left in the lurch once again, Jacques decided he would take the opportunity to visit a friend from his student days. The thought of Armand's laughing face and impish sense of humour enabled him briefly to cast off the growing weight of responsibility. There was a long-forgotten lightness in his step as he walked across the city to the abbey of Saint Germain.

'Brother Armand!' he said enthusiastically as he was shown into his friend's private study.

'I'm pleased to see you.' The voice was flat, unwelcoming. 'Sit down.'

Jacques sat down awkwardly, disconcerted by the formality. His friend's stiff face and tonsured head bespoke a new seriousness that had taken him unawares.

Then Armand addressed the gate-friar who had accompanied his guest. 'You may leave now.'

As soon as the friar was gone, the old mischievous grin broke across Armand's face. 'Six years!' he exclaimed.

'Ten since I came to Paris.' Disappointment vanished. Apart from the tonsure and sharply etched crow's-feet when Armand smiled, his face was unchanged.

'You remember the night we met?'

'Scrumping in the royal orchard. You couldn't do it now. Not the sort of thing a deputy abbot does, is it? Anyway, the new palace walls have covered up our secret entrance.'

They shrugged off years in friendly laughter.

'You won't recognize the college now,' Armand said, 'and Rue St Jacques has disappeared under new lecture theatres.'

'But I recognize you, my friend. Though you had me worried for a moment there. They tell me you are destined for great things. This is no ordinary abbey.' He indicated the ancient walls as he spoke.

The deputy abbot smiled demurely.

His expression amused Jacques. He was one of the few who knew the private side of Armand, which included drinking, laughing loud and openly at his own jokes, and an almost physical pleasure in his pranks which Jacques had readily shared. He also had a sharp legal and theological mind which had made him an exemplary student of commentaries and sentences. But above all he was totally loyal to his friends. These thoughts reminded Jacques of their time together in Paris. 'Is *our* hostel still there?'

'I'll show you,' Armand replied with unexpected enthusiasm. 'We have two hours until sext.'

'Excellent.' Jacques felt uncomfortable in saying nothing of his duty to report to the royal banquet rather than to midday prayers.

They walked towards the Sorbon.

'See, our bakery has disappeared! Do you remember when they used to give us those slabs of unleavened bread on our way back from Matins? There it is, a hostel for Dutch students.'

Jacques noticed that other shops and the counters of artisan workshops were also changed or had disappeared altogether. But he was pleased to see the shop where they used to buy shellfish when his father sent him money for feast-days. Now his privileged status allowed him to carry money, especially on such journeys as this. He leaned his elbow on the slate counter as he used to do, and called for service. He was delighted to see the same moustached Breton appear at the hatch and bought two small bowls of mussels.

'Now this is sinful,' the deputy abbot protested in jest.

'But taste them. It takes six years off my life. I feel as though I were on my way to dispute my doctoral thesis: "Whether for the knowledge of a thing the existence of the thing itself is required or whether that which is not can be the object of the understanding".' He recited the title with mock seriousness.

Armand laughed with the unrestrained pleasure of a student. The bond was still close between them.

77

'Sounds silly now,' Jacques observed. 'But it was impressive then. Noble words, impressive rhetoric, my Latin as fine as it has ever been. Even the rector couldn't put me out of my stride with his clever questions. How false it all was.'

'Yet how important. Remember, I was the water-carrier's boy from Rouen and you the son of a provincial baker. We learned to compete with noblemen and princes, with the minds which God has given us. The Sorbon prepared us for our present tasks just as our mothers' milk prepared us for life . . .' Armand paused, like one who was trying to remember what he had forgotten to ask. 'But tell me, what brings you to Paris?'

The question sounded innocent, but Jacques sensed that it was carefully prepared. Yet Armand was perhaps the only man he could trust fully at the moment. 'A curious investigation.'

'Curious?'

'Into a preceptor of the Temple, an Italian.'

'Aren't those trials all finished now?'

'That's what makes it curious. He's been investigated at least three times, and nothing important has come of it. Now, suddenly, for reasons he keeps to himself, our Lord Bernard has got it into his mind that this Templar is harbouring some great secret.'

'Great enough to take you away from your duties after all these years . . . and bring you to Paris?' The afterthought made him look keenly at Brother Jacques. 'That's why you're here, isn't it?'

Responsibility could not be shrugged off for long. Jacques was embarrassed, remembering his Superior's words concerning *Opus Christi*. He could trust his conscience to Brother Armand, but not his most recent suspicions. The immensity of his new solitude horrified him. 'Yes, there's a missing link,' he said vaguely, 'a fact, a detail, which Bernard de Caen seems to believe our Templar will reveal sooner or later.'

'You have some idea?'

'Not yet. We have no idea where to look. But I suspect it will lead to Italy . . .'

'Italy? That's odd.'

Jacques looked at him sharply. 'Why?'

'You're the second person who's mentioned Italy this morning. All *rumours* lead to Rome, it would seem.' He looked around quickly, took Jacques' arm, and drew him into an empty doorway. 'News has come that Henry of Luxembourg is dead.'

78

'The Emperor? Where? What happened?' It was stunning news.
'In Tuscany. On campaign. And it was all very irregular. The first
odd thing is that he was murdered; the second, even odder to my mind,
is that he was killed by a Dominican friar who gave him poisoned wine
at communion.'

Jacques found it disconcerting that he was not shocked by this detail.
The extraordinary was becoming routine. 'When did this happen? Do
you know?'

'In the month of August . . .'

Just as the knights were leaving Aigues-Mortes. Then they had been
too late for his campaign.

'. . . he was buried in the cathedral at Siena.'

'And now we'll need a new Emperor.' Jacques spoke in a barely
audible whisper. He feared that Philip the Fair would step into the
breach. Would that *he* never reached Rome.

'You sound as if you know who it will be.'

'That is up to the Pope to decide,' Jacques commented, although
he guessed the Pope would have little say in the matter.

'It never has been before . . . and anyway, is there a real need for
an emperor?'

Jacques was surprised that his friend dared to make such a
suggestion. But at the same time he was pleased that he was trusted,
and knew that he would always be able to trust Armand. Just like the
old days. 'The world is not ready yet, although it might be soon. No,
somebody must be emperor.'

'Has this to do with your mission?' Armand asked.

'Perhaps. I really don't know.'

'But you believe so?'

Jacques hesitated, and looked his friend straight in the eyes. 'Yes.
I do.'

'Then know, my friend, that you may always rely on me. For
anything. I feel that you are entering treacherous waters, and may
one day need a friend.' He pointed to a chapel on the other side of the
street. 'Shall we pray together?'

It was an elegant way to cement their trust, Jacques reflected.

But his mind was soon elsewhere. As they crossed the street he
stopped, turned and gazed on the sprawling royal complex below them.
That was one centre of power. To the right beyond the river, where
the royal banner flew ominously from the Temple tower, was another.
The third was back in Avignon. These three centres were linked as

if by invisible threads, and he was convinced that each of the three played a part in the mission he had been assigned by Bernard de Caen. But there was a fourth point needed to complete the matrix of threads and, when that was discovered, the caster of the net would possess real power. Jacques felt his clenched palms grow sweaty as he realized that the unknown fourth point was the objective of all this diplomacy.

Even as he prayed he saw the royal palace in his mind's eye. Today at midday he would be there, not, it was true, at the king's table but nevertheless inside the royal refectory.

13

'In which royal court would men such as ourselves be served like this?'
The man who had introduced himself pompously as 'Renaud Essart,
Seneschal to His Majesty King Philip of France' spoke proudly as soup
after soup was served.

'It is indeed generous,' Jacques agreed. On his left sat a silent canon
who had just returned from the Holy Land. Would this seneschal were
so quiet, he thought to himself.

He marvelled as wild boar soup, verjuice made of sorrel and vinegar,
hare soup with pomegranate seeds, and a thick soup of peas and beans
each arrived with the seneschal's explanations. But Renaud's pride
grew even greater when another dish was served: 'Bet you've never
had that before, Brother,' he roared, to the amusement of the others
present. 'And like as not you'll never see it again. The cost of this *soupe
dorée* would feed the starving of Toulouse for a year.'

Jacques looked up sharply, surprised by this reference to Toulouse,
although the man's accent had already betrayed a generic southern
origin. Then the perfume of the gilded soup wafted across his face:
delicate, exotic, but stirring a family memory. His father had once
told him that it was made by toasting slices of the costly pure white
bread of Chailly, throwing them into a jelly composed of sugar, fine
white wine, egg-yolks and rosewater, then frying them and covering
them with more rosewater, sugar and saffron. But he was now unable
to distinguish the rich spices, many of which he had neither seen nor
tasted in his life.

Now entire baskets of Chailly bread, which his father always spoke
about in a kind of awe whenever Jacques mentioned Paris but which
he himself had never eaten, were brought to the table to eat with the
soup. It was given to them as freely as the stalest and roughest black
breads were thrown to the poor.

King Philip, together with the ambassadors from Aragon, royal
princes and great nobles sat at the high table, while the lesser nobility,
courtiers and important royal officials made up the three long tables
which ran perpendicular to it. Pride filled Jacques' breast as he saw
his Superior seated at the royal table.

Along the centre of the tables was a line of large silver plates with sweetmeats, almonds, pomegranates and orange dainties. Between them were silver saltcellars and sauce-boats, with flagons and drinking cups. Jacques was awestruck by the abundance of gold and silver; it hardly seemed possible that a man in desperate need of the Templar treasure could furnish a silver dish and a knife and spoon to each guest.

The centrepiece was a swan, which stood on a separate table in front of the King. Jacques had never seen anything like it. It sat, cooked but recomposed as if alive, on a sea of green-painted pastry as large as a bed. Its beak had been coated with gold leaf, while the entire body shimmered in sunlight with what seemed to be silver painted over it. The wings were sustained by invisible struts. Through the haze of smoke and the movement of bustling serving-men Jacques perceived it as a great imperial eagle poised for flight.

Voices at his table steadily increased in volume as fine wines, mead and the powerful local beer known as *godales* were served continuously. None was louder than that of Renaud Essart: 'Have some wine, Brother,' he roared, giving his neighbour little choice as he filled the cup to overflowing. 'The likes of you and I rarely get a chance like this. Brought up from Burgundy special, you know.'

Jacques was not impressed. He had never envied others their food, and would have been just as happy with haricot beans and garlic. But he found himself wondering how Nicolas de Lirey would have reacted.

He was relieved when waiters brought fish, since the seneschal wished to boast of his knowledge to the whole table and that gave him temporary respite. 'The turbot and sole were sent from Calais, and the *lotte* brought up from Brest by the King's agents especially for today. You'll never eat fish like this again,' he roared. 'I've served at Brest, and know what I'm talking about.' He then explained in detail how each fish was prepared.

When he slid back along the bench Jacques could see that he was about the same height, with the same strong arms visible under his tunic as he grabbed the wine jug to fill his cup. A man who clearly enjoyed the physical pleasures of life, with a slight fatness in his neck and chin which suggested over-indulgence for a man of his profession. His hair was jet black and full; perhaps he was in his early thirties. A good full laugh revealed half his teeth were missing, but he still managed a smile which began to endear itself to Jacques. He was probably an honest enough man, with no trace of guile in his almond eyes. 'Look at that!' he suddenly shouted in admiration. A line of waiters in long white tunics paraded through the hall with immense platters of game. 'They talk about wealth in Italy,' Renaud observed to his neighbour, 'but there is nothing like this even at the palace of the Visconti. This is real power!'

Jacques looked at the seneschal with new interest. He was about to draw out Renaud on how he could possibly know the inside of the Visconti palace when his question was drowned by applause as the swan was ceremoniously cut with a silver sword. On their own table waiters arranged plates of stork, thrush, starling, quails and plovers. Spices were brought, and slices of bear, roe deer and red deer on wooden boards.

Through the commotion he watched the king, at that moment with his right arm outstretched – a gesture which could order wine or destroy a city. He knew that Renaud had been right, and saw with a clarity which took him unawares that this whole display was an intimation of raw power for the benefit of the envoys of King Jaime. Monastic discipline had taught him to eradicate personal pleasure and the desire to dominate others. Yet it was there beneath the skin, he knew, as he sat in that hall and found himself reluctantly admiring the absolutism of the king's rule. It was a recognition that shook him to the very core of his being.

'Are you all right, Brother?' Renaud Essart enquired. 'Is it the wine?'

He shook his head. Then remembered his unanswered question. 'Do you know Italy, Seneschal?'

'I do sir, as well as any man here present today,' he said, proudly. 'As a matter of fact I returned from Milan just two days ago.'

'Milan?' Jacques sought to disguise his interest.

Renaud Essart looked round him conspiratorially, and then drew closer to Jacques. 'On a secret mission,' he whispered.

His breath stank, and his sweaty body disgusted Jacques. But he was intrigued by the seneschal. 'You're from Toulouse, aren't you?'

'Well, bless my soul! How did you ever guess?' Renaud lifted his cup, and Jacques responded. He knew that refusal to join these endless toasts would cost him the seneschal's openness.

'My first abbey was Mirepoix, and I've often visited my Order's house in Toulouse.' He used the white lie to avoid allowing the seneschal to guess his role, for nobody would talk to an inquisitor in

83

the province of Toulouse. The elimination of the Cathars had touched every family there.

'Bless my soul,' Renaud roared, 'we're nigh neighbours. Let me fill your cup.' He reached across the table roughly, making sure everybody realized what a good man he was. Then he moved along the bench closer to the friar. 'Yes, my good Brother, I've seen and heard things in Italy that would shock many a prelate and lord here. Things I would never tell anybody, except an honest friar and man of the south such as yourself.' He had switched to the *langue d'oc*, and a new confidential tone.

Jacques fought to overcome the foul stink of the man. 'That's very good of you,' he said simply. He would not upset the seneschal by asking questions, but interrogate by listening – as Bernard de Caen called it.

'The king has a hundred agents scouring the country even now. Who knows if I won't have to go back myself? And will you guess what we're looking for, Brother? It's something that would interest one of your kind, I'll bet.'

Jacques overcame his sense of revulsion and leaned closer.

'A holy relic. That's what it is.' Renaud breathed into Brother Jacques' face, then grabbed a sugar plum and washed it down with an entire jug of malmsey. 'You're a fine man, Brother Jacques, as honest a friar as I've met.'

The inquisitor in Jacques sensed that this was the moment to press. 'The king already has the greatest of holy relics,' he objected quietly.

'The True Crown of Thorns. Yes, I know, but they say there is a greater relic still, and the king would give anything to possess it.'

'Why could that be, I wonder?' Jacques' own mind was befuddled by the wine which the seneschal continued to pour into his mug, but he struggled for innocence in his words.

Renaud regarded him warily, then burst into loud laughter as if he judged that there could be no danger from this simple friar. 'Between you and me, you see, our lord the King has a great plan. And he needs this relic to make it work. He's a great reader of the psalms . . .'

'What of it?' Jacques feared the wine had got to Renaud's brain. There was nothing evil about reading the psalms.

But the seneschal smiled. 'They say he's fonder of one psalm than of all the others, the one which begins, if I remember rightly . . .' He paused, placed his mug carefully on the table, sat up straight and forced his drunken features into concentration. When he spoke, it was with the formal tones of a priest reciting in confident Latin: '"May God be gracious to us and bless us . . ."

'"And make his face shine upon us",' Jacques completed the verse.

'That's it, you see,' Renaud said with satisfaction.

'That's what?'

'The key.' Again, that phrase. 'He believes that with the consent and protection of the Face of Christ nothing will stop him. He cannot fail.'

'But where is this face? What is it?' Jacques could barely contain himself now.

'I don't know, Brother. I've never seen it. But it's been seen in Italy not fifty years since. I dare say I'll be back there myself before winter's done.' Then, with his natural suspicion gaining a hand, he added: 'Mind you, it's just a rumour.'

Jacques stared through the haze at Bernard de Caen, who was deep in conversation with other prelates.

The seneschal abruptly leapt from the sitting position to attention. Jacques was at first puzzled, but then guessed that the banquet was over and stood with the others. He marvelled that Renaud's ingrained sense of duty had functioned through so many jugs of wine and such chaos: at the total command of body and soul which the king's person exercised. Through the smoke and movement he could just make out King Philip and the ambassadors leaving the hall in formal procession.

Once the royal party had left, the hall emptied fast. Renaud Essart made to leave with his fellow officers. But just as they reached the end of the table he turned back to his dinner companion. 'Mark you well, Brother Jacques,' he shouted, 'when you are next in Paris come to find the Seneschal Renaud of Toulouse. You will be welcome, and may trust me.'

Jacques resolved to do so, and sensed that it would not be long. A pattern was forming. The Pope's urgency and Bernard's secrecy were now comprehensible, if not fully understood. He felt himself slowly but irrevocably being drawn into the *Opus*, a feeling of belonging which sent pleasure through him throughout his walk to Abbot Gilles' house.

He was anxious to return to Avignon, and to Pietro di Ocre.

14

Jacques' new sense of belonging was confirmed when he reported to the papal wing of the Black Friars' convent in Avignon with Bernard de Caen the day after their arrival. The highly polished friar deferred to him with the same obsequiousness accorded to his Superior. He was no longer required to wait outside, but followed Bernard de Caen into the papal quarters. The guards with two-handed swords seemed shorter to him now; they represented neither a barrier nor a threat. From within, the sense of papal power was palpable. Jacques was enveloped in its aura, and perceived Avignon through the filter this power created between him and the dust and filth outside.

Even Nicolas de Lirey seemed to treat him with respect, he was surprised to notice.

Nicolas himself was amused to notice how easily a nod of his head could appease the inquisitor. He pushed back the shock of thick black hair which fell over his forehead, and followed behind to ensure his inner smile did not reveal itself.

A slippered usher led them through an arched doorway into the Pope's freshly whitewashed study, which was pervaded by the persistent dampness of recent plastering. Jacques noticed the regular tapping of masons finishing details in the covered cloister outside. Then he realized that the interior walls were not in fact whitewashed but had been prepared for mural painters to work on. It was a sign of purpose and duration which surprised him, since he thought Pope Clement desired to escape King Philip's reach from across the river and return the Holy See to Rome.

In spite of its newness, the room was already a comfortable private study. Its size suggested a small refectory, with a door at each end and a large stone fireplace along the wall to Jacques' left as he entered. On each side of the fireplace, stacked with fresh logs to dry ready for winter, were large wooden throne-like chairs with high backs, arm-rests and leather seats; beyond it a broad table with paper, bound volumes of manuscript and writing materials. On the other side of the room was a portable wooden altar, with velvet cushions placed on the flagstones beneath it. In the centre of the room was a large refectory table at which His Holiness Pope Clement now sat.

He was alone; a still, ghost-like figure in that great room, but on the table in front of him were three bowls, several drinking cups, silver spoons and a carving knife which suggested a more convivial personality. A semi-transparent jug shaped like a heron caught Jacques' eye. Near it were serving dishes with fish stripped like discarded combs. A bowl of paradis apples stood beside a silver finger-bowl. It appeared the Pope had hastened guests from the room in order to hear the news from Paris. He greeted them in a friendly manner. 'My dear Abbot, I'm pleased to see you in Avignon again. Is this the young man you have spoken of? Come!' The gentle but full, throaty voice made him sound like a benign grandfather summoning his favourite grandchild to his side. 'Sire Nicolas.'

But Brother Jacques did not allow this impression to influence his comportment. He genuflected with genuine respect and charity.

'Yes, Your Holiness,' Bernard de Caen replied with his eyes fixed on the floor as he stepped forward. 'Brother Jacques Fournier. Originally of the Cistercian Order, but for many years attached to the Dominicans of this abbey.' His arm stretched gradually towards the younger inquisitor, as if to embrace him. 'He is now part of my own staff,' he added.

Jacques shot a glance from the corner of his eye without lifting his head. He had not conceived it quite that way, but he was gratified to hear Bernard's acknowledgement.

'You may be seated,' Pope Clement said. Again that benevolent voice, and a flicker of real curiosity on his grave countenance. He indicated a high-backed wooden chair, then gestured to Nicolas to sit as well. Not a word was exchanged, but Jacques sensed respect and communion between them.

Although the Pope's demeanour was pleasant and friendly, his deep-set, worried eyes betrayed different feelings. His roundish face and balding head were familiar enough, since Jacques had often seen him from a distance as he made his rounds of Avignon. But he had never realized how small the Pope's mouth was. More curious than this, however, was the fact that the isolated tuft of hair which grew just above his forehead seemed to move in sympathy with his words. He was wearing a simple white habit similar to that of the Cistercians, but with tiny golden buttons which ran from the collar and disappeared under the table.

The Pope rose and walked to a small writing desk from which he took a folded sheet of paper. He opened it, and was about to pass it to Bernard de Caen. 'This is the reply you brought from His Highness King Philip.' But he hesitated, as if a new thought had struck him, and withdrew it abruptly. 'Tell me about your return journey.'

'Routine, Your Holiness,' Bernard stated flatly. 'Brother Jacques will explain.'

It was like torture. 'Well, Your Holiness, it was routine as Lord Bernard says,' he began nervously. 'Thanks to the mounts provided by the papal stables we made excellent speed.'

'I can see that. Did you notice anything of special interest? Preparations for war, for example?'

Jacques reviewed the journey rapidly. At the same time he tried to dry his sweaty palms with his fingertips. He glanced at Nicolas, wishing he possessed the same self-control, but there was no compassion in that pallid visage – just detached curiosity in the sharp black eyes and a touch of contempt in the gently tilted head. He turned back to the more comfortable face of the pope. 'There were many royal parties on the road, and one large band of English knights . . .'

'Travelling north or south?' Pope Clement snapped.

'South, Your Holiness.' Jacques was taken aback by this attention to detail, but it served to jolt his memory. 'There was one thing . . .' he began slowly, recollecting the scene.

The papal gaze focused on him, as intense as that of Bernard de Caen and Nicolas. The homely softness vanished. It was like talking to starving wild cats in the dark. 'At Chalon we boarded flat-bottomed river boats for the passage to Avignon. We sailed all day and went ashore to hostels for the night. Every day we passed barges carrying uncut timber up-river, so one night Briac the guard and I spoke with a barge-master who put in to the same quay. "It's for shipbuilding of course, Brother," he explained; "the King wants a new fleet before summer." Later he told us that all the royal shipyards are working at full capacity.'

'Nothing else?'

'No, Your Holiness.' The torture was over, and he knew from Bernard's admiring gaze that he had done well. He watched the three men carefully.

'Fascinating,' the Pope said. 'Now, Brother Bernard. The letter.'

Nicolas stepped forward quickly and took the letter which Pope Clement proffered. He wondered as he did so whether they would be able to forestall the King's plans. Since his family had fallen out of favour with King Philip his own prestige had declined. He was a young man, and needed wealth to renew the family honour and rebuild their castles and estates. There was at present no war in which he could enrich himself quickly, and his only chance was an alliance with Bernard de Caen. The churchman needed him, and if his ambition to throw off the shackles of Philip's power over the Church were to be successful then his own power would instantly increase. He must side with the Pope to achieve his ends. And now there was this new thing of the relic; who knew where that might end? The risk was high, but then so were the stakes. If the worst came to the worst he would join one of the new mercenary companies in Italy: but that was a long way off yet. He bowed slightly towards the Pope, showing just the right allegiance but without sycophancy, then stepped backwards and passed the letter to Bernard de Caen.

The Inquisitor-General accepted it with a nod, and read it attentively. Then he lifted his face into the Pope's waiting gaze. 'It is much as we expected, Your Holiness.' He passed the letter in turn to Nicolas.

Jacques felt himself to be in an uncomfortable no-man's-land. Here he was at the centre of ecclesiastical power, yet the crucial piece of information was withheld from him. Suspicion of Nicolas de Lirey's role – and his true relationship to Bernard – flared again within him.

'It is an insult to our person and the Chair of St Peter,' Clement exploded. The effect astonished Jacques. Three deep furrows in his forehead shook with anger; his eyes were screwed up until it seemed they would burn through anything placed in front of them. 'His pretensions to the treasure of an Order of the Church place him in the fire and brimstone of hell with the worst heretics. We must not allow it!'

No one dared to speak.

As if satisfied with the effect he had managed to achieve, Clement suddenly calmed. The furrows rested, his eyes opened and became friendly. The corners of his tiny mouth opened almost imperceptibly.

Jacques blinked. Was it possible? The Pope was the head of the Holy Roman Church, yet here was a timid and anxious man who himself seemed uncertain of the future, living in borrowed quarters with little real power. He wished to impress his visitors, and would like to challenge the King of France on his own ground, but he gave the impression of playing theatrical games. The show at Paris may have been put on for the ambassadors, but there was substance behind it. The strange awareness of the fact that the world around him was changing rapidly suffused him again. It left Jacques cold, as if in a trance. But without fear.

Pope Clement continued, this time quietly and slowly. 'I must thank you, Lord Abbot, for the skill with which the letters were composed . . .'

Letters? Jacques was doubly surprised this time: that his mentor had been responsible for writing the text; and that there were other copies.

'Our envoys to Jaime of Aragon and Edward of England have returned . . .'

So that was where they had been sent.

'. . . We believe that with time our diplomatic endeavours will be successful. The problem is, of course, as you well know – and it would be futile of me to pretend otherwise – that we have little time.' He paused, and looked into the eyes of Bernard de Caen again. 'How did King Philip react to our proposals to divert the Templar funds to our other orders, should we agree to dissolve them?'

So that was it, Jacques understood with a start. Gain Philip's pleasure by suppressing the Order of the Temple, but at the same time save their treasure and land for the Church – all with the blessing of the kings of Aragon and England. He had to admit that it was a brilliant plan, but would it be so easy to trick such a man as Philip the Fair? For the moment, however, even as he absorbed this astonishing intelligence, it was more fascinating for Jacques to see how Bernard trod the razor's edge between truth and stirring the papal anger.

'He seemed anxious for the business of the Templars to be finished,' Bernard said thoughtfully; 'almost as anxious as Lord Guillaume de Nogaret.'

Pope Clement's brow tightened at the mention of this name.

'Furthermore, Your Holiness, there were signs of a certain military movement in Paris. There was a new training ground between the royal palace and the Temple. Large numbers of active officers were present everywhere, and there was a general sense of alert about the entire city. I hope it is not already too late.'

Jacques recalled the archers, and the shouts in the royal courtyard. He sensed Nicolas lean forward with fresh interest.

Pope Clement inclined his head sadly. 'Other sources confirm what you say, alas. Jaime and Edward will be afraid to discredit King Philip as we desire if they too know of these preparations. We must reiterate our full support for the completion of the trials immediately. And then write to the Kings again. Offer them Church property. Allow them to confiscate some of the Templar lands of little value to us. Anything that will block Philip of France.'

'That will be difficult, Your Holiness,' Bernard observed. 'His preparations have been careful, and the Inquisition in France supports him in every move.' He stopped, looked down at the table in front of him as if uncertain whether to continue. It was as if he did not want to place his head on the block alone.

Clement understood. 'Well?' he demanded. 'What is it that you are hiding from us?'

Bernard de Caen looked up again. 'My agents in Paris have reported strange events,' he began slowly.

Jacques felt he could have sliced the tension in the air.

'The sense of alert I have spoken of suggests that His Highness the King is preparing for action concerning the Templars, but I'm afraid Brother Jacques' intelligence about the ships confirms strange rumours in the city . . . things I should rather not mention in Your Holiness' presence . . .'

'Out with it!' Clement snapped.

'It seems he is waiting for a sign. For months his most trusted officers and agents have been searching throughout his kingdom and beyond for a relic . . .'

There was little his Superior did not know, Jacques saw. He wondered nervously whether Bernard knew of his long conversation with Renaud Essart. Should he have reported it? His palms began to sweat again as Pope Clement continued.

'Well?'

'. . . there is a relic which the superstituous king believes essential to the success of his plans. Without it he will not move; when he finds it, I am afraid the consequences will be terrible for us.'

Jacques felt he could sense contempt in his superior's voice. First for King Philip, but also for Pope Clement himself; as if Lord Bernard believed he could have withstood the King's threat better himself.

Clement was barely in control of himself. His fists were clenched on the table; his face flushed with blood. 'What is this relic? What in the name of God does he want?'

'I don't know yet, Your Holiness,' Bernard de Caen said softly, 'but given the predilections of the king and his ancestors, I believe it must

91

be an especially sacred relic, something directly linked to Our Lord Jesus Christ himself and kept in secrecy for centuries.'

'Is that possible?' It was Nicolas de Lirey who spoke, risking the Pope's anger. Something so holy must have been known to men such as St Louis, he thought.

Jacques listened with fascination, for it was the first time that Nicolas had revealed that he too was in the dark. It really seemed that Bernard was concealing details from the Pope as well. He had always assumed that the *Opus Christi* was in the direct service of the Pope. Now this exceptional reticence and secretiveness, almost as though Bernard de Caen and his *Opus Christi* were conspiring against their putative master. He found himself wondering whether his Superior could be that ambitious, but immediately dismissed the thought as irreverent and turned to watch the Pope as he spoke.

'Well? It's a good question.' For an instant the Pope's body was as still as a cat about to pounce, on the knife-edge between resolved calm and fury. He seemed to stare at Lord Bernard almost plaintively, hoping it could not be true.

'It is unusual, I agree,' Bernard said thoughtfully. 'Such a relic could not have been kept secret in France, or even in Europe. No, it has been in the East, perhaps in Byzantium. It may have come to Rome with Boniface of Montserrat's crusaders; or to Venice. If the rumours I heard in Italy many years ago are anything to go by, then it is a genuine and very powerful relic. The Lord alone knows what it is.'

At this, Pope Clement's entire body shuddered as he rose to his feet and thumped the heavy table continuously until it shook beneath the force of his fists. 'Find it!'

Brother Jacques was struck by the humility with which Bernard de Caen left the room. He seemed to be in the best of moods. 'Thank you, Nicolas,' he said to Jacques' companion in the most affable voice Jacques had ever heard. 'I'll join you presently.'

Nicolas inclined his head courteously, and left them alone in the antechamber.

Once they were alone, Bernard rounded upon Jacques angrily. 'Have you told me everything?'

'Yes, my lord.'

'Well?'

'I have reported to you everything Pietro di Ocre has said.' That was true enough. He had only omitted Renaud Essart's comments and his own thoughts.

'He has said nothing about this relic?'

'No, my lord.'

'Or San Eusanio?'

That name again. Once more Jacques knew that Bernard de Caen was holding back something, and that fact salved his conscience. 'No, my lord.'

'There must be something. Find it!'

'I'm doing my best, my lord.' The words Pope Clement had used brought out the same obsequiousness in himself, he noticed.

He felt Bernard's wrath subside as they reached the main corridor, and when his Superior turned to him again there was worried doubt written across his face. 'You will continue to do your best, won't you? We must find this thing.'

Jacques shivered. 'I understand,' he said, using his skill in rhetoric to avoid empty assurances.

For a few moments they walked in silence. Jacques tried to guess what Bernard thought of him now, and whether he had acted correctly. To judge by the expression on that chubby face he would have thought so, but he was beginning to see that in this new situation facial expressions – and even words asserted as truth – were not to be trusted. There was one lingering doubt. 'Lord Bernard,' he began quietly.

Bernard de Caen turned to him again, screwing up those green eyes until it seemed they would leap from their sockets. He was already on guard.

'About this relic.'

'Yes?' Bernard's voice registered suspicion.

'Do you think there can be any connection between that and King Philip's plans for a campaign next summer?'

Bernard de Caen bristled with the barely controlled anger of an officer to a subordinate. Jacques felt a tremor run through his body. 'Where did you learn of that?'

'Rumours, my lord.' He did not wish to reveal how closely he had been listening during the royal audience.

'On this mission, young man, you'd be well advised to stick only to facts. Rumour will only lead you astray. Bernard paused briefly. 'We'll discuss the whole matter tomorrow morning, Brother Jacques. Thank you for your collaboration.'

93

'I need time to think,' Jacques translated for himself. 'Yes, my lord,' he said aloud. So that was it: King Philip had given his men until next summer to find the relic. On its possession he would base the success of his campaign, and if the Pope found it first the royal plan to achieve imperial dominion over the world would be thwarted. Jacques smiled to himself as he realized that he was one step ahead of Bernard de Caen, because Renaud had referred to it as a 'face'. He wanted to press his Superior further, but Bernard's closing words had been spoken as a dismissal. There was nothing more to be learned now.

Jacques stood watching the chubby figure of Lord Bernard, waddling from side to side like a duck with bright sunlight glinting off his bald crown. A ridiculous figure: yet he was a man whom Abbot Gilles treated with awe and Pope Clement with caution; a man who inspired fear as no other Jacques had ever seen. He began to perceive the source of Bernard's power, and the fact that power could be grabbed and manipulated within the Church as much as outside it: here was raw political power, manipulated by Bernard and underpinned by the work of the *Opus Christi*. It was a shock at first, but the demands of the papacy were temporal as well as spiritual. The strange new world around Jacques was beginning to come into focus, and was quick with excitement as the conviction grew within him that the key was in his possession in the person of Pietro di Ocre.

He turned to see the slender figure of Nicolas de Lirey emerge from the shadow of a column just as Bernard vanished. 'Were you waiting here?' Jacques asked bluntly.

'Naturally.' Nicolas concealed his embarrassment with practised ease. 'I wish to have the latest news.'

That was honest enough. But Nicolas' interest presupposed a deep motivation. Jacques tried to catch him off-guard. 'What makes this matter of such importance to you?' he asked.

Nicolas inclined his head forwards. There was little point in hiding the truth. 'Our Lord the Pope is setting for a battle with King Philip the Fair. Now he is the puppet, but he wishes to be the master. I believe he may well succeed, and I will do anything, anything at all, to limit the King of France's power.' Nicholas began slowly to walk away, then quite suddenly turned and straightened his stooping shoulders. 'He must not conquer Europe,' he snapped venomously.

'Why such hatred?' Jacques was taken aback.

There was no need to dissemble, for the hatred was real enough; and it would be a good thing, Nicolas reasoned, to throw some titbits to the inquisitor. 'My father was a knight in the King's service. He was with him when he married Joan of Navarre and became King of Navarre and Count of Champagne. After more than twenty years' loyal service he was dismissed on a whim after some false information from one of my father's rivals. My only desire is to vindicate his name.'

'Is it that important?'

Nicolas laughed loudly, and pushed his shock of hair back over his forehead. Let the baker's son understand. 'I cannot claim such noble descent as our good preceptor – if what he says is true – but good and noble nonetheless. The estate of Charny was granted to the family of Raymond de Mont-Saint-Jean two hundred years ago; so I, too,' he was aware of his own voice rising in pride, and emphasized his words clearly, 'am related to a Grand Master of the Temple, the Guillaume de Beaujeu who succeeded Thomas Berard. And to Hugh III, Duke of Burgundy.' He paused for effect.

Jacques' mind was now racing. Could Nicolas then know something of this 'relic' through his own family history? He began to understand why this secular knight had been chosen by Bernard de Caen. But there was a long way to go yet. He would need to butter up Nicolas. 'Very impressive,' he said. He knew the words were banal, but could think of nothing else at that moment.

Nicolas did not notice. His thoughts were in the past, names rolling through his mind like ships through a stormy sea: now visible, now lost in a trough, then suddenly appearing with the painted prow showing off the family arms from the crest of a wave. 'That is not all! We can claim links with Andrew II of Hungary, the counts of Savoy and Jean de Brienne, King of Jerusalem. For two centuries now we have been amongst the rulers of France, and it will take more than a Capetian to destroy us. He has burned the honour of Charny: but from the ashes will rise the house of Lirey! The Charnys and Lireys will not die.'

So he was the enemy too, as much as Pietro di Ocre. The past and the aristocracy.

Jacques watched with fascination as the pallid face of his aristocratic companion took on colour for the first time since he had known him. This litany of family history had moved Nicolas sufficiently to give him an aura of prophecy. Nicolas' role was becoming clearer, but was he too an instrument of the policy of Bernard de Caen?

A new thought occurred to Jacques. Nicolas had been lurking in the cloister, which was not his natural environment. 'What have you been doing today?' Jacques asked. For a moment, the notion that the young knight organized Bernard's clandestine encounters with women flashed through his mind. A layman and aristocrat would be ideal for that.

Nicolas smiled. 'I've been seeing to our prisoner's needs,' he replied evasively. Colour drained from his face again, and his hair had fallen back over his forehead. 'Would you like to attend on him this afternoon, Brother Jacques?'

Even as he opened his mouth to answer this question, Jacques saw how skilful his companion had been in diverting his attention. But it didn't matter. He would allow Nicolas his small victory. 'No, thank you, Sire Nicolas. I should like to rest and pray after our long journey. Tomorrow will be time enough.'

At first Jacques was ashamed of the blatant deception. But as he walked across the cloister towards the main entrance of the convent, he sensed that this ease in telling white lies was an integral part of a new personality developing within.

It was his turn for deception. He needed to talk to Pietro alone.

15

The preceptor's keen interest as Jacques entered the cell suggested a readiness to talk. It was a clean and well-lighted room with a good straw mattress and a wooden stool. Pietro himself had been cleaned up and given a new shirt, and had been provided with a copy of *The Lives of the Saints*. There were few reminders of the broken man at Aigues-Mortes.

He stood up as the inquisitor entered, watching him expectantly. 'More questions?' he asked.

The irony and near-pleasure in his voice reassured Jacques. His sense of guilt at the lies he had told Nicolas dissipated. 'A conversation, rather,' he replied gently. Then, more harshly, to the gaoler who had accompanied him, 'Bring a stool and leave us alone!'

Jacques decided he could do away with the usual preliminaries. The transfer from the dungeon might already have wrought the desired effect. The prisoner was ready, the moment right, and he had no desire to push deep yet. 'I've never heard of an initiation by the Grand Master in person,' he began casually.

Pietro rose to the bait like tame fish in a pond. A glint in his eyes betrayed intense family pride. 'It was unusual,' he agreed, 'but he was my uncle, and in any case it was Jacques de Molay who insisted.'

'Did you already know him well then?'

'Not at all,' Pietro smiled, 'but in later years we were on many campaigns together. He trusted me as he trusted few men.'

'Will you tell me about your reception?' Jacques then asked softly.

'You must have read dozens of transcripts about our reception ceremony.'

'I'd like to hear about yours,' Jacques insisted gently.

Pietro drank from a jug beside him on the bench, then sighed. 'There can be no harm in that,' he conceded. 'Where would you like me to begin?'

'When you decided to take the Templar vow.'

'I'd always known I would. From the day of my birth.'

'But there must have been a decision at some time.'

Pietro gazed past the inquisitor. 'Yes, I suppose there was, and it was only the day before my initiation.'

'In Ocre?'

'Yes. My uncle had just returned from Acre on his way to the Paris Temple.'

'And he asked you to take the vow?'

'On the contrary! He did everything he could to stop me. But it was written in the stars. And that night in the hall of our castle there was no way he could stop me.'

'Why were you so keen?'

'Who wouldn't have been after listening to his tales of battle? I was a young lad of eighteen and there in front of me was one of the greatest warriors of the day. I drank in his every word like a sponge. He was like Methuselah talking of glorious feats of chivalry in past centuries ... Mind you, he was a fine strong man who still sat straight in the saddle. And he could ride for days on end while younger men begged to dismount and sleep. His face was broad and bearded with fine bulldog jaws that no one ever forgot. But the first thing to strike everybody was his laugh. Still today, forty years later, whenever I hear such a laugh, deep and resonant as if the man's stomach is going to burst, I turn in hope.'

'It's odd he never encouraged you to take the vow,' Jacques reflected aloud.

'Not really. My brothers were young, and I was destined to hold our castle. So he did everything possible to make it appear awful. "It sounds fine and heroic here," he would say, "but battle in Outremer is largely a matter of dust, insects and finding water." He was right, of course, as I know for myself now, but it made no difference to me then. My only thoughts were of the Temple and the Holy City. Now, after these years in prison it amuses me to remember that young man. So full of youthful flame, like a boy in love. How the world seemed corrupt, and the Order pure! I would have laughed myself to death if someone had suggested that nearly half a century later I would find myself in the dungeons of his Accursed Highness the King of France.' He spat on the floor as if to cleanse his mouth of the name.

'But if he was so much against your joining, what made him change his mind?' Jacques asked quietly.

Pietro di Ocre looked up sharply, then smiled. 'The memory of my father, whom he loved deeply. That evening he told us about St Louis' crusade. My father was with him then, you see, although he refused to his dying day to tell me about it. You can imagine how thrilled I was. "Yes, they were good times," my uncle said; "I was Master of the London Temple then. Your father was as good as one of us on that campaign. I myself saw him cutting down the saracen with his sword." My heart jumped, and I ached to take the vow there and then. I pleaded with him. "No," he objected, "with Tommaso in Rome and Tibaldo too young, you have your duties here in Ocre."' Pietro paused as if trying to recollect the exact words. 'But I think he was already half-convinced, for the next day he relented. And we held the ceremony the same night. Before he left for Paris.'

'In the castle?'

'No. A church nearby. In the crypt. San Eusanio, it was called.'

'Was?' This was the very saint that Bernard de Caen had asked him about.

'And it still is, although it no longer belongs to my family.'

The inquisitor let the comment pass. But he made a mental note to find the reason for this change later. Instinct told him that now Pietro was relaxed his guard would be lowered and patient listening would reveal new information. 'Describe the ceremony to me,' he said softly.

'It was at sunset. My uncle was dressed in a white mantle and a heavy golden chain with his insignia of office. The five knights accompanying my uncle were present, including two young men destined for a great future, Geoffroi de Charny and Jacques de Molay.' Jacques noticed the pride which flushed the preceptor's voice as he spoke these names, and was interested to discover that Pietro knew the present Grand Master so intimately. 'My uncle led me to some steps leading to the crypt. "Wait here," he said, and went down alone. When de Molay led me down shortly afterwards there was an eerie atmosphere. A strange light pervaded the crypt as the sun gradually sank behind the mountains west of the village. But it was not so much the light and warmth, I realized, but the reverence of the knights which struck me. They were silent, facing my uncle, who stood behind the altar containing the bones and relics of San Eusanio.

'Then the ceremony began. "*Biaus seignors frères*," my uncle began, "you have seen that the majority of those present have agreed that this young man should become a brother. If there is someone amongst you who knows something which would prevent him becoming a brother according to our Rule, let him speak now." His companions were silent. He waited for the sound of his voice to disappear amongst the columns. Then he turned towards me: "Brother, do you wish to belong to the company of the house?" I can remember the shiver of excitement which ran through me at those words, even though I have myself pronounced them many times myself since that day.

'"Yes, Sire," I said, naturally.

'"And are you aware of the rigours of our life, of the rules of the house, and the commandments of charity? You see us with fine horse and fine harness and eat well and drink well and possess fine clothes, and it therefore appears to you that you will be much at your comfort. But you do not know of the harsh commandments which obtain here within: because it is a hard thing that you, who are master of yourself, should become the serf of another. If you wish to be on this side of the sea, you will be sent to the other side; if you wish to be in Acre, you will be sent to Tripoli."'

The preceptor was in a trance. Jacques listened with fascination, but thinking more of San Eusanio than of the ceremony. So far, it was much like dozens he'd read. Perhaps it had been a waste of time after all. The secrets he sought were buried more deeply yet.

'By that time no threat of hardship could have restrained me. So I swore solemnly in God's name and in the name of the Blessed Virgin Mary that I would always be obedient to the Master of the Temple, and to whichever brother of the Order was put above me; that I would preserve chastity, the good customs of the Order, and never be in any place in which any Christian is killed as the result of my wishes; and that I would not for better or for worse leave this Order without the express permission of my superiors. Then my uncle concluded the ceremony with these words, which I have since repeated often myself: "Now that we have told you the things that you should do and of what you must beware, and those that cause loss of the house, and those that cause loss of the habit, and of other rules; and if we have not told you everything that we should tell you, then you may ask it. And God permit you to speak well and do well!"'

'Then it was over?'

'The normal ceremony, yes.'

Jacques sat forward; at last his patience would be rewarded.

'The knights left us alone to pray, after which my uncle unlocked a small door fitted behind the tomb and stood as if he were addressing the chapter. Then he kneeled with his back to the altar and to the cross. He opened the casket and spread the dried bones of San Eusanio in a semicircle before us. "Kneel beside me, Pietro," he said. Then he began to recite what sounded like a prayer, but in a language I had never heard before. It continued for some time. When he stopped, he began to talk to me without looking. "Pietro, you have today made the first step in a series that will bring great power to you and to our family. Now you must study."

"'But I joined to fight for God!" I protested. I was anxious to travel to the Holy Land at once, like all young men in those days.

"'That is one of our duties," my uncle said, "but there are others of greater importance. As you will discover."'

These details of bones and strange language made Jacques uneasily aware of his ignorance concerning the Templars. Talk of mysteries, the Holy Land and secret duties seemed to emanate from another world. His emotions vacillated between contempt, as a trained interrogator, and utter fascination with this talk of nobility and power, as befitted a man of humble origin. For the moment he had a specific purpose, and would try to draw Pietro on the object they were seeking. Later, he promised himself, he would come back to this strange ceremony. It was vital not to lose the rhythm he had established. 'Did he say anything else?' he prompted.

'Just one thing. Before we left the crypt, he asked me to stand beside him on the other side of the altar. We said a final prayer together while I gazed on the faces of God and the Devil on the capitals in front of me.'

'What prayer was it?' Jacques pressed softly.

Pietro hesitated, and the inquisitor feared he might stop there. But then he smiled confidently. 'I heard it for the first time that evening. But I soon learned it by heart, for my uncle used it at all private ceremonies. In the crypt at San Eusanio it was always the last prayer he said.'

'Recite it to me.'

Pietro di Ocre looked up in front of him, as if studying the two heads he had just described. Then, in a strange distant voice that Jacques had not heard before, he began:

'The images are manifest to man,
but the light in them remains concealed
in the image of the light of the Father.
He will become manifest,
but this image will remain concealed by his light.

I shall give you
what no eye has seen

101

and what no ear has heard
and what no hand has touched
and what has never occurred to the human mind.'

Pietro stared entranced as his words faded into the vault. Then his eyes dropped abruptly. He sighed heavily and turned towards his inquisitor. All strength was drained from his face.

The prayer had a certain beauty, Jacques admitted to himself. Yet the promises it made were worthy of the heaviest sentence the Holy Office could impose. This was abominable heresy, ascribing words and sentiments not present in the scriptures to Our Lord the Father. Promises which smacked of Cathars, Bogomils and propagators of dualism.

A tremor of apprehension shot through Jacques. The picture was beginning to form in his mind's eye, but there were still too many gaps in his knowledge for him to rest on his laurels. Above all, he needed to see Bernard de Caen again.

· —— 16 —— ·

Brother Jacques took a deep breath as he entered his Superior's study. Once over the threshold, the pressing need to draw information that only Bernard could provide gripped both mind and body in a kind of trance. Invisible lead weights drove his sandals into the floor. He looked behind him, but there was no solace in Nicolas' lean and austere face. He forced his feet towards the desk. How was *he* to interrogate the master interrogator?

But Bernard was affable again, almost jovial. 'I'm delighted to see you both. Come, sit down.' His smile was charged with the love and joy of an angel of the first hierarchy. For an instant, Jacques envisioned him in a painting, dressed in red with a burning candle in his hand. His anxieties dissipated.

'We've come to report, my lord,' he said when the vision faded. The sound of heavy breathing behind his neck ruffled him again. He tried to will Nicolas away.

'Report! You look like two young men with no cares in the world,' Bernard laughed, 'a pair of pagans at play.'

Jacques wanted to reply, but refrained.

To his surprise, Nicolas spoke: 'We come from prime, my lord,' he said, pushing back a shock of black hair from his forehead. Then he lifted his head.

It was a gesture he often made when he grew pompous, Jacques noted. But why should a jest like Bernard's bother a secular knight? Nicolas had taken no vows. He glanced quickly at Bernard, expecting anger. But the prelate's seraphic smile was still there. It was a good moment to begin. 'We are making some progress with the prisoner,' he said.

'Excellent. Tell me,' Bernard replied. Then he sank back into his chair to listen.

The sounds of iron striking flint and keen axe-heads splitting damp logs punctuated the crisp morning air as Jacques talked. Wafts of smoke from piles of burning leaves drifted into the room. More than once he wished he were outside with the other friars doing manual work, far removed from the complexities of politics and the corruption of power.

103

'So that is your conclusion?' Bernard asked when he finished. His smile had disappeared now. Tiny beads of perspiration glistened on his forehead.

'. . . that there is a deeper heresy? Yes. But that is not all. There are too many loose ends. And they all lead back to Ocre,' he added, recalling Armand and wishing he could have been more specific. 'I've been wondering about the monastery of Santo Spirito at Ocre.'

'Wondering?'

Still Bernard seemed open, willing to talk. Jacques went on, determined to take advantage of this unexpected friendliness. 'You know it well, I believe.' He avoided the intonation of a question.

Bernard sat with his hands clasped across his stomach, his face unshaven and hair wet. 'Not so well. It was a long day's ride by mule from Casanova in the summer and virtually cut off during the winter. The terrain is hard and rocky, and in winter the winds will cut a man in two. In five years at Casanova I don't think I visited it more than half a dozen times.'

'Was it under the patronage of the Counts of Ocre?' Brother Jacques asked.

Bernard looked at him shrewdly, carefully weighing his words. 'This seems to me like an interrogation,' he smiled, 'but I suppose you do need more information. What is it you wish to know?'

'Nothing secret. I'm just curious to know about the monastery and the Counts of Ocre. Who founded Santo Spirito and why – that sort of thing.'

'There's little wrong with that,' Bernard agreed. 'If it'll help you with your search. Santo Spirito was founded by Count Berardo, grandfather of your prisoner. A hermit lived in a cave on a sheer rock face nearby. When Count Berardo returned from the Holy Land, it seems that he adopted the hermit as family seer and built the monastery in gratitude to Our Lord for his safe return. Then he gave it to our Order. No one knows why . . . perhaps to gain respectability for his foundation. That's what they used to say. Anyway, he built or rebuilt other churches in the area at the same time.'

It was Nicolas who asked the question on Jacques' lips. 'Why did it need respectability? Wasn't his patronage enough?' He had been following with interest, noting how the inquisitor was overcoming his handicap and drawing information from Bernard de Caen.

Bernard silenced him with a glare, and ignored his question.

Jacques regarded his companion afresh. This genuine curiosity suggested that he was not after all merely a spy. Otherwise he would never have accepted such a task. But for the moment he pushed the question from his mind to concentrate on Lord Bernard. Jacques willed his eyes away from the knight, then rested his head on his clasped hands, gaining time as he sought to frame an innocuous question. His Superior's reaction had been strange, but, to Jacques, not surprising. Now he felt the beady green eyes gazing at him, but they no longer penetrated; neither did they inculcate fear. He would try to elicit the answer Nicolas sought, but with a different question. 'Who exactly were the counts of Ocre?'

'A local feudal family,' Bernard said, with a suspicious emphasis on the first adjective which implied far greater importance. His attempt to dismiss them did not come off. 'Important in their own way, of course,' he carried on, 'and extremely wealthy after the crusades.'

Jacques went on as if he had noticed nothing, looking blandly at his Superior. 'What I don't understand is why the scion of such a family became a simple Templar.'

'I do not believe he was intended to be just "a simple knight", as you put it. And he was not the only son,' Bernard added softly. 'There were two others. The younger son, Tibaldo, died as a young man. At the time there were rumours that he was murdered. The elder son, Tommaso, joined the Church. He became the Cardinal of Santa Cecilia. A remarkable man, in fact . . .'

'You knew the Cardinal of Santa Cecilia?' Nicolas asked.

At first Jacques was annoyed at this interjection. Yet the possibility that the answer would be affirmative reinforced his suspicion that Bernard knew much more than he was prepared to proffer unasked. He watched Bernard anxiously, recalling Pietro's mention of his brother.

'I met him,' Bernard admitted, 'but I didn't really know him.' There was no mistaking the reproach in his eyes as he replied to Nicolas. 'It's strange that his name should come up again today. When we were in Paris, the Inquisitor-General Guillaume de Paris asked me about him too.'

Now the shock could not have been greater, and Jacques failed to conceal it. So that was where Bernard had gone when he had been left alone, and had taken the opportunity to visit Armand. But more than this, Bernard de Caen's uncharacteristic openness perturbed him. This case seemed to involve his Superior emotionally in ways he could not yet fathom. It made the task of unravelling the truth more difficult. There would be no easy route; yet this recognition made him all the more determined to find it.

Bernard himself seemed to sense his unease: 'You must not be surprised, young man,' he said quietly. 'Lord Guillaume and I have known each other for many decades. It was only natural that I should pay him a visit.'

A visit? Was it natural to pay one's enemies a visit?

Again, Bernard interpreted the silence with uncanny precision. 'In the *Opus*,' he said, 'you must be prepared for strange travelling companions. You have heard of the occasion when King Philip's soldiers attacked Pope Boniface at his summer residence in Anagni?'

Jacques nodded. When he was in Paris as a student that incident had been portrayed as one of the great scandals of history. It always seemed to him a good reason never to trust the French king. Now he had to shake himself awake, for Bernard de Caen had already turned the tables: even as he had replied to Jacques' questions in his docile manner he had been leading the younger inquisitor where *he* wished to go.

'Well, the world is never as simple as it seems,' Bernard went on, 'and there was good reason for the attack. Some years earlier we had made a secret alliance with Cardinal Gaetani, as he then was, against what he presented as a dangerous conspiracy against the Church. We supported him: he won, rose to the Holy See himself, and then reneged on his agreement.'

Jacques recognized the implications of this statement. Above all, he was fascinated by the pronoun 'we' Bernard had used in speaking of the alliance. 'I never realized that,' he muttered.

'Neither did I,' Nicolas added. But it did not affect his loathing for King Philip, who was the real villain of the Anagni story as he saw it.

Again, Jacques noticed, he was obviously speaking the truth.

'There are many things you do not know. Must not know. But some things that I wish you to know, for they will save the Holy Church from the designs of King Philip.'

'You spoke of an alliance with him,' Jacques said. As he spoke, he sensed Nicolas de Lirey stiffen beside him. An odd reaction.

But before he could look at him Bernard de Caen laughed. 'That was twenty years ago. The papacy was still in Rome.'

Jacques' mind spun with this new information: Bernard had once

106

been an ally of King Philip, and Guillaume de Paris; now they were virtually enemies. Yet he was chosen to deliver Clement's message. And he paid a private visit to the Inquisitor-General. It made no sense. 'The conspiracy . . .?' he began.

'I'm pleased you begin to understand,' Bernard said.

Jacques feigned understanding, but in truth understood little. It appeared that the counts of Ocre had seen their fortunes rise with the crusades, increased their ambition, and made an attempt at total control of the Church. If this was true, then it was an astonishing story; as astonishing as that of Icarus. He began to see the importance of Pietro di Ocre to Bernard de Caen. At the same time he was pleased that Bernard had decided to fill in some of the gaps.

'We never discovered the full extent of the conspiracy. The immediate plan was to take control of the Church via a puppet pope – who was indeed elected to the Holy See. Rumours circulated of far more ambitious plans.' He switched to his normal utterance, dropping his casual attitude. His eyes almost flamed as he stared first at Nicolas, then at Jacques. 'You see, my young colleagues, wherever we looked, whatever clues we followed, the same name appeared: Thomas Berard. He had been dead then for twenty years, but his chosen successor, Guillaume de Beaujeu, had followed him as Grand Master of the Temple. One nephew was preceptor for Southern Italy, and another the cardinal at the heart of the conspiracy in Rome.' Lord Bernard never spoke thus openly without good reason. Jacques glanced at his companion as this reason became apparent to him. He was beginning to understand the source of his Superior's power.

'For twenty years I have been convinced that the secret key to that conspiracy, and the damaged relations between Church and France for over a decade, lay in Ocre,' Bernard went on. 'Fifty years before, they were a minor family; by a hair's breadth they missed control of the entire Church.'

In an unprecedented gesture, he unclasped his hands and took the arms of the two young men. He had gained a victory, and told them exactly what he wished them to know.

'Last month Guillaume de Paris asked me if I knew of any secret relics which might once have been in the area of Casanova.' He paused, staring ahead as if lost in contemplation of a holy image. 'I did once hear of something said to possess extraordinary power,' he said dreamily, 'from a monk in a nearby abbey. That may well be what we are seeking.'

Then, suddenly, he snapped out of this reverie as though he had willed himself to return to his former self. 'Anyway, Guillaume is as keen to find them as is His Holiness Lord Clement. And I am more than ever convinced that our Templar prisoner could help us if he wished. If there was such a relic, then he would know of it. But we must find the means to loosen his tongue . . . some hint, a suggestion that we know as much as he does.'

Pride and satisfaction swelled the churchman's normally squeaky voice. But for the first time, Jacques sensed that Bernard, too, was indispensible.

He guessed the drift of his Superior's argument, and saw that he was meant to. Lord Bernard wanted him to believe that his actions were spontaneous while he, in fact, dictated them. But it made no difference now. Once out of Avignon Jacques would be his own man. This was the real point of no return. The words came easily with a deep sense of relief and excitement: 'It looks, my good knight of Lirey, as though we must leave for Ocre!'

'Do you believe the months of travel will be justified by what we find?' Nicolas asked when they were alone in the cloister.

'There is nothing to be found here. I'm sure even torture will be useless without some lever to open Pietro's mind.'

'And that can only be found in Ocre?'

'Yes.' He glanced at Nicolas.

'You've always wanted to go there, haven't you?' What was it about the place that attracted the friar?

'Not always. But now I'm convinced that the answer will be found there. It seems King Philip thinks so too, from what we've heard.' Then another thought came to him, and for the first time he dared to ask a direct question about his Superior. 'Speaking of answers,' he began cautiously, 'I wonder what made Lord Bernard so amenable this evening. He seemed over-willing to answer every question and grant each request. I feared he would not allow me to go to Ocre.'

Nicolas laughed quietly to himself, then drew Jacques closer. 'Lord Bernard has his Superior as surely as you have him for yours,' he said, 'and he's only human.'

Jacques looked up, puzzled.

'This day Lord Bernard has been caught *in flagrante delicto*, as the lawyers say. His only recourse is to show extreme willingness in executing the Pope's desires.'

Jacques' feet seemed to take root in the cobbles. 'What on earth are you talking about? Make sense, for the sake of Our Lord! What offence?'

'You haven't heard? The entire convent knows. Pope Clement's messenger found Bernard with his woman.' There was an admixture of amusement and admiration in Nicolas' voice, but no shock or disgust.

'His *woman?*' Jacques exclaimed. But disbelief was already tempered by his memory of the Gascon's friar's gossip.

'Power does strange things to men who are not born with it,' Nicolas said portentously.

'But he has taken holy vows.'

'Vows?' Now Nicolas failed to hide the contempt in his voice, but it was not for the Inquisitor-General's lust. 'Men like our Lord Bernard do what they wish to do once it is within their means, vows or no vows. But when they're caught at their game must they make amends. He wanted desperately that you – and I – should depart for Italy at once, to appease His Holiness.'

'He only needed to order it.'

'That would have been too obvious. It must appear to be the consequence of the work we have already done; something that would have happened anyway.' Then, with embarrassment, aware that he might have spoken too much, Nicolas continued. 'Be that as it may, with your blessing I shall retire. There's much to be done, and little time.'

Jacques regarded his companion anew as he departed, as though a shower of rain had swept away previous layers of knowledge. His affirmation had been genuine enough: aristocratic disdain had been stronger than his loyalty to Bernard de Caen. So although he to some degree be Bernard's spy on this mission, there was a fissure in his allegiance which Jacques might be able to exploit.

The journey to Ocre augured well.

17

To Brother Jacques' delight, renewed saracen pirate raids near Marseilles rendered the fast river and sea route to Italy hazardous. In addition, for months there had been rumours of imminent war between Pisa and Genoa. The prospect of a sea voyage would have pushed his simmering sense of apprehension to boiling fear. Furthermore, Bernard de Caen had encouraged them to take the more difficult route into Piedmont over the Alps. 'With luck, you will reach the plains before the heavy snows fall,' he had argued, 'and it will be safer. Moreover, you will travel in disguise and must reveal your identities to no one – save the abbot of a religious house in case of emergency.'

Jacques was only too willing to accept this advice. He and and Nicolas travelled in the anonymous, brown woollen riding clothes of members of the minor nobility going on pilgrimage. They were equipped with heavy cloaks and blankets. This feigned elevation in rank allowed Jacques to ride a rouncy such as he had never ridden before, and justified the presence of armed guards to curious bystanders. Nicolas at first treated both mount and clothes with disdain, but once out of Avignon he seemed to take to the journey. They were also accompanied by a dour guide from Chambéry for the Alpine pass, and a Dominican who had been brought up in the Abruzzi and spoke the local dialect. The friar was to remain behind in the Black Friars' monastery in the new city which was under construction near Ocre.

As they travelled east from Avignon Jacques was lulled into optimism by fine autumn sunshine. Nicolas de Lirey was as happy as a sandboy in the saddle, and the whole world seemed at ease. Peasants were treading their grapes on the lower slopes: in the foothills he could see them outside the hamlets still picking them.

In one village they saw boys scrumping. Jacques pointed at them. 'They deserve a good beating,' he said severely.

Nicolas laughed. 'What? Did you never scrump or poach when you were a boy?'

Jacques glared at him.

'I did, and I'm not ashamed of it. When my father sent me to the school at Cluny . . .'

This surprised Jacques. 'You mean to say you studied with the Benedictines?'

'Indeed. It's not strange for the son of a knightly family in Burgundy. It's only three days' hard ride south from Montbard to Cluny. In fact I almost took holy vows myself at one stage.' Nicolas laughed at the memory of his eighteenth summer, when he had discussed it with the abbot. But pressure from his mother, and a young lady who appeared fortuitously – possibly arranged by his mother - had distracted him from his ambition. Then had begun his private and most secret crusade against King Philip. 'But at least they taught me to read, and to write in a fair hand.'

'And scrump?' Jacques asked mischievously. He began to see his companion in a new light, though it was hard to imagine him in ecclesiastical robes.

'No,' Nicolas laughed again, 'that was to supplement my diet when I strayed off our family lands. But don't tell me you never did it.'

'As a child,' Jacques admitted reluctantly. Later it had been portrayed as a terrible sin. But he had been punished, and now felt the stripes of his father's belt across his backside. 'I was well beaten for it,' he explained, as though that would expunge his error.

'Excellent. Then at least you're part human.'

This prompted Jacques to continue. 'And sometimes from the royal orchard in Paris,' he confessed.

'That's even better,' Nicolas chuckled; 'that's fine indeed.'

For the rest of that day they rode easily together.

Soon the broad highway, which could accommodate three ox-wagons side by side, narrowed to a single-wagon road. When they entered the first mountain valleys the blood month had turned. As the echoes of the bells of matins or prime faded in the cracks and gullies of rock walls alongside the road, they were replaced by the screams of pigs at slaughter. These screams unnerved Jacques.

For several days he had noticed horsemen behind them. Each time he turned in his saddle they were there, visible but just far enough to make identification impossible. When he and Nicolas stopped for the night they were always gone; then towards the middle of the following morning they reappeared. At first he had assumed they were simply fellow travellers on a busy road. But the screams made him look again, and those distant horsemen – four or five, he fancied – hovered there in the distance as a permanent threat. He strove to resist this unwelcome

111

sentiment, but it would not go away and at frequent intervals he turned to look. They were always there.

One evening they arrived at a small town just in time to enter the gates before curfew fell. 'What is this town?' Jacques asked the guide.

'St Jean de Maurienne, sire.'

Jacques smiled, for although it was he who had ordered the guide to address him thus it still rang strange in his ears.

'A resting place for pilgrims to Rome,' Nicolas added. 'I've heard of it.'

'Then here we will surely find hospitality in the monastery,' Jacques said, ignoring the hint of superior knowledge. 'Perhaps we should declare ourselves?'

'This is hardly an emergency,' Nicolas admonished.

In the past such sarcasm would have wounded Jacques. But he knew his companion was right: they had strict instructions not to use the papal letters they were carrying except in an emergency.

He rode on, wondering at how easily Nicolas' haughtiness could resurface after days of good humour. They found lodgings in the guest-house of the monastery without endangering their mission. A supper of freshly slaughtered pork baked with apples, and served with the convent's best wine, restored their good relations. Jacques was amused by the fact that he was actually living like a nobleman, but he kept his thoughts to himself.

From the cloister an egg-shaped mountain was silhouetted against moonlight. A bitter wind rushed down it like boys on sledges. But the corridor in the lee of this wind was lighted by torches, and offered respite. There, after supper, Jacques and Nicolas found themselves alone for the first time since their journey had begun, wrapped in heavy cloaks. They sat in a niche of the cloister's inner wall.

'These long days are dull,' Nicolas complained. There were no guests of any distinction or interest. After days of virtual silence this village offered little respite.

'We have a long way to go yet.'

'We could talk . . .'

'There'll be time for talk once we reach Ocre.' But he too was bored by the journey, and weakened to temptation. It was a surprising opening gambit. 'I suppose it would be better if we didn't have to keep ourselves in disguise,' he suggested.

'I'm afraid we have no choice.' Nicolas didn't like to say that the real problem was Jacques' company. In spite of the occasional spark

112

of comradeship, Nicolas felt as remote as ever from the ambitions baker's son.

'I'd sooner sleep outside these nights than share a bed with three others, and ten beds to a room,' Jacques remarked.

'Now there's a good Cistercian.' Nicolas' irony was sharp, but avoided contempt.

'If I remember rightly, you yourself complained at the inn yesterday.'

Nicolas glared at Jacques, but his face showed a recognition that he was trapped in the game of wits. He laughed.

It was a genuine and infectious laugh. For a moment suspicions and differences were forgotten. As it subsided Jacques fancied he could feel a new warmth in his companion, like fresh crocuses pushing through late winter snow. Pork and good wine had added colour to Nicolas' pallid face.

Then they sat quietly. But after a few minutes the bitter wind cut into their legs under their tunics even there, as if it had found them out in their niche. Yet inside was little better, with no heating save that given off by the kitchen chimney-breasts. The church was colder still.

Nicolas began to pace to and fro, holding his arms clasped across his chest. 'Did you see the biforium?' he asked as he turned back to face his companion.

Superstitious nonsense, Jacques thought to himself. Then he looked sharply at the moonlit face: was the aristocrat provoking him again? He chose his words with care. 'It's hard to believe that they might really be the fingers of John the Baptist. That seems to me stretching credulity a little too far.'

'Do no relics have meaning for you?' Nicolas asked. He was surprised at this scepticism in a friar, and an inquisitor at that.

'Some,' Jacques said cautiously. He was trying to guess the reason for such a direct question.

'Those in the Sainte Chapelle, for instance?'

'If their history is known. It's not surprising that certain objects associated with Our Lord were preserved as objects of veneration. Many are authentic.'

'Which?' Now there was no malice. Just simple curiosity.

But Jacques did not rise to the bait, for he still did not fully trust his new companion. He found himself longing for a Dominican *socius* again. 'The problem is classification. There are so many in circulation today that many must be false. But fortunately it is not our task to classify them.' That should deal with Nicolas.

113

But Nicolas went on: 'But surely it is your task, as inquisitor into heresy.'

'Not at all. The objects themselves are never heretical. We inquire into the ideas of heretics, not their possessions.' Jacques paused, and looked around the cloister as if expecting to find someone watching him. 'Nevertheless, it is true that the dependence of people nowadays on the power of relics is absurd.'

'And the relic we are seeking? What do you think about that? What do you think it can be?'

'Shall we go inside? We have another hard day in the saddle tomorrow.' This was no time to discuss the object of their journey.

Nicolas laughed at this blatant evasion, but accepted it. 'Hard is the right word. Tomorrow we have to leave our comfortable saddle. The road after St Jean is little more than a mule track, the guide says. And soon we begin to climb.'

Intimations of a storm to come reached Jacques in the last refuge before the Mont Cenis pass.

The wooden cabin was barely lighted by embers as he and Nicolas sat with the other guests eating a breakfast of dried chunks of bread, which they softened by dunking them in a bowl of red wine. The embers took the chill off the cold morning, but still they shivered as they ate. The guards and muleteers who had been hired for the crossing sat furthest from the fire. Jacques leaned against the chimney-breast with Nicolas and their guide. He would have been happy to rest his aching limbs there all day, but the guide was anxious to leave as soon as possible.

Intermittent creaking noises accompanied their breakfast.

'Is this thing going to fall down on us?' Jacques asked. He had felt uneasy since they had entered the cabin, and longed for the plains which he knew awaited them beyond the mountains.

The guide laughed. 'No. It's just breathing. The damp is increasing. It doesn't look good for us.'

'What do you mean?' Jacques asked anxiously.

'The weather's changing. Might snow. We'll certainly get rain up there.' He jerked his thumb towards Mont Cenis. His face broke into a devilish grin as if he were amused by the prospect of bad weather.

'And if we leave immediately?'

A piece of brushwood flared up from the embers, illuminating the guide's smallpox-pitted face as though someone had lighted a torch.

'No difference. It's a full day's journey across the pass. And no shelter. We'd best eat well. At least we won't starve if the brigands steal our horses and food.' A toothless chuckle whistled from his mouth.

Rain began soon after they left the refuge; at first a light drizzle, it increased as they climbed and a freezing wind blew up. Jacques drew the hood of his cloak about his face and saw the guards tying theirs with rope across the forehead. But the bitter wind still drove the rain into his face. Only as they turned to ride the next section of the zig-zagging track was there respite from the rain.

The path narrowed until there was barely space for a single mule and the small party was strung out over a dozen loops, so that, while Jacques could hear the guide ahead and Nicolas behind, he could see nobody. Mist rose from the moss beside the track and heather on the moors to either side. All tree cover had disappeared, the last solitary pines seeming to fall away behind them. The cloud level appeared to get ever closer. Although it was now two hours after dawn there was little light. It was bitterly cold. 'Just keep moving steadily,' the guide insisted; 'whatever we do we mustn't stop.'

There was some respite when they reached the plateau beyond the pass. The going underfoot was good, so they could mount their mules and travel faster in a group. But half-way across the plateau, the track turned into the wind. The driving cold rain became sleet, and they were forced to slow their pace.

Watery sleet gradually hardened until it stung Jacques' face in spite of the hood drawn across his features. The wind increased so that it seemed as if some demon were blasting it at him, trying to prevent him from crossing the pass. Finally the sleet turned to snow, coating the cloaks and pack-horses now visible behind him with a thin film of white, picking out men's eyebrows and beards with the skill of a painter highlighting his work. The rolling moors around him were suddenly sprinkled as if with sugar.

Then they began the descent.

'It's steeper this side,' the guide announced. 'Dismount, and walk in single file.'

Jacques narrowed his eyes against the snow, bent his head low and trusted the mule in front of him to lead him along the path. Wind buffeted his cloak to right and left, sometimes finding its way in from his feet and billowing up to the rope tied around his waist. Beneath him the track barely accommodated two boots side by side; in several places it had slipped away altogether. He noticed how the mule would stop, pick ahead with its forefeet, then sway its body over the slope to keep balance as it stepped over these small landfalls. He learned how to imitate the mule, and felt safer.

In front, the guide had disappeared into the mist and cloud; behind, Jacques assumed that Nicolas and the guards were following. Visibility was now limited to a few paces. He could make out the form of spurs which forced the track out from the mountainside, and saw occasional, snow-coated rocks to his right. To his left, there was nothing but swirling mist, and ahead and behind there was nothing. He fervently prayed that no one else would be on the track that morning.

Then a mule set up a hellish braying. An avalanche of rocks hurtled down the path, punching at Jacques' calves before plunging into the void. Simultaneously, he heard the rasping noise of hoofs struggling to make purchase. Finally, there was chaos.

A dead weight hit his left shoulder and knocked him flat into a rift eroded by a rivulet that crossed the path at that point. A horrified scream came from the object as it flew past into the mist. Sharp pain flashed through Jacques' right arm, while his left shoulder was numb from the blow. He gasped for breath and began to pull himself to his feet, instinctively grasping the reins of his own mule like a blind man seeking the door.

Then the second weight hit him. This one did not fly straight at him, but rolled over the small spur inside the bend. Although Jacques was exhausted, and weakened by the previous blow, he did not fall back to the ground. This bundle was lighter and did not bray. It simply rolled over him and on down the slope. Shock and confusion were knocked out of his mind by a piercing human scream.

Jacques stepped across the track and saw a bloody hand in the gorse just beneath it, gripping with such tenacity that the bones shone through like those of a new-born fledgling fallen from the nest. He threw himself on the track so that his body smothered the stream, then grabbed the wrist with all his strength. It was not sufficient to haul the body up, but he held on desperately as he recognized the slender white fingers. There could be no mistake: it was Nicolas de Lirey who was suspended over the ravine, and whose life depended on the strength in the young monk's hands. Jacques closed both hands tightly over the gory wrist, and shouted with all the breath in his lungs. Atrocious pain stabbed through his right arm, but he was beginning to regain feeling and strength in his other shoulder.

Somehow he hung on.

The deadweight beneath him tugged at his wrists, and he had the sensation that the gorse on which Nicolas had broken his fall was starting to give. The small patch of muddy earth in which the bush grew began to slide down with the rest of the slope. Gorse and Jacques together had been enough to sustain the body. Now Jacques felt every stone on the path rub and stab lingeringly against his chest and thighs as he began to slither slowly towards the edge. But he never for a moment loosened his grip on Nicolas: he prayed, and held tight.

Death seemed inevitable. He thought of his parents, and of their sacrifice for him. He was frightened, because his mission had not been completed. He saw the bright eyes of Bernard de Caen, felt the breath of his disdain as if he were Death itself; but then was no longer afraid of him because he saw Bernard with his woman. And that vision frightened him even more, because he saw with astonishing clarity the anatomical details of a person he had never met, so realistically that it could not be a dream. And he found that in the face of death instead of God and His Son he desired the woman. And he cared nothing for his vows. It was the last thing he thought before he prepared himself mentally for the fall onto the rocks below.

Then, so quickly that it seemed to him the whole incident had taken a matter of seconds, he felt the guide beside him. 'The Devil!' Jacques shouted. 'Hold us!'

At the same time the probing forefoot of another mule touched his thigh. The mule snorted, stepped forward a pace, and stopped directly above Jacques' body. The first guard came soon afterwards, standing over him like the Colossus. Jacques looked up in relief. As he did so, the mist above the spur cleared for an instant and he fancied he saw a horseman there: a knight, in the colours of King Philip. Then the vision disappeared again. Jacques shivered with cold and fear. It must have been a dream, he reasoned. All strength was drained from him.

Lying on each side of him, the guide and guard took a better grip on Nicolas' wrist. Once they got a firm hold, it was a simple matter for them to pull Nicolas up onto the track. His lean cheeks were sunken like those of a death-mask, and his legs lacerated by grazes from the gorse. His wrists bled steadily. There was no colour in his face.

He was then wrapped in a blanket, and the guide bandaged him and gave him spirits.

Jacques dragged himself up, and sat on the track with elbows on his knees and hand supporting his face. He prayed quietly for Nicolas, and gave thanks for the strength which the Lord had given his own arms. As he did so, his companion looked up: the faintest of smiles appeared on those death-like lips. Jacques stared ahead, watching fresh snowflakes covering the splattered crimson and restoring peace to the mountainside.

His entire body was shaking uncontrollably.

It was time to trust his companion with his suspicions. 'Now I'm certain we're being followed,' Jacques said. He looked out of the window, glad that daylight had come. Since they had come to the infirmary of this convent beneath the pass he had woken every night in a pool of sweat, shaking with fear. The mattress on which he lay had never dried out completely.

'What makes you think so?' Nicolas asked sceptically. He was deeply grateful to Brother Jacques, and had adjusted his opinion of the man's worth. But that was no good reason to accept his delusions without question.

Jacques shifted his body painfully so that he could see Nicolas' face. 'I saw horsemen following us from the moment we left Avignon. And when you fell in the mountains, I swear I saw a horseman – a knight – in the French King's livery, watching us from a hillock not far from the wide track across the plateau.'

'It was not in your dreams?' A typical monkish vision: always shadowy figures, whether virgins or saints; especially in the snow. Yet Nicolas recognized reluctantly that the horsemen might equally well belong to Templar knights.

Jacques was embarrassed. He guessed that Nicolas had been watching him during the night. Across the room, he could hear the infirmary brother reciting recipes aloud as he brewed herbs for his salves and medicinal drinks. For the past few days Jacques had been drinking a potion for the ague made of plantain roots, wine and water, and eating nothing but cakes of barley meal. He wondered what Nicolas might have heard as he kept wake. 'It was snowing hard,' he said, trying to sound convincing, 'but I'm sure I saw them.'

Nicolas studied him. 'Perhaps you're right. But you know what that means?'

'That our "accident" was no accident?'

'I'm afraid so. Let us keep careful watch when we leave this place. If someone really is following us, they will make themselves visible sooner or later.' The words were spoken in sympathetic agreement, but Nicolas' lean face registered doubt. He carried on, as if he were aware of his expression and wished to erase it: 'The Brother who has been tending you suggests we wait a few more days. Your shoulder is badly bruised . . .'

'And you?' He pointed to Nicolas' bandaged wrists.

The infirmary friar was now heating cups in preparation for bloodletting on another patient.

'Nothing to stop me riding,' Nicolas said. 'In a couple of days we'll be on the road. I'm not one of these new courtier knights, all perfume and curls.'

Jacques registered the contempt in his companion's voice but made no comment. 'What of the others?' he asked, remembering the guards and muleteers.

'The guide has gone back to Chambéry, and the others are in the guest-house here.'

'Then we can leave.' Jacques gained strength as he spoke, as if he could ride to Ocre with the force of his will alone.

'In a couple of days,' Nicolas insisted gently. He stood up and walked towards the door. But before opening it he turned and grinned. 'And thank you,' he said simply. Yet three words had rarely cost him so much.

When he had left, Jacques looked out. Through gnarled apple trees he was glad to see the mountains behind them. Now they would be able to make good time across the plains.

Nicolas de Lirey sat on a bench in the orchard. He leaned back into the air and stretched his spine for relief against aching pain. That heavy blow in the small of his back had been far worse than cuts and lacerations, although he had said nothing about it. He tried to massage himself, but soon gave up. Sleeping, standing, sitting; it was still there. Only this chill wind seemed to dampen it.

A heavy blow. But from what? He closed his mind, and in spite of the pain sought to recall that moment exactly as it had occurred. He was leaning back then too, following as his mule picked a steady path down the mountainside. To him, the path was invisible at that moment; seconds earlier he had leaned down to check the path. To no avail. Gusts of wind brought swirling snowflakes which obscured even his mule's taut ears from view. Then he had felt the weight in his back: sudden, noiseless, unannounced by a shower of stones. It had felt smooth, as if he had received a swingeing blow from a club. But that could not be the case, for a hypothetical assailant would have

119

been as blind as he had been in the mist and cloud. And it would have been hard to find firm footing on the steep, snow-covered rockface beside the path. Then Nicolas recalled that thick forest had covered the slope above the path. An avalanche of rock was unlikely on such terrain; perhaps a landslip, an entire hillside, but not a shower of large rocks.

Yet there had been no attack, no attempt on the life of Brother Jacques. An assailant could easily have pushed him off the edge, together with gorse-bush and Nicolas himself. Perhaps it had been a discreet warning? Or their imagination? The incident was like a bad dream now, and all his efforts to recall those instants of pain and near-death failed to retrieve helpful detail.

Stabbing pain forced Nicolas to stand up quickly for relief. At the same time intuition told him the avalanche was man-made. That reduced his questions to one: who?

Bernard de Caen had been as explicit as he had ever been when Nicolas had been briefed for this investigation with Brother Jacques. The main purpose of their quest was to thwart King Philip, and for that reason he, Nicolas, had been chosen. Now he reflected that the French king had men scouring Italy for months, and at this late season of the year they would be obliged to use the same pass through the mountains. But even within the Church there would be other claimants, perhaps from Rome, as soon as word of the searches leaked further. Furthermore, there was a good chance that surviving Templar knights were trying to find it as a last ditch attempt to regain credibility and save their doomed Order. The more Nicolas thought things over, the more he accepted the inquisitor's claim that he had seen men on horseback over the pass. Any number of men could have thrown whatever was thrown, or loosened rocks higher up the slope; it could even have been one of their own guards who held back and climbed a man's height up the other side of the rough spur.

No, Nicolas decided; it had been no accident. He must be on guard. He could trust no one.

Save Brother Jacques. He looked towards the infirmary. The inquisitor had shown himself to be a man of courage, as well as intelligence and strength: two excellent qualities, but both useless without that rare kind of courage. Nicolas had been surprised, and ready to die even as he hung there by his wrist. He was embarrassed by the pressing awareness that he would not have risked his own life for the friar as Jacques apparently had for him. He had never felt comfortable with the man, and doubted his ability to resolve the mystery of Ocre and lead the *Opus Christi* to the relic its Superior so keenly desired. For weeks now he had watched and listened with constant scepticism: yet Pietro di Ocre *had* begun to talk, and they were now on their way to Ocre. When they returned Nicolas hoped he would have fresh information to help prise open the preceptor's mind, and Pietro would have had two or three months in his new cell to ponder the benefits of collaboration.

The intuition Jacques so often mentioned was as strange and persistent as a water-diviner's rod. Nicolas began to see that Bernard de Caen's choice was just. And the advice of Jacques' mother was equally sound. It was rare to find such virtues as theological acumen and physical courage in a single being – and a baker's son at that! Nicolas smiled to himself, thanking the baker's son once more deep within and deciding that he would seek to be more friendly. Yes, he reluctantly admitted to himself, Brother Jacques was proving an excellent ally. And he suspected that soon they would need all their combined courage.

Courage; and luck. Nicolas well knew the kind of men they were up against: desperate, fanatical, terrified of failure. There would be more attacks, as sure as Easter followed Lent – and there might not be a convenient gorse bush next time.

He turned towards the infirmary.

As he walked Nicolas thought of his father, cursing under his breath as a vision of the gelid face of Philip the Fair began to form in his mind's eye in place of the rugged, ruddy features of Brother Jacques. They must find the relic at all costs. Gorse bush or not, they must head south with haste.

18

The walls of Milan rose from the misty countryside like a mirage promising safety after their experiences at Mont Cenis. Knight and friar exchanged a mute glance of relief at the bustling traffic which engulfed them now after the bleak open road from Mont Cenis.

Brother Jacques had never seen such a city, which seemed larger and more thriving than Toulouse or even Paris. Inside the gate he and Nicolas were questioned by suspicious guards, and forced to disclose the contents of their baggage to the customs. From that moment on, they were surrounded by frenetic crowds: shoppers, artisans at work outside their workshops, mounted soldiers and children, all as urgently busy as bees. In their slow progress past the castle he was buffeted to and fro by builders' carts and the emblazoned carriages of the nobility.

The inhabitants were dressed richly in fine silks, velvet and damask cloth. Men wore huge rings of precious stones, bejewelled buckles on their belts, and wide hats, usually of velvet, which threatened to collide with each other as their wearers swaggered in the streets. The women were equally extravagant, and wore their cloaks open to show off the fine dresses they wore underneath, as if the cold were of no consequence. Jacques saw hair-styles which belied description, with tresses gathered into shapes which seemed like birds in flight or serpents coiled upon a woman's head, each one studded with pearls or gold. Splendid carriages with the new double axles and springs seemed almost unremarkable in this maze of wealth, all painted in rich colours with family stems proudly in evidence on the front and back as well as on the doors, as in France. Some were announced by heralds, who cleared the way for a platoon of thirty or forty private soldiers. Then would come the coach, drawn by six fine bays, as fast as the busy streets would permit. If the occupant were a member of the ruling Visconti family, pedestrians kneeled humbly by the roadside and doffed their caps.

They passed through an area where blacksmiths and armourers worked at forges open to the street. Beside them lay great sheets of metal and unworked rods of steel. The results of their labours hung ominously on the folded-back doors of the workshops: an infinite variety of fine plate armour with all the accoutrements which made a modern knight safer in battle: vambraces, rerebraces, spaulders and basinets. On the walls inside were lances, swords and knives. Jacques felt as though he were gazing on rows of invisible knights.

Soon they came to a fine basilica with a brick campanile which seemed to stretch into the sky. Jacques and Nicolas left their horses and stepped down into a long porticoed atrium which led up to the main facade, which had a broad double door for each of the three naves. It was the most splendid church they had seen since leaving Avignon. 'This must be the basilica of St Ambrose,' Jacques observed. 'Let us go in and give thanks to Our Lord for a safe arrival here in Milan.'

They passed through the gloomy nave, which was charged with the vanishing scent of incense and quiet mumble of citizens who came in for a moment to pray. Then they went down into the crypt and knelt together before the tomb of the city's patron. They prayed for the safe completion of the first half of their journey, and then for God's protection on the next.

Beyond the church was a bustling market. Again the image of bees came to Jacques. 'Like the bees of St Ambrose,' he joked.

But Nicolas stared blankly at the friar, obviously unfamiliar with the story.

'When St Ambrose was a child in his cradle, in Gaul,' Jacques explained, 'a swarm of bees flew around him and some even crept into his mouth. The people said it was a good omen, and since he was to become Bishop of Milan and a Doctor of the Church they were right. And now the people swarm like bees around his tomb.'

Now Nicolas smiled reluctantly. 'Yes, you're right,' he said, 'but Ambrose for me means pain.'

It was Jacques' turn to stare.

And Nicolas' to laugh. 'I ruined my eyes poring over his epistles at Cluny. My tutor thought they were the finest of Latin letters.'

Jacques was surprised, for he had read nothing of St Ambrose's writing. There was nothing to say. He pushed forward into the market crowd.

An infinity of stalls crowded in on them. Huge loaves of bread sticks of dried salt cod, and every imaginable kind of fruit: grapes, apples, pears, quince, red and yellow plums. Beside them were vegetables – turnips, cabbage, celery, spinach, fennel and immense yellow pumpkins – more than Jacques had ever seen together. Vintners had come in from the country with barrels of the new wine, white, red and golden, strapped to their carts – some with narrow shafts to be drawn by the men themselves. There were stalls with sacks of dried legumes, chickpeas, broad beans, white beans, brown beans and lentils, and others with sacks of flour. Then there were fishmongers with lake fish, eels and freshwater prawns, often accompanied by women who fought a losing battle to keep live frogs in the large baskets in which they were carried; and meat both live and dead – living chickens, ducks, pigs, horses, and freshly slaughtered capons, peacocks, quail and blackbirds. At the very end of the market, thronged and surrounded by eager purchasers, were Jewish merchants selling dates, saffron, pepper and other spices imported from the lands of the Saracen.

Above all, they inhaled the steam thrown off by immense cauldrons of hot vegetable soup and smoke from the grills of roast chestnut vendors. After such abundance it was a relief to come to the end of the market and turn towards the south of the city.

Near the fluvial port which gave access to the rivers and canal system south of Milan they entered a busy street full of inns, hostelries and bawdy houses. 'The Street of the Venetians, where traders who come up the Po lodge. There you'll find rooms, a good table, and any other pleasures of the flesh you desire,' the alpine guide said with a wink, before leaving them.

Amongst the jostling crowds Jacques noticed a woman dressed in bright cloths of red and azure. From a distance she seemed familiar, but he knew it was ridiculous. She disappeared as a wagon laden with timber passed between them. When they reached her she was looking at the counter of a shop. He was about to ride past when she turned and looked up towards the new arrivals. She did not recognize him at first; but he was in no doubt.

'Are you not the widow Ida?' He had to shout over the crowd.

'Why!' she exclaimed when she realized who had addressed her, 'I would never have recognized you. How strange you look without your habit.' She bent her head and feigned admiration. Then a look of fear appeared in her eyes. 'You're not here to look for me, are you?' she asked. 'I'm an innocent housewife, and go to church twice a week for confession.'

Her voice was as warm as he remembered it, and her face honest enough. Would she be like the woman in his vision?

He dismissed the thought. 'Good woman ...' he began. He wanted to sound comforting, but was conscious of the absurdity of the adjective. 'I and my colleague here are on pilgrimage to Rome.'

'Ah, so that's why you're not –'

'Widow Ida!' Jacques stopped her. Then he dismounted and stepped close to her. 'We're just pilgrims,' he whispered.

She laughed. 'Of course you are. Welcome, good pilgrims!' she shouted. Then she too leaned closer and whispered. 'That's good news. I tell you what. You can sleep with me tonight ... no, don't object. It's as clean a bed as you'll find in this city.'

'But there are others, I presume?'

'Blonde and brunette, as you wish ...'

'Beds, I mean! Keep your voice down, woman!' He glanced around quickly. Nicolas was absorbed in the sights and sounds of the street; he seemed to be taking no notice, watching, with sincere curiosity, a carriage of wealthy Milanese go by. Their guards were watering the horses in a wayside trough.

Ida's laughter registered disappointment. 'If you wish to sleep with a dozen stinking Venetian boatmen ...'

'Our guide spoke of the Boar Inn ...' He spoke loudly so the papal guards would hear him, enjoying her banter but keen to keep her well at bay.

'Pah! A stinking vice-hole. Full of vermin. And you'd go there?'

'He said he knew Milan well, and that it was the best.'

'He obviously knows this city as well as he knows my fanny,' she spat.

Jacques turned away, certain his face was as visible as a hill-top beacon to all and sundry. The woman knew no limits, yet he was pleased to see her. He turned back: 'Keep your voice down, woman,' he repeated, 'for the love of our Lord.'

Ida went on in the same tone. 'If you're searching for a good inn, Brother, then The Three Pigeons is the place for you. It has good rooms and clean beds ...' Suddenly she stopped, leaned closer to him, and added: 'But there's none as clean as mine.' She then leaned closer to him and whispered: 'And none more welcome than you. With any girl you like!'

Jacques looked anxiously at Nicolas, glad that street noise smothered their conversation and pleased that he had been away from Avignon when she was on trial.

125

At that thought, memories of Ida's trial flashed through his mind. He had never quite believed the stories told about her then, of her hunting out priests and friars. But here she was using quite the same words again. 'We . . . ' he began with indignation.

She lifted her right hand in an imperial gesture. 'No excuses. One word and it's arranged.' She winked at him.

'We have urgent work to do,' he argued, amazed and amused by her effrontery. Yet he recalled his vision of Bernard de Caen and his woman at the brink of death, and knew within that he desired a woman himself.

'One of your enquiries?'

Jacques nodded, humouring her. It was pleasant to hear her warm voice after the hardship of their journey. But still he was afraid of the feelings within him. 'I'll come to visit you another time.'

'You never change,' Ida said with downcast eyes and fake sadness in her voice. Then, brightly gathering her skirts, 'Well, young man, when you need me, remember that you'll find me at the sign of The Three Pigeons.'

She giggled, and disappeared into the crowd.

Jacques was relieved and perturbed at once. He saw a guard coming towards him. 'One of my trial victims,' he explained, embarrassed.

'They're all as friendly as that afterwards, are they?' came the reply.

'We should make haste for the Boar. It's late,' Jacques answered, turning away. 'Nicolas. Let's go now.'

A curious blended vision of the naked woman of Mont Cenis and of Ida plagued Jacques as he ate supper that evening. He was far from home, divested of clerical garb and subjected to a whole gamut of new emotions. He recalled the comments of Nicolas when he learned of Bernard's secret liaisons: '. . . power does strange things . . .'; '. . . men like Lord Bernard do what they wish to do . . .' Here in Milan, *he* was in command, and had power. Close to death he had desired a woman, and to his constant shock that evening he knew that he wanted the experience. He would make his peace with God later. There could be penance for the breaking of holy vows just as for everything else. He smiled wryly at the thought of condemning himself.

Jacques left Nicolas and the guards at the Boar and galloped back to the port.

The Three Pigeons was thronged with drunks and pleasure-seeking Venetians. But Ida saw him instantly, as if she had been waiting only for him. 'About time too!' she exclaimed with delight. 'I've just the thing for you. Come!'

'Weren't you . . . ?' he began nervously.

'Me, darling? I'm for later. We've got to break you in first, haven't we?'

Before there was time to object, she had drawn him into the smoky kitchen. A coarse woman with her legs thrust widely apart on the earthen floor and sleeves rolled up to her shoulders was kneading dough. At first she reminded Jacques of his own mother, but there was something raw and attractive about her which he had never seen before. Near her, on the cooking range, was a blackened iron pot, but it was not until he had already passed her that he noticed the familiar smell of haricot beans and garlic. He breathed deeply and happily, and followed Ida.

She showed him into a small, dark room which was empty save for a mattress and a wooden clotheshorse. He hesitated under the door lintel. 'Don't be afraid. She's a lovely girl,' Ida admonished him. Then, softly, caressing him, 'I wish it was me.'

Then, as if by a miracle, she was gone, and the door closed behind her.

Left alone, Jacques' first instinct was to flee. Years of trials flashed through his mind, and the memory of his own vows. He gripped the door handle, but as he was about to open it he recalled Nicolas' words about the vows of Bernard de Caen: 'men like our lord Bernard do what they wish to do once it is within their means. Vows or no vows.' It was a question of power.

The girl came.

There was no time for remorse. Jacques was glad she was quick, and silent. He wanted to dominate her, take her violently, but he was uncertain how to begin. He fumbled in the gloom, but soon gave way to her expert, kneading fingers. She took him, and made him feel her, then opened his hose and kissed him until he thought he would explode. While he lay there thinking once again of the vision at Mont Cenis, she pulled him onto her and without knowing how Jacques realized with a shock of pleasure that he was inside her. Now there *was* a curious sense of domination, and although half-conscious that it was the girl who led the way the thrusting action which came naturally to him seemed to him an act of pure power. She drew him on and

127

caressed him, and he followed, until he was no longer able to think. Jacques abandoned himself to physical joy with the enthusiasm he had previously given to prayer. It was the embodiment of his dream, and in that moment all fear vanished. He could have died without fear.

Then, abruptly, it was over.

He was not sure what had happened. He found himself, to his shock and embarrassment, panting half-naked atop the kind of woman he had been condemning for years. She smiled with yellow teeth and moved his hand between her legs. 'Think about me, deary,' she said with an incongrously sweet and innocent voice.

She stank. Jacques recoiled sharply and leapt to his feet, covering himself with his hands. Turning his back on the naked form sprawled across the mattress, he dressed quickly and left the room without once turning back.

Ida saw him immediately. 'That was quick,' she observed. 'But now you're a new man anyway,' she added with admiration.

In that she was right, Jacques thought to himself. 'It was a mistake,' he snapped. 'Never again.' But even as he spoke he found himself studying Ida afresh, as if he had never seen her before.

There had been pleasure, and he knew it would not be the last time. A single penance would do service for multiple offences. For the moment, however, there was nothing he desired more than to put this shame behind him and hurry south.

19

The rock of Ocre seemed to Brother Jacques to rise from the plain like an upturned ship set into the earth with its bow pointing skyward. The crenellated walls of the castle circled the highest part of the rock like a crown. From the village set in a hollow at its foot rose a sheer rock-face loftier than the twin towers of Notre Dame. There appeared to be no direct access to the castle, but a mule-track zig-zagged up to the saddle behind the rock which joined it to the mountains beyond.

As his mule picked its way round precipitous bends on loose scree Jacques was glad of the clear azure sky. It was hard to push Mont Cenis completely from his mind, but there was no place for attackers to hide in this sparse scrub. Occasional shouts from below and a faint odour of manure drifting up with the breeze bespoke human proximity. On the valley floor villages were scattered across the plain, pushed towards the foothills by the loops of a river which meandered sluggishly like a silver ribbon in the bright sunshine. Beyond the plain, at a good day's ride, barren foothills rose sharply towards a range of mountains whose peaks were capped with snow. Behind him, Nicolas de Lirey, the Dominican interpreter and the papal guards were strung out along the path in reassuring order.

Rounding a sharp bend, the monastery of Santo Spirito suddenly appeared ahead of him like a vast wall, two storeys high but windowless. It was set on a tilted escarpment which led up to the saddle behind the castle, and was built of massive limestone blocks hewn from the mountains. There was no gate-house, and no guest wing or stable buildings were visible. To Jacques it did not look like a Cistercian house at all, especially the heavily fortified gate complete with sentry post and oil chutes above it.

Nobody appeared when they reached the gate, so Jacques pulled the rope that hung loosely from the sentry post above it.

As he waited he looked up into the oil chute, and noticed a threadbare bird's nest clinging to the inside. It was obviously some time since the monastery had been threatened. Then, beside the chute, he caught a glimpse of pale reddish flowers. He strained his eyes, and was surprised to see a bunch of what in Saverdun were known as wild artichokes. They were grown there as a defence against thunder and lightning, and never died even in the harshest of winters, but they were also often planted as protection against black magic. Surprised, Jacques lowered his gaze and moved forwards to look through the grille. Inside, he was even more astonished to see more of the same flowers, cultivated inside terracotta vases. There was neither doubt nor coincidence: they had been carefully planted and preserved, and placed beside the main gate. Ironically, their dusty pink petals were the only note of joy on that massive stone facade.

A brown-robed serving man appeared at the grille. '*Che vo*?' he asked.

'"What are you wanting?" he says.' The Dominican friar seemed to lose control of his French as he translated.

'Tell him we have a letter of introduction to the abbot.'

The serving-man took it reluctantly. Then, without uttering another sound, he was gone.

Presently, a tall young monk appeared, ruddy-faced and dressed in the working habit of the Cistercians with an apron over his shoulders. He shouted an order in the local dialect to a gatekeeper who, now Jacques realized, must have been there since they arrived, silently observing them.

'Brother Jacques Fournier? Sire Nicolas de Lirey? God be with you. You are welcome to Santo Spirito.' The monk addressed them in Latin.

'Not a very warm welcome so far. Do you agree?' He half turned in the saddle to address Nicolas.

'Not the warmest.' Nicolas didn't bother to return the glance. His eyes were focused on the castle of Ocre, whose walls, impressive across the plain, he now saw to be badly decayed, either by weather or by man-made erosion. He had expected something grander, and although the walls suggested an immense enclosed area there was nothing within of elegance or style. The monastery too was the blandest, most inhospitable building he had ever seen. The excitement of anticipation which had carried him thus far with enthusiasm now waned. It seemed unlikely that the solution to a great mystery would lie in this rough, isolated valley, or under the protection of these uncouth rustics.

The Dominican grunted as if he sensed this contempt. 'You must expect no more from these people. They trust nobody, not even their own.'

Are you not one of them? Nicolas thought.

Their Cistercian host turned away, and led Jacques and Nicolas across the small courtyard into a square, two-storeyed building, and up a steep staircase to the first floor. On the landing, he knocked twice at the only door.

'Come in!' a gruff voice commanded.

The monk pushed the door open, and ushered Jacques and Nicolas inside. 'My lord,' he addressed the bald man sitting by the window, 'these are the two visitors from Avignon we have been expecting.' Then he turned towards the visitors. 'Abbot Placido,' he announced.

Inquisitor and knight exchanged looks like swords. How could it be that these men were expecting them when they had travelled with all possible haste? Yet again Bernard de Caen had somehow outwitted them.

The abbot sighed deeply as they entered. His face was puffed into a triple chin, and he needed time to recover a regular rhythm of breathing after he had shouted to them. The cuffs of his habit were worn and dirty, in contrast to the heavy gold signet ring which he wore on his right index finger. He was wearing open sandals, as the Rule of the Cistercians prescribed, but broke the Rule by sitting against the chimney-wall. 'Well?' he asked grumpily. 'What can we do for you?'

'I believe the letter of introduction . . .' Jacques began.

'Yes. Of course.' The abbot looked him over carefully, then studied Nicolas. 'We receive few visitors from France nowadays,' he said irrelevantly. 'I look forward greatly to hearing your news.' There was no enthusiasm at all in his voice. He snatched a deep breath, then looked towards his window.

'We shall be pleased to oblige.' Jacques spoke with the reverence due to the abbot of a far greater monastery than Santo Spirito.

'I gather you are to conduct an investigation . . . or is it perhaps an inspection?'

Jacques studied the abbot closely. What more did he know? 'The letter from our lord Bernard requests nothing beyond your hospitality for the short period we shall spend in the area,' he said warily.

'And full access to our library and archives . . .' Abbot Placido spoke as if his monastery held one of the great libraries of the Church.

131

Nicolas nodded politely, throwing a glance at Jacques which seemed to say: don't worry, I know this kind of man and he won't cause any trouble.

Jacques relaxed. Perhaps he was over-reacting. 'There are some matters of local concern which interest us. For instance, certain papal letters and indictments of which the copies were lost during the transfer to Avignon.'

'You will of course have the free access you request,' Abbot Placido answered in a bland voice. 'Now, if you will excuse me, it is time to prepare for our chapter.' He rang the small brass bell beside him.

The library was no larger than Jacques' cell in Avignon, and the archive was contained in a single cupboard.

He took on the more difficult job of ploughing through miscellaneous letters and the monastery accounts. Nicolas was assigned the task of reading papal bulls and letters, one bundle for each pope since Santo Spirito's foundation. 'Look for anomalies, or direct references to the family of the counts of Ocre,' he said; 'anything unusual.'

Nicolas ignored the tone of command, since this was, after all, the inquisitor's territory. It took all his concentration to read through the bulls, and more than once he had to ask for assistance with the flowery vocabulary used in the documents.

From time to time as they read, a monk would enter on some pretext and watch for as long as he deemed prudent. Few of them uttered anything beyond the merest greeting; some entered, remained, and left in total silence. None troubled to read any of the numerous manuscript volumes in the book cabinet or to feign interest in the archives. At the end of their second day at Santo Spirito, Jacques was sure that he had seen the entire community at least once. He had spoken with perhaps half a dozen, but had enjoyed no more than ten minutes of conversation in all. They had not seen Abbot Placido again, either at divine offices or in the refectory.

It was as dusk fell on the second day that Nicolas made his discovery. 'Now here is something curious.' He was as surprised as the inquisitor that it was he who had found something.

Nicolas stepped towards the single narrow window of the room, holding a parchment, held it to the light and read aloud: ' ". . . and as the result of an inquisition made in that district by Brother Godefroy of our most sacred Order of St Dominic into his heretical activities . . ."'
He felt ridiculous reading this ecclesiastical Latin to a priest and

132

inquisitor; but Brother Jacques said nothing. 'It goes on, "the said Gualtierus of the Counts of Ocre is perpetually banned from entering the said church in the parish of San Eusanio at the risk of eternal condemnation ..." It bears the signature and seal of His Holiness Innocent IV. But as far as I can see, there are no details of the supposed heresy.'

It would be remarkable indeed if you did see, Jacques thought to himself. Laymen seemed to believe that heresy was stamped on documents like a customs stamp, whereas the worst abominations were only to be found by subtle reading between the lines. Heretics were rarely ignorant men. Yet he hoped his doubts were concealed. 'What is the year?' he asked thoughtfully.

'"The Year of Our Lord one thousand two hundred and fifty-four",' Nicolas read slowly. 'But there is a renewal by order of Pope Alexander IV, dated five years later.'

'You realize what this means?' It must have been an exceptional crime to warrant an individual condemnation.

'That Gualtiero di Ocre was banned from entering his own church.'

'... by a personal papal bull. The only thing that could justify such an action is a heresy severe enough to threaten the Church itself.'

'Not only,' Nicolas observed.

'Not only what?'

'There were two popes, for five years later the ban was renewed ...'

'Which means that the heresy persisted. What on earth was it, do you think?' Jacques said, more to himself than to his secular companion. But even as he spoke, he saw the answer to his question. He kept it to himself. 'Then, the year after the ban is renewed, our preceptor is initiated in the crypt of the very same church.'

'What were they doing there, in the name of our Lord?'

Jacques said nothing, but his companion's phrase had suggested a new line of enquiry. 'That we must discover,' he replied elusively.

'How?' Nicolas asked. As he spoke he closed the volume of papers he had been reading. He inclined his head slightly like a schoolboy listening to his master: or was it like a spy listening for every hint to the truth?

Spies? Popes? And here they were, three days journey from Rome. Jacques thought of Henry of Luxembourg, killed as he attempted to get to that city. It was astonishing to be so near, and yet so distant; a city where even the religious were no longer safe. Henry had tried to take Rome, and now King Philip was trying – as once the allies of the Counts of Ocre had tried. It was uncanny that two popes should take such a direct interest in this small, remote church, not to mention Bernard de Caen.

'We must visit San Eusanio,' Jacques stated as if it were the most natural thing in the world. 'Alone.'

20

There appeared to be no living being in the village, which stood on a hillock within a bend of the river below Ocre. Jacques asked his companion to tether their horses to a fountain in front of the church. While he waited he studied its imposing facade of rough stone blocks hewn from the local rock, in the expectation that curiosity would soon bring forth the population.

The church was built of the same blocks as Santo Spirito, with a simple rose window in the top half and a square campanile to the right. On either side of the church, flush with its facade, was a solid wall perhaps a hundred paces in length that culminated at both ends in circular towers. But the most curious feature was the crenellated wall about half the height of the facade which led back on each side of the church to two further circular towers. He had seen nothing like it. The church was fortified, standing within a square, walled area with its facade built into the western wall.

As no one came, he walked along the side wall parallel with the nave. Nicolas went ahead like an eager child. The crisp air seemed to invigorate him. 'There's another wall behind,' he shouted excitedly.

'I thought there would be. It's a fortified church. Quite unique, I think.'

'What do you think could be inside?' Nicolas was astonished at his own enthusiasm.

'Now? Probably nothing.' There seemed to be no limit to the mysteries of this family of Ocre.

They reached the door again, having made the full circle of the fortified complex.

Still no one had come.

Jacques crashed the brass knocker against the church door. But there was no reply. He walked across to the fountain, where he drank icy water from his hands. Then he waited with the patience that years of interrogation had instilled in him.

At length an ancient priest appeared from one of the corner turrets, bent almost double with age and hobbling with a gnarled stick which echoed his own form. He came towards them without looking at them, every irritible gesture actively wishing them gone. 'What do you want?' he asked brusquely when he drew near.

'A few silent minutes in prayer, Father.'

The priest grunted, drew a key from his ragged cassock and opened the door for them. He stepped inside without saying anything, and leaned back against the doorpost.

As friendly as the gate-friar at Santo Spirito, Jacques thought to himself. It was clearly the warmest greeting they would receive in this ancient place. He led the way into the gelid interior. Ancient Roman columns dividing the nave revealed a far older provenance than the more recent facade suggested. An acrid smell of damp mixed with incense pervaded the atmosphere. The nave was almost bare: only two small chapels had frescoes in them, while most of the bays along the stone walls were unused. Ahead of him, steps led up to a raised dais which bore the high altar, whose only ornament was a life-sized wooden sculpture of the Virgin Mary.

He noticed what appeared to be a recently blocked-up doorway that must once have led down to the crypt, and wondered idly why it should have been bricked up. The crypt had not been closed off, since another set of steps led down to the right of the altar. Jacques drew a deep breath of contentment at reaching the place he had so often thought about, and went down the steps. He felt Nicolas following closely behind, as if he were afraid of losing him.

The crypt was permeated by the stilly malefaction of centuries. It lay at right angles to the nave above, and Jacques walked quickly to the point where the older steps would have entered it. Standing there, he counted three rows of five columns, each surmounted by a capital with different decoration. Straight ahead of him was the altar, directly beneath the high altar, and behind that an apse with stained glass in the four lights of its double window. Dull sunlight was sufficient to illuminate an ebony reliquary under the altar; presumably that of San Eusanio.

Jacques was fascinated to discover that the central entrance was not the only one that had been blocked up in recent years. To the right of the crypt, level with the wall of the nave above, there had been another entrance; this one, he noticed, with an elegant arched doorway. He wondered where it had led to, and what strange rites Gualtiero might have practised there in order to require such a secret entrance.

Finally, he walked to the apse and stood where, according to Pietro's description, the Templar Grand Master Thomas Berard had stood that evening more than forty years before. He realized that it was exactly under the high altar, and then, with a thrill of excitement, saw that the two capitals Pietro had described were intact. Nicolas de Lirey was at that moment standing where the neophyte Templar must have stood, and for an instant Jacques had a weird sensation of having been there himself many years before.

He examined the capitals. Just as Pietro had recounted, they represented God and the Devil. As Jacques looked more carefully, he saw that these sculptures were minor masterpieces carved by an artist of rare skill. The God-figure looked down at a slight angle towards the spot behind the altar, as if blessing whoever stood there. Its face was tilted almost imperceptibly forwards, as if trying to look down from the column. It was beautifully sculpted from soft stone, with fine lineaments and an aquiline nose which emerged softly below delicate eyes after the Byzantine style.

But the most remarkable feature was the hair, which issued like drapery high above the head, descended, then fell away from the forehead and onto the shoulders as if lifted by the gentlest of breezes. Finally it seemed to melt into the stone again behind the thin neck.

'This ought not to be here,' Jacques muttered to Nicolas; 'it merits a greater setting.'

His companion stared in silence. It was indeed an eerie place, impregnated with mystery. He had noticed strange symbols on the pavement flags, such as had been described to him by his father when he came back from the Holy Land. It was as if Saracens had been buried there.

'And look at this!' The other head was as hideous as the first one was beautiful. A grotesque parody of a human being, which began with a recognizably human chin and then widened to what seemed a mule's head with huge ears and cone-shaped horns pointing sacrilegiously towards the altar. The eyes were distorted vertically with eyebrows like spikes, while the nose was a shapeless, roundish mass.

Jacques stood as Thomas Berard must have done, intently studying the two faces while Nicolas went towards the bricked-up door.

As he gazed, his head raised towards the capital on the left, a faint spell of dizziness came over him. Jacques' entire body seemed to vacillate and sharp pain sliced through his forehead. All his ideas and the musings of past weeks seemed to be concentrated in that single gaze, which sucked out his soul like an eddying mill-rush. The intense quiet coupled with a feeling that the ceiling was pressing down upon him unhinged the delicate balance of his body. The sensation lasted a moment, but seemed to him an age. That astonishingly beautiful and serene face exercised a strange power, like that which radiated from the Cross after prolonged contemplation and spiritual exercises. It was as if he had glimpsed an image of the Lord, he concluded with a start.

An awesome power. Jacques stumbled, felt instinctively forward to where he knew the altar top would be and gratefully leaned upon it. He held the marble top firmly with both hands and shook his head in disbelief. Slowly, equilibrium returned. He glanced furtively behind him and was pleased to see Nicolas still studying the doorway.

Nicolas seemed to feel Jacques' glance, and joined him by the altar. 'God bless my soul,' he exclaimed, 'your face is as white as a winding sheet. Have you seen a ghost?' Even as he said it, he realized that his question was inappropriate in that place.

Ignoring him, Jacques gave a cursory glance at the reliquary under the altar and left the crypt. His body was chilled to the quick, and his unease was enhanced by the feeling of eyes boring into his back as they walked into the winter sunshine.

Two toothless crones dressed from head to foot in black stood outside the door watching them, together with the old priest.

'Tell me, Father . . .' Jacques addressed the priest in Latin, trying his best to make his voice sound steady and matter of fact. Nicolas stood to one side. This was priests' business. He felt strangely useless, ignorant; the quest was bringing new sensations to him, and by no means pleasant ones.

'What?' the old priest asked bluntly.

'Could you tell us who San Eusanio was?'

'Why do you want to know?'

'Simple curiosity. It's not a secret, is it?'

'I suppose not. He was a martyr to the Romans. He came from the south and converted the people of this valley. The Romans killed him. Flung him from that rock.' He pointed towards the castle of Ocre.

'I see. Did he leave any writings?'

'No,' the priest answered bluntly. He was totally uninterested. 'I'll be on my way now. Good day.' He shambled off, followed by the crones.

As he disappeared into the tower, Jacques noticed two shepherds sitting by the fountain with their dogs stretched panting in front of

138

them. They gave no sign of life, but sat expressionless as if they were stone figures added to the fountain for embellishment.

Nicolas' movements were dramatic by comparison. He had been pacing nervously back and forth, examining every angle of the building, but now he suddenly stopped, as if transfixed, and marched back to the portal. 'Look! Can that be an accident?' he exclaimed.

'What is it?' Jacques replied abstractedly.

'Stand here, on the steps, and look at Santo Spirito over there . . .' The monastery appeared as a grey block on the scrubby hillside. 'Now look to the right, at the hill outside the village . . .' Again, Jacques followed his instructions. 'You see? There's another church, fortified like this one.'

'Yes?' Jacques' heartbeat quickened. He had never heard Nicolas so excited in their months of companionship.

'They're part of a geometric plan. Can't you see?'

'It may be so,' Jacques replied with scepticism. He needed time to reflect, and walked towards the shepherds. 'Could you tell us the name of that castle on the hill?'

'The Castle of the Madonna,' one of them replied gruffly as if everybody ought to know.

'And who might be the owner?'

'Whoever cares to live there,' the shepherd laughed. 'There's no one ever goes up there save on the saint's day.'

'Then tell me, who built it? It's not so old, after all.'

'Nor is it indeed. My own father watched them building it . . . and before there was no more than a wooden cross . . . isn't that right?' He turned to his fellow shepherd for confirmation.

'So who built it?' Jacques asked again, irritated at not getting an answer.

'Old Count Gualtiero, of course.' The shepherd spoke as if the count were still alive.

'There you are!' Nicolas said triumphantly, as if he had solved the riddle.

They set off for the castle as one man.

The walls were breached and crumbling as if damaged by a recent battle, and the buildings within were dilapidated. Black fire marks scarred them like groping fingers. Only the chapel appeared unscathed, but its door soon gave way to Nicolas' shoulder. The interior was well kept: the altar was covered by a clean white cloth

139

with no visible signs of dust, and there was a vase of chrysanthemums that could be no more than a week old. Instinct told Jacques this chapel was important in the scheme of things, but there were no clues to substantiate his feelings.

Outside again, they climbed to the crest of the ridge of the strange, barrow-shaped hill just beyond the church. From that point they could take in the whole valley with a single sweep of the eyes.

Jacques fixed his gaze on Santo Spirito, which, from that point, appeared to be suspended on the rock-face directly beneath the crown of the castle walls. He was thinking of the strange vision in the crypt, and the sound of his companion slithering across the scree below him was irritating. Nicolas was darting here and there as agitatedly as he had been in front of San Eusanio. 'What is it?' Jacques shouted. His voice was lost on the wind.

A hawk swooped between them, fighting to gain height with the extra weight of a thin snake which dangled from its beak.

Beneath him, their horses drank from the spring where they were tethered.

Jacques watched as the ungainly black figure half stepped and half slid along the hillside. Then Nicolas stopped abruptly. Jacques felt the urgency in his stance, and was not surprised to see his companion rushing back as quickly as he could.

'Brother Jacques! Brother Jacques!' Nicolas gasped, 'I've got it.' Then he paused for breath, leaning forward onto his knees. 'You see down there on the plain, the church by the farm there, beside the bridge?'

He peered along Nicolas' arm, and nodded.

'Well, together with the other three points, San Eusanio, Santo Spirito and the chapel, it makes a perfect shield. And at the centre of that shield is the castle of Ocre. Is that a coincidence too?'

'It's curious,' Jacques admitted.

'More than curious.' Nicolas was breathing normally now. 'I've seen the like of it before, in Provence.'

Jacques leaned forward, pleased with his companion now. 'And what did it mean?'

'Earth magic.' Nicolas waited for the words to sink in. 'It was a Cathar castle. They believed this form would make their land impregnable. And what's more, I've heard say that the Order of the Temple was not loth to use it in the Holy Land.' He squatted, picked up a dead twig, and began to trace geometrical figures in the dust. 'Triangles and pentagons are good,' he explained, 'but the best of all is a shield or diamond shape consisting of two equal triangles. It doubles the power.'

Jacques stared at him. It made little sense to him. 'Power?'

'These people believe that you can dominate all men and objects within the figure. And if it is especially strong, cast this power well beyond the figure. So you possess the four points,' he went on, tracing small squares at the four angles of a diamond in the dust, 'construct altars on them . . . in a church or an abbey . . . and form an invisible but potent chain around the protected area. But at the sharpest point of the shield there must always be something . . . an ancient site, a temple, a place giving life – like a spring or a holy relic . . .'

'A relic?'

'Indeed.' Nicolas paused in astonishment, showing that he too had seen the connection. But he said nothing. 'That is the key. The sites cannot be random. The church or altar itself must be charged with some special power.'

'In this case, that something is – or was – in San Eusanio, if you're right?' This was the most abominable use of holy relics, an appalling heresy.

Nicolas' eyebrows raised in assent. He knew he was right, and that Bernard de Caen was right. For he had seen another example of the same phenomenon, which he had chosen not to mention to the inquisitor, on the Charny estates at Montfort. His father had once explained it to him.

'It's absurd.'

'Of course it is. But they believe it.' And so, Nicolas realized with a shock, does Bernard de Caen. Could Bernard have learned about the Montfort shield from his father? If so, then that was why he had been sent here with Brother Jacques. Bernard knew that he would see and understand. But what did it mean? What should he see next? He moved away to hide his confusion and his embarrassment at holding back information from his companion.

Jacques watched as Nicolas walked further along the ridge, and now stood erect with his cloak flapping violently in the wind. His enthusiasm concerning the position of Santo Spirito and this castle was exaggerated . . . unless experience or knowledge allowed him to perceive more than he admitted. Once again, Jacques found himself wondering whether Nicolas was fit for the task. He had once spoken of a great-uncle in the Order of the Temple, and in many ways that would have been a more logical place for him than as Jacques' reluctant companion. Why had he not joined too?

Nicolas came back again with triumph stamped on his face. 'There's much more,' he shouted. 'Look there! What can you see?' He pointed towards the hills at the end of the plain.

'The walls of Aquila . . . Brother Bernard told us about them.'

'Do you remember what he said about it?'

'That it was founded only fifty years ago . . .'

'It was built quickly. Then within five years destroyed and built again.'

'So?'

'Can't you see? The city was built, destroyed and rebuilt within five years. Exactly the same period in which Count Gualtiero was banished from his own church twice and his son was initiated in it.'

'But that proves nothing.'

'Indeed it doesn't,' Nicolas agreed, unshaken in his conviction. Without telling the Montfort story it would be hard to explain. Yet that was a family secret, and the origin of his father's undoing. 'But it does suggest a line of inquiry. I feel in my bones that this is more than coincidence.' He paused. 'Now, remember what we noticed standing at the entrance to the church down there in the village. We couldn't see beyond this mound then . . .'

Jacques listened sceptically.

'Well, now it's obvious.' Nicolas' voice dropped to a conspiratorial whisper as he saw it clearly. There was no need to bluff or obfuscate any longer. 'If you were to stand at the door, Santo Spirito would be at 45 degrees to your left, and this castle at 45 degrees to your right. Then, straight ahead, would be the city of Aquila!' he concluded with triumph in his voice. 'I'm certain that this new city was to be a new centre of power: as impregnable as the castle of Ocre, and controlling a much vaster area. Perhaps even a challenge to the Holy Roman Church. I know you will not believe me, and I admit there is no proof. But instinct tells me I am right. Give me time and I assure you we will find the proof.'

Jacques was pleased by the sudden change of pronoun to include him. But what he had heard was beyond belief. He was ready to dismiss Nicolas' theories as nonsense when he recalled a phrase of Pietro di Ocre that he had never understood: 'and we would have had the Church'. Could there be something in it? He needed to think, and to plumb the depths of Nicolas' apparent knowledge of these things.

'It's cold now,' he said. 'The sun is sinking fast, and there are storm clouds gathering over the mountains. I think we should get back to the abbey.'

Jacques had one foot in the stirrup when wild-looking men sprang from the flowerless gorse bushes, brandishing staves. He spun against his horse's flank in surprise. When he regained control of his mount, Nicolas had already been knocked to the ground: two of them held him firmly while a third struck at the young knight. Jacques realized that they had been concealed in a dry gulley running parallel to the track and obscured even by the bare bushes.

He leapt down. The only protection around was a wall sheltering the spring. With a violence driven by fear which astonished him, he seized a stave from one of his assailants and took a stand with his back to the wall. Terror coursed through him: he thought of Nicolas' gory hand in the mist, and then of the girl in Milan. He thrust his stave towards two men who approached him, attempting to catch them under the padding in their hose. Parried by one, he cracked the head of the second, who looked up in wide-eyed amazement as his pointed felt hat flew into the gorse.

Others appeared, their dark faces furious with hatred and matted long hair making them appear like demons sent to scourge Jacques for his recent sins.

They were charged with a venom whose source he could not understand until he saw that they were mostly parrying blows rather than attacking with intent to do serious injury, as if they had been instructed – possibly paid – merely to scare him and his party. This in turn meant that whoever had followed them from Avignon had both a large purse and good contacts in the Ocre area.

It was a disturbing thought, but Jacques forced himself to forget it for the moment and look around him. Ten paces away he noticed Nicolas still pinned to the ground. Beyond, there was chaos.

He shuddered. A taller man, apparently the attackers' leader, now faced him. For a moment their eyes locked, and Jacques saw into his soul: he was one of nature's violent ones. But something within himself gave him the strength and courage to resist.

In the turmoil that ensued, he was vaguely aware that the number of horses had tripled. One of the new animals, a giant bay, had a long white blaze on its nose which seemed vaguely familiar to him. But there was no time in the fray to reflect. Then he saw Nicolas on his feet, shaking himself down. It was like a dream, or premonition of death: but at the same time he saw the attackers retreating down the hill under the violent blows of three stocky men. One of them was particularly huge, and brandished a double-sided sword against the staves of the smaller men. In his other hand he held a vicious-looking mace.

Then he realized where he had seen the blaze: in the papal stables at Avignon. Jacques stared in awe-stricken fascination as Briac's broad-backed figure scattered the enemy before him like dried poppy-heads. He knew that when the man turned, his belt would bear a bright yellow buckle. As he rested against the wall, other details began to slot into place: the man's presence explained the apparition on Mont Cenis. Had the incident been fortuitous, after all? It was obvious that this soldier must be one of Bernard's most trusted men. But what were his orders?

In a matter of minutes, the attackers were dispersed amongst the rocks and gorse. Here and there on the hillside, dark figures could be seen scrambling towards the valley like vagrant sheep rejoining their flock.

Nicolas was badly bruised, but nothing more. He now sat watching the stragglers in disbelief. Jacques shook himself, and looked quickly over his body. It was merely dirty, and covered with tiny scratches from the rough stone wall. The real damage was within. His reaction to the violence had been a non-reaction: he had been neither shocked nor afraid, nor even amazed at the situation in which he found himself. He had known a numbness, a fatalistic acceptance of the necessity to fight, but not fear, not shock. He had simply fought. The fact that the attack had ended was more shocking than the event itself: he was disturbed at what was happening inside him; more so even than in Milan. It was as if his vows no longer existed; all was subordinated to the *Opus Christi* – and to power.

Then Briac returned.

'God be with you,' Jacques greeted him sincerely. He made the sign of the cross when he noticed blood. 'Are you injured?'

'Not a scratch!'

'You wounded them?'

'Easy blood,' Briac laughed. 'We just drove them off, but it's hard to avoid broken skin.'

His bearded face was smiling, and bore no recent wounds. He was already breathing in a relaxed manner, as if the fierce activity of the past few minutes had been a mere exercise, but a thick purple welt across his forehead and two old parallel scars that ran from scalp to chin down the left side of his cheek made his face a terrifying sight to see close up. He had sheathed his sword, and was wiping his dagger with a handful of dried grass.

'It was a lucky escape,' Nicolas observed. 'We might have been killed.'

Briac looked at him, clearly amused. 'No, sire, that was not luck. They were peasant levies with orders not to kill. Armed with nothing but staves and clubs. It was a warning. Otherwise they would not have fled so easily.'

Nicolas realized at once that he was right. It annoyed him that he had been so taken with triangles and memories of Montfort that it had not been as obvious to him as well. With a little care and observation he would never have been taken so easily: like a neophyte, while the friar had bettered him again. 'What other arms might peasant levies have carried?'

Jacques watched as the sarcasm in Nicolas' voice made Briac stop and study his companion just as he had once done.

'I'll warrant they had pikes hidden nearby. And these men were strong. With pikes and mantlets I'd just as soon not face them. But they were here to scare you off.'

Jacques sensed that he was right. 'Our Lord Bernard de Caen has trained you well,' he remarked.

Briac smiled, but said nothing.

'Will you stay with us, now that you can no longer pretend you are not here?' Nicolas asked. He sensed the power of the man, and knew they would be safer with him and his men. He regarded Briac warmly.

'Our orders are to follow you from a distance. That is what we shall do. You won't see us again, unless, by St Sebastian, there is need.'

There was a note of coldness in Briac's reply. Jacques studied Nicolas closely while he spoke, suspicious of the friendliness in his companion's face. He was certain that Briac and his men had followed them from Avignon, but realized that the explanation might not be simple. At first he had assumed it was to protect them, yet a nagging doubt had surfaced in his mind: could it be that they were being followed in order to make them do as Bernard de Caen wished? Was Bernard in turn suspicious of his spies' growing friendship, and desirous of creating a double insurance? The more he thought it through, the more it seemed that this was the case since the 'enemy'

145

now knew that there was a guard with them. The element of surprise was lost.

Then what did this man know? He turned to Briac. 'Have you any idea who they were?'

'Shepherds!' Briac spat. 'They stank of the fold.'

'But someone must have sent them.'

The guard was embarrassed now. He looked briefly to the west, where the sun was rapidly sinking towards the mountain range above Ocre. 'We'll leave you now, Brother. There'll be no more trouble today.'

As quickly as they had come, the three men now disappeared amongst the rocks and, within minutes, silence was restored. Jacques could hear the wind scurrying through the ruined castle.

A hawk circled high above them, searching for prey.

'Someone must have sent them,' he repeated to himself. Then, aloud, 'Who do you think they were?'

'Someone doesn't want us here,' Nicolas replied obliquely. He was convinced by now that Briac had been right. 'Yet these were local men by the look of it. Disguised, yes; but I'd say they were local.'

Jacques' gaze instinctively turned west, where the newly built walls of Aquila glimmered like a crown around the city.

'There is the manpower,' Nicolas agreed, following his gaze. 'A city risen from the ashes of Pietro's family, which would hate to see any resurgence of the power of Ocre. But at the same time . . .'

'. . . they could have had no idea who we were,' Jacques completed his sentence, 'unless they were informed from Avignon.'

Nicolas nodded gravely. 'Or Paris.'

'King Philip? Surely not?' It was uncanny to hear his own inner suspicions voiced by another.

'Perhaps. There is no limit to his power.' Nicolas looked sombrely towards the distant city again, his eyes hardening into a glare. Then he glanced at Jacques. 'Or someone within the Church,' he suggested quietly.

'That's absurd,' Jacques snapped. How dare Nicolas make such a suggestion? A knight he might be, but he was still a layman. Yet the seed of suspicion was already within him, and now began to grow in spite of his disgust.

Nicolas remained silent.

Jacques regarded him quizzically, then recalled that his companion was himself in the service of Bernard de Caen, and therefore of the

146

Church. This made it all the more absurd, that a layman, temporarily attached to the most secret organization in the Church, should suspect an enemy within, while his real enemy was obviously the King of France. Another thought occurred to Jacques: Nicolas' innate antipathy towards Briac might explain his exaggerated reaction. He decided to test this hypothesis. 'Briac will always be there now, I suppose.'

'That's what he said.'

'Does that bother you?'

'Should it?' Nicolas' face was innocent enough as he spoke.

Was Nicolas feigning too? He was certainly avoiding an answer to the question. It was time to try a more direct route. 'Are they here to protect us, or to observe us?'

'God only knows.' Nicolas shook his head slowly.

Once again, his reply seemed sincere enough, and that was enough to confirm Jacques' deepest fears. He was entering a quagmire of loyalty in which only the quick of mind and strong of heart would survive.

Night fell suddenly on the way to Santo Spirito. Jacques halted for a moment, and looked back to San Eusanio. While the rocks above them were now in shadow, bright orange sunshine broke through the clouds to bathe the valley. The Castle of the Madonna floated above the darkness, illuminated like a fairy palace. The highest mountain peaks beyond were tinged with a brilliant pink. Then, as the sun dropped steadily over the mountains behind them, a dark shadow crept with the stealth and certainty of an invading army up the valley, engulfing villages remorselessly. With the suddenness of an eclipse, all was darkness. Jacques shivered as a wave of cold air passed over them. Silence was only broken by the sharp metallic sound of horses' hoofs picking at the gravel path. Then, as the monastery came into view like a black shadow against an even blacker wall, he became aware of a gentle, shimmering light which seemed to emanate from its walls. Jacques sat rigid in the saddle as the light increased, eerily aware that beyond that wall was the cemetery, then the chapel. But there was no divine office at that hour, and the single light prescribed by the Cistercian Rule could not create such an effect. For now it was no longer shimmering: having reached its maximum intensity, it remained fixed as a steady glare. With a slight tremor, Jacques recalled his spell of dizziness in San Eusanio.

But as suddenly as this light had broken, a full moon appeared through a break in the clouds, illuminating the grey rock like a silver torch. A screech-owl howled amongst the rocks above them; below in the village, dogs barked at the moon.

'It goes against all reason, but I believe there is evil in this place,' Jacques commented sombrely as they reached the monastery gate.

—— 21 ——

Brother Jacques had learned that the living archive of Santo Spirito was a certain Brother Matteo, who was said to be ninety years old and to have lived in the monastery since he was fourteen.

He used the dubious authority of Bernard de Caen's letter to draw the old monk to the library. The next problem was Nicolas. 'Would you please make sure nobody comes near this door? I'm afraid we can't trust these monks.' Jacques knew his last words must sound sincere enough for Nicolas not to suspect he was being excluded from Jacques' conversation with Brother Matteo.

'Outside, you mean?'

'There's no other way, I'm afraid. We can't let them get a hint of what we're doing here.'

'I suppose not,' Nicolas agreed reluctantly, although he was convinced that whoever had brought news of their arrival would have known something of their journey's purpose. But in a sense he was pleased to leave Jacques to do the hard work. His time would come, and for the moment he could sit in a window-seat in the short corridor leading to the library and study the landscape in the valley below.

He waited until the old monk hobbled into the corridor on a curved ash walking-stick whose gnarled deformities echoed his own form. With all the courtesy he could muster for what he perceived as a foolish and useless old peasant, Nicolas took his arm and led him to Jacques. Then he was more than content to be left alone.

Jacques looked up with pleasure at the honest, open face of Brother Matteo. Someone had dressed him in a freshly starched habit, in which he sat uncomfortably, like a child dressed up for a wedding, on the high-backed chair which Jacques had prepared for him. His face was as cracked as a dried-up lake-bed, and sparse white hairs fell singly about his head in abandon, as if allowed a licence of their own. His right arm shook constantly once he had laid his stick against the chair, but the other was firm as a rock even when he lifted it to gesture. 'Yes, it is true,' he began in careful Latin, 'I came here to Santo Spirito when I was a boy of fourteen.'

'From a village nearby?'

'Not a day's walk from here. We were eight brothers, so there were enough to work the land and tend our sheep.' He paused for breath, his eyes glistening like dew. 'They've all passed on now, God bless their souls.'

Jacques listened attentively, wishing to draw him into confidence. 'The abbey was flourishing when you came here, I believe.'

Gradually, the old monk warmed to his questioner. He began to talk with the openness characteristic of those who are beyond politics and ask no more than a willing ear. 'Yes indeed; our founder, Blessed Placido, was himself gone to Heaven, but many of the original brothers were still here then. They were good years: there was never any lack of funds for building and repair when our patron Lord Gualtiero was in residence.'

'Was that often?'

'No. He was forever on his travels. His family lived in the castle, but Lord Gualtiero had greater ambitions. One year he was with the Emperor Frederick in Sicily; the next with King Henry of England at Winchester . . .'

'Surely that was before your time?' Jacques had realized that Matteo's reflections mingled personal experience with hearsay.

The old monk looked at the inquisitor remissly. 'That's true enough,' he conceded, 'but I do remember the day Lord Gualtiero returned from Jerusalem with Richard of Cornwall, son to King Henry. I was only eleven, but my father brought me to the Ocre road to watch them. There were a hundred knights led by Lord Richard, every one dressed in silks and ermine and bearing the great curved swords of Saracens. I never saw such a great parade. And our own Lord Gualtiero at the head with the King's own brother.' He hesitated, as if these memories were tarnished by a less pleasant fact. 'That was when things began to change, people say,' he then added.

'Began to change?'

'The failure of the crusade with Prince Richard was a great tragedy to Lord Gualtiero. He saw the Holy City in the haze of distance one hot summer's day and never forgot it. It changed his life: he rebuilt San Eusanio, built new walls for our convent, founded churches throughout the valley, and filled them with relics he had brought from the Holy Land. Often, they said, he would sit dreamily as if looking at Jerusalem on the hill in the distance.'

'So his ideas . . .?'

'. . . were nothing but dreams? You must remember, Brother, that it was a time of great wars. A a man like Lord Gualtiero could not just sit and dream. He united the villages and convinced them to build a strong new city. It was to be filled with churches and monasteries, as a sacred refuge for the people of the valleys and mountains nearby. The first church was consecrated and the walls nearly complete, with a thousand hearths within, when the new Emperor Conradin razed the city to the ground.'

It was a remarkable tale, which would have seemed pure fantasy to Jacques a year ago. Now there was more substance in what had previously appeared an exaggerated sense of pride in Pietro.

'These are mountain folk. Brave and strong as you like, but no match for the trained troops of the Emperor. The inhabitants were sent back to their villages and flocks and the new city of Aquila disappeared as soon as it had been built.'

'But why did Conradin come here?'

'I don't know, Brother,' Matteo spoke apologetically, as if afraid of losing his new listener, 'unless . . .' His voice petered out. He too stared dreamily into the distance.

'Unless what?' Jacques prompted gently.

Matteo seemed to drift back into a deeper, more secret past as he spoke. He looked briefly out of the window, smiled to himself and then turned back to Jacques. 'If you would really like to know my opinion . . .' he offered.

'Please tell me.' Jacques felt the hairs on the back of his hands stiffen. He knew he was close to the secret, and hoped the old monk would not suddenly clam up.

'It is an old thing, and I wouldn't like Abbot Placido to know that I have spoken about it.'

'You may trust me fully, Brother Matteo.' Jacques leaned forward. 'Whatever you say will be for my ears only . . . and for he that sent me here.'

Matteo stared at him. His face registered suspicion, as the inquisitor had hoped. 'And who might that be?'

'His Holiness Pope Clement V.' It was not quite true, but he hoped it would have the desired effect.

'Ah! So that is the reason for all this secrecy.' Brother Matteo accepted this statement as if there could be nothing more normal; it reminded Jacques again of his proximity to Rome. 'I thought there must be something important about you, young man. You're destined

151

for high office yourself, I'd say . . . Anyway, I'll tell you. My days are coming to an end now. Mind you, what I'm going to tell you is nothing more than a personal intuition.'

'I understand.' *Please don't stop now*, Jacques thought.

'The idea was, you see, to build a New Jerusalem near Ocre. It was Count Tommaso who saw it first. One morning, after his first visit to the Holy Land, he looked out of the castle to the north-east and was struck by the strange formation of the land.' Matteo's voice warmed as he spoke of the Grand Master of the Templars. All hesitancy and doubt had gone. 'You can see it for yourself if you go up to the castle. Look towards the new city of Aquila. See how the hills are shaped like Golgotha and Calvary, with the city high on its own hill. The new fountain issues to the south like the Fountain of the Virgin; and the garden of the monastery of Collemaggio is placed like that of Gethsemane, so the basilica of Santa Maria is on the site of the tomb of the Blessed Mother of Christ. That was how Count Tommaso saw it that morning, and how he wished to build it.'

'He succeeded?' Then Nicolas' ideas about earth magic, geometric patterns and power were not far wrong.

'For a while, yes, he did. The New Jerusalem was built in our valley. It would have been one of the great cities of the world if the Count had had his way.' He spoke flatly, without nostalgia.

This idea was at the very heart of the Ocre heresy. Jacques remembered Pietro's pride, and his ambiguity. 'But why would people accept this New Jerusalem, here in the mountains of the Abruzzi?'

'Well, I myself never saw it, but the word in those days was that Count Tommaso had got for himself one of the most holy of relics, greater than anything King Charlemagne had found in Constantinople, and greater even than St Louis brought back from the Holy Land . . .' Matteo paused to study his fingernails, as if determined to make the most of this rare captive audience. 'It was said to strike terror into the hearts of the bravest men, and give infinite power to whoever held it. There were lots of stories at that time about a sacred head of the saracens. Some said it was the head of Christ himself; others that of the Prophet Mohammed. You will excuse the blasphemy, Sire Inquisitor?' Anxiety showed in the old man's eyes for an instant. 'Anyway, we discussed it for years, but as far as I know nobody ever saw this thing.' He paused again, as if trying to remember somebody who might have seen it.

A tight knot had formed in Jacques' stomach as he listened to the old monk. He wondered how much of this Bernard de Caen knew, or had guessed. 'Then what happened?'

'Well, they began to build the New Jerusalem. It was laid out in the form of a cross, with the longer arm pointing towards Ocre. There were to be four convents, one at the limit of each arm; a temple at the centre of the cross, and a great church in the place of the Garden of Gethsemane. Never had a city been built with such enthusiasm. I remember as if it were yesterday. Thousands of masons and labourers worked on the building: nothing was grown in the whole valley that year. The Counts of Ocre brought in lentils from the lands of their cousins in the Marsica. Entire trains of ox-carts arrived in the new city from Celano, and grain was brought by ship from Apulia.' He paused for a moment, reliving the excitement. 'But then the troubles started.'

'Troubles?'

'Rumours spread with the new walls. Tommaso and Gualtiero were becoming too powerful. There were fears they wished to dominate the church in Rome. Now, people said – and, mark me, I believe they were right – if this is to be Jerusalem, then what of Rome? Now you, Brother, a learned and well-travelled man, will understand that if the monks of Santo Spirito thought these things there were others of greater station who feared them.' Again, the pause, the glance out of the window. 'If you ask my opinion . . .' He let the words hang in the chill air between them.

'Do not fear. Tell me your opinion.' Jacques spoke softly, coaxing memories from this man who had been there.

'Ambition is a dangerous sin, as Saint Bernard our Founder taught us,' Matteo began, with new confidence. 'Count Gualtiero was a powerful man and lord of a hundred castles. But his life at the great courts of the day led him to aspire to greater power. Yet I suppose it wasn't surprising, for quite ordinary men feel this ambition in the presence of the great.'

In the quiet of the library, the ancient Cistercian's words took on an air of admonition. Jacques felt a deep surge of conscience within his soul.

Matteo seemed to understand through the sixth sense which men of great age sometimes gain. As if to fill the silence, he continued: 'So King Conradin's army arrived one morning. The people thought it was a friendly visit after Gualtiero's years of loyalty to the Emperors. His

153

army marched in through open gates, then expelled the people from their own homes. When every last women and child had left, they set fire to the houses and began demolishing the new city walls. The people fled to the mountains, for there was no respite from destruction within earshot of the peals of the city bells. It was like a ghost city, with ruined walls enclosing open countryside. The magic had gone.'

Jacques began to understand. 'That was when the vocations began to fall?'

'Yes. After the death of Lord Gualtiero. The next year his brother Tommaso returned from Jerusalem. From that summer, no Count of Ocre ever resided in the castle. It was taken by Charles of Anjou, who resided there for three months and then razed it to the ground. These self-same eyes saw him in this convent that year.' Matteo touched his eye-lids, as if his action would add credibility to his words.

The very year Pietro di Ocre was initiated into the Order of the Temple, Jacques realized. Now he saw the point of the second, promised initiation. He also recalled the exaggerated fear which Pietro di Ocre had shown on learning that he was to travel to Avignon. A new thought came to his mind. 'Brother Matteo, do you happen to recall when the Castle of the Madonna was built? And the walls around the church of San Eusanio?'

The old monk smiled a toothless smile. 'That I do, Brother. It was the year before I came to Santo Spirito. I remember it well because my brothers worked on the towers at San Eusanio and I passed many a day with them.'

'Was Count Tommaso in Ocre then?'

'Indeed he was. That was the first summer he came back from Jerusalem, with Richard of Cornwall. He was then Master of the Temple in England. It was a great year for our Counts. New frescoes were painted, and great corridors built. What you now see as a ruin was a great palace then, mark my word.'

'Just one more thing, good Brother, before you attend compline,' Jacques said, delighted with Matteo and his information. 'Tell me, the relic you spoke about, the one which gave the counts of Ocre this power –' He felt foolish as he spoke the words, but knew that the old monk believed in it. 'Was it ever seen again? Was it taken away?'

'No, sire. And not for the sake of looking. The Emperor Conradin sent troops to search castles and churches, and even our monastery. Then Charles of Anjou did the same. But it was never found, of that I'm sure.' The last phrase was firmly spoken, with a certainty which

154

showed Matteo's loyalty to the counts of Ocre. Jacques knew that it would be useless to push for further information.

When Matteo had left, he mulled over the interview as he waited for Nicolas to come in. The pattern was filling. King Philip would have learned of this relic from his brother Charles of Valois, perhaps even many years ago. His knowledge had lain dormant for decades, and the recent urgency of his actions derived from his plan to place his family on the great thrones of Europe. It was imperative for the future of Church and Empire that the relic be recovered before the King laid his hands on it.

'Well?' In spite of himself, Nicolas was anxious to learn what had been said.

'They wanted to build a New Jerusalem.'

'What?'

'. . . a New Jerusalem . . .'

The news flabbergasted Nicolas de Lirey, but did not totally surprise him. He had heard of such schemes from his father; there had once been talk of such a city at Montfort. 'The old man told you that?'

'He's an interesting man. Old, but not as foolish as you might think.' Jacques paused to let the gentle admonition have its effect. 'He certainly filled in some gaps in my knowledge. Mind you, without your insight into the thinking of these counts I may not have discovered much,' Jacques admitted. He was intrigued to observe Nicolas' knowing reaction. How much did he know?

Nicolas lowered his head, trying to appear grateful for Jacques' information without being servile. 'How might that be?'

'Your triangles and shields are but part of the whole matter, it would seem. I must say that I was sceptical before this conversation.'

'Matteo confirmed them?'

'Much more, good sire, much more. These counts of Ocre were strange men indeed, and wished to reproduce the city of Jerusalem here in their own valley as a substitute for the city they couldn't recapture. If your ideas about earth magic are right, then they meant to gain hold over the entire region . . . and possibly even Rome itself.' Jacques paused again for effect.

But before he could continue Nicolas spoke softly to him. 'Then it must have been something remarkable. Really quite remarkable.' He now saw Bernard de Caen's fears in a new light, and perhaps his ambitions. He had heard once that the Inquisitor-General aspired to

155

the highest of all positions. Could it be that he saw this relic as the means to achieve his ends?

Jacques regarded his companion curiously. There was a new glint in his eyes. '*It?* What do you mean?'

'The relic, of course. Did he tell you about that?' Nicolas pushed his doubt about Bernard from his mind. It could not be possible.

'Yes.' Now Jacques began to sense Nicolas' interest, but something in the knight's change of voice had alerted him. He chose his words carefully now. 'Apparently it's an image, a head of some description.'

'Matteo told you that? Does he know what happened to it?'

'No,' Jacques replied thoughtfully, speaking as he reached his own conclusion.

'Does that mean . . .?'

'That we'll return to Avignon? I'm not sure yet.' Jacques' wrists ached at the very thought of it. The relic was here: of that he was now certain, but he was equally sure that the key to finding it lay with Pietro di Ocre. In that his Superior had been right, whether through knowledge or a hunch.

Duplicity was becoming second nature to him, it seemed. Bernard de Caen's lesson in withholding decisions and facts until it was essential to pass them on had been well absorbed. Jacques was reluctant to inform Nicolas, but he knew that they must leave at once.

One morning, in a convent where they had taken refuge on their journey, Jacques was astonished to see Briac again. Unarmed, clean and smiling. 'Briac! What are you doing here? Is there no longer any danger?'

'There is always danger, Brother Jacques. But today is the day of Our Saviour and my men wish to pray and feast like other Christian folk. We are now over half-way to Avignon . . .' He paused, a twinkle in his eye: 'I don't think those shepherds will follow us here,' he grinned.

'But *you* have followed us. I fancied I saw you once on a hillside near the road . . .'

'That may be. It's not you we're hiding from.'

'Who then?' Jacques looked around quickly to see if the lean, stooping figure of Nicolas de Lirey was visible. It seemed the guard wanted to laugh, but he restrained himself. There was little point in arguing. 'Come, let us leave the cloister,' Jacques said quietly.

Nearby, nuns sat weaving new habits from that autumn's wool.

They strolled in the herb garden. 'You are from the Pays de Foix, I believe?' Jacques was pleased to slip back into his mother tongue.

A suspicious frown corrugated Briac's forehead. 'What if I am?'

'Don't worry; this is no inquisition. I haven't been checking on you.' It would be awful to have Briac for an enemy. 'It's your accent, by Saint Sebastian!'

Now Briac laughed openly. His favourite's saint's name reassured him. 'Then you know my village?' he asked.

'Father Guilhem was my own confessor.'

'*Our* Father Guilhem?' The incredulity in Briac's voice was nothing in comparison with the huge beam that appeared on his face. It seemed his grin would crack the massive head in two.

'But you're not from our village . . .'

'No indeed. From Saverdun. My father was Jean the Baker.'

Briac thought for a moment. 'Yes, I've heard of him,' he said without conviction. Then he turned to safer ground. 'I myself was baptized by Father Guilhem,' he said proudly. He continued to smile like a child with a new toy, watching the inquisitor whom he had rescued with a kind of local pride. 'They say you're marked for greater things,' he said.

'Who?'

'Around . . .'

'And yourself? How do you come to be in the service of the Pope?'

'It's a good position, and my family are proud of me too.'

'My parents are dead, God bless their souls.'

Briac lowered his head respectfully. 'Then the people of Saverdun will be proud of you,' he suggested. 'We must stick with our own in these strange times.'

'Yes, we must indeed,' Jacques agreed. The guard's assumption of local pride gave him an idea. 'You are a good soldier yourself, Briac. Are you destined for better things?'

'Me?' The man laughed. 'Who would want to better my position?' He regarded Jacques cautiously. 'You're not trying to bribe me, are you?'

'Did I ask you to come here?'

'No, that's true enough.' The great grin returned to the weather-beaten face.

'And did you not say yourself that we should stick together in these strange times?'

'But I don't know you from Adam.'

'Father Guilhem does,' Jacques reminded him. He was not sure how to progress, since he did not wish to offend Briac's loyalty to Bernard. How did one make a bribe? Should he leave some silver from his purse in a niche of the cloister, and then walk away?

His uncertainty was resolved by Briac. 'What is it you propose?' he asked bluntly.

Jacques felt his cheeks grow warm in the winter chill. 'Let us say there are certain facts which you see from a different perspective, even small things . . .'

'You mean let you know anything I hear?' Briac asked bluntly. 'Keep you informed, like?'

'If you wish to express it in that way, then yes.' There was no point in going back, so Jacques reached into the purse which he carried on the belt inside his habit, and took out some silver florins. 'Here,' he began, warming to this new role, 'let us call this a Christmas gift.' He passed the silver coins to Briac, who accepted them without a word and hid them quickly inside his leather tunic. 'There will be more.'

'That suits me, Brother, and you may trust me as you can trust any man from the Pays de Foix. But I think we should go in. It's unusual for such an important visitor to stroll in the gardens with a guard.' He chucked softly and patted Jacques on the arm familiarly.

'Yes, you're right,' Jacques agreed. 'Mark me well, Briac!' Even he was aware of a new conspiratorial tone in his own voice. 'This mission is of vital importance to me, and in the next few months I shall be needing the help you can provide. If I am successful, I will be able to guarantee you promotion beyond your dreams. Remember that.' He stared Briac out with the penetrating gaze he usually employed on his prisoners, amazed at his own bluff. 'Now let us go in.'

When they arrived together at the refectory door, Nicolas was waiting for them in the porch. 'I didn't realize you were staying in the monastery too,' he said to Briac.

'Me? In the monastery?' Briac's laughter shattered the silence. 'I brought my men here to feast the day of Our Saviour. There's pork and blood pudding to be had. And who should I meet as I arrived but my good Brother Jacques.'

'And now he can talk to you, Nicolas,' Jacques quickly added, leaping at his chance.

To his credit, the guard immediately understood the game. 'Come, let us go in. Brother Jacques still has work to do.'

The reluctance on Nicolas' face was manifest, but he went, without a murmur of protest.

Relieved, Jacques walked alone in the walled garden, which was greened by ancient cypresses even in the midst of winter. Sheltered from wind and driving rain, shrubs and herbs flourished in the medicinal garden. Late-flowering oregano and thyme spiced the air and added colour to the dark leaves of comfrey and winter savory. At the centre of the garden stood an ancient beech; a family of squirrels sat nervously among its roots, chewing at pieces of bark and beechmast.

Jacques stopped where a channel of crystal water burbled through a tiny arch in the wall. This place was more akin to Abbot Guibert's monastery than the austerity and isolation of Santo Spirito. Now, after months of travel and with King Philip's summer deadline no longer so distant, he yearned for that peace again: the tranquillity of the sleeping *dortoir* as he lay awake waiting for the summons to Vigils; the steady rhythm of life with no sudden decisions or reversals; the sense of community and trust in chapters; the sharing of hard work and small joys; the singing of psalms as they left the refectory after the midday meal; the communal *boire*.

He discovered within himself the desire for such an abbey to command. He would fill his library with fine volumes: the *Chronicles of the History of Jerusalem*, the real Jerusalem; stories of the crusades; the *Commentaries* of Bishop Grossteste; and the works of Albertus Magnus and Thomas Aquinas. Bernard de Caen had already hinted at such a possibility in the event of success. Now it seemed to draw closer, and the thought warmed him. Jacques was beginning to understand the depth of the heresy of the counts of Ocre, and was convinced that through them he would discover the 'face'. But beyond that was an even stronger desire to discover the truth.

He followed the channel of shimmering water to a pool where a thrush sang with exaggerated joy. Bubbles rose to the surface and silver-like fish fled when he stepped on the edge of the pool. His mind automatically reviewed the charges as he stood gazing at the smooth surface of the water, reflecting green from moss-covered stones around it. The bubbles vanished, and the last temerarious fish darted into the safety of lily leaves. Jacques found himself staring at his own greenish image.

The heresy of both Ocre and the Temple was based upon the worship of a face, perhaps the one that he had seen in San Eusanio. But that in turn was the representation of another, much holier, image. The image on the relic everyone was searching for. What was it? Where was it? Would he be able to find it in time? But even as he ran through these questions he saw that the real problem was another: how to prise the information from Pietro di Ocre and then exploit it to the full without ever allowing Nicolas or Bernard to see the whole picture. Then, still staring at his own image, he understood that the magic head of the Order of the Temple was the same as the face at Ocre, a fact that neither Bernard nor the King seemed to have grasped. With a shock, Jacques knew that he must play a double game and keep his own counsel, for only total secrecy would enable him to succeed. Goose-pimples rose on his arms as he saw a glimmer of the route to the kind of power he had never believed would be open to him. Now it was a palpable reality dancing in front of him like his image in the pool . . .

When he looked up, the garden seemed suffused with a new light. The thrush still warbled nearby, and Jacques was as happy as the thrush.

He walked towards the refectory with a new eagerness in his step, wishing that he could be transported instantly to the prison at Avignon – as some of the wise women he had interrogated earlier had claimed was possible. For now he possessed the lever to open the Templar's mind.

· —— 23 —— ·

Pietro di Ocre's cell was light and clean, with a new straw mattress which he had rolled up against the wall like a cushion. A freshly painted crucifix was nailed to the wall, and a lingering scent of pine suggested to Jacques that the cell had been swept recently. He glanced back at Nicolas to share the satisfaction that his orders had been fulfilled to the letter, then motioned his companion to wait in the doorway.

The prisoner himself was as neat as the cell: his beard had been trimmed, and once dishevelled hair had been cropped close to his skull. Morsels of bread left on his plate suggested that he was not hungry.

Brother Jacques moved closer. 'Good morning, Preceptor. I see you are being treated well,' he began brightly. He waited for a reaction, but none came. Then he turned his gaze away from the prisoner, and spoke quietly: 'I hope you've had plenty of time to consider your position.'

'There's little else to do here.'

Jacques smiled. 'Then I hope you are beginning to see the advantages of collaboration.'

'Little . . . or nothing.' Years of imprisonment and interrogation had obviously taught Pietro all the tricks. He was answering, but saying nothing; staring vacantly ahead as he spoke.

Jacques realized that a new approach was necessary. He turned silently and walked slowly to the door. 'The stool,' he whispered.

The hair on Nicolas' hands bristled. He was being treated like a serf. He had already felt ludicrous walking past the guards with a stool in his hand as if he were a mere page-boy again. Now he fought back anger as his religious companion lifted his forefinger to his lips to enjoin silence. Sometimes it was like a children's game, he thought, but he passed the stool to Jacques silently.

Then Jacques entered the cell again. He sat down deliberately, shifting the stool until all three legs rested firmly on the ground, and began to speak abstractly as if addressing the prisoner, avoiding all eye contact with Pietro. 'I had a long conversation with a certain Brother Matteo in the convent of Santo Spirito,' Jacques said slowly; 'an interesting man, who you may remember from your childhood . . .'

'I know no one of that name,' he answered haughtily.

'An ancient monk . . .'

'I know him not.'

'Be that as it may.' Pietro might well have forgotten, since Matteo had known him only during his childhood, but at least he was answering now. 'He spoke to me of your father, and of certain plans of his. "Ambitions" was the actual word he used. I found his story fascinating . . . was it not, Nicolas; that idea of founding a New Jerusalem?'

'Fascinating indeed,' Nicolas nodded sagely, surprising himself even as he spoke by his enjoyment of the unexpected role. He had been reluctantly admiring the way in which the inquisitor so easily got his prisoner to talk. The game worked. There was much to be learned, and he must suppress his instincts to interrupt or hurry proceedings along. He would listen quietly.

Pietro seemed unaware of the trick. 'Is there something amiss in that?' he asked. There was neither surprise nor perplexity in his voice.

'Perhaps not,' Jacques answered softly, 'if it were to remain at that. But it didn't, as I'm sure you know.'

'My father was a devout Christan . . .'

'I've no doubt of that.'

'. . . and fought in the Holy Land like many another knight. Yet you speak as if he committed some heresy.' Pride edged into contempt on Pietro's last word.

'Other knights did not aspire to re-create the holiest of cities,' Jacques observed. 'And it seems his ambitions went well beyond that.'

The preceptor sneered, and attempted to divert his inquisitor: 'Who is this Jacopo? I've never heard of him. A monk at Santo Spirito knew nothing but convent gossip.'

'Gossip is one of the main founts of information.' It was one of the axioms inculcated in Jacques many years before in Paris. 'A careful reading of your interrogations, together with documents in Santo Spirito itself, substantiates the story of Brother Jacopo.'

Nicolas was impressed, and could not resist a comment. 'Indeed, it's quite remarkable,' he agreed. His own intuitions were reinforced by Pietro's wariness and the snippets of information he had gleaned at Santo Spirito.

Brother Jacques looked askance at him for an instant, but carried on: 'Anyway, for the good fortune of the Holy Mother Church, the whole story ended there. We might well say a prayer for Charles of Anjou, who managed to stop him.'

The veins on Pietro's neck stood rigid like soldiers at attention. 'Oh no, Sire Inquisitor, it didn't end there!' he said with menace. 'You are clever enough, I admit, and this Brother Matteo informed you well, God damn his soul, but this time you are wrong. It didn't end there!' But as quickly as he had risen to the bait he dominated his anger, as if ashamed of accepting the inquisitor's provocation. He spoke softly: 'You are a clever man, Brother Jacques, but such things are beyond you.'

Now Nicolas knew. He sympathized with the prisoner, and was momentarily saddened by his recognition that Pietro had under-estimated the inquisitor just as he himself had done. But the thought of Bernard de Caen's orders cut through his sympathy like a sword through butter. His task was clear. The breach was made, but his inquisitor-companion could not benefit from his own skill. He stepped into the cell, drawing the door to behind him and stood by the window, where he could look straight into the prisoner's eyes and also see Brother Jacques beyond. 'Why don't you give us *your* version?' he asked the preceptor gently.

Pietro looked up slowly. Was there a moment of shared understanding? 'I suppose there's little to lose now,' he conceded. He sank back onto his furled mattress. 'It's true that Charles of Anjou destroyed our castle at Ocre, and that his alliance with the Emperor Conradin was designed to destroy my family. But even he never understood the whole of my father's plan. Fifty years later I can tell you that no one ever did, or ever will . . . for it's not over yet.' He shook his head slowly, and defiance flared in his eyes, then subsided again.

A question was forming in Nicolas' mind, but he blocked it. He must listen and assimilate Pietro's tale. Moving away from the window, he nodded almost imperceptibly to Brother Jacques, acknowledging that now the flow was renewed an expert questioner was needed.

'It's not over yet,' Pietro repeated dreamily.

'Go on.' It was now Jacques who spoke gently, fearing the preceptor might suddenly change his mind if he paused too long.

'You know the story of Pope Celestine?'

'Yes indeed,' Jacques replied warily. He had been a student in Paris when the hermit-pope's abdication was the scandal of the year.

'Well, he was chosen by my father,' Pietro continued. 'Did your Brother Jacopo tell you that he was a monk at Santo Spirito? It was

164

he who founded the Basilica of Collemaggio which you saw. But my family paid for it! We arranged for him to study in Rome, at the Convent of Santa Cecilia ... he was groomed for the papacy and – do you know the great irony?'

The inquisitor's mind raced as he attempted to reassemble the pieces of the puzzle and tally the truth of these assertions with other information.

Now there was triumph in Pietro's voice. 'Yes, a fine irony, for it was Charles of Anjou who persuaded Celestine to accept the Holy See. They said he was a simple hermit whom Anjou plucked from the mountainside.' He chuckled with genuine pleasure at this thought. 'My father would have liked that! But Pope Celestine, Sire Inquisitor, was murdered because Cardinal Gaetani of Rome, may the devil curse his name, discovered our plan ... No! Wait! I can tell what you are thinking. Pope Celestine is supposed to have abdicated. But I tell you he was forced to give up his pontificate. Then, in prison, he was drugged and murdered in his sleep. The bastards drove an iron nail as long as my hand into his skull. Poor soul!' He crossed himself rapidly, then went on: 'My brother Tibaldo was thrown to his death from the rock of Ocre in the same year; and Tommaso was drowned in Rome. Study the lives of my family and friends: you will find that not one of them survived that year.'

'You did,' Nicolas observed tartly. Sympathy was now replaced by a sense of duty. The prisoner was not, after all, a French aristocrat, whatever claims he might make about his ancestry.

'I?' It seemed that Pietro would react violently, but he simply chuckled. 'I was in Cyprus, at the Temple of Nicosia.' He paused, as if overwhelmed by his memories, then added: 'But there is more ...'

'Go on,' Jacques pressed. He turned his open palm towards Nicolas to avoid further comments.

'Anjou was informed too, and thus his brother-in-law Philip the Fair. Then the king sent Guillaume de Nogaret to insult Gaetani when he became Boniface VIII. Have you ever asked yourself the real reason, brother?'

'No ...' Jacques admitted. History was being turned inside out here. It was like seeing the world afresh, from Ocre.

'Has any pope's name ever been further from the truth?' Pietro laughed at his own joke. 'Work it out for yourself, inquisitor. You're the clever one here. I'll just tell you one more thing, and it regards my own Order. Do you know why our Grand Master still languishes in your dungeon of the Inquisition in Paris?'

As he spoke it seemed that Pietro entered into some kind of delirium. Yet a mosaic was slowly emerging from these apparently unconnected facts. Jacques would need to fit the pieces together later. 'I've no idea at all,' he said with total honesty.

'It's simple. You see, we still hold the key – the same key that my father, Count Gualtiero, held many years ago now. Celestine was murdered for it. King Philip thought Boniface had it, and destroyed him; now he believes the Order of the Temple has it, and is trying to destroy us.' He stopped abruptly, studying the impact of his words on the two men.

It occurred to Jacques that the preceptor would himself have made an excellent inquisitor. 'Go on,' he said.

'I'll tell you something, Brother Jacques. You're a clever man, and you know as much of this as any other man alive. But you're only half the man my father was, and he'll be laughing in his grave when he sees you fail. No one will ever discover the truth, although many, now and in the future, will delude themselves. The secret of the Order of the Temple is the secret of Ocre. And try as you will, you will not find the key to the secret of Ocre.'

Jacques regarded Pietro with disbelief. This total identity between the Temple and Ocre was astounding. He turned away so that Nicolas would not see the perturbation which must be evident on his face, and passed quickly out of the cell.

Outside, the vespers bell began to sound, each chime followed by an eerie, higher-pitched echo from the vaults of the corridor. 'I will, I will,' Jacques repeated softly to himself in unison with the strange double toll.

24

'A little comfort has certainly made him loquacious,' Nicolas observed as they left the prison. 'Do you think there's anything in his stories?' In bright, clear air it all seemed less plausible.

'That the pope was a puppet of the counts of Ocre? Why not? I've heard stranger things before, and in this case the facts do tally.' The inquisitor strode forward, secure in his conviction.

'To some extent,' Nicolas conceded. It was a reluctant admission. The Frenchman with noble blood in him refused to acknowledge the possibility of such influence being held by a minor Italian family.

Abruptly, Brother Jacques stopped and turned back. 'But there is something else which convinces me.'

Nicolas veered to one side to avoid tramping over the inquisitor's feet. 'What would that be?' He knew that he had failed to disguise his scepticism.

But Jacques ignored the implicit taunt. He sensed he would soon need the layman's assistance, and that he must trust *someone*. 'Pietro is an ignorant man. Neither learned, nor imaginative,' he said, choosing his words carefully.

'Does that make his theories true?'

'In a sense, yes.' He was pleased to see surprise registered on Nicolas' face. 'You see, I don't believe for a moment that he's capable of making it all up. *Somebody* was a master strategist – I dare say his father, Gualtiero. But Pietro is not. What he says is true enough as far as he sees it.' He spoke the last words with the certainty of a pondered judgement at the end of a trial. He moved towards the convent steadily, as if an important conclusion had been reached, but more slowly this time. Nicolas was about to ask a question when Jacques suddenly continued, as if in an afterthought: 'Furthermore, his manifest sincerity when he speaks of the past confirms the existence of the relic.'

'The relic,' Nicolas repeated mechanically as if it were an antiphon. It was so easy to forget the relic in this midst of this conspiracy.

'He has also confirmed something else for us. That King Philip learned about it many years ago. We may also assume that Pope

Innocent knew when he banned Gualtiero from his church. Certainly Pope Celestine did, and perhaps Pope Boniface.'

'So it was barely a secret . . .'

Some washerwomen passed them. Jacques waited, then led the way into the Black Friars' convent. 'Secret enough!' he said when they were alone again, 'but not common knowledge. It must be an image of intense potential, something that strikes terror into the hearts of great men and confers power upon its possessor.' He thought of the head in San Eusanio as he spoke. That, he now realized, must have been a copy of the original relic. And if that was a copy . . .

Nicolas unwittingly broke into his thoughts. 'But where is it, do you think?'

'Ha! That is what we must discover. And I believe Pietro di Ocre still holds the key.'

'Will he tell us? Just like that?'

Sometimes, Nicolas' ingenuousness was disconcerting, Jacques reflected. 'Just like that, no. But indirectly, perhaps yes. We must keep our wits about us.' Yet even as he spoke he made a decision: that when the moment of revelation came, he would be alone with Pietro. He would contrive to finish his task without his secular companion.

He sat down in an empty niche in the cloister, ignoring Nicolas. His mind reeled. As clearly as he saw the solitary gardener turning compost ready for spreading, he understood the use of a relic to win over friend and enemy alike. He recalled a lecture in Paris by Albertus Magnus on properties of objects and how they may be used to command other objects. He had not believed then, and refused to believe in them now. But the counts of Ocre had been convinced that this holy relic would give them the power to take over the Church; now Philip the Fair believed that possession of the same object would enable him to conquer the world.

Half of Paris – half of Europe – was searching for it, and he must find it first.

The thought of Paris caused him to draw a scroll from inside his habit. He looked across the corridor, and saw the young knight discreetly waiting. He sensed a new respect in this discretion, and warmed to him for an instant. 'This, Nicolas,' he said, 'is a letter from our Lord Bernard. He has been obliged to leave for Paris.'

'The needs of diplomacy are pressing, I see.' It required all Nicolas' will-power to suppress his anger. What was this now? Was *he* not the spy who should inform Brother Jacques, and be informed before him? Nothing was as it seemed any longer.

Jacques sensed the inner conflict, and smiled to himself. 'We'll have to wait, I'm afraid, before reporting the success of our mission.'

'That might be several weeks, or even months.' Nicolas' words were spoken harshly, as if he hoped to take revenge for his losing face by emphasizing his own companion's impotence. But the realization that Jacques was no better informed than he was coursed through Nicolas like the blood of a freshly beheaded hen. 'Why must we wait?' he almost shouted in his enthusiasm. 'Wouldn't Paris be the logical place to take Pietro? We need to force the secret into the open, don't we? Well, the best way to do so would be to take the preceptor to Paris, and allow him to see his former colleagues.' He had drawn nearer to the inquisitor, within a hair's breadth of shaking sense into him through his shoulders.

'Perhaps you are right,' Jacques agreed reluctantly. It would mean direct disobedience of Bernard de Caen's orders. How would the Inquisitor-General react? But even as he asked himself the question, instinct overcame fear. For if his intuitions were correct, then such insubordination would be forgiven; if wrong, then his career in the *Opus* would of course be over. Yet it was worth the risk: he could allow Pietro to smell the possibility of success and then trap him when he became too confident; moreover, that way he could at the same time keep close to Bernard de Caen and *his* projects. This time, Nicolas was right.

His mind was made up with a finality that surprised even him. 'This is no time to sit here meditating. Tell Briac to make preparations for our departure.'

Delight won over fears of publicly perceived servitude as Nicolas bowed. 'At once.' He then threw his hair back over his head with a quick nod, and left in search of the chief guard.

Brother Jacques sat alone, considering the new implications of the situation. It was clear that Bernard believed as firmly as the others in the power of this image: he must surely have learned of it during his time at Casanova. It was, after all, on his personal initiative that Jacques had been sent to Aigues-Mortes. Yet his task had never been made explicit, as if he were expected to unravel the problem in some way without understanding its nature. He began to suspect that he was not supposed to understand: he was not sent there for his skill in reasoning, but for his ability to draw the truth from notoriously recalcitrant heretics. He imagined the chubby face of his mentor and wondered how much of the story *he* knew. Moreover, the fact of the Inquisitor-General's new departure for Paris was in itself disturbing, given Bernard's intimacy with Guillaume de Paris: two men who had gone to Pope Boniface with de Nogaret. He would inquire into the date of Bernard's promotion to his present office with Pope Clement.

His prisoner's change of attitude was even more disturbing. The preceptor had grown almost arrogant during questioning, as if he thought he was fooling his inquisitors. Pietro still believed that the possession of this relic would lead him to personal victory, even after seven years spent rotting in a dungeon. He had received the ordeal of water twice, and the ordeal of fire once, Jacques recalled from the dossiers, but had never mentioned Ocre or this power before. Now he seemed keen to co-operate with them! Could it really be that Pietro thought he could keep the ultimate secret for himself?

Jacques realized that he too must play this dangerous game of cat-and-mouse. Then he would be at the centre of events. The thought of it warmed his heart in the chill cloister, and he rubbed his rein-calloused palms together to spread the pleasant sensation through his body. Then he chuckled quietly to himself, pleased at the new confidence which had led him to make the decision to travel to Paris.

25

Storm clouds blackened the sky as they followed the flooding Seine northward through Burgundy. Villages nestled grey in the folds of dark hills like ashes piled against the soot-black flue. Constant torrential rain obliterated conversation and doused both supply-sacks and their cloaks. An ominous sense of evil seemed to seep into Brother Jacques' very bones with the pervasive greyness and damp.

Briac led the way. Jacques and Nicolas followed in the guard's wake, cowled against the elements. Behind them, two shires pulled a heavy four-wheeled wagon with their prisoner, who was protected from the rain by leather stretched over the wooden planks. They lost count of how many times Briac joked that Pietro was the only one to be dry. But since the perch stuck firm in the mud of humped-back bridges at least once a day, the Preceptor was often forced to join them in the downpour while the wagon was huffed and heaved over by Briac's men. Most of the time these guards rode unobtrusively behind them.

Across the fields beside them streaks of manure were carried like boats towards the river by sheets of surface water from the careful piles where it had been laid in readiness. Mill-wheels spun freely in the bank-bursting current, sculpting it into white braids which brightened the monotonous grey landscape. The torrent would plunge into the funnel of a village, rip ivy and climbing rose bushes from containing walls, and then beyond the village burst across fields and gardens like a tidal wave. Peasants sat glumly under broad eaves, sharpening ploughs and hoes. Even the crows took shelter. Jacques bent his head and rode determinedly, all thought smothered by the driving rain.

It was Briac's stentorian command which stopped him dead in his tracks. 'The flanks! Guard the wagon! Quick!'

Then there was mayhem.

Jacques pulled up his rouncy, and turned off the track so that he could look back at the wagon.

It was surrounded by foot-soldiers; tall northerners in hauberks and mail hose, some of them wearing iron poleyns to guard their knees. Two of them had jumped onto the transom and taken control, while the driver lay sprawled in the mud with his face buried in a puddle.

More roughly-dressed men in long shirts covered by leather jerkins, their legs planted like trees in the mud, while their heads were protected by nothing more than felt alpine caps, surrounded the cart. But amidst them was a more sinister figure: a single man wearing a mail helmet, and bearing both sword and shield, commanded from the rear. Men were fanned in front of him, fighting outwards with a discipline and control which suggested great skill, yet their weapons were a mixture of clubs and spears, and even agricultural tools.

Before he could study them longer, Jacques was knocked violently from his mount and instantly pinioned to the grassy earth beside the road by what felt like a spear against his shoulders, which revived the forgotten pain of the Mont Cenis bruises. He had to force his head up to stop it dropping into the chill mud of the track.

From that position he could see a series of muddy legs and arms battle violently around the wagon. Nicolas was struggling against two of the foot-soldiers beside it. Meanwhile Briac's guards were being held back as the two men who had jumped the wagon wrenched Pietro di Ocre from his shelter onto the ground. Helpless, Jacques watched as his prisoner was dragged across the road into the undergrowth by his legs. As Pietro disappeared from his view, it seemed that all was lost. A confused succession of the events of the past few months passed before his eyes as it was said happened to a drowning man: the prison at Aigues-Mortes, Bernard, Pope Clement, Ida, Mont Cenis, the girl ... He felt he too was close to drowning as his face was roughly pushed even further into liquid mud. He went under. Could this be God's punishment for his sins?

At that moment the blood-stilling roar of Briac's anger penetrated both mud and dread. With an effort, Jacques forced his head up once more to peer through the rain, fearing that his guard and ally had been killed.

But Briac was far from dead, and fought as if driven by demonic fury. His mouth seemed to be stretched open by invisible cords as he alternated between shouts of primordial rage and gasps for breath. In his right hand he held a sword long enough to require a double-handed grip from ordinary men; in his left hand a poleaxe with a broken haft. He sat as stiff as buckram in the saddle, fighting simultaneously on both sides. One man soon fell under a blow to his mail helmet from the poleaxe. Another, a younger man with terror written scarlet across his white face, turned and ran. Briac edged his horse forward slowly, cutting a remorseless swathe through the enemy.

172

His guards now followed his lead as Briac felled another man. Then he roared an order to three of his men to follow Pietro and his captors and they ran into dripping giant ferns beyond the track, their bodies enwrapped, demon-like, in mist and horses' breath. Meanwhile Briac took on another attacker, cracking him across the helmet with awesome force. Jacques watched, his eyes almost bursting in astonishment. Now he understood why Briac was known to all as 'the Beast'.

Just then, a shorter foot-soldier managed to sneak under Briac's blows, and begin to hack at the tendons of his mount's forelegs. The horse screamed, reared on its hind legs, and fell forward, catapulting Briac into the mud. While he struggled to regain his balance with the two heavy weapons in his hand, the same man swung at him from behind with a scythe. Jacques tried to shout, but no sound came from his throat. The blow fell across Briac's upper right arm, slicing the woollen tunic just below his mail shoulder-piece.

But this cunning assault was to no avail. The other guards had been whipped into equal fury by Briac's example. The tall knight seemed to sense defeat and roared a command to withdraw. Then, as one, the attackers beat a slithering retreat as quickly as they had appeared.

The pressure lifted from Jacques' shoulders. He pushed himself up from the mud, and was relieved to see Nicolas beyond him doing the same. Rain still fell in sheets, and he stumbled in the slippery ruts in the road. One of the guards was examining the cart's transom and front axle. Two of Briac's men were shouldering Pietro di Ocre towards the wagon.

'They wounded me, the bastards!' Briac shouted as he came across to Jacques. His sleeve was red with blood that washed over his hands with the rain and then dripped onto the mud beneath; but he ignored the wound. 'I'll have them for that, sooner or later.' He ran out of breath, stood firm with hands on hips, and looked around the scene nonchalantly. 'You are both unhurt, I see.'

Nicolas brushed mud from his cloak and the sleeves of his tunic. 'They were rough, but clumsy,' he observed, 'like boys.' He smiled at the thought of the rough-and-tumbling scuffles of his own childhood in the fields near Lirey and pushed his clotted hair back over his head.

Jacques was not so sure. A sharp pain in his back made him want to stretch out in the mud again for relief. As far as he was concerned, the struggle had been for real. Briac's wound was no boy's prank. Yet he was amused to realize that the guard was offended by the notion that these attackers had dared to wound him, rather than suffering from the pain of the injury itself. He tried to humour him: 'Have they gone for good?'

'For their own good, by God's blood, I hope so.'

'The preceptor?'

Briac laughed. 'No harm there. Perhaps a little shock will do him good.' A huge wink threatened to split the great scar down his face. 'We'd better find shelter soon. The wagon's finished too, so our prisoner will have to face the rain.' That thought seemed to warm him.

Jacques looked at the wagon, which sagged forwards where the metal pin holding transom to perch had snapped under duress. The front axle now curved towards the earth. Then a new thought struck him. 'Any idea who they were, Briac?'

'Peasant levies, by the look of them,' Nicolas remarked.

'Not this time, sire.' Briac glared at him, with barely disguised contempt in his eyes. 'They were dressed like levies. On that score you're right. But they fought like knights.'

'Boys, more like it!'

'Knights, as sure as I stand here,' Briac asserted with finality, 'with all respect, Sire Nicolas.' He stood firm while one of his guards tied cloth round the gaping wound in his forearm. He turned away from Nicolas with evident distaste. 'I wouldn't swear to it, Brother Jacques,' he whispered, 'but I reckon I've seen their leader before. In Paris.'

Nicolas looked down, so that his curling lips were invisible to the others. How could Briac challenge the judgement and knowledge of fighting technique of a knight's son? But he said nothing.

The tension between them seemed to cut a swathe of silence through the rain. Jacques thought of Solomon's dilemma. 'That's a tall claim,' he said carefully. Yet he too had sensed something familiar in the man's stance. And the mission was vital. He looked at Nicolas, and saw that his anger was subsiding; then towards Briac, a slight smile on his face as he realized that his own adjective had prompted his thought: 'You mean the tall one?'

'That's your man!' Briac looked at Jacques with surprise which quickly changed into respect. 'What's more, I wouldn't mind betting that he's one of King Philip's soldiers.'

'The King?' Jacques' voice registered astonishment. This really was an absurd suggestion. Perhaps his wound was affecting Briac more than the guard believed or showed?

But Briac insisted: 'I'd bet on it,' he said forcefully. Then he pushed the guard away as the rough field-dressing was finished.

'The King tried to kidnap Pietro di Ocre?' Jacques forgot the rain for a moment, and thought aloud as if Briac were not there with him. He turned towards Nicolas.

'But he doesn't want us to know that he was behind the attempt.' Nicolas reluctantly spoke his thoughts aloud. It was all beginning to make sense, since they were carrying neither treasure nor merchandise – just Pietro di Ocre. Then perhaps Briac was right, and he *had* been fooled by the disguises. He himself had been hasty in his judgement of Briac: a churl, yes, but a brave man and a good soldier. 'We were supposed to think they were local robbers,' he said slowly.

Both Jacques and Briac stared at him, but it was the inquisitor who spoke: 'Which in turn means that King Philip must be well informed of our movements.'

'I dare say he is.' Briac still spoke quietly so that his men would not hear, and glanced towards Nicolas as he spoke.

Brother Jacques followed his gaze. Could it be? Jacques thought that while Nicolas had certainly spied for Bernard de Caen he would not do so for the King of France, the man who had appropriated Nicolas' birthright. Yet someone had. He turned back to Briac. 'How many of you are wounded?'

'Just two, and myself. Nothing serious, though by Saint Sebastian I shan't be able to wield my sword again for a week or two.' He feinted with his arm as if in battle, watching his own hand with the curiosity of a baby who had just discovered it, but experience soon gained sway and he looked straight into the rain. 'We'd best find shelter soon,' he suggested.

'You're right. We must leave at once.' Jacques began to move towards his horse.

'Brother Jacques . . .'

The voice was soft, but tense. The inquisitor turned back sharply.

'If they'd been using their own weapons, we'd never have beaten them off.'

There was no fear in Briac's voice; but a quiet certainty which was even more disturbing. There was nothing to be said in reply, just a silent mutual recognition of the magnitude of their task and a quiet shared moment of apprehension. Jacques glanced at Nicolas, and saw that he agreed this time, then he moved quickly towards his horse, assured by this reinforced trust.

They travelled forwards cautiously, cowls thrown back to increase their field of vision. The rain was now only a minor evil. Beyond the next bend in the river Jacques could see a hamlet on the opposite bank and, almost imperceptibly, they increased their speed in longing for the succour and warmth of a roof.

Jacques peered ahead between a line of willows which partially shielded the banks. The river raced through the village like a mountain torrent in spring. Thank heaven for the bridge, he thought; without one we'd never make it. He spurred his horse towards the willows.

Jacques' horse drew up sharply at the bank of its own accord. Sheet rain beat against his face, distorting his vision. He pulled a sleeve across his eyes and then held it against his forehead to maintain a clear field. His heart sank.

The bridge was gone.

He dismounted, still with one arm across his forehead, and stared in disbelief. There was no other half of the bridge: just what had been visible from the road a hundred paces away. At his feet a vault began a lazy arc towards the village, but it came to an abrupt end after no more than two paces, to be replaced by eddying foam and spray. He could sense Nicolas behind him but willed himself not to turn. This was a delusion he preferred to keep private. He stared ahead, the dizzying movement of the water hypnotizing him.

Beyond lay the village – fires and broth. Suddenly the newly kindled warmth within Jacques vanished, and the damp penetrated to his soul. Purple streaks appeared on the backs of his red hands; his cowl was pressed chill and sodden against his cheeks. His feet squelched as he turned away from the river. He looked into Nicolas' dark, forlorn face and those of the others beyond. But there was nothing to say.

They trudged back to the main track. It seemed to Jacques, walking beside his horse with Nicolas, that the mud grew thicker with each step – as if they were entering some hellish quagmire. The wind now drove the pelting rain into his face, stinging it into numbness. Pietro was better off lashed to a pack-horse with his head facing the earth, he thought ironically. They walked slowly in a huddled group for a full hour before they came to the next sign of habitation, a simple farmhouse set on a rising slope beyond the grey sheets of flooded field. Night was beginning to fall, so that there was no choice but to turn from the road to beg shelter.

The farmer came out as they approached. He was dressed in a mantle and floppy felt hat, and brandished a huge club studded with nails. Jacques understood not a single word when he addressed him. He turned to Briac for help, but he seemed equally baffled. Then Nicolas stepped forward and spoke quickly in the same guttural tongue. 'He wants to know who we are and where we're bound.'

'Tell him; you've no need for my authority,' Jacques said lightly. He recalled that Nicolas' family had once had lands in Burgundy.

As Nicolas spoke to the farmer again, Briac drew closer to Jacques. 'Look at that belt,' he whispered; 'there's more knives in it than I've got fingers. I shouldn't want to meddle with the man.'

Jacques regarded the guard with amusement. Apart from the obvious hyperbole, it was difficult to imagine Briac suffering fear of anybody.

Then Nicolas turned to them again. 'His name is Rollanz,' he explained. 'He's not very happy about giving us shelter, but he's a good enough man. He says the corn shed is full, but that Briac and the guards can sleep in the hay barn behind the house. We will be guests in his house.' He spoke the last sentence with marked lack of enthusiasm. There was nothing he desired less than to be the guest of such a man.

'Better than a muddy field,' Jacques reminded him. His companion's feelings were not hard to understand.

The farmer had walked towards them while they conversed. 'You will stay with us,' he said to Jacques. He now spoke slowly and clearly in French, making sure the friar understood by illustrating his words with vigorous gestures as if talking to a child. 'You can give us the news,' he added.

A rickety external staircase led up to the family quarters above the stables. Rollanz beckoned them inside. He sat at the table in the middle of the room and motioned Jacques and Nicolas to sit opposite him as he poured mead from one of the jugs. Briac had joined them for supper, and sat quietly at the other end of the table. Rollanz' wife spread their sodden clothes over the cooking range beside the fire.

Jacques drank the mead. It was foul-tasting, as if made without honey. He smiled politely at the farmer.

A young girl emerged from the darkness and placed a slab of unleavened bread at each place. Then the farmer's wife ladled thick soup from the cauldron onto the slabs until it spilled onto the table. Jacques sniffed the food in front of him, conscious of the farmer's gaze as he did so. This time he failed to stifle a grimace.

177

'It's Lent,' Rollanz said. Then he looked at his own *tranchoir*. The explanation seemed to satisfy him.

It stank. Everything left over in the larder had been thrown into the cauldron; pieces of rancid cheese and other unidentifiable flotsam floated in the soup. Jacques thought of the smoked back of tuna and salted herring which were the lenten staple with the Black Friars. Even his mother had been able to buy dried herring when the travelling salters from Bordeaux passed through the village.

He tried to ignore the taste and smell of the food. He noticed that even Briac ate little, concentrating his attention on the mead which Rollanz poured for him liberally. As they ate, the girl placed the remains of what looked like roast chicken on the table between Rollanz and Jacques. Then she brought some pieces of darker meat and set them down.

He watched her intently, ruefully recalling the girl in Milan. She was shapely and inviting.

Then he saw Nicolas grimace at the food in front of him.

Rollanz noticed too. 'Widgeon,' he said grumpily.

'In Lent?'

'Comes from water,' Rollanz stated flatly.

Jacques answered automatically. 'But it's a bird all the same.'

'As sure as I'm a man. But the Lord said that fish and fowl were created together. So it's a fish too.'

'A bird cannot be a fish. That's absurd.'

'The Bible says so. And that's good enough for me. These are things we country folk know. This kind of duck is a kind of fish. So we can eat it in Lent and pray to Our Lord.'

Jacques laughed openly for the first time in weeks. 'That's strange reasoning,' he said. The logic of it amused him.

'You learned men talk of reason,' Rollanz said. He could not keep the scorn from his voice. 'But we know what's what. These small ducks are not like other fowl. They're born in water. If you leave a rotting boat in the river, you'll have widgeon before you know it. That's a fact as true as that I sit here.' There was a note of finality in his voice which discouraged further argument. He licked the leg bones clean noisily.

The room was now entirely full of smoke and steam, so that it seemed like the forge at Mirepoix. Jacques laughed within at the incredulity and superstition of these peasants. He forced himself to drink the mead in order to wash the taste of wood smoke from his mouth.

When they had finished, Briac stood up to take his leave.

178

Jacques drew him close. 'Remember,' he said softly in *langue d'oc*, 'you might have to eat like this for ever. But you might also become an officer. It's up to you.' He stopped to see the effect. Briac's craggy face burst into a happy smile. 'Now take care of Pietro!'

'Don't worry. You have a good rest. We'll guard him,' he assured Jacques.

Jacques and Nicolas were led into a room behind the chimney. It was warm, and almost smoke-free. An immense high bed took up the entire space. They clambered across it to sleep beside the wall. Rollanz lay beside them, and then his wife and daughter. Two smaller girls and a shy-looking boy they had not seen before were soon stretched across the bottom of the bed like entangled tree roots.

The others soon slept, but Jacques lay awake thinking over the evening's conversation. It was many years since he had heard such nonsensical notions about water-fowl and fish. Yet even these things, he realized, were nothing compared with the superstitions of the great: kings who would not embark on a military campaign without a holy relic; knights who planned to conquer the Church with an image. Rollanz and his wife were no worse than the rich who went to astrologers for advice on when to build a palace or city, witches who sold love tokens, priests who sold consecrated hosts, and a bevy of heretics, magicians, conjurers and charlatans such as an honest man could never imagine. They were simpletons who knew no better. But there could be no excuse for such men as King Philip and Guillaume de Nogaret.

26

Paris seemed to Brother Jacques to be a city in readiness for war. Stone
flags rang with hoofs and iron-bound cartwheels, while the dialects of
provincial levies mingled with the babel of city life. Military barges
could be seen moored beneath the royal palace and squadrons of
knights cantered through the main thoroughfares, careless of the dust
their mounts kicked into the faces of vendors and shoppers. Alleys
near the market thronged with quartermasters and their clerks buying
provisions, while simulated campaigns were being enacted on the
training ground outside the royal barracks between Seine and Temple.
'Looks like a real battlefield,' he remarked to Briac as they passed by.

'Too well-organized,' Briac laughed, 'with spearmen and archers
under the Temple walls, and knights by the river. Too easy. On
the battlefield, Brother, it takes a master of strategy to see what's
what. Look at them by the river, in perfect formation. Wouldn't last
a minute!'

'But they'd charge in that formation . . .' Jacques had taken
advantage of a free morning to cement his alliance with Briac, and
was fascinated by this military information.

'Not nowadays. It'd never work. Six squadrons together would be
wasted on any ground . . .'

Jacques could see only four squadron pennoncelles, but assumed
Briac had other information. 'And the foot-soldiers?' he asked,
remembering those who had attacked them on the road.

'Knights can't fight without them any more. Since Courtrai the royal
army has used the Brabanter technique. With one of them polearms a
skilled man can bring down a knight as easy as a boy brings down a
conker with a stick.'

He could hardly have described his own fall into the mud better,
Jacques thought. 'So they're good men?'

'As good as can be found.' Briac paused, watching a fresh simulated
charge by the river banks. 'And word is they'll be in action before long.'

'Oh?' Jacques said, 'against . . .?' He let the question hang in the air.

The guard laughed again. '. . . the whole damned world, by the
sound of it.'

'Let us not exaggerate,' Jacques mocked him.

Briac turned sharply. 'It's no joking matter, Brother.' He lowered his voice as a group of soldiers passed them. 'They say envoys are being prepared at this very moment. The King's informed his allies of an imminent offensive. It looks like there'll be a summer campaign . . . though God knows where.'

Rome, Jacques thought to himself. A summer campaign. It was all too likely. He shuddered as if there had been a sudden drop in temperature. Just then the bells for terce begin ringing in the nearby Augustinian convent, and he realized it was time to hasten to King Philip's audience hall. The chagrin he had felt earlier at being excluded by protocol from the delivery of Pope Clement's letter was dissipated by his new knowledge.

27

As Brother Jacques entered the royal antechamber a shriek that seemed to come from the Devil himself froze waiting heralds, ushers and soldiers like a tableau in front of him. He lifted his body instinctively forward onto the balls of his feet, until the quiet susurration gathered in volume.

Men gaped at the painted and gilt double doors of the audience hall as if some drama were unfolding before them. Scenes of hunting and bucolic happiness contrasted sharply with tension that could have been sliced with a knife. 'I'm glad I'm not in there,' an elderly courtier remarked as Jacques moved towards the doors.

'The King?' an officer asked incredulously, 'was that the King?'

The courtier nodded. 'It's him all right,' he murmured. 'There's no other voice like it.' And then, feeling the puzzled gaze of a score of men burning into him: 'Though it's true he never shouts like that.'

Jacques shuddered again. Could the rage have been directed against Bernard de Caen?

A group of courtiers arrived, dressed in scarlet robes and mantles, and flat black velvet hats which seemed to add severity to their faces. They joined the throng of nobles and knights waiting there until it seemed the antechamber would burst. 'Who are these men?' Jacques whispered to the elderly courtier. He was furious at being excluded from the royal audience this time. Outranked in the presence of Nicolas de Lirey, who had been admitted to the audience.

'Court registrars and presidents,' he replied. 'There is to be a Seat of Justice this morning.'

At that moment a flurry of cloaks, swords and guards pushed into the surprised crowd. Jacques recognized the stern, ghostly face of Guillaume de Paris as it floated through the antechamber amidst his personal bodyguard: like a stray goat caught up with a flock of sheep, he thought irreverently. With mysterious promptitude, the double doors of the audience chamber opened.

Then they closed just as abruptly, engulfing the party. Jacques realized he had not even attempted to glance inside.

His eyes were drawn to the doors as if by the attraction of power within. But there was no hint of what happened behind in those pastoral scenes, and now no sound passed through them. He stared with the others, his eyes roaming almost of their own accord through the painted country lanes and rings of dancing peasant girls.

Within, the audience hall was thronged with courtiers, ushers, envoys, and the baillis, provosts and seneschals of the realm. When they arrived, Bernard de Caen and Nicolas de Lirey had been escorted to a distant, roped-off corner where those who awaited the royal summons were to stand. Then Nicolas had left Lord Bernard, and begun to forge a way nearer to the royal dais, so that he would be able to follow the audience better. He lifted his head high, and raised an arm imperiously before him; no one denied him passage.

The splendour of the hall dazzled him after months of dreary monasteries, wayside hostels and inquisitorial prisons. He had quite forgotten the joys of luxury and revelled in the touch of velvet and satin as dukes and princes passed him. Yet it also saddened him: for he could not forget that he had first come to this great hall as a young boy in the company of his father, when he had been literally spellbound by the display of gold and silver. There, amidst it all now as then, was the canopied throne: set on its raised dais and draped with rich crimson cloth studded with pearls, it was protected by a silk canopy like the open marquees set up at a tournament. The red velvet border of the canopy was embroidered at intervals with the arms of the House of Capet, and beneath the border was a fringe of gold cloth shimmering in bright sunlight. His eyes absorbed it all, halting at each detail as if his father's voice were still guiding him.

Now, however, the elegance and luxury was tarnished by a feeling of palpable apprehension in the perfumed air. Knights renowned for their dash and daring appeared curiously muffled as they sought to stand back from the royal dais when once they would have pushed forwards. Ruffed and embroidered hoods on the gowns were dross amongst such tense expectation. It was only the younger fops, apparently unaware of the political scythe which was about to cut through the hall, who vied with each other to show off their new garments: for the most part loose scarlet or royal blue cloth blouses, with the latest slits down the side to reveal fur and satin linings. As alike as herons in the marsh. Was it the drama of the occasion, Nicolas reflected, or the changes that were taking place within him that made the display of brocade slippers with their fashionable curling Polish points look so silly to him? And the flat caps with a short hood behind. The most dramatic of them flared over the shoulders like a cockscomb. Once he had envied these wealthy scions of great families; today they were absurdly out of place. As Brother Jacques would be in such a setting, he thought complacently.

A flourish of trumpets awakened him from his reverie. It began amidst the noise of a hundred babbling voices, and ended in a quiet whisper. Nicolas looked up. Even the horses and hounds of the hunt in immense tapestries suspended along the walls of the hall seemed to pay their respect as the sound of the bugle reverberated over the brightly painted and gilt wooden barrel vault.

Then a single trumpet sounded a sennet. Now the hush was total. Elderly courtiers near the dais with the Constable and Chamberlain kneeled in homage. At the back of the hall, where there was no space, men doffed their caps and bowed their heads forward as best they could.

Six halberdiers as tall as any men Nicolas had ever seen formed a kind of cage within which King Philip of France entered his audience hall. A far cry from the time he entered alone or with Queen Joanne on his arm, he mused with a profound feeling of contempt for these 'new' knights.

As soon as he was seated on his throne, the king summoned an usher, who passed on his instructions to a herald standing at the back of the dais. 'Lord Bernard de Caen, Envoy to His Holiness Pope Clement,' he announced so that everyone in the vast hall could hear. There was clearly no time to be lost.

Nicolas fancied he saw the king snarl as Lord Bernard moved forwards, head inclined so that his double chin nearly rested on his chest. It was impossible to distinguish the few words which they exchanged, even in that silence. He watched as Bernard de Caen passed the scroll to His Majesty.

Still leaning on the arm of his throne, King Philip opened the scroll and turned away to read it as Bernard stepped back the required three paces. Nicolas noticed his instinctive obedience of court procedures with pleasure. So many men nowadays were incapable of following the simplest rules which were ingrained in a real French nobleman from birth until they were – as natural as kneading dough to a baker's son. He smiled wryly to himself as he thought of Brother Jacques outside.

Then to Nicolas' astonishment King Philip stood up and surveyed the noblemen beneath him. 'What is this?' he shouted. 'Does His Holiness pretend to rule in France? To dictate policy to the descendant of Hugh Capet and Philip Augustus? The grandson of St Louis. What is this impertinence?' He paused, and seemed to relish the ripple of grave and noble nodding heads which passed through the hall. 'We understand, of course, that the Brothers of the Temple are dearly-beloved by the Keeper of St Peter's keys, and it is no wish of ours to offend the Holy Church. But these men have been found guilty of the most abominable heresies. There *will* be a trial. What is more . . .' again he paused and looked round the hall as if seeking opposition to hurl his wrath upon. Then he rose to his full height, pointed his right arm directly at Lord Bernard, and shouted in a voice that sent tremors through Nicolas' body: 'At once!'

Lord Bernard bowed and began his slow, backward progress from the royal dais to his place amidst the courtiers. Nicolas could hear his shuffling slippers as if their bearer were stepping through an empty chapel. Courtiers and ushers around him seemed frozen into statues, their elegance stripped away to reveal the fear-stricken men beneath.

Nicolas continued to watch as Bernard joined a prelate whom he recognised as the Archbishop of Sens, notoriously the king's pawn. He stared as the two men huddled together in urgent conversation, and wondered what on earth the Inquisitor-General for Provence could have to say to such a man.

The king again beckoned an usher forward and whispered to him. The man hastened across the dais, and in turn whispered to the herald. 'Lord Guillaume de Nogaret!' he called.

Nicolas watched as the Keeper of the Seals came forward. 'Well, my lord? It is now months since your promise should have been redeemed.'

De Nogaret bowed. 'We are close, Your Majesty, and our officers in Italy are carrying out their researches diligently. It is only a matter of time, perhaps weeks.'

'Weeks! That's far too long. I must have results immediately. We must move before the summer.' Philip's voice was rising to such a pitch that nervousness began to spread through the crowded hall. 'Who is in charge of this operation?'

De Nogaret turned towards the huddled officers, seeking his man. 'Essart! Present yourself to His Majesty King Philip. At once!'

Nicolas watched as one of the king's officers shuffled forward nervously, head bowed. When he rose to his full height Nicolas saw that he was a tall, finely built man with a touch of noble breeding in his thin face and delicate Roman nose. He wore a tightly fitting hood which covered both hair and ears, but the carefully trimmed goatee on his chin was mottled with grey patches suggesting age and hence years of service. He was dressed in an under-tunic with no signs of office, and the scabbard on his broad leather belt was empty. His face was stricken with fear.

'You are Essart?' King Philip asked loudly so that all could hear. He spat the name like an angry viper, with venom in each syllable. The king's face seemed to light up like an oil lamp, pale skin turning flame red as another thought came to him. 'Well?' he shouted, 'did you find it?'

'Find it, Your Majesty?'

'The image, seneschal, the image you were sent to find.'

'No, Your Majesty. It was an impossible task.' The man bowed his head gravely. Nicolas warmed to him, for he knew the king's wrath and feared the worst.

There was not long to wait. 'What? Impossible?' the king roared. 'Months of time and enormous expense, and all I get is "no, Your Majesty"!' He mimicked Essart maliciously. 'How dare you address me thus?' The royal fury was growing apace. King Philip turned to an officer near the throne. 'Hang the man, damn him, have him and his insolence silenced at once,' he shrieked.

'I did my best, and, with Your Majesty's leave, believe no man could have done better,' Essart protested.

'Insolence upon insolence!' the king roared. 'Take him away at once!' His arms were shaking violently.

Guards moved forwards to obey the royal command. Nicolas expected the king's rage to silence the man. But it had the opposite effect. He looked up proudly and shouted back, now careless of his own life. 'How in the name of hell do you expect me to find something when I don't even know what it looks like? Hang me if you will, sire, but I go to my grave with a clear Christian conscience.'

'Be silent, scum!' The King's entire body shook as he emphasized the last word. He waved his arm, and turned away.

At least he won't be hanged after all, Nicolas reflected with pleasure. There was reason behind his insolence, and King Philip knew it. That was why he shifted from threat to insult; even he could not sentence a man thus in front of his entire court.

'Your Highness,' the poor man replied, in a last plea, 'there was little alternative.' Nicolas de Lirey felt for the officer, thinking of the humiliation his own father must have suffered many years before. It was almost unbearable to watch the trembling figure.

'You may consider yourself dismissed from the royal service,' the King intoned. Then he screwed his face into a hellish grin and shrieked at the top of his voice: 'Dismissed! Finished.' He turned away as Essart left, as if to gaze on the more pleasant sight of obedient courtiers.

It was so easy. So quick. Like a noose. Nicolas prayed for his father.

But King Philip had not finished. He now summoned de Nogaret forward. The Keeper of the Seals obeyed with a slight hesitancy in his normally arrogant gait, not quite managing to hide a reluctance which seemed evident to Nicolas. He looked curiously hindered by the black bell-shaped cloak which he always wore, with its slit right side thrown over his arm, and the tippet-shaped ermine collar which the power-seeking young lawyers of Paris emulated. From behind, his beaked nose issued from his thick hair as if he sought comfort from his fellow nobles: like a cock searching for grain around him, Nicolas thought irreverently. He was clearly uncomfortable in this public questioning, where his own responsibility could be less easily disguised than in the private chambers and closets of the royal palace.

'Well?' the King asked simply, but with a ferocity which struck fear into all present. 'When will this relic be found?' Then he stood again. His pallid cheeks turned crimson as the velvet collars of his courtiers; he stretched both arms forward with his palms open towards de Nogaret and began to shake as if all control of his body was lost. For once, Nicolas felt sympathy for the Keeper, who stood before his monarch and long-time protector, with his prominent lower lip trembling, like a truant brought before his tutor. 'You, Guillaume de Nogaret, whom I have trusted as my own brother, are proving yourself as incompetent as the others!'

Then, as if his wrath had subsided, King Philip returned to his throne. Colour drained from his face, and he sat there as quietly as if what had happened were a routine audience. Yet there was a tension beneath his placidity which threatened every man in the room. No one dared to speak.

187

It was at that moment that the entrance doors were thrown back, and a party of men entered.

All heads turned, and strained to see who the new arrivals were. Tension was replaced by native curiosity. For no one would dare make such an entry without a royal command.

Above the hubbub Nicolas heard the herald's voice. 'Guillaume de Paris requests permission to approach the throne of His Majesty King Philip of France,' he announced gravely.

All eyes turned to King Philip, who had sunk back onto his throne. The danger was passed, and the Inquisitor-General for the Province of France came forward.

There was not a trace of fear in him. If anything, his stance as he stood before the royal dais was more haughty than Nicolas had noticed before. Moreover, his usually white and pudgy face was burned as red as that of a serf, as if he had spent weeks in the saddle. Now where had *he* been?

He stood in bleak contrast to his surroundings in a plain black Dominican mantle. When he spoke, his words sounded clearly with overweening pride evident in the emphasis he placed on every word. 'Your Majesty,' he began, ensuring that everyone would hear him, 'we have located the image you seek.'

There was a stunned silence.

'Information has arrived posthaste from my agents in Italy that it is to be found not far distant from Rome. Furthermore, from sources within the Holy Roman Church before Our Lord Clement wisely decided to accept Your Majesty's protection . . .'

Nicolas noticed that Guillaume de Paris turned more than once in his pride to gaze upon the Keeper of the Seals. He wondered what ancient vendetta must lie between two arrogant men who had served the king together for so many years, yet it was hard to feel sympathy for de Nogaret for long.

'. . . we have learned that it is indeed a most sacred relic that has been kept in great secrecy and safety since the day of Our Saviour's crucifixion.'

'The image of Our Saviour Jesus Christ.' King Philip spoke the words softly, with the intonation of a prayer, but strongly enough for Nicolas to hear them fall into that shocked silence. Now it was public knowledge and events would run fast.

This time it was Guillaume de Paris who looked surprised, as if he had hoped to announce something unknown to his sovereign. Yet with a grandfather like St Louis and a lifelong interest in the relics of the Sainte Chapelle which he built to house his collection, it was no marvel that Philip the Fair should have this information.

What did stun Nicolas was the King's next action. He motioned to Guillaume to stand aside, and sent an usher towards the corner of the room again. To Nicholas' astonishment, it was Bernard de Caen who was led to the royal dais. He was summoned forward to the throne and bent to listen to King Philip's words. The heads of the two men were as close as lovers, incongruously, Nicolas thought, as if cold anger had been miraculously transformed into affection. It bespoke evil, he surmised at first. But then he recalled Bernard's loyalty to his father. Surely he could not be the king's ally? There must be a good reason for these confidences, and sooner or later Nicolas would know what was behind it. His musings were interrupted as Bernard left, as suddenly as he had arrived.

When the Inquisitor-General for Provence had returned to the roped-off area, King Philip beckoned Guillaume de Paris to move forward again. 'Why have we heard nothing of this before? It's seven years that you have had them,' he said, once more addressing the entire hall.

'We discovered the truth from the Templars, Your Majesty. The "head" which appears in our records so often, and which they were said to worship most blasphemously, was believed by them to be the original of this image.'

King Philip passed over the extraordinary deduction which could be made from this statement, to Nicolas' surprise, but there were obviously other things on his mind. Heresy was Guillaume de Paris' realm. 'The Templars! After seven years! Why has it taken you so long to discover this secret? They are only human.' Unlike me, he seemed to assert.

'It is easier to draw blood from a stone, Your Majesty, than to get information from the Temple.' There was a sneer of pleasure in Guillaume's words, as though he looked forward to that evening's events with particular delight. 'But we have succeeded at last.'

The shrill voice of the king froze every man in the hall. 'Then burn them! Damn them! I've had enough of these accursed Templars. They will be burned tonight! Go to it!'

With a wave of his hand, King Philip announced the end of the audience. He looked out onto the sea of courtiers, then turned and left the dais. As he disappeared towards his private apartments, Nicolas heard the sharp tones of his voice, as if he were issuing orders to his officers.

Then the king was gone.

Behind him, in the antechamber, Brother Jacques noticed whispers gradually rising again into a murmur which reverberated through the vaults. Shouts from grooms in the courtyard punctuated this constant hum. Tension began to rise again, as though the intention of the men within the audience chamber to leave the hall was somehow transmitted to the antechamber.

With uncanny timing the doors burst open. It seemed for an odd and irrational moment that events within were being conditioned by those outside. Suddenly there was a single concourse of humanity as courtiers spilled out like beans from an upturned sack. Brother Jacques turned shoulders-on and stretched one leg behind him to serve as a buttress against the crush.

Amongst the courtiers was Bernard de Caen, deep in conversation with a silver-haired prelate whom Jacques did not recognize. He tried to push forward towards them. 'Lord Bernard! Lord Bernard!' he called earnestly.

The Inquisitor-General turned, saw him, but did not stop. For an instant he felt Bernard's gaze upon him, those green eyes penetrating his innermost thoughts as they had during his first interview. Then, without waiting for Jacques to reach his side, the rotund figure seemed to roll its way through the crowded antechamber arm in arm with the Archbishop.

Next Jacques saw Nicolas de Lirey, his forearm held in front of him like a shield and his head aloof from the crowd pressing in on him. With apparent ease Nicolas cut a narrow but sufficient passage in the wake of Bernard de Caen.

Jacques imitated the technique, though he realized that he lacked the haughty carriage of his secular companion. But it worked anyway, and he quickly found himself face to face with Nicolas. 'Any news?' he snapped. Anger at his exclusion still smouldered within.

'The Templars are for the stake.'

'At once?'

'This very night.'

They were pressed together like salted herrings in a basket. 'Did His Majesty make a decision in our regard?' Jacques then asked grumpily. The inevitable fate of the Templar knights had only been a matter of time.

'We can't keep the Archbishop of Sens waiting,' Nicolas snapped impatiently. He lifted his forearm higher and disappeared amidst a flurry of velvet caps. The old haughtiness had returned again.

Jacques was cut to the quick, for it was Bernard himself who had ordered him to be in the antechamber. 'Wait for me. There is much work to be done,' his Superior had insisted; and Nicolas de Lirey had assured him they would leave the royal palace together. Yet there could be no doubt where Nicolas' fundamental loyalty lay – and this rebuff was proof of it. Furthermore, now that he thought about it, the uncharacteristically friendly greeting he had been granted by Lord Bernard on his arrival in Paris was in itself suspect.

Something as big as a door and hard as granite collided with his back. Jacques was stunned, and found himself being carried towards the exit with the crowd. But a fresh realization came to him even as he was buffeted through the main doors and, as soon as he found space outside to step aside from the flux, he bent his head amidst the chaos and asked forgiveness for his selfishness. For, he had realized with the shock, the Archbishop of Sens was the prelate who had condemned the fifty-four Templars to the stake. And now his own Superior, whose avowed task in Paris was to thwart the King's plan to destroy the Order of the Temple, was publicly flaunting his intimacy with the very man who had accelerated the trials.

As Jacques stood transfixed in thought, an officer in royal livery thrust his way past. The man's eyes were fixed in front of him, yet something about his dark face and long, confident strides jogged Jacques' memory. He studied the officer, who was unusually tall, trying to place him.

Jacques felt a heavy hand on his shoulder and flinched, certain for an instant that a sinister destiny had caught up with him, that his omniscient Superior had sensed his scepticism. He forgot the officer, who had now vanished into the throng. In the same brief time, the attacks at Ocre and on the road to Paris flashed before his inner eye, and he wished Briac were there.

He turned to meet his nemesis.

'Good Brother Jacques!' An unsmiling face greeted him.

Jacques had so feared arrest or death that the man's voice seemed meant for another. He glanced quickly around. There was no doubt that the soldier was addressing *him*. Then he relaxed, and recognition came: 'Renaud!' he exclaimed with genuine joy.

'Do I look like a ghost?' the seneschal laughed. He doffed his cap and then opened his ermine-trimmed cloak with both hands. 'Good solid flesh,' he chuckled as he beat his chest, 'and a friend of yours to boot.'

Jacques willed himself to smile, but as he looked over his erstwhile boon companion he sensed a certain nervousness in the man, as if the seneschal were clinging to the inquisitor in desperation. There was sadness in his eyes, but his behaviour allayed Jacques' fears.

Renaud slapped Jacques' shoulder heartily. 'Let us walk and talk, Brother. I've not had such good conversation since last you were in Paris.'

It had been a monologue rather than a conversation, Jacques recalled, and marvelled that Renaud remembered him at all. But he was glad enough of the company, since Renaud would be able to give him all the details of what had happened in the audience chamber, which Nicolas' brusque dismissal had failed to supply.

They were borne by the flow of courtiers and soldiers until they were able to turn away and cross the river towards the Temple; then they walked upstream opposite the royal buildings and the Sainte Chapelle. The newly built Louvre Palace rose in front of them. Late winter sunshine took the chill from the air, and the river shimmered beyond silhouettes of fishermen. The high water level showed that heavy rains continued south of the city.

At the last island, which cut into the fast-running current like the bows of a ship, they paused and looked across the river together. Upstream from the cluster of buildings forming the Augustinian convent was a lateral ditch connecting the two branches of the Seine. Beyond that was a triangular piece of land with neither buildings nor cultivation. Workmen were driving stakes into the ground, while others unloaded faggots from an ox-wagon and threw them across the ditch. 'Good men will die here tonight,' Essart commented.

'Shall we pray for their souls?' Jacques suggested without particular interest in the seneschal's words. It seemed the right thing to say.

They entered a nearby church. When they had knelt together at the high altar Jacques prayed for the soul of St Germain, for whom the church was named, and for St Genevieve, the patron saint of the city. Then he began to consider the unknown condemned men but, almost without knowing it, he found himself asking forgiveness of St

192

Bernard, whose Rule he was transgressing in his present activity. At the same time he told himself that the Founder had been a knight by birth, and had condoned the killing of infidels by warrior-monks in the service of the Church: the Knights Templar.

Then he understood.

'Seneschal?' He was aware of a tremor of anxiety in his companion which Renaud could not disguise. 'What is the name of this place?'

'The Ile-des-Javiaux, Brother.'

'Those stakes. The *good* men you mentioned. Who are they?'

Renaud smiled wryly. 'Still want to pray for them, do you? It's too late to save 'em, I'm afraid.'

'But who are they?' Jacques spoke slowly, fearing the answer.

'You must be the only man in Paris who doesn't know,' the seneschal laughed. 'The Master of the Temple and his preceptors.'

'So *that* was the cause of the king's anger?'

'The consequence,' Renaud corrected him.

Jacques looked sharply at the seneschal, realizing with a shock of annoyance at his own blindness that Renaud was suffering some unspoken stress. 'Something very strange must have happened,' he observed, questioningly.

The seneschal nodded agreement; although he said nothing, Jacques felt a new communion between them. They stood as if by a prearranged signal and walked towards the door. Jacques felt Renaud's intense scrutiny, but didn't return his gaze. Then he felt light pressure on his arm. 'Are you like the others, Brother Jacques, or can I trust you?'

'As if you were in the confessional.' Jacques turned to face the seneschal. There was bitterness deep within the man. Anger and uncertainty. But also a bursting need to explain. 'Tell me,' he said; 'you can trust me.'

His words seemed to soothe Renaud, who sighed deeply. 'I've been in the royal service for nigh twenty years,' he began in a heavy voice, 'and I've always admired the King. I've seen him grow from a near-novice into the ambitious man he now is. The last few years I've been especially close to him, working on missions that very few members of the royal guard are allowed to be on . . .' He looked anxiously at Jacques. 'You will understand that these things must not go beyond these walls, of course, that I would not talk like this to anyone, by St Sebastian, except a friar and fellow countryman . . .'

193

Jacques was certain that the floodgates were open, and that, with careful coaxing, the questions which plagued his mind would be answered. 'Shall we sit down?' he suggested, indicating a stone bench beside the church door. This might take a long time, and they were safe there. Some canons of the collegiate church passed them, but paid them no attention. In these days a royal officer and a friar were common enough company.

'I've been dismissed from my post,' Renaud announced baldly.

'What on earth for?' Jacques was more interested in the details of the day's events, but felt an instinctive sympathy for the evident suffering of his one-time companion.

'That damned relic,' Renaud said absentmindedly. 'I should've known it would come to no good. But that's how it is, good Brother. Had I found it, I would have been smothered with riches. But I didn't. And here I am out of a job after twenty years.' Then, as an afterthought, he said, 'Mind you, I wasn't the only one. I just happened to be there when His Majesty lost his temper. Never seen such a thing in twenty years of service, I haven't. But that's what you must expect in royal service: riches one day, and head in a noose the next.'

The hyperbolic reference to two extremes Renaud had never known amused Jacques. But now he was genuinely interested. 'Tell me how it happened, Seneschal.'

'There I was in the audience hall, standing quietly and minding my own business, when I hear my name called out: "Messire Renaud Essart, Seneschal of Toulouse". It was Lord de Nogaret. He looked at me apologetically when I moved forward. But even I could see that he had no choice.

'"Are you Essart?" the King demanded. I was trembling from head to foot. "You are the officer responsible for the search?"

'"Your Majesty," I replied. I bowed as low as I could. What else could I do?

'"But the image has not been found. You may leave, Seneschal," the King said. "You are finished." God only knows what *image* he was talking about. I've no idea myself after all this time.

'Anyway, "Your Majesty," I replied. And bowed. I've seen it happen before, Brother, and I've known the king long enough to understand there was only one thing to do. I bowed lower still and retreated from the dais. Lucky to be alive.' He touched his throat with forefinger and thumb. 'Men have lost their heads for less,' he added laconically, 'but

194

it's odd to think that I am no longer an officer of the King . . . that there is no need to return to Toulouse.'

'Where will you go?'

'Well, I had half an idea,' Renaud said awkwardly. It was clear he did not wish to go any further.

'I may be able to help you,' Jacques suggested. 'I must leave now, but would be pleased to see you this evening, after nones. Here at Saint-Germain-l'Auxerrois?'

Renaud beamed. 'You're a good man for a friar, Brother Jacques, and I'll be here, and we'll pray together for the souls of these good knights.'

Without another word, the ex-seneschal set off at a brisk pace towards the Temple. For a while Jacques followed him, barely able to keep up. He noticed that workmen on the small island were beginning to pile faggots at the base of the stakes. He was glad when the moment came to turn away across the river.

Now the King was close. Although Essart had not mentioned the name, and perhaps King Philip himself would not have pronounced it openly, the image *must* be the same as that of Ocre, the goal of his and Nicolas' quest.

Half-way across the bridge, a further thought caused Jacques to come to a halt: the face in the antechamber. The tall, dark-skinned officer who stepped so arrogantly through the hall had been present both in Ocre and in Burgundy. It had been difficult to recognize him in court dress, but there was no doubt. It was he, unshaven and dressed like the others, who had led the shepherds attacking them at San Eusanio; and again in the storm. So the King's men were *very* close, and had been following him for weeks. Yet at the same time this intelligence was reassuring, since it meant that they knew no more than he did.

And Jacques needed reassurance.

On the road to Paris it had seemed to him that the questions were beginning to transform themselves into answers and that the end of his mission was nearing. But now there were new questions, of a type he would never have dared to ask six months ago. Why had Bernard de Caen remained in the royal audience hall on that occasion after his diplomatic mission was accomplished? And above all, why should he, rather than any other of the prelates and officers present in the hall, have been called to the royal dais after Guillaume de Paris' news? What could be his connection with the information about the image? Had he known all along? Why was he apparently acting against the interests of Pope Clement? Jacques knew that he would have to ponder these matters in greater peace.

But time was short.

And there was no peace for, to his surprise, Nicolas de Lirey was waiting in the Cistercian house. 'I expected you to be here already when I returned,' he said sharply.

For once, Jacques ignored him. This was no time to play up to his companion's sense of superiority. 'I learn that the King was furious.'

Nicolas looked up. 'Learned? Or heard from the door?'

'Learned,' Jacques said firmly. Now he too would play the diplomatic game, and had no desire to be lorded over by Nicolas. 'I too have my sources.' He turned to drink from a bowl on the table.

'Indeed, my Lord Abbot,' Nicolas said softly.

Jacques spun on his feet. 'How did you find out?'

'Is it a secret?'

'No, I suppose it isn't.' It was such a new role that Jacques had not yet adjusted to it.

'Well, now you're not so nervous about it, let me offer my congratulations.' He paused, and smiled sincerely at Jacques: 'Abbot of Fontfroide ... it sounds well.' And improves your status, he thought to himself. To be the friend of an abbot was better than associating with a mere Cistercian monk, and an inquisitor to boot. Nicolas was filled with a spontaneous desire to bolster the new abbot's confidence. 'Our Lord Bernard was most proud of his decision, and of Pope Clement's agreement.'

Jacques drank again, gaining time. 'Proud of me?' The words slipped out, quiet but firm, as he placed the bowl back on the table. He thought of his curt dismissal in the antechamber. And even the moment of the announcement earlier. Was he imagining things, or had there had been an expression not distant from contempt in Bernard's eye as he gave the news about Fontfroide? If so, then he had been wrong to gloat over his elevation to an abbacy. It occurred to him that it was no real prize but, rather, a titbit thrown to him to encourage him in his mission. What, after all, was an abbey against the risk of losing control of the Church? Jacques began to walk away. He needed peace to reflect, not conversation.

But Nicolas continued: 'Will you attend the Seat of Justice?' he asked.

This stopped Jacques in his tracks. What was the young nobleman leading up to? 'Who is presiding?'

'The Archbishop of Sens.'

'Ah!' That meant that Bernard de Caen had left the royal audience with the very man who was to provide the formal sentence of the Order he was supposed to protect. What would he do next? 'No,' Jacques replied, 'there's little point, is there? It's a foregone conclusion. King Philip will have his way. The stakes are pitched before the trial begins.'

'The royal fury knows no bounds today. "*Homo extra corpus est suum cum irascitur*" . . . "when a man grows angry his reason rides out". I never believed I would see the King fall prey to such a proverb . . .'

Jacques couldn't resist a smile at this show of Latin learning. Nicolas was staking his claim to respect and confidence, though he could not understand the reason. He sat on a bench by the table. Perhaps it was after all a good moment for conversation. 'Tell me what happened,' he prompted gently.

Nicolas had been instructed not to reveal the details of the audience, but he felt a strange new sympathy towards this inquisitor working so much in the dark, and it was as well to assure loyalty from both sides. 'There's little to say, really. Lord Bernard's message from His Holiness the Pope threw the King immediately into a foul mood. "There *will* be a trial, and at once!" he shouted, "whatever His Holiness the Pope says". Any other man might have given up there and then, but Bernard is a shrewd one, for he didn't leave the chamber, he simply waited, as though he was sure the king would relent. And sure enough, when the other business was over, King Philip called him over for a secret consultation.'

Jacques nodded. He wondered what Bernard de Caen would have to discuss with the king *after* his official message was delivered. Yet Nicolas would not know, he surmised, regarding that lean, impenetrable face; and if he did, it was something he would not reveal. Then a new thought occurred to him. 'I thought the only purpose of the session was to resolve the problem of the Templars. What other business was there?'

'Lord Guillaume de Nogaret was called to account for the progress of his researches. You should have seen the scene: "So where are we? After all these months?" the king shouted. "What more do you need?

Cannot a man of your experience, with all the men you need, find this relic?" De Nogaret had no answer to this, and tried to play for time: "We are close, sire," he tried to argue, "and the results will be seen soon enough, in a matter of weeks, I am sure . . ."

"'Weeks!" the king stormed. "I want results immediately!" He demanded to be told who was in charge of the operation, a poor seneschal by the name of Essart, who has lost all after a lifetime of service . . .'

Brother Jacques controlled the smile which began to form on his face. 'The king was demanding that the relic be found,' he prompted.

'Indeed. That was the first sign of his anger. Every man in the hall was shocked into silence, and the king's voice was as clear as crystal.'

'What did he say?'

'He wanted to know when the relic would be found. With each word his voice rose a pitch, and his face was transformed as I have never seen before. It was a terrifying sight, God help me. His cheeks reddened, his arms began to shake, and he bellowed at de Nogaret. He smashed his sceptre to the ground as he did so, pointing a quivering finger, and shouted: "You are proving yourself as incompetent as the others!" Then he stormed across the dais.' His enthusiasm grew with the telling. 'What was even more frightening was that he suddenly turned back to stone, sat on his throne and bade the Keeper come forward as if nothing had happened.'

'"*Potissimus irae fructus peonitentia*",' Jacques commented softly . . . "Anger begins with folly and ends with repentance . . ." Tell me what happened next.'

'God knows what would have happened. But at that very moment Guillaume de Paris was announced.'

Jacques recalled seeing that dramatic entry from the outside.

'He claimed that his agents had located the relic!' Now Nicolas was enjoying his superior knowledge.

'*What?*' Jacques began to shake exactly as Nicolas had just described. 'What did you say?'

Nicolas spoke slowly, relishing each word: 'He reported, my dear Abbot, that it is an image of the face of Our Saviour Jesus Christ, a genuine relic preserved since the day of his crucifixion. In Italy. A cloth. What do you think of that?'

'So it's in Italy, after all?' Jacques spoke aloud, but to himself, fighting to recover his wits. It made sense. He had heard stories about burial cloths used during the burial of Jesus, and that such cloths were supposed to have existed in Edessa and Constantinople. But this must be something special.

'As we have always thought,' Nicolas reflected aloud. He did not wish to inform Jacques about the private conversation between King Philip and Lord Bernard, for it would reveal his own ignorance. 'But within weeks now the whole world will know. The ambassadors to King Jaime of Aragon and King Edward of England were present. There is little time indeed now.'

'But perhaps enough,' Jacques observed. The burning of the Templars would be a useful diversion and he was sure they had the key in Pietro di Ocre. 'Most interesting,' he said to Nicolas with all the gratitude he could muster in his voice.

There was nothing else important, he sensed, to be gained from Nicolas. A plan was now forming in his mind, with a rationality which he was pleased to recognize but an implicit ruthlessness which disturbed him. The first step was to interrogate Jacques de Molay before it was too late. But he must first divert Nicolas de Lirey to some other legitimate task. 'I'm told there is a place where we can overhear the imprisoned Templars,' he began hesitantly, 'and we must hasten there at once.'

Nicolas pushed back his hair, wondering what would come next. Pique that the inquisitor's interest had suddenly dissipated, that his information was no longer vital, formed a lump in his throat.

'But there's a small task I would like you to carry out first.' Orders came more easily with his new role, Jacques noticed as he spoke. 'Would you please go to the Governor's office at the prison, and obtain the transcripts of the Grand Master's inquisition? We may find a lead in it.'

'At once.' The request seemed innocuous enough.

'I'll join you there,' Jacques added as he watched Nicolas stride through the door. 'And another thing . . .'

28

Nicolas accepted the task without hesitation, although he wondered what Brother Jacques wanted to do with the transcripts. Sooner or later he'll need me, and forget his distrust, he thought to himself as he walked away. The Abbot of Fontfroide was certainly on the right track, but as yet unaware of the ramifications of his mission.

A securely-tied bundle of documents as high as a pair of riding boots was placed on a table in front of him in the Governor's office. As soon as he was left alone, he untied it and leafed through the transcripts, but a combination of minute monastic script and inquisitorial abbreviations made it hard reading for him. And he doubted that there was much to be gleaned from such old interrogations.

He pushed them away, brushed dust fastidiously from his cuffs, and thought of Brother Jacques – or the Abbot, as he should now consider him. Perhaps he had overreacted in the antechamber, he reflected; yet at the same time he had been obliged to show himself loyal to Bernard de Caen. By duty and by birth: to the man who had been his father's friend and could redeem his downfall; to the son of a French nobleman. Yet he was aware of an easiness deep within as he considered these two antithetical figures who now loomed so large in his life: the prelate and the baker's son. The strange events of recent months were overturning all the premises of his role in this mission.

He had come to it out of duty to his father's memory, and to seek revenge against King Philip the Fair. Nicolas had latched himself onto the inquisitor, prompted him, assisted him, and even learned from him as they travelled together. Brother Jacques had proved to be a sharper man than Nicolas had expected and seemed to have as good a chance as any man of resolving the problem they faced: the man he was sent to observe.

Bernard de Caen's orders had been explicit. His voice came to Nicolas' mind now as he sat in the silent office: '. . . as the son of a friend and knight, there is no better man than you.' He had been told of Santo Spirito, and of the nature of the relic – things Brother Jacques had been left to fathom out for himself – and for months had enjoyed his superiority of information. But now it was lost, and this fact disturbed him. Brother Jacques was now an abbot, with autonomous powers of decision. Where was he at this very moment? He hadn't bothered to say; or had he deliberately hidden his destination? Whichever was the case, it was now Nicolas who needed assistance. Yet Lord Bernard had also become more enigmatic. Nothing new was forthcoming, and mystery fostered mystery.

This morning had been the worst. Nicolas chuckled to himself as he recalled Jacques' irritation at being excluded from the royal audience. As if he had expected to learn something useful. He, Nicolas de Lirey, knight of France, had been present, had seen from the distance as an outsider, and failed to understand the one thing that might have been of importance to them. It was true that he had read the papal letter, but even Jacques had guessed that it was nothing more than a plea for clemency for the knights of the Temple. No, the public business of the audience was of little interest. The real business had taken place in those few minutes when Bernard de Caen had been called forward by the king, having angered him shortly before. Nicolas had laughed within when courtiers whispered that the chubby man in hushed conversation with King Philip was destined for the Holy See, even though it reminded him of a conversation overheard months before. It was absurd.

He stared at the papers in front of him as if he wanted them to stand up of their own accord and provide the answer to his dilemma, but the lifeless, yellowing sheets only proffered questions. Was his aim to thwart Philip the Fair, or help Bernard de Caen? Nicolas realized with a shock that if his real aim were the former, then Brother Jacques was the man to back. Their ultimate duty was now to find the image. Nicolas shook his head in disbelief at this topsy-turvy world, ran his hand through his hair, licking manuscript dust from his lips and looking around the office to see if there was water available.

Then he heard Jacques being announced in the corridor outside, and drew the bundle of transcripts closer.

29

The Grand Master of the Temple appeared unconcerned about his imminent fate. As he stood on the threshold of the tiny cell, Jacques had the uncomfortable feeling that *he* was being assessed as a potential recruit. It was hard to believe that the prisoner was manacled to the floor by the ankles, and it needed a real effort of will to step in and assert his authority. 'I am Abbot Jacques Fournier, of the Order of Citeaux,' he began. It sounded pompous even to his ears.

The prisoner looked away contemptuously. His profile was dominated by a huge beaked nose, slightly uplifted.

'I've been reading your confession with great interest,' Jacques began cautiously, recalling the charges from other trial transcripts he had read. 'Item: that at your reception you denied Christ, whose image was presented to you on a crucifix, that you spat on the said image ... Item: that you yourself in later years performed the same ceremony with neophytes ... and committed other enormities which I shall not mention this day for the sake of your soul.' He paused, watching for a reaction. As he did so, his conscience reminded him of Nicolas' useless errand. His companion did not deserve such treatment; or perhaps, as Lord Bernard's spy, he did. Jacques forced his concentration onto the Grand Master in order to avoid this unpleasant thought. 'But I note that the questioning was carried out by Brother Guillaume de Paris, so I'm inclined to take it all with a pinch of salt.'

The Grand Master continued to stare blankly at the wall, without the slightest flicker of interest.

Jacques then stepped across the cell so that he could see the Master's face. De Molay did not flinch. And he was beyond threat, since he was to die that evening. It would be necessary to try another opening gambit.

'You were received into the Order at Beaune, I understand, by Amaury de la Roche, Master of the Order in France, and Humbert de Pairaud, Master in England. Is that so?' He spoke softly, allowing the names to linger in his mouth like a nostalgic roll call. 'That must have been during the Mastership of Thomas Berard, if I'm not

202

mistaken . . .' He continued to watch the Master carefully. 'Anyway, you mention a certain "irregular" part of the ceremony. That is most interesting, and I myself have spoken with other knights of your Order who confirm what you say. It involved a head, or an image of some kind, I have been led to understand . . . which existed in all the main preceptories, in the chapter-room. Quite fascinating. But I understand there was one image in particular . . . perhaps one from which the others were made as copies – some on crucifixes, some on wood panels, some even in bronze, as far as I understand.' Jacques was casting desperate straws, seeking confirmation of his hypothesis in the slightest gesture. 'I believe I know now where the original is kept,' he added confidentially.

There was still no reaction.

He moved so close that he could see each corrugation on the Master's battle-ravaged face and then the whites of his eyes. He could hear the deep, steady breathing, and caught a breath of a curious odour that might have come from the Holy Land. 'I've been speaking with a certain Pietro,' he then said casually, 'your preceptor in Apulia. He's here in this prison now, you know . . . Pietro di Ocre.'

The wrinkles of the crow's-feet at the corners of the Master's eyes moved almost imperceptibly. Had Jacques not been so close and concentrating with all his will he wouldn't have noticed. Then the old man's eyes flickered briefly, as though his muscles were fighting to hold his gaze straight against the curiosity of his mind.

It was enough. And Jacques was sure there would be no more. He gathered his habit and stepped backwards carefully. At the door he joined his hands in prayer, bowing his head towards the Templar. He prayed silently, sensing the inner strength of the man. The Grand Master had not uttered a word, but had unwittingly corroborated his hypothesis. He made the sign of the cross. 'God bless your soul, Master,' he said.

30

Nicolas was waiting for him in the Governor's office. He sat at a table reading a pile of discoloured manuscripts. 'The transcripts you asked for,' he said.

Although it was midday and the room was light, a torch blazed in a wall-holder behind him.

'Have you issued the orders as I asked?'

'Certainly.' Nicolas indicated the torch. 'But do you not wish to see these?' He proffered some yellowing sheets.

'Later.' Was there a hint of suspicion in Nicolas' voice? The inquisitor again wished he had thought of another excuse to keep Nicolas occupied. He would have to be even more careful at the second stage of his plan, when it would be vital to avoid the slightest suspicion. 'Everything's ready?' he asked, avoiding further embarrassment.

'The orders have been given.' Nicolas paused for a moment. For a moment duty overwhelmed his secret doubts about his immediate superior. 'Do you not think we should inform Lord Bernard? He knows nothing of this.'

'The responsibility is mine,' Jacques replied. That's because you have no idea where he is, he thought. 'Let's go down.' He turned towards the wall where an archive-cupboard had been shifted to reveal a black curtain behind it.

'But the transcripts . . . ?'

'They won't be necessary. I had an unexpected chance to see the Grand Master in person.' He was glad Nicolas could not see his face.

The shock of this information created consternation rather than anger in Nicolas, administering a quiet jolt to a state of mind which felt it could no longer be startled, like a gentle wave after a shipwreck. So it had been planned this way, and the transcripts were nothing more than a ruse. Yet at the same time Brother Jacques had informed him of his meetings with de Molay when there was no need to. So any comment would be wasted breath. Seeking action to disguise the jolt, Nicolas took the torch from its bracket, moved forward past Jacques to the wall, and tugged the curtain aside. Then he thrust the torch in front of him and he entered the roughly hewn aperture behind. 'Come!' he said. The soft echo of his voice within the rock suggested a calm which was surprising even to him.

Jacques watched silently, wondering how far he could trust Nicolas, then followed him into the passage which led in from the concealed door.

After a dozen paces it ended abruptly at a circular black hole in the floor. He gathered his habit, and stepped tentatively down the spiral staircase which became visible in torchlight as Nicolas descended, leading the way. He felt his way along the wall behind his companion. It was easier than at Aigues-Mortes.

A narrower passageway led off into darkness at the bottom of the staircase.

At regular intervals of about ten paces were apertures no bigger than a man's face. Jacques stopped at one, pushed his head against the wall until the hole fitted like a mask and tried to peer in, but recoiled sharply as his face snared in a spider's web. His shoulders crashed into the opposite wall while he tore at the sticky filaments which clung to him like tremulous ghostly fingers.

'Sssh,' Nicolas whispered. 'We've passed five openings now, and the Governor said it would be the seventh cell. We'd better leave the torch here and move on without light.'

'Is that wise?' Jacques demurred.

'They'll see us otherwise.'

'True.' Nicolas was right, but still Jacques was reluctant. He peered forward, searching for obstacles in the diminishing cone of light.

He let his habit fall to the ground and began to grope his way along the darkening passage. Flints embedded in the walls cut into his hands. He felt the first aperture and glanced behind him, shuddering involuntarily as he saw the ghost-like form of Nicolas, with his arms raised in front of him, silhouetted against flickering torchlight. He determined not to look back again, and felt his way to the seventh aperture.

Voices came to him like murmurings of autumn leaves in the breeze. Jacques smiled to himself: his gambit was working. He leaned against the wall, and pushed his face into the pitch darkness of the small opening, wiping cobwebs from his face and listening intently. In the chill of the dungeon, he could feel warm trickles of blood on the back of his hands.

205

Nicolas was beside him, nudging his way forward. He couldn't understand the inquisitor's motive in this absurd enterprise, but didn't want to miss anything. He wondered whether all inquisitorial prisons had such corridors as these behind the cells. 'Are they in there with him?' he whispered. He too felt the warmth of blood, and sought to free his hands from cobwebs.

'Somebody is,' Jacques replied.

'Will they fall for it?'

'They're desperate men. In a matter of hours they will die. This is their last chance.' He paused, pushing away the last traces of cobweb. 'Listen. There are at least three distinct voices.' There should have been four.

One voice commanded. Jacques had never heard de Molay's voice before, but guessed that he was listening to the Master. 'It is too late,' he was saying, 'by seven years.' The voice was heavy with resignation.

'. . . events beyond my control, *our* control,' a second unknown voice said.

'Nonsense. All is not yet lost. We must think of our Order and its future now.' Jacques recognized Pietro di Ocre's heavily accented French. Given the situation, such optimism was astonishing.

'You have never lost faith?' the second voice asked. It was either Hugues de Pairaud or Geoffroi de Charny.

'Certainly not. In the name of my uncle I have harboured our secret these seven years,' Pietro went on. 'My own life is of little importance, and even the worst tortures of the Inquisition never dragged a word from me. Our cause is too important.'

Jacques turned instinctively towards Nicolas, but he was invisible in the darkness. He strained to hear better.

'Even today, when we are hours from our death? There is no future,' Jacques de Molay commented. It was a weary voice, resigned to death.

'There *will* be a future. Our own deaths are not the end of the cause,' Pietro asserted.

Again, his tone surprised Jacques, who thought he had known his man. There was a long moment's silence before Pietro continued.

'Yet in some ways I am glad that we have come to the end, and that we shall be together. The years have made resistance harder, and I must confess to you that I'm not certain I could withstand further torture without revealing all. My will is at the limit, but my courage

206

is not ended. I shall die proudly. Every man and woman present will see the courage which makes a Templar Knight.'

'Well spoken,' the third voice said. 'Let us all give them and the bastard King of France a sign of our courage. Let us publicly deny the false confessions they made us sign and die as true knights.' A general murmur of agreement followed this assertion.

Well spoken indeed, Nicolas thought to himself. He was tempted to make a comment to Brother Jacques, but recognized the risk of discovery. He felt an instinctive kinship with these doomed knights, yet in the darkness of the secret corridor he felt an even stronger companionship with the inquisitor. Was it merely because these men were to die, while the other would live?

Jacques sensed Nicolas' reaction, and smiled to himself as he guessed the reason. But to him, Pietro's hint that he would not be able to withstand further torture was of far greater significance.

The voices continued: 'No man will surpass me in courage this evening,' someone else stated peremptorily. At first Jacques took it for another knight's voice, but then he realized it was the Grand Master again, speaking with reinvigorated boldness. 'Now to our present business,' he went on with an enthusiasm which must once have been normal to him. The change was disconcerting. They might have been in a secret chapter years ago, before the arrests. 'We must save the Image of Our Lord from King Philip, and use it to rebuild the power of our Order.'

'The Image of Our Lord', Jacques repeated silently to himself. He heard Nicolas mutter in the darkness. What was this image exactly? And where was it? Most extraordinary was the total faith which these knights had in its power.

'The problem is', Jacques de Molay continued, 'how we can save it and place it safely in the hands of our brethren at large.'

'Perhaps I have the answer.' It was the second voice speaking again after a long silence. Jacques listened eagerly. 'I believe the solution has come into our hands this very day.'

'How can that be?' It was de Molay who spoke, and Brother Jacques shared his sentiment this time. 'Tell us!'

'A Dominican friar came to me in my cell this morning, claiming to have been sent by the king himself. He had a proposition to make.'

Nicolas turned abruptly towards Brother Jacques, in his excitement forgetting that he could not be seen. He pushed his first suspicion from his mind: even Bernard de Caen could not stoop to such

207

duplicity. He fancied the inquisitor's breathing was heavier now. It was certain that these knights knew what the 'Image of Our Lord' was, and where it could be found. He leaned into the stone, as if that would improved his hearing.

'What proposition?' Pietro was asking with equal excitement. His enthusiasm after so many years of prison was extraordinary.

'That I should sign a truce on behalf of our Order. It was too late, he argued, to save our Grand Master – whose death was demanded now by the people of Paris, so he said – but he would be prepared to negotiate the release of Hugues and myself and a hundred brother knights in exchange for information. They would be allowed to live in total freedom within the realms of France on condition they did not conspire against the throne.'

'And what is the other part of the bargain?'

'He wants to know the location of the Image.'

'Ah!' Jacques de Molay snapped. 'Now I see. I will die, and you will go free. That's a fine plan.'

'It is the Order we are concerned with, my lord, not our own lives.'

'It's a ruse! You must never trust a friar.'

Nicolas smiled in the safety of the gloom.

'But we could trick him,' Pietro di Ocre observed. 'In truth I myself am not certain where the Image is to be found after all these years. I could guess . . .'

Go on, guess, Jacques thought to himself in the darkness. He felt Nicolas tense beside him.

'. . . but in any case false information will gain enough time for our knights to find it. We'll send his men to Rome, and then our own men to the right place, for I'm sure it must still be hidden in Ocre.'

'Excellent!' de Charny exclaimed. 'Master?'

'Can we send a message out of this prison?'

'There are guards who will carry a message for the right sum . . .'

'Good. Then this will be our course of action: we shall send a letter to Berengar de Pollencourt, who with two brother knights awaits our news hard by Paris. We will dispatch them to Ocre with the best indications possible, which Pietro can provide better than any man alive. Then we will play the king's game. Geoffroi will negotiate with him, and seek freedom for our knights, if not for ourselves. Tell him what you will, for it is enough that we gain a few weeks start.'

The Grand Master's voice rose in volume and firmed in timbre as he continued. It was as if he were addressing a chapter before a great battle, performing a rhetorical swan song. 'Our faith in Thomas Berard, who was present at my own initiation, and in his nephew Count Pietro, is fully justified. We shall go to our death proudly and in the love of Our Lord, confident that the Order of the Temple will survive. Brother Berengar is a fine man, and will find the Image which gave life to our plans. He will then command the free knights of Spain and Italy and go out to propagate our innocence. They will take the Temple of the Counts of Ocre as model, and rebuild it wherever Templar knights reside so that the Image of Our Lord will shine upon our brothers and give them strength in adversity.'

The prophetic certainty of his words stung Jacques into reluctant admiration. He felt Nicolas' breath on his cheek, and knew that he shared the sentiment.

'And now we shall go to die in peace of mind and in the love of God,' the Grand Master added quietly.

Silence followed these words. Once again Brother Jacques was astounded by the power the image could provide to people who believed in it. Even at such a distance and after so many years.

There was nothing more to be learned. He shook Nicolas' arm to sign that they would leave.

Nicolas was more than willing to depart. It was a relief to return to the Governor's office, which was airy and spacious after the close, dark corridor. Jacques drank from the jug of water on the table. 'Go you straight to Lord Bernard,' he ordered Nicolas, 'and report what you have heard.' It would be little good trying to persuade Nicolas to hold back information, he realized, and in any case time was now on his side. 'I myself have a small task to perform.'

31

'Lord Jacques! Lord Jacques!' The cries were distant, for someone else. It was only the familiarity of the voice which reminded him that he was an abbot now. He turned to see Briac the Beast running towards him. He was pleased to see him and to switch into their own tongue. It represented a world of shared trust in this quagmire of suspicion.

But as he drew near, Jacques saw a mixture of excitement and panic on the guard's face. He felt his body stiffen.

'I've important news, my lord,' Briac gasped. 'Three Templar knights led by a certain Berengar are said to have fled the city for Italy. Killed the guards at the Orléans gate, and rode out.' He paused to get his breath back, but failed to contain his agitation. 'They say the King has offered lands and silver for the man who captures them.'

'When did this happen?'

'Two days ago, sire. The very day we arrived in Paris. At dawn. But I only heard today.'

Jacques put a palm to his forehead, half-expecting he would find himself to be feverish. What on earth was happening? Who was pulling the strings? He had just been listening to plans for an event that seemed to have occurred days ago. He stared at Briac in disbelief. 'Are you sure?'

'As sure as I'm standing here.'

Briac's presence embarrassed Jacques. He needed solitude. 'Go back to the barracks and see what more you can learn,' he ordered. It was the first thing that came into his mind, but his own ease of command surprised him.

'Yes, my lord.'

'Good man. Mark it well! Now, I must be off to our Lord Bernard at once. Look to it! And be prepared yourself, for we may leave Paris ourselves any day now.'

When Briac was gone, he stood gazing at the towers of the royal palace, then at the walls of the Inquisition prison. With a start, he realized that someone was manipulating the Master of the Temple and his cohorts, pretending to aid them, gaining information, and then keeping one step ahead of them, acting in league with Berengar and the other knights. And clearly that person was the mysterious Dominican who had visited Jacques de Molay in the name of the king. Yet it could have been another, his intuition told him . . . his own Superior, Bernard de Caen. It was absurd, but the suspicion nagged at him.

Finally, as if sensing some unseen gaze upon his shoulders, he turned towards the hill where Bernard de Caen awaited him in Abbot Gilles' house. Suddenly, uncannily, Jacques perceived the triangle made by these three points, like those Nicolas had seen at Ocre, and he realized that he was was at the centre of this triangle. The baker's son from Saverdun ranged against three of the greatest powers of the land: King Philip, Guillaume de Paris, Bernard de Caen. It was frightening. And exhilarating.

He shook his mind awake and strode forcefully towards Abbot Gilles' house.

It was guarded. Anonymity thrown to the wind, Jacques approached the door with trepidation. But as he crossed the threshold he could hear Bernard de Caen's impatient voice, and entered quickly.

The Inquisitor-General for Provence was seated at a table with Abbot Gilles, Nicolas de Lirey and the abbot's personal secretary.

It seemed to Jacques an age since he had been called into the abbot's quarters at Mirepoix, and had been struck rigid by the gaze of this short, quiet man. Bernard's aura of power had suddenly evaporated. With a start, Jacques found himself studying the details of Bernard's head for the first time: the nervous twitch which made his left eye flutter briefly as he began to speak; the oversized ears with tufts of hair darker than that on his half-bald head; the chubby neck which appeared almost to spill out over his collar.

Yet his presence was reassuring; his concern manifest in his agitated gestures. Surely Jacques had been wrong to doubt his Superior's loyalty? He was pleased that his doubts were fading, for he owed his abbacy to Bernard. When this mission was over, he decided, he would depart at once for Fontfroide. He relaxed, warmed through by a new confidence, curious to learn what Bernard had to say and wondering whether Nicolas had found time to relate the details of the first part of his plan.

Lord Bernard didn't waste words. 'The knights of the Temple know about the relic,' he began brusquely, 'and are making a final attempt to retrieve it. They appear to believe that they will be able to save their Order in this way. Three knights left Paris under the cover of the darkness the day before yesterday. Their destination was Ocre.'

So Bernard knew the true departure date, Jacques thought, and the destination. Could it have been he who sought to beguile and cheat Geoffroi de Charny?

Bernard de Caen thumped the table. 'We must find it first!' he shouted. Then, suddenly, he was calm again. Jacques felt the full intensity of his gaze. 'I have ordered my men to prepare animals and supplies for the journey. You must leave as soon as possible. How much time do you need to make ready?'

'Two or three days,' Jacques replied. There was no question of objecting. He glanced at his secular companion.

'That should be enough,' Nicolas agreed.

'Make it two!' Bernard snapped. I will arrange for you to have the fastest horses. It is imperative that you succeed.'

Jacques again glanced towards Nicolas, glad that someone else would bear some of the responsibility.

'I need hardly add that His Holiness Pope Clement will provide his full support for this mission. He has renewed his letters patent for this journey. They should remain secret as before, if possible. But should you need assistance you may apply to any monastic house. Your every wish will become a command.' He paused, and studied the faces of the men before him one by one. 'Furthermore, Abbot Jacques, you will realize the extreme importance of this task for your career. You are acting on the highest authority of the Church, on a mission which may prove to be of vital importance. The odds are against us, but God will be on our side. Let us pray that with His help your mission will be successful . . .'

They bowed their heads together as Bernard de Caen led a brief prayer.

Then Jacques felt a hand on his arm, and was surprised to find himself drawn aside. 'Success will of course be to the credit of the Church and the *Opus Christi*, but we will not overlook your own advancement.'

Before Jacques could think of a suitable reply, Bernard was gone. Now he was talking to Abbot Gilles in the far corner, his arm linked to that of his host and his bald head inclined conspiratorially to the abbot's shoulder.

212

He felt a tremor run along his spine. Abbot Jacques! And already further promises. What could he mean – a bishopric? Was there a limit? Then he found himself wondering where the impulse behind this mission originated: with Pope Clement, or with Bernard himself? Bernard had always been perfectly informed, and furnished with letters patent already prepared in Avignon, horses, extra manpower and able to make promises of office . . . as if he were perpetually one stage ahead of the game. The thought of Bernard's apparent omniscience led Jacques to a fresh idea. He crossed the room quickly. 'Do we have any information about their route?'

'Indeed we do,' Bernard replied. For the first time Jacques was struck by the fact that Bernard and Nicolas de Lirey had this phrase in common. 'Our agents inform us that the Templars will head for the St Gotthard Pass. One of their last operational commanderies lies just beyond it, and they hope to gather more men there. But we have also learned from other sources that the pass has been blocked by late snowfalls. So it should be easy enough to overtake them by travelling round the Alps . . .'

There it was again: that apparent omniscience. As he listened, he recalled again the Dominican who had visited Geoffroi de Charny, and Bernard's own penchant for dressing in the habit of that Order. But now there was more urgent business. 'Round the Alps?' he asked.

'To sail from Chalon down the Saône and Rhône, and thence from Marseilles to Genoa . . .'

'I will travel overland,' Abbot Jacques stated with a boldness and authority which surprised even him. A hint of vomit blocked his throat as he recalled the journey from Marseilles many years before.

'As you will,' Bernard said. He seemed to sense the finality of Jacques' reply. 'You can disembark at Avignon and take fast horses via Grasse.'

A new thought occurred to Jacques. 'Does His Majesty the King know of this journey?'

'Certainly not!' Bernard snapped.

'That is well.' The shift in Bernard's tone renewed Jacques' suspicions. Jacques was glad that he had learned of the discrepancy in time from Briac, otherwse he would have revealed himself too easily. What game could Bernard be playing? *Somebody*, he realized with a start, had allowed the Templars to believe they could outwit both King and Church, using them as a hare for the hounds.

Jacques observed Nicolas, whose lean face remained impassive, betraying no sense of emotion or even interest. Was it just aristocratic detachment? Was he better informed than he? Or was Nicolas too feeling the ambiguity of the situation, changing sides in his inner thoughts? Jacques wished deeply that it were possible to confide more fully in Nicolas. But he knew within that he must keep his own counsel, and wait. He longed for the independence that the journey would provide. 'Come, Nicolas, there is much to be done,' he said.

It was time to enact the next part of his plan. First he would send Nicolas off to organize their departure. Then he would accompany Renaud to the evening spectacle.

32

It seemed the whole of Paris was going to the Ile-des-Javiaux that
evening.

Abbot Jacques was shoved, elbowed and kicked along by the milling
crowd of soldiers, students, women and children which thronged the
bridges leading to the Ile de Palais and converged into a single mass.
He looked back constantly to ensure Renaud was still with him. When
he could see through a gap in the throng he marvelled at others who
crossed the river standing precariously in flat-bottomed ferries. It was
a fine evening, which encouraged the first late outing of the year.

At first he had felt uncomfortable in the black Dominican habit he
had chosen to wear to make himself less noticeable. His own white
linen habit would have made him too conspicuous, and with so many
of the Black Friars in Paris it was the perfect disguise. Abbot Gilles
had suggested it, and provided the habit as if it were the most natural
thing in the world. It was clearly how *he* passed unobserved in France.
Elevated to a new dignity, Jacques smiled wryly to himself, he was
obliged to disguise himself as a Dominican inquisitor. But soon he
learned to relish the sneers of the people with a deep ironic pleasure.
Behind him, the ex-seneschal was dressed in the anonymous brown
tunic of a regular soldier.

They crossed a bridge of planks which had been thrown across the
ditch. The tiny island resounded with the hubbub of a great fair. Land
that was bare the previous day was now marked by well-trodden paths
lined with booths and stalls selling beer, mead, skewers of meat and
all manner of sweets. Jacques was amused to see fake pilgrim badges
from Compostela for those who did not wish to make the journey. Card
sharps and dice-men drew newly paid soldiers as dung attracts flies.
Jugglers, charlatans and tricksters had set up shop wherever there was
space, and where there was less space, beggars and cripples squeezed
in.

The stakes were now surrounded by carefully constructed piles
of faggots with bunches of dried furze thrust into them. Jacques
studied them with grim curiosity. A simple ladder, consisting of
a pole with small cross-pieces nailed on to serve as steps, leaned

against each stake. Near the top was a small flat board nailed to the post.

'Do you think King Philip will bother to watch?' Jacques asked as they drew near.

"Course he will. He's been waiting for this moment for months . . . if not years.' Renaud was standing on tiptoe to see above the crowd that pressed around them. 'Here they come now!' His voice was charged with the enthusiasm of the people.

The prisoners were sitting on an open cart drawn by oxen, lashed to a wooden beam that ran from transom to tail-guard. Jacques was fascinated to see that the haggard faces and long unkempt hair of these once powerful warrior-monks evoked compassion in the greater part of the crowd. Few men mocked them or taunted them; no boys threw stones, as they usually did at convicted criminals. As they stepped down from the cart the knights seemed to acquire a strange dignity which transcended their tattered clothing. The sun had almost sunk beneath the houses across the river, and the Templars were silhouetted against its deep ochre glow.

As guards led each man to his stake, the murmuring voices began again. A boy with a small sack of sulphur ran between the prisoners, smearing their chests and arms with the greenish-yellow powder. A gasp of admiration rippled through the crowd as the knights climbed nobly to the small boards fixed above the faggots.

'Who's the white-haired one?' a boy's voice asked. He was seated astride the broad shoulders of his father, a stocky man who brought the smell of the forge with him when he pushed close.

'No idea, son,' the father replied.

In front of them a priest turned to look at the man's face. 'They say he's a preceptor from Italy,' he said, 'and perhaps the most depraved of all. It is good that he should suffer with his leaders.'

'Ah!' the man said. 'Did you hear that, son?'

Jacques looked about him anxiously, seeking the lean face of his companion in the crowd. He hoped Nicolas would be distant from the stake since he was the only man who could thwart the plan which was forming in his mind to draw the truth from Pietro di Ocre. He glanced nervously at Renaud Essart, but the seneschal had turned to look at the royal palace. 'There you are,' he said. 'I was sure I'd be right!'

Jacques followed Renaud's gaze, leaning against the blacksmith so that he would not be pushed forward. On a balcony on the east facade of the royal palace stood a small group of men. Even from that distance the erect figure and blond hair of King Philip were unmistakeable. Three other men stood with him. Jacques fancied he could make out Guillaume de Nogaret. The others were dressed in black, and he guessed that one of them would be Guillaume de Paris.

'The king! The king!' the blacksmith shouted as he too turned to see what had engaged his neighbour's curiosity. He pointed to show his son the figures on the balcony.

'Yes, and he'll be glad when this is over I'll bet,' said the man beside him.

'What 'yer mean?'

'You didn't hear? I was there this morning at Notre Dame, when they was trying these knights. And I can tell you it was a close thing. The whole of Paris was ready to defend them, and the king's men were looking scared. I'll bet he's right nervous up there now. They ain't dead yet.'

The blacksmith looked at him in surprise. 'You know it all, my friend.'

'And I know more,' the man said proudly. 'The king can't wait to get his hands on the Templar money. And when he does, it'll be worse for us. For there'll be wars again, and new taxes, and we'll wish we'd stopped him . . .'

'Us? Stop him?' the blacksmith laughed. 'Listen, if you know everything, tell me, who's that white-haired knight there?' He pointed to the stake on the left.

He obviously didn't trust the priest.

'He's an Italian,' the man said, leaning forward as if he were giving confidential information. 'Pedro di Ocre his name is, and word has it he's one of the most powerful of the Templars.'

The blacksmith sneered in evident disbelief and drew his son away. 'Never 'eard of 'im.'

'Ain't it Hugues de Pairaud, Visitor of the Temple?' another man asked.

The first man feigned indignation. 'It *was* supposed to be, my friend. And I dare say the people here think it's Hugues, for who's ever seen him in the flesh?' He paused, and then leaned closer to his new acquaintance. 'But I've heard from someone as knows,' he whispered with a conspiratorial air, 'and that there is the Italian Pedro. I'll swear to it.'

His listener seemed almost convinced. 'But why didn't they announce the change? Like you say, the people'll always think it was Hugues de Pairaud.'

'He's right,' Renaud observed.

The first man shrugged his shoulders. 'That's not for the like of us to know,' he murmured as if he were in on the conspiracy. 'But look! The priest has come for extreme unction . . .' His remaining words were lost.

Jacques caught Renaud's attention, and placed his index finger over his lips. Then he turned with the crowd to watch the priest as he approached the Grand Master. The priest's words were too faint to be deciphered, but Jacques de Molay replied in a stentorian voice as if addressing the people gathered below him. 'Yes, I pray you to turn my body towards the Church of Our Lady, that I may die with my faith in the Mother of Our Lord Jesus Christ.'

After brief words with the provost in charge, his last wish was granted. The other prisoners were left facing upriver. Then the provost looked towards the royal balcony until he received a wave of authority from Guillaume de Nogaret. 'Set fire!' he ordered sternly.

De Molay rose to his feet and shouted imperiously: 'No!'

The guards stood stock-still with the burning furze, as if awestruck by the Grand Master's authority. Jacques smiled to himself, admiring de Molay's sense of timing. It couldn't have been bettered. He watched spellbound as every eye in the crowd was drawn irresistibly towards the gaunt figure balanced miraculously on the tiny platform. 'Citizens of Paris,' de Molay roared, 'I come here to die at the hands of your king. And I am not afraid to die here this evening. But first I wish to deny once and for all the charges made against the Order of the Temple and against my person . . .' The provost had sent guards from the back of the crowd to stop him. The people had pressed closer to hear every word, but could not break through. Jacques felt his body would be crushed by that of the blacksmith. 'The Temple is innocent of all charges,' the Master went on, his voice edged with the power of desperation, 'and the crimes of which we have been accused are nothing but lies. The Rule of our Order is just and holy, and leads us in the steps of Our Lord. I myself have been tricked by the lies and deceits of His Holiness Pope Clement and His Highness King Philip into betraying my Order, and I die now as just punishment for this.

But the Order, I repeat, is innocent of all accusations made against it.'

King Philip's soldiers could not stop the crowd cheering these words. Jacques felt Renaud beside him. 'Who would ever have imagined the old man making such a speech?'

'No one,' Jacques replied. But he smiled within as he recalled the Master's words in the dungeon.

Another prisoner stood up: 'I too . . .' he began.

'That's Geoffroi de Charny,' Essart commented, 'a face I know well.'

But the Preceptor for Normandy had no chance to emulate his Master. One of the King's officers had covered the short distance from the royal palace at the gallop and now forced a passage through the crowd with his horse. He dismounted beside the provost, who turned white with fear. 'Fire!' he commanded. In an instant the guards had set fire to bunches of furze in their hands and in perfect synchrony thrust them into the faggots.

As the flames spread rapidly, Hugues de Pairaud forced his resounding voice into one last great shout: 'Our bodies are due to the King of France; but our souls to God!'

At that moment, the vespers bell began to ring in the nearby church of the hermit brothers of St Augustine. An uncanny silence fell once again over the crowd of spectators. Jacques prayed silently to himself for the souls of the Templar officials. As he looked up again he thought of that day, which now seemed years ago, when he had first entered the prison at Aigues-Mortes to interrogate Pietro di Ocre. Then too, the vespers bell had been chiming. He recalled the ominous chill in his heart as the sound of that call to prayer had been cut off from him by the massive prison door. He wondered how many more vespers he would miss before he could return to his favourite office of the day with his previous peace of mind.

The wind gusted up the Seine, while the greater part of the faggots had been placed downstream, perhaps to dramatize the spectacle for viewers in the royal palace. The furze flared dramatically, but blazed wastefully away from the prisoners' legs.

Defiantly, Jacques de Molay thrust his arms into the flames. His speech had endowed him with fresh courage and nobility. He appeared like one of the huge figures of Christ on oriental crucifixions, with his hands clasped in prayer and his head uplifted towards Notre Dame.

Jacques pushed forwards, wishing to hear the Master's last words. He held a hand in front of his face as the heat became intolerable, and closed his eyes as the sulphur on the Grand Master's chest flared noisily. In an instant the man's face was black as charcoal, and his lips swelled up so that he could barely speak. But he continued to repeat, as if he were at church reciting his Hail Marys, 'Lord Jesus, have mercy on me ... Lord Jesus, have mercy on me'. Slowly the voice faded as flames encompassed him. His whole head seemed to be on fire, with burning hair creating a kind of halo. Then his lips shrank back to the gums and the voice ceased altogether. But the burning face continued to smile seraphically even as the right arm flared up brilliantly and dropped away to the ground.

Jacques turned away feeling he was on fire too. His face was scorched as if by the southern sun, and he sweated uncomfortably inside his woollen habit. But he was satisfied that there had been no heresy in this man.

He looked at the other stakes, where burning trunks were almost totally enveloped in flame. Fat and blood now dripped from the arm stumps onto the fire beneath. The last agonizing groans had died away, and not one of them had cried for help. 'Brave men all,' he remarked when he rejoined Renaud in the midst of the crowd. 'There is nothing more to be learned here.'

As they were bustled back along the river bank by the crowd Jacques noticed that King Philip and his guests had disappeared from their balcony. 'One to you, and one to me,' he said to himself.

'What's that?' Renaud asked.

'You'll see.' Jacques wished he could tell him now, for he felt close to the seneschal this evening, but he could trust no one that far, except perhaps Brother Armand. And the seneschal's time would come, he reflected. 'Renaud?'

The soldier seemed surprised by the new form of address. 'Yes?'

'I'd like you to come to Italy with me. You'll be well rewarded.'

'I'm your man, Brother Jacques,' the seneschal said simply. It was as if he had been waiting for those words all evening.

Now the team was complete in Jacques' mind.

At the bridge, he left Renaud and walked briskly up the hill towards the house of Abbot Gilles. From the doorway he looked back towards the Ile-des-Javiaux. He was pleased that there had been no sign of Nicolas all evening, although he was sure his companion had been amongst the crowd.

220

Now darkness had fallen, leaving three dying fires like beacons warning boats away from the island. Jacques shivered, noticing a chill in the air as his body cooled down after its scorching. But pride still warmed him within, and he entered the lodging in the knowledge that daybreak would bring him to the next stage of his plan.

33

First light picked out Jacques' saddlecloth when he was already half-way to Saint Germain-des-Près. He turned instinctively to see the reassuring bulk of Briac behind him. Their horses clipped through streets peopled by ghostly figures of bakers' boys delivering bread, and washerwomen on their way to the river bank.

Through a break in the houses he glimpsed the bare Ile-des-Javiaux. There was no sign of life, nor even a wisp of smoke; it was as if last evening's events had been a dream.

When they dismounted at the abbey, Briac took the reins of his palfrey and began to lead it towards a water-trough opposite the gate. 'Where are you going?' Jacques asked.

'To care for the horses.' Briac frowned in puzzlement.

'But I need your assistance.'

'Here?'

'Come! Grooms will take care of the horses.'

Briac looked up at the abbey walls, mystified. Then he obeyed, at first with suspicion in his eyes, but when grooms emerged and led the horses away he seemed impressed by the respect shown towards him.

'Lord Abbot,' the duty gatekeeper greeted Jacques, who was annoyed by this, since he had arranged with Brother Armand that his visit be strictly secret. Yet he realized that the gatekeeper and other serving-brothers would need to be given some information about his visit.

Nicolas de Lirey pulled his mount to a halt a hundred paces from the abbey gate, safely hidden by the plane trees which lined an avenue leading down to the Seine. By chance he had been in the stables, trying a new saddle for the long journey to Ocre, when the order to prepare horses for this dawn expedition had been given the evening before. It was odd enough that a friar – even an abbot – should pay a visit during the hour of lauds; stranger still that he should require a bodyguard like Briac in the streets of Paris. Odd enough to justify pursuit.

He watched as Briac made to lead the horses away from the entrance. Perhaps Abbot Jacques was so proud of his new palfrey that he wouldn't trust the abbey grooms?

But to Nicolas' surprise grooms came running from the abbey gate, and Briac entered with the new abbot. Nicolas tethered his mount and moved slowly forward under the planes, wetting his face against the broad dewy leaves of the lowest branches. On the avenue two water-carriers passed with their barrow, but showed no interest in the curious figure under the trees. A bell began to sound within the abbey. The only plausible explanation that had come to Nicolas' mind as he followed at a distance through the streets was that Jacques was making a last visit to his friend, Abbot Armand. But there would be no need for Briac to enter the abbey with him; the protocol was wrong.

Nicolas stopped directly opposite the abbey gate, not a stone's throw from the grooms who tended Jacques' horse. The building seemed more like a fortress than an abbey, and he recalled that the deepest dungeons of Paris were dug into the rock beneath. Could they be connected with this dawn visit? Traffic was steadily increasing in the avenue. He leaned against a trunk and studied the closed gate until the tolling of the bell ceased; the only sound then was the scuffing of hoofs and footsteps in the dust.

The massive walls of the abbey were unforthcoming. There was little point in waiting now, and at least he knew where Abbot Jacques had gone. Soon he would be due at a final conference with Bernard de Caen. Nicolas walked back to his horse. With one last glance at the abbey walls, he mounted and rode slowly towards Abbot Gilles' house.

Perhaps there was nothing in it? The times were strange, and a visit by Jacques at any hour to such an old friend as Armand was certainly no stranger than Bernard de Caen being huddled in private conversation with the King of France, his avowed enemy.

The thought of Bernard brought another memory to Nicolas. Last night in the stable, as he listened, transfixed, to Jacques' orders he had thought of the only other time in his life that he had engaged in the dishonourable activity of spying. He remembered it with distaste, for his own behaviour rather than for what he had heard, but that was when he had heard Bernard de Caen talking to his sister in Avignon. The most remarkable assertion he had ever heard, something for which the Pope's envoy could conspire with the King

223

of France? Could it have been true, or had he misheard? That was true conspiracy, and he was sure Jacques was incapable of such cunning. No, it was nothing more than a simple visit.

But why was Briac there, he repeated to himself as he rode through the busying streets.

Armand was waiting for Jacques in his study. 'You're lucky our abbot is in the country,' he said, 'otherwise it would have been difficult to arrange, even with your new rank.' His eyes took in everything from the Dominican habit to the leather bag Jacques was carrying. Then he looked apprehensively at Briac as the huge guard bent to pass under the door lintel.

'This is Briac, my most trusted man,' Jacques said quickly, to allay suspicion. He sensed the guard's surprise as he spoke.

'I hope you'll be quick,' Armand said, ignoring Briac. He pointed towards the corridor outside. 'You'll find the room near the top of the stairs. On the right.' Distaste was marked on his face now. He handed a key to Briac without looking at him.

Jacques was mortified. Yet the circumtances required exceptional measures. His eagerness to follow his plan through was stronger than his concern for Armand's feelings. But he acknowledged his friend's loyalty and made a clumsy attempt to thank him. They embraced each other with all the warmth of sparring partners, and it was with relief that he left the study, embarrassed, but keen to get on with the business in hand.

He and Briac walked as quickly as they could in the gloomy corridor, halting by the stairs Armand had indicated. 'Open it,' Jacques ordered brusquely.

Briac fumbled with the lock for a moment, then pushed the heavy door open, and grinned at Abbot Jacques. Something glimpsed from the corner of his eye wiped the grin away. 'My God! But I thought . . . ' he spluttered. He stood aghast, grasping the doorjamb.

'That Pietro was dead?' Jacques grunted at the guard's reaction, then entered the room with what seemed even to him a perverse sense of enjoyment. 'So did the crowd. But it wasn't hard to find a man who resembled him. Old men are much of a muchness after years in prison, and the provost had never seen him before. I had our Pietro drugged and carried out of the prison in a burial shroud last night. The fellow who died was already inside. It was a simple switch.' He spoke the last words with pride at his new skills.

224

Briac stared agape, alternating his gaze between prisoner and inquisitor like a marionette.

'That's enough staring,' Jacques snapped. 'Now close the door and keep watch. No one should come into the corridor. But if they do, knock at once.'

'Yes, my lord,' Briac said with enhanced respect.

When the door was closed again Jacques faced his prisoner. This would be the hardest moment of his deception, and would require due penance afterwards. He tried to sound friendly, and fanned the dying embers in the fireplace as he spoke: 'Well, preceptor? I've kept my part of the bargain. Your fellow knights are dead and you virtually a free man.'

The revived embers cast a soft glow in the cell.

Pietro lowered his head and made the sign of the cross. Then he looked up proudly. 'I'm surprised you came. But I too will keep my word. That was the first thing I learned from my father.' He paused, looking at his unshackled arms and legs in disbelief. 'I trust you, inquisitor, and now I know it's too late. So I'll tell you the truth.' Again, there was a long pause, then Pietro looked up again. 'Tell me, how old are you? Thirty? Thirty-five? Forty? It's hard for an old man to judge.'

'Towards the first figure.' Jacques was curious to see where the Templar was leading.

'Too young: I thought as much. For all your brilliance, you will never understand. No one will ever understand now. But I'll keep my word. And then I'll be free . . . '

'To go to Italy . . .? Yes.' Jacques cleared his throat uncomfortably, then add, gently: 'What is it I'll never understand?'

'The old days, when a knight's word had value.' The preceptor's voice softened, as if he were dreaming. 'Acre, Tripoli, Castle Pilgrim; *that's* what you'll never understand. Once, you know, I was within a day's ride of Jerusalem. I would have given my soul to the Devil to have entered the Holy City and restored her to Christian hands. It was all we dreamt of then. But no one seems to care now . . . the days of true chivalry have passed. Men sing and combat for a woman: but no woman – however beautiful – can compare with the Holy City.' There was a damp glint in his eyes as he spoke, but his voice was firm. 'Then there was Acre. I was there when it fell to the filthy Saracens. The last Christian city in Outremer. It had the form of a crusader's shield, with two sides looking onto the sea and the third side facing the

plains behind. With that city fell the flower of Templar courage . . .
it was hideous . . . we fought for Christendom and lost. Many great
men were lost that day. Others, like Jacques de Molay and Geoffroi
de Charny fought valiantly and were wounded. And yesterday were
burned by a king who neither fought nor sent an army to help.' He
laughed nervously and stared at Jacques. 'The man who now believes
he should be Emperor,' he spat. His lower lip twisted with contempt,
and he closed his eyes as if in a trance. 'I can still see it as if it were
engraved inside my eyelids . . . '

'See what?' Jacques coaxed. It was diffifult to follow the preceptor's
train of thought. He had clearly been mulling over the details for
weeks as he prepared for death.

Pietro's eyes opened slowly. 'It was the first Sunday in April that
the Sultan arrived before Acre. They said there were sixty thousand
horsemen, and over a hundred thousand infantry. When I looked
out from the Temple tower, the tents were thick as ants across the
plains to the south of the city, blackening orange groves and orchards.
The sultan's own tent was pitched barely beyond the range of our
mangonels, near the Tower of the Legate. It was a terrifying sight,
since we had not more than fifteen thousand fighting men, and of
them only a thousand knights. We sent the women and children to
Cyprus on our ships, and prepared for battle. Catapults were built
and walls strengthened. Supplies of oil and grain were replenished
by sea. The Temple stood on the tip of the peninsular, surrounded
by water on three sides, so it was comparatively easy to bring new
supplies in by ship . . . '

It was like listening to a reading of the *Chronicles of Jerusalem*. These
events had clearly been fermenting in Pietro's mind throughout his
years of imprisonment.

'. . . one night I was myself part of a sortie into the Moslem camp.
I recall it as if it were yesterday, although it's now two decades since.
There was a full moon that night, and a stiff breeze off the sea that
covered our footsteps. We took rowing boats from the Pisans and
crossed the harbour. We reached the Sultan's own tent before we were
discovered. Someone tripped over a guy-rope. He cursed loudly, and
the Saracens were upon us like wild dogs. There was no choice but
to flee towards the city walls. I saw men sliced in two before me as I
ran. Knights who had fought before Jerusalem, in Galilee and against
the Seljuks, tripped and fell like helpless boys, and the saracens drove
their long daggers into the fiery hearts of true Templar knights as if

they were slaughtering fowl. I myself was sliced in the arm. Look!' He pushed his left sleeve up to show a thick scar, a palm's span in length, stretching diagonally across his forearm.

'It was then that the members of our Order began to lose heart. Saracen engineers undermined the walls of the city. One by one the towers fell. Then Sultan Al-Ashraf ordered the final assault on a Friday, their holy day, as is their wont. By then they had assembled a hundred siege engines and filled the moat with faggots. That morning, shortly before dawn, we heard the distant rumbling sound of a thousand giant drums, which seemed to come from the bowels of the earth like an earthquake. After that came the throwers of Greek fire, and archers. Then fifty thousand men swarmed over the city walls like angry wasps. They took the Accursed Tower, then attacked along the Street of St Anne, which led to the very gatehouse of the Temple compound. It was a fearful sight: they killed man, woman and child with no discrimination. Our Grand Master was killed in the attempt to take the Accursed Tower back from them; I stood with him in the breach and saw him slay a dozen saracen scum as truly as I sit here. My own life was saved because I helped to carry him back to our fortress . . . '

'William of Beaujeu? He succeeded your uncle, I believe?' Jacques prompted.

For an instant, the preceptor stared at Jacques suspiciously, but nostalgia quickly regained its sway. 'Yes indeed,' he answered with genuine pride in his voice. 'He was often a guest at our home when I was a small boy. In fact, it was my uncle who appointed him Preceptor of Apulia.'

The old Templar's enthusiasms were perhaps misplaced, and his loyalties questionable. But there seemed to be little evil in him, just as Nicolas has previously said.

'We lost three hundred knights that day,' Pietro di Ocre continued. 'I've never seen greater bloodshed. Men fled like young girls, hanging on to the ropes behind ships that could barely move out of the harbour for their weight. Those who didn't drown were cut down and slain on the quayside. When night fell the only building still in Christian hands was the Temple, with a hundred brothers inside. We spent the night repairing breaches and preparing catapults, and held out for a week, until the walls began to shake as the Sultan's engineers began to dig under the foundations. We managed to fill in two tunnels with broken masonry from the walls, but they kept digging. Jacques de Molay and

227

I were in charge, and still held the battle standard of the Order, but in the end we were forced to retreat. God forgive our souls and those of our brother knights who died in the carnage!' He crossed himself as he spoke.

'How did you escape?'

'We had ships of our fleet standing off the Temple. And a galleon, the *Falcon*, commanded by the sergeant-brother Roger Flor.'

'Was your treasure taken away on the *Falcon*?'

'Treasure?' Pietro roared with laughter. 'Had there been anything in the treasury by that time, the likes of Roger Flor would have taken it. No, Sire Inquisitor, there was nothing in the coffers of the Temple. Everything was spent on supplies and weapons for the siege.' Again he chuckled to himself, looking at Jacques as if feeling sorry for him. 'The only treasure we left for the Saracens were four golden lions which stood on the towers at the corner of the Temple. They were forgotten. We didn't think of money that day, you see, but of our honour and the loss of Outremer. That's what you inquisitors and the King of this accursed country fail to understand. That battle was the last time true knights fought in earnest!'

'You really believe that?' Jacques knew the question was superfluous, but wanted to keep the preceptor in full flow.

'True knighthood ended at Outremer,' Pietro replied simply, as if it were an incontrovertible fact. Then he turned away, again dreamily. 'That is why I'm glad it has come to an end. There are no more great men: remember Armand de Peragors, William de Villehardouin, Bohemond de Antioch, Robert de Artois, Raoul de Coucy, Alfonso de Poitou, Geoffery de Sargines, Oliver de Termes, Odo Poilechien; the Knights of the Temple: Pierre de Sivry, Gautier de Payns, Ansell de Rohaire, Raoul Moyset, Hugues de Pairaud, Amaury de la Roche, Gerard de Gauche, Gui Dauphin, Gautier de Liancourt; even King Louis of France. Each man a true knight!'

The strangely distant quality of his voice transformed the list into a litany.

'The world is changing, young man. Knightly privileges are now given to merchants' sons. Many great cities have abolished all privileges of knightly birth. Anyone can aspire to knighthood today. The world is full of republics of merchants where true values have been lost. How can a man who spends his life buying and selling, trading and haggling, understand knighthood?'

228

His voice reminded Jacques of the contempt which Nicolas de Lirey had often shown for the new knights they met – and towards Jacques himself, the baker's son. Nicolas could have spoken these words, and this fact made him overreact to them. 'I have read the romances of knighthood,' he said sharply.

The preceptor roared with laughter this time, as if he were a free man on his own lands. 'Those are tales for priests and merchants!' Jacques recoiled from the splattered saliva of his vehemence. 'I am telling you about *real* men, *real* wars; battles fought within my own lifetime for the glory of God and his Holy Land. These merchant-knights and story-telling knights will never retake Jerusalem! They dress themselves in silver and gold, and pride themselves on the beauty of their saddles, spawning avarice rather than respect. The knights of the Temple were men with faith in their souls who struck terror in the hearts of the Saracens. There will be no more crusades, for there are no men worthy to take up the cross in battle. This accursed false knight-bastard-king wishes to lead a new crusade, they say. If he does it will fail, and the curse of the Templars will be upon his head. Jerusalem will remain heathen until it falls into ruin.'

In spite of himself, it seemed to Jacques that in that cold and damp room Pietro's words rang with prophetic resonance.

'You see, my uncle was right. The only alternative was to build a new Jerusalem. That was the stimulus of true Christian knighthood: the ultimate objective of all the prowess, courtesy, loyalty, hardiness and generosity of which men nowadays speak. To seek knighthood for the wrong reasons is as evil as simony in a clerk, or heretical beliefs in an inquisitor ...' He looked amusedly towards Jacques, as if pleased with his analogy. He was not such an unlearned man as they had thought. 'When my uncle returned from Outremer he knew that we would never recapture the Holy City. He built the New Jerusalem as a centre of knighthood, a focus for the new Church which he and his friends envisioned. He nearly succeeded. We had the Pope, and came within a hair's breadth of having the Church. And do you know why?' He looked at Jacques.

A tremor shot through Jacques as he listened. He knew he was close now. 'Tell me,' he whispered.

'Because we had Jerusalem. The original was lost: the Temple was in ruins; the holy places were subject to saracen blasphemy; Christ's own house was destroyed, and the garden of Gethsemane burned to dry desert. We transferred the dream, and brought with it the holy objects which made Jerusalem a site of pilgrimage. We put together the relics of Jerusalem and Constantinople – and would have taken those of St Louis too!' Pietro's voice had been rising until it now reached a silent, tremulous and frightening anger: 'That's what Anjou never understood. He thought only of himself. But Thomas Berard, Conte Tommaso di Berardo di Ocre . . .'

Jacques shivered at the resonance of Pietro's uncle's name in his native tongue. It joined the earlier litany in his imagination.

'. . . wished to preserve the seat of Christendom. But now it will never happen. We so nearly had the Church, but now we have nothing. The Order is broken, my family has lost its lands, and I am here relating all to an inquisitor in exchange for the right to die on my own lands. The last knight!' An unearthly, nasal sobbing sound issued from the preceptor as he finished. He dropped his head into his hands.

The strange blend of absurdity and truth in his words dumbfounded Jacques. Inexorably, like the chill of death, from deep within welled up an awareness that such men looked back to an age of knightly perfection which no longer existed. They could never compete with ruthless adventurers like Guillaume de Nogaret, or even King Philip. Mercenaries with neither qualms or loyalties like Roger Flor were the men of the future. To compete with them one must use the same weapons. With piercing clarity he saw that Bernard de Caen had understood this fact, and that his perception of it motivated the *Opus Christi*. From the outset of his mission men had been prepared to attack representatives of the Church and God, would not stop at killing priests and inquisitors. These were the men who would control the future world, and must be faced on equal terms.

That, Jacques realized with a start, meant finding the image. It was time to press on. 'You mention the relics from Jerusalem and Constantinople. Was the image that everyone is seeking one of them?'

Pietro regarded him sharply, then smiled. 'It was indeed,' he replied.

'When did you first see it?'

'The year before my uncle died, some ten years after my initiation. One evening after chapter he asked me to remain alone with him in the crypt.'

'At San Eusanio?' Jacques guessed. He was surprised how easy it was; how readily Pietro had accepted the pact. It was his last desperate effort to retrieve his family's power.

230

'I only ever saw my uncle at Ocre,' Pietro replied indirectly, 'and I shall never forget his expression that night – the last time I saw him alive. "There is something I must show you," he said. He opened a door I had never been allowed to enter . . .'

The bricked-up doorway. It must be. 'Go on . . .' Jacques said anxiously. He was afraid the preceptor would lose himself in his memories. But as he spoke, the *name* of the church echoed in his mind. Who was Saint Eusanio, and why was he of such interest to the counts of Ocre?

'There was another chapel, smaller, with two plain altars. Not a single cross was to be seen and on each altar was a golden vase of fresh flowers. The floor was richly carpeted with those flowery carpets you see in the East. The walls were freshly painted white. And inside one altar there was a strange box . . .'

'Is the altar still there?' Jacques' excitement was barely concealed.

'No. It was removed when Charles of Anjou plundered the church. The chamber was bricked up.'

Jacques felt his chest throbbing. 'The image was inside this box?'

'When we had prayed together, my uncle led me behind that altar,' the preceptor replied indirectly. 'He took a key from inside his shirt, unlocked the altar and placed the box on top.'

'What was the box like?'

'Square, flat. About two palms square, and the height of a bible. It was made of dark wood. But the top was open, and covered by a silver grille like a prison window. The silver was worked by hand with designs like those on a mosque. It looked like a heathen object at first, but then I saw something white inside. A cloth . . .' His voice faltered. 'I couldn't see it properly until he tilted it towards me and bright sunlight fell on the cloth. It was one of the most frightening moments of my life, for I was looking at a face which I knew to be that of Jesus Christ our Saviour. My knees shook in terror, and light filled the crypt as in a miracle.' Pietro paused, as if in disbelief at his own words. 'With that face, Brother, you could incite fear and obedience in any man. It is the most powerful object in the world.'

This was pristine heresy, but Jacques refrained from the sarcasm which would have come easily to him. The old Templar was as superstitious as King Philip and Guillaume de Paris . . . who both believed in this image and its power, he recalled. 'What happened to the image?' he asked directly.

231

'My brother, Cardinal Tommaso, concealed it before Anjou ransacked the church. I never spoke to him, nor heard from him again, bless his soul. He was murdered while I was in Cyprus.'

Jacques recalled the earlier interrogation. 'Murdered?'

'As surely as Pope Celestine was murdered. And by the same hand.'

'Evidence?'

'The fact that I am here. My Order and my family ruined. Had Tommaso been alive and Celestine on the Holy See for ten years we would have succeeded ... Rome would have had the pope we groomed for the Holy See. *We* would have controlled the Church, and could have made ourselves Kings of Italy – like the first Berardo – and perhaps even more ... if we had had the time.'

Jacques stared, flabbergasted at the audacity of this plan. 'Did Tommaso know of the move against Celestine before the pope's death?'

'I believe so. The coronation was in Aquila, you see. And Charles of Anjou himself was there that day. Some days later, the pope fled south. He never went to Rome, and never returned to Aquila. They must have known by then.'

'Tommaso was at the coronation?'

'He was made Cardinal the next day.'

In the same year they all died. And the image disappeared. Now only one detail was lacking. 'You speak of your uncle as if he were alive today,' Jacques began carefully. He did not wish to upset his prey. 'He sounds a fascinating man ... and he was careful in his choice of followers ... But tell me,' he went on with all the art at his command, 'now that you have told me much of the story ... where is the box hidden?'

'No!' Pietro shouted defiantly. 'That is something I will never tell you!' His voice shook as he shouted, and the entire force in his body seemed to swell up into his reply. The truth was indeed buried deep, though his desperation suggested he knew quite well that he had revealed nearly everything to his inquisitor.

Instinct told Jacques that the preceptor would never tell him under these circumstances. Time was short and he would soon have to depart for Ocre. There was a solution: torture – but that was repugnant to him. Or was it? With shock at his own self-discovery he saw that the idea of torture was no longer abhorrent. He touched his eyelids with the tips of his fingers and pushed them down as if to conceal from himself what he knew he must do. *Opus Christi* required it, since it was for the good of the Church, and thus of God and all mankind. He pushed harder against his eyes until he could feel the pulse on his fingertips, peering into his memory to conjure up a vision of that evening in the dungeon at Aigues-Mortes what seemed like years ago. Then, when his eyes began to hurt, he opened them again and looked on Pietro, fully aware for the first time of how much he himself had changed. And then, he reasoned, we shall be sending the preceptor directly to his Maker and to eternal peace, which could hardy be worse than the torments he has already endured here on earth.

He shook his head sadly. Ruthless times necessitate ruthless measures, he reflected ironically. 'Briac!' he shouted. 'Find water and grease, quickly,' he ordered when the guard entered.

Briac soon returned. 'Bind him to that bench, and rekindle the fire. Here's rope.' He handed over the leather bag.

The guard looked at Jacques in astonishment, and then at the bag, but he obeyed the order.

Abbot Jacques sat quietly in the corner while Briac worked. Pietro said nothing. There was neither surprise nor delusion on the prisoner's face, which was as pale and expressionless as a death-mask.

The embers were soon spread evenly like a bright red carpet across the fireplace. There was little smoke. Together Briac and Jacques lifted the bench with Pietro di Ocre strapped to it until it stood at right angles to the fire. Briac had placed a rough wooden board against the end of the bench to act as a screen.

'Apply the grease,' Jacques ordered. He recalled Pietro's assertion that he would not survive further torture, but he hoped the mere threat would be enough.

The preceptor lay back placidly, staring at the brick vault. With his arms folded across his abdomen he looked for all the world like the effigy of a bishop on a sarcophagus. For a moment, Jacques hesitated, out of piety, but urgency soon overcame compassion.

Briac removed the board. Then he pushed the bench towards the fire. Jacques drew a sand-glass from an inner pocket of his habit, turned it over, and placed it on the table as the first grains began to fall.

The prisoner's face was impassive. Pain seemed to have no effect. Jacques and Briac watched in silence, like small boys at a frog race waiting for the first movement, he thought.

233

Presently a quiet sizzling sound echoed about the room. The receptor's face flushed with the pain, and his lips hardened as he sought to resist. The sizzling dropped a tone as it modulated to a steady roasting sound. The silence of the room was destroyed by a horrifying scream that seemed to come from a dozen voices. It rose from the inner man as the sum of years of protest; his beliefs in knighthood, his Order and his family were concentrated into a terrifying shriek of protest against this treatment. When it receded, tears had appeared at the corners of his eyes. Jacques noticed with detached interest that his victim had gone well beyond the normal level of resistance. He motioned to Briac, who replaced the board.

By that time the soles of the Templar's feet had been burnt off, and the flesh immediately beneath them was grilled to the point at which beef was usually eaten. He would never walk again. But then, he would never need to ... 'Well, Preceptor? Where is the image hidden?'

Pietro di Ocre grimaced. 'You may kill me now,' he said weakly, 'for I have nothing more to tell you. And it is clear I shall never get to Italy.'

'Just one word, or I'll have Briac the Beast here pull your body apart piece by piece until there is nothing left but your tongue.' Jacques stepped back, shocked by his own language, but there was nothing to hide now, and everything to gain.

'Find it yourself!' As Pietro spat the words, his eyes closed and his mouth fell limp. They had overdone it. The prisoner's resistance had not been so high after all, and he had slipped into the temporary refuge of all torture victims.

'Bring water!'

At the second bucket Pietro's eyes opened again.

Remorse nearly won Jacques over, and he had to shake his head to remind himself that Pietro was indeed guilty of the most abominable heresy. 'Tell us what we wish to know, and I will promise you burial in a Christian cemetery. I myself will perform the funeral rites, I swear here by Saint Germain and in the presence of Briac. If you do not do so, then I shall arrange that your body be broken into pieces and scattered to the four winds, and you will rot unrecognized for eternity like the worst of heretics. The choice is yours ...'

As if in defiant answer, a thin voice began to intone like a demon issuing from the body of the preceptor. 'May the Lord save my soul, for I have gazed upon his countenance and do love him ...'

234

The words came with a weird passion, and Jacques was struck by the joy and certainty which illuminated the prisoner's face. Then Pietro began to chant the prayer he had recited in Avignon:

'The images are manifest to man,
but the light in them remains concealed
in the image of the light of the Father.
He will become manifest,
but this image will remain concealed by his light.

I shall give you
What no eye has seen
and what no ear has heard
and what no hand has touched
and what has never occurred to the human mind.'

Jacques sat enthralled by the unearthly voice. The image had indeed remarkable powers, he thought. As the old Templar began to speak his eyes had softened, the lines wrought across his face by age and imprisonment seemed to vanish, and his body relaxed. All signs of pain miraculously disappeared. It was greater than the power of nostalgia, as if the memory of it could heal sorrow and agony. Could that have been the image which terrified courageous knights and drove a king almost mad with desire for its possession?

It so, then this prayer indicated the solution of his problem, for Pietro had heard it and gazed upon this image at Ocre.

Jacques moved towards the door, trembled as he grasped the catch, and prayed to the Lord for his soul as he prepared to commit the ultimate sin.

Briac seemed alarmed. 'What shall I do?' he asked, pointing at the Templar.

Abbot Jacques stopped abruptly, astonished that Briac, whom he had come to regard as an exemplar of ruthlessness, should show compunction about his obvious duty. 'Remember, Briac,' he said, not without a lump in his throat, 'that this man was executed last night.' Then, as if it were an afterthought: 'The deepest dungeon of Paris is beneath this abbey, I understand, and Brother Armand tells me there is an ancient cistern even deeper where unwanted corpses have always been disposed of.'

He was struck by his own callousness as he left Briac to his task.

235

34

Abbot Gilles' house was guarded. All pretence of secrecy now thrown to the wind.

Bernard de Caen failed to disguise his annoyance as Jacques was escorted inside. 'Ah, there you are; Nicolas and I were discussing the details of your journey.' He closed a delicate leather manuscript cover on the table before him, obviously feigning absent-mindedness, and hid his hands under the table as if removing the evidence. His forehead glistened with tiny beads of perspiration.

'We're to leave at dawn,' Nicolas added, 'if that's not too early for you. There is no time to be lost.'

'I am ready now,' Jacques replied calmly. Had Nicolas known of his visit to Saint Germain? Anyway, it no longer mattered. There was nothing more to be done in Paris. 'So there is no problem for a dawn departure.'

'Excellent.' The legendary calm had returned to Bernard's face. He placed his chubby hands back on the table. 'Nicolas has been provided with letters for the journey.'

A new thought crossed Jacques' mind as he listened; something he would not have dared to express when he left Bernard's company for Aigues-Mortes the previous summer. 'Where will you be, should we need to send letters, my Lord Bernard? In Paris, or in Avignon?'

A faint pig-pink suffused his Superior's cheeks. 'You will know when it is necessary,' Bernard replied pompously. His tone was that of an angry schoolmaster admonishing a student he had once admired for coming out into the open as a rebel. Then, as if aware that he had been unnecessarily harsh, his voice suddenly softened. 'There is one thing I should like to make very clear to both of you. You know that this mission is of vital importance to the Church, and that we are acting with fullest authority of His Holiness in this matter.' He paused, fixing each man in turn with his beady green eyes. 'We must recover the relic for the Church,' he then asserted, 'and it is equally important that we thwart the renegade Templars on their way to Ocre at this very moment. Above all, we must block the imperial dreams of King

Philip. Whatever price we must pay will be paid, without question. Is that clear?'

'Yes, my lord.' For once inquisitor and knight spoke in unison.

'I am not of course in a position to make promises,' Bernard continued. 'But I can state with certainty that any recommendation I should make when this affair is completed would certainly be met with favour by His Holiness. I make no promises, mind you, yet I dare say a bishopric would not be beyond your reach, Abbot Jacques.' He allowed the word to roll around his mouth and issue slowly, enjoying his moment of supremacy. Jacques was discreetly reminded of his power in this and other matters. 'And for you, Sire Nicolas, a suitable appointment – and lands – in the papal service. Is that clear?'

Again they spoke together: 'Yes, my lord.'

'Then God be with you.' Bernard looked down at the file in front of him while he waited for Jacques and Nicolas to leave.

35

A new shared intimacy prompted Jacques to open his soul as they walked down from Abbot Gilles' house. 'I had a last chance to question Pietro di Ocre,' he said as though it were the most natural thing in the world.

'Indeed?' Nicolas regarded Jacques closely as he walked slightly ahead. As his companion he should have been present, he thought. But then, he was not an inquisitor, and had not attended every interrogation of the preceptor. 'What did you learn?'

'Not much. But I discovered a quite different man.'

Nicolas looked at him with genuine interest. 'Did he tell you where the image is hidden?'

'No.' It was only a half-lie. 'But with regard to his sense of values, of the old knighthood ... I think I begin to understand what he means.'

What was Jacques leading up to? It must be his new rank which was causing him to view afresh the people around him. 'I'm not sure the preceptor himself knows what he means much of the time.'

'He was lucid enough when he wished,' Jacques continued. 'He had fascinating information about the fall of Acre, and the Templars in the Holy Land. An honourable Order of Knights, according to him, attached to the ancient values.'

'Then we'll have plenty to discuss on the road,' Nicolas observed coldly. This sudden conversion was as suspicious as his previous scepticism, if it was genuine.

'There'll certainly be time.' Abbot Jacques sensed that this was not the moment to press his point. Once out of Paris, when there would be no one for Nicolas to report to, would be time enough. He longed for the independence of action that the journey would give him.

The brisk walk had made him hot. When he saw a fountain on the other side of the street, he asked Nicolas to wait a moment.

It was odd, he reflected as he crossed the street, that he felt so close to his companion in these simple exchanges. For a moment, he thought back to Pietro di Ocre's nostalgic musings on knighthood. Nicolas belonged to the old order, and would always do so. It was stamped on him as clearly as the image of the King was stamped on his coins. Although Jacques had never fully trusted the young aristocrat he now saw that Nicolas had been curiously loyal to him through these difficult months. There was no doubt that he reported back to Bernard de Caen, but he managed to do so in a way that did not affect their day-to-day working relationship. In his own way, he was loyal to Jacques too.

Unlike Bernard. For whatever his doubts during the meeting, Jacques was certain that Bernard de Caen was not revealing all he knew. He never had done. From the very first, Jacques had been sent on this mission without knowing the real reason behind it; had he not been capable of guessing the real reason after questioning Pietro, he would have been sent back to Avignon. So what were Bernard de Caen's final intentions?

The answer lay in Ocre. That much was clear.

He bent down to drink. As he did so he was shocked to see his own face clear as a painting on the smooth dark surface of the water. Light surrounded the basin, but left the surface dark, like a perfect mirror. He stared at his own image for an instant, as if he were watching someone else. The face on the water was leaner than that he had known before, with slightly hollow cheeks. The skin seemed somehow harder, with lines drawn deeply and firmly across the image. He fancied his eyes were sharper as he watched them, unblinking, on the water. On the whole he was pleased with the new tautness of expression, which exuded what appeared to him a certain authority.

Then he shrugged off this unpardonable vanity, and drank deeply of the cool water that had borne his image.

He knew that he was ready.

36

'But how is it possible?' Rage swelled up in Jacques' throat, nearly choking his words. 'Lord Bernard counselled us to travel round the Alps to overtake them, since they would be slowed by late snows. On *our* route the Saône and Rhône were in flood and the boatmen swore they had never seen them so rapid. The horses waiting in Avignon were the fastest available. And we left our baggage train behind at Grasse to gain time. Yet here in Milan we hear rumours . . .'

His voice stifled. He looked up at the cobweb-strewn ceiling of the hostelry in which they were sitting. Trapped as hopelessly as those flies, he fumed to himself. His back ached, his thighs were chapped from the saddle, and still they might be late. He repeated the last words dreamily: ' . . . we hear rumours . . .'

'*Messire Essart* hears rumours,' Nicolas corrected him, 'and they are only rumours.' The sympathy he had felt towards the seneschal when he was dismissed had long since disappeared.

'Be that as it may,' Jacques snapped, 'I trust Renaud.' He wrestled down his anger and frustration, realizing even within its grip that it would be perilous to alienate Nicolas. Each man was vital to the success of their quest now. 'In a word,' he continued in a quieter voice, also aware of the gaze of their table companions, 'the Templar knights may already have passed through this city. What is the meaning of it? You should know!'

'Why should *I* know? I've no idea. You must believe me.'

Nicolas' indignation seemed genuine, so he was probably speaking the truth, Jacques reasoned. 'But you must have some idea,' he insisted. 'Think back to your last meetings with Lord Bernard. He may have hinted at something . . .'

Nicolas shook his head. 'I can't understand it at all.' He too was puzzled. With the mountain passes blocked, there was no faster route than the one they had taken. He gazed at their host, who was pouring wine, as if in search of inspiration from that cheerful face. 'Perhaps we should check the rumours first,' he suggested brightly.

'I suppose you're right,' Jacques agreed, relieved that the mounting anger in his breast had begun to subside. In effect second-hand rumours were scant evidence. Yet at the same time he thought he detected a new note in Nicolas' voice: was his insistence on the rumours simply based on mistrust of Renaud Essart? Or could he have known all along that the knights were ahead of them? Yet even that presupposed the physical possibility of the Templars travelling faster than they.

He recalled Nicolas' strange demeanour during the journey. While usually he never lost a chance to assert his superiority of birth and knowledge on such occasions, for days he had barely uttered a word. During the hair-raising boat ride Jacques had squatted in the bows as calmly as if he were in his own cell, never looking out. It had taken him days to adapt to the sudden lurches as the fast-moving current changed direction, and the spine-shuddering jerks when the boatmen erred and their flat-bottomed boats crossed the main current and entered a temporary lull on the inside of a bend. But Nicolas seemed not to notice. He sat in silence with a sullen look on his face. Jacques was inclined at first to attribute this to the boat journey itself. Even in the inns where they stopped each night his companion continued to behave in the same sullen manner, speaking rarely and usually gruffly.

'We'll reach Milan before those Templar renegades if we keep up this speed,' Jacques had suggested to him one evening.

'Indeed,' Nicolas had concurred.

'We're lucky to have had such good information about the snow on the mountain passes, aren't we?'

'Yes.' It had been like squeezing blood from a stone.

'Lord Bernard has such good sources,' Jacques had continued, trying to provoke a reaction.

It worked. There was a glimpse of doubt, or perhaps even fear, in his companion's eye. 'Lord Bernard?' Nicolas had queried. There was embarrassment on his face as he repeated the name, as if three syllables had brought him back to life.

Jacques had been intrigued. But no further blood was forthcoming, even though Nicolas himself had asserted before their departure that they would have time to talk. His mouth was closed as tight as a clam, save for banal comments on progress and table each time they made a halt.

Now, in Milan, and nearer to their destination, the thought of that single brief exchange nagged at Jacques, together with the memory of the argument between Nicolas and Bernard that his unexpected arrival at Abbot Gilles' house had stifled. What had they been discussing with such vehemence? Could it have been that Nicolas was resisting the instructions he had been given for this journey? It was essential to find out the truth, and here his companion seemed more amenable. 'Nicolas?' he began cautiously. 'There's something I've been meaning to say to you. We're alone here in Italy. Lord Bernard will not be able to assist us in difficulty. We must work together.' As he spoke, it seemed to him that suspicion lurked in those deep dark eyes like trout in a shady pool.

'Aren't we? As far as I can see we are together, and will be so until Ocre.' This constant tension was wearisome.

Jacques ignored the disdain in his companion's tone. But was there a suggestion of further knowledge in those eyes? Perhaps not. He knew that he was wrong to seek treachery in every movement of eye and mouth. He must needs trust Nicolas. 'You are right; we must check the rumour. I shall go at once with Renaud, and you with Briac. We shall seek confirmation . . . or denial.' He added the last phrase with hope in his heart.

Instinct told Nicolas it would be a hopeless task, but he agreed. It would be better than sitting here distrusting one another. 'I'll leave at once. Briac! Here!'

Jacques summoned Renaud. 'We'll pose as French sergeant-brothers on the run,' he suggested to Nicolas while he waited. 'That should be enough to explain our curiosity.' Then, as soon as Renaud was ready, they rode to the abandoned Templar commanderie.

They had to scramble in through rubble that had fallen from the floor of the gatehouse above. Someone had plundered the doorposts and hinges for use elsewhere, while the doors themselves had been broken up for firewood. The courtyard inside was as barren as the hills of Ocre. Thick grass and clumps of nettles as tall as a man occupied the ramshackle outbuildings. The only living beings were ancient servants of the brothers who once lived there and now spent their time sitting in the shade of the walls. According to them, no sign had been seen of the knights they were pursuing. 'They're speaking the truth,' Renaud joked. 'Who'd come back to this mess anyway?'

Jacques glanced at the men and nodded. 'It was worth a try,' he observed. But it was more to encourage himself that he spoke. He wondered how Nicolas and Briac were doing: probably ensconced in another hostelry.

Next they rode to the Street of the Venetians, again meeting no luck. Innkeepers and stall-holders claimed to have seen nothing. 'Foreign knights?' was the universal reply. 'This city is full of them. But not those you're looking for. No knights of the red cross.' Jacques was beginning to consider revealing his presence at Chiaravalle, since the monks there may have had news; but it was no real emergency yet, he reflected, for he, Nicolas, Renaud and Briac would have to continue their own journey south in any case. He was reluctant to reveal his presence in Milan.

They passed an armourer's workshop, with lengths of mail and helmets hanging on the outside wall. Inside, smoke bellowed from the forge and enveloped the artisans at work. For an unnerving moment serried suits of armour seemed peopled with soldiers, each tilted on its nail as if about to charge down at Jacques. It was then that the inspiration came to him. He thought of the last time he had passed that way, and of his destination then. 'At the sign of The Three Pigeons,' he muttered to himself as he remembered that visit.

'What did you say?' Renaud looked at him inquisitively.

Jacques then realized that he had spoken aloud. 'Just an idea,' he said, 'a woman who may well have information.'

Renaud stared at him, nonplussed.

The Abbot spurred his palfrey forwards, eager to escape that questioning gaze.

His mind hesitated on the threshold of the inn; but his body was carried in by a group of thirsty barge-men. 'Wait here with the horses, Renaud,' he shouted from the door. 'I won't be long.'

He felt he was entering hell. The very walls exuded steam and smoke. Men ate and swore rumbustiously. Sweating, smoke-encased women stirred cauldrons at the huge fires. There was no quiet corner, and no empty table. Brightly-dressed maidens served at table: smiling, offering. Jacques found himself searching their faces for the girl who had initiated him. Then he heard Ida's infectious laughter. Enwrapped in a gown of vermilion which put the others in shade, she was supervising the serving of a noisy group in the centre of the room. 'Ah!' She smiled as she saw him, then winked with genuine pleasure. 'I knew you'd come back one day.' There was no trace of surprise in her face.

'You misunderstand ...' Jacques began. He looked anxiously about the crowded room, spurred by was he knew was an irrational fear that he would be recognized. He was glad they were travelling in disguise.

'Of course I do. But don't worry. Ida will take care of you. Now come along!' She left the client she was about to serve open-mouthed, and beckoned to Jacques as if it was the most natural thing in the world.

He followed her into a room behind the stairs.

Ida shut the door quickly behind him, and pushed the heavy bolt across. Smiling, she stepped backwards to a large padded chair and sat down. 'Well,' she said, 'do you want me now? Or should we drink first?'

Jacques was perplexed. In the months of this mission he had gained a new sense of his own importance. He had learned how to conceal his emotions and now enjoyed the power which his position as Abbot gave him. Giving orders to such as Briac and Renaud came naturally. But in front of this seductress he was as nervous as an adolescent. Whatever his intentions. Words blocked in his throat.

Without the slightest remorse, he allowed her to undress him. As she fondled him and kissed him, he tore off her underclothes with a vehemence which shocked him when he saw her standing naked before him like the woman in the dream.

He was in command. He felt it was something he had always known how to do. Time, Ocre, the Church: all were forgotten in a spiral of passion such as he had never imagined possible. He knew now that he was not being seduced, but seducing: it spurred him on to feasts of strength beyond his wildest imagination. He gasped with a sense of raw power as he climaxed, and found strength to continue until Ida screamed with pleasure too. And then, without shame, he brought her to pleasure again as the other girl had wished.

He lay back with a wonderful sense of exhaustion, and contentment.

But as he did so, his conscience impinged upon pleasure. Renaud Essart was waiting for him outside. He stood up quickly, and started to dress. 'I want to ask you some questions about travellers you have seen lately,' he said as he pulled on his hose.

'We see them every day, deary.'

'I'm thinking of some Templar knights.'

'Templars?' Ida regarded him with a new curiosity.

'Three knights, who I'm told passed through Milan.'

'They did indeed, deary. And Templar brothers pass through well,' she laughed. 'I saw them with my own eyes, wearing their full insignia they was, with shields and the red cross on their shoulders. And one of them was a fine figure indeed. But they never stopped here, I'm afraid. You won't catch them, sir inquisitor!'

'Why not?'

'They galloped like the wind.'

So the rumours Renaud had picked up were confirmed. Jacques made to leave the inn. There was no more time to lose.

'Anyway, that was a good day,' Ida continued as he began to walk towards the door. 'There were more knights from Paris that day, and *they* did stop.' He paused on a hunch, feigning interest without alarming her. 'One of them said he was a personal friend of the King of France. Right tall tale that was, but he was good enough.'

'A friend of the King?' Jacques walked back to her.

'Yes, my dear. He was in this very inn two days ago. An excellent evening it was.' She pouted her lips.

'What do you mean?'

'I screwed one of them. Right here on this very chair.' She let her hand run along the cover. 'The others weren't having any of it.'

Jacques shuddered, instantly regretting what he had done. He sat down, feeling suddenly weak. She was not unique to him, and he saw his illusion of having power over women for the sham it was. The thought of another man with Ida tarnished his pleasurable memory. He concentrated on her face to avoid his eyes falling on the instrument of sin. 'How many of them were there?'

'Three others. Pensive types. Stubborn as asses and impossible to interest. Bit like you used to be, deary.' She pouted her lips at him again as she began to dress.

'So they were here?'

'Couldn't have screwed him if they weren't, could I?' she laughed.

Jacques ignored her question. 'When did they leave?'

'Yesterday. At dawn.' She looked dreamily at him. 'I suppose it wouldn't be worth going with men like that . . . and anyway the one I had was pretty good.'

'What was his name?' He was now detached, urgently thinking of Ocre and no longer disgusted with himself.

She looked at him pertly, then held out her hand. He passed her a silver *denarius*. When she had put it carefully inside her dress she smiled at him again. 'Gerard. Said he was a personal

245

friend of the King of France. Go on, I said, you as likely be . . .'

'He said that?' Jacques interrupted.

'That's what I'm telling you,' Ida replied. 'If you won't believe me there's no point in listening.'

He ignored her. 'What did he look like?'

'Tall, young, strong . . . and a fine piece of grain. Dark-haired. He lisped when he spoke. Strange French too. He was younger than the others, but they obeyed him without question.'

'Did he say where he was going?'

'South.'

'Nothing else?'

'It was a secret mission, he said.'

'He didn't say what? You're sure?'

'As sure as I'm standing here.' Ida spoke in a whisper. 'Yes, I suppose the others would have been a waste of time.'

'What did you say?'

'Nothing, deary.' Again she laughed the deep, hearty laugh which Jacques could not help but enjoy. Oddly, it reminded him of his mother. He got up to leave.

'Thank you,' he said sincerely. He was thinking of this new information, but she ran her fingers over him as he stood above her, evidently understanding otherwise.

'No. Not now,' he shivered. Although he was tempted, he pushed her away. He was beyond caring about her now.

And she no longer played up to him, he noticed with a flash of annoyance. She had turned off her charms as easily as she had switched them on, and was now chastely buttoned to the neck. 'We'd better go back, deary. I've work to do.'

Yet he could not deny a deep satisfaction. Their encounter had drained the simmering fury within his breast. He felt that he would do better what he had to do. Furthermore, he was not ashamed to admit to himself that it was for love that he had gone to The Three Pigeons. The information was a bonus.

As he left the inn, Jacques imagined his face must be like that of one of the miscreants he had tried when they faced neighbours and relatives from the dock. Nicolas de Lirey and Briac were waiting there by his own mount. The horses whinnied nervously as if they knew what he had done. He fancied he saw a knowing look in Nicolas' eye. But Renaud seemed to notice nothing. 'Did you find anything out?' he asked quickly.

'It wasn't easy.' He laughed within at his lie, then told them what he had learned. 'And you?' he addressed Nicolas.

'Nothing at all. The people here pay little attention to travellers, it appears.'

Abbot Jacques was pleased with the hunch that had led him to visit Ida, but now he tried to push her from his mind. 'Who could this Gerard be, do you think?'

'Gerard? Gerard? I'll have to think. It's a common enough name,' Nicolas replied. 'Renaud?'

The seneschal shook his head.

They mounted, and rode in silence, following a canal south from the fluvial port away from the city.

Beside the canal, men and women were sowing new crops. Jacques imagined they would be oats, peas, beans and perhaps barley. Cows were now coming into milk again, and he noticed that fresh milk and cheese were on sale at farms they passed. The days were growing longer, he had been pleased to notice in the last few days, and the increased light would allow them to travel further.

Nicolas was lost in thought, but Jacques didn't press him, hoping that his thoughts were devoted to uncovering the identity of the mysterious Gerard.

It was some time before he suddenly drew up his horse. 'It might have been Gerard de Troyes,' he suggested. 'King Philip would entrust him with a mission like this. He fought well in Navarre, and has been a seneschal for a good ten years now. And he knows Italy well.'

Jacques looked up. 'Knows Italy? Are you sure?'

It was Renaud who answered. 'Sir Nicolas is right,' he asserted with conviction. 'I myself was here with him. Last year he commanded one of the search teams. Rome was his brief, if I remember aright.'

'In the late autumn?'

'Yes, Brother.'

Then he could have been in Ocre – and in Burgundy. Jacques glanced at Nicolas, and knew his thoughts were identical. 'Tell me, Renaud, is he a tall man, taller than the average soldier, thin faced, dark . . .'

'You've seen him?'

'. . . who speaks with a lisp?'

'That's your man. Gerard de Troyes. I couldn't have described him better myself.' Renaud's mouth gaped in astonishment.

'Now we know who we're looking for, it'll be easier,' Nicolas said. 'I'd love to have a word with this Gerard. And I think Briac here owes him something, don't you?'

A ferocious grin appeared on the guard's face. He feigned drawing his sword, and cut the head off an imaginary figure beside him with such gusto that he nearly fell out of the saddle.

Abbot Jacques smiled. That was the right attitude. He turned back to the seneschal: 'Thank you, Renaud. Your information is most useful.' The confirmation of the rumours was bad enough and this additional news dismayed him more than he wished to admit to himself.

There was no further need to dally in Milan. 'Come, we have a long way to go yet,' Jacques shouted and, as he spurred his horse to the gallop, he thought he could discern the great Abbey of Chiaravalle through the poplars to his left. When eventually he made a visit, he thought, he would arrive there in state.

─── 37 ───

As Abbot Jacques looked up at the south gate of the new city of Aquila an uneasy and inexplicable sense of guilt came over him, as if he had in some way been responsible for the demise of the family of the counts of Ocre. For this was to have been their New Jerusalem. And here by the gate that led to their castle was the chapel of Santa Maria del Ponte, built by Gualtiero for the Templars. Beneath the church a stone bridge bore the main road over a stream and south away from the city. A desire to pay homage prompted him to dismount and enter. Nicolas followed him silently.

Renaud, Briac and the guards remained in the saddle.

The chapel had a simple whitewashed interior, with a stone altar and a worm-eaten crucifix made of three horizontal sections of plank nailed together, the middle one broader for the outstretched arms of Christ. But as soon as he saw it, he knew something was wrong. Even here there was an anomaly, as in everything connected with the counts of Ocre, although he couldn't identify it at first. Jacques studied the painting, and found it attractive: the huge head bore thick black lines of suffering, while the body seemed too thin for such a massive neck and arms. It was crude in comparison with the painted crucifixes of Avignon and Paris, and he assumed that the artist was a local man. But it served its function. He bent his head and prayed with humility.

When he looked up again, he felt warmth on his back. He opened his eyes to see a spiralling cylinder of dusty sunshine streaming in from the plain rose window above the door. With a start, he saw that the crucifix had changed colour, especially where the area around Christ's wounds had turned deep blood-red.

Then he understood the anomaly.

There were three nails, not four, as was usual. Jacques smiled inwardly at his own earlier apprehension: for this was no heresy, but simply the ignorance of a local painter. Yet while he knew that it was a minor thing he was forced to admit to himself that it had disturbed him. Nothing here was quite what it appeared to be. He glanced at Nicolas, and wondered whether he too had noticed.

Jacques was still kneeling before the altar when the chapel was suddenly filled with the din, clatter and shouted orders of what sounded like an entire army. Above all he was struck by one harsh voice, which appeared to command them. That shrill, high-pitched tone chilled his bones even in the warmth of sunshine. It was familiar, although he could not place it instantly.

Nicolas too recognized it. He glanced quickly at Jacques and leapt to his feet. They strode to the door together. Outside, men and horses all but obliterated the tiny square before the church and brimmed over to fill the road up to the city gate. Bright sunshine blinded their eyes so that they could not recognize the men. Jacques held up his right hand to create shade, seeking out Renaud Essart and moving towards him while Nicolas stood by the door. 'Who are they?' he shouted.

'Frenchmen,' Renaud replied, 'but I can't see their commander.' He too was squinting into the sun.

From the shelter of the porch Nicolas had less difficulty. 'Several of these officers are familiar to me,' he called to Jacques, who felt a chill deep in his guts as he began to understand why they were familiar. 'I fear', he began softly, 'that these men . . .'

At that moment, Abbot Jacques thought he saw a familiar form on horseback in the throng of soldiers and black-robed friars who he now saw amidst them. But it seemed impossible. 'Look, Renaud,' he shouted, drowning out Nicolas' voice, 'the helmless man over there. Could it be . . . ?'

'By my oath, you're right!'

It was Nicolas who pronounced the name: 'Guillaume de Paris!'

'May the Lord help us,' Jacques whispered in the shock of recognition. He had expected to see the officer Ida had described, and was seeking a tall, young man. He was sure to be somewhere there as well. But this unexpected presence was of much greater importance, and it unnerved him. Hoping he was wrong, he looked again. There could be no doubt. The shrill voice ought to have been enough, he now realized.

His feet seemed to take root in the square as the Inquisitor-General for Paris bore down on him, and he sought solace with his hands in the rough limestone wall behind him. To each side of Guillaume rode a royal seneschal armed to the teeth, their right hands resting on their swords as if by prior agreement. Behind them rode half a dozen prelates of the French church whom Jacques did not recognize; but their harnesses and apparel bespoke immense wealth. He studied the impassive grey face of the Inquisitor-General and waited for that voice which could chill a brave man to stone. Would it be arrest? Disgrace? Loss of the abbey he had not yet seen? Death in this wasteland with no one to report it?

Guillaume de Paris pulled his horse up and stared hard at the monk. Jacques absorbed, rather than watched, while his lips first pursed as though he were about to spit and then modulated their expression into a sneer of contempt. It was only a matter of seconds, but it felt like an eternity. Then Guillaume turned his face away as though the men before him had ceased to exist, pulled the reins to turn his mount, and moved away. His retinue imitated him in absolute silence.

'A fine exercise in intimidation,' Jacques remarked to Nicolas when the horsemen were well out of earshot.

Nicolas nodded his agreement at this sentiment. Then a new thought came to him. 'But his presence here provides us with two essential pieces of information.'

'And what may they be?' The shock was beginning to diminish. He was glad that Renaud and Briac were there with them.

'First that His Excellency the Inquisitor-General has no idea of where to look. Otherwise he'd have no cause to show himself.' The irony in his voice was unmistakeable.

'And second?'

'That he is staying within the city walls.'

'And so?'

'So it would be best for us to keep well away from the city.'

'I see,' Jacques said thoughtfully. He did not wish to go to Santo Spirito yet, although he realized that the abbot there might be able to help him with information. Yet Nicolas was right. He made two rapid decisions, one dictated by logic and one by intuition. 'Briac,' he called. Then, as he walked towards the guard, he felt his calves aching as though he had been climbing mountains all day.

'Sire?' Briac was standing apart with his men.

'There is a small house of my Order in the valley between here and Ocre.' He glanced towards Nicolas, who nodded agreement.

'Yes, sire.'

'We shall rest there tonight. Now take two men, go straight past that house to Santo Spirito, and inform the abbot. See whether he has any information about the Templars. Then come back to the house as soon as you can. Is that clear?'

Briac nodded. Then he turned his mount away.

'That's just as I'd've done,' Nicolas commented. Implicitly he had made the decision in advising the abbot.

'Shall we leave too?' Jacques said, watching Renaud Essart and the remainder of Briac's men cross the bridge as though they had been awaiting such a command. Briac himself was just beyond it.

The castle of Ocre soon came into view, squat on its mountain-top in the distance. Jacques recalled with a thrill of excitement that Santo Spirito was behind the rock and that San Eusanio was hidden away to the left. He now thought of the entire valley and its surrounding mountains as Pietro di Ocre's land, and tried to perceive it from Pietro's point of view. As he did so, he recalled his hunch concerning the character of the saint for whom church and village were named. Now was the time to find out.

He turned to Nicolas. 'There is something you could do at Santo Spirito if you are willing,' he said.

'But of course. Go through the papers again?' Nicolas was more than happy to oblige. First, because he too believed that the solution to the riddle of the hiding-place of the image might be in the monastery; second, because it would give him some freedom of action.

'Good,' Jacques said simply. Then: 'Briac!' he called to the small party ahead. 'Nicolas will come with you.'

Jacques spoke to his companion again. 'It might be nothing more than a foolish notion,' he said, speaking quietly now, 'but I'd like to know more about San Eusanio. Who was he? Where did he come from? Why was he made a saint? What might be his importance for the counts of Ocre? Go with Briac, and see what you can find out at Santo Spirito. They must know.'

There was no need for a reply. Nicolas nodded, urged his horse into a canter, and was gone.

'At the house for dinner!' Jacques shouted after them. But Nicolas and Briac were already out of earshot. He needed time to reflect on Guillaume de Paris' presence in Aquila.

252

38

When he saw it again, Jacques chuckled quietly at his own description of the stone structure as a 'house'. It was little more than a two-roomed hut which the monks of Santo Spirito used during sowing and harvest, when the hours of daylight were too valuable to waste walking to and from the monastery. But he was pleased to note its position, beside a brook and protected from wind by a wall of loose stones that had been gathered during centuries of ploughing. In front of the door was a well-trodden square with a stone water-trough for animals. Inside, a wooden platform was raised from the earthen floor, with rolled-up straw mattresses stored for use beyond the reach of field mice.

Outside, a low stone wall created a sheep fold on two sides of the building. Horses were already loose within the fold, and guards were throwing forage to them. Others were posted beyond the house, on the road and amongst banks of sedge which led down to the brook. Nearby was a small, stone-roofed hut, where the monks kept tools, and stored produce gathered, until carts collected it to take to the monastery.

In the distance he could make out the grey mass of Santo Spirito, nestling precariously on its spur like a brick which looked ready to topple into the valley beneath. On the track which led up to the monastery he fancied he saw moving black specks which could be Nicolas and Briac.

The massive wall seemed less forbidding to Nicolas now, although they were still forced to endure a long wait outside. The same grumpy monk led them to the abbot, who greeted them with equal coldness, but the mention of San Eusanio worked like a magic spell. The abbot himself came from that village and worshipped the local saint.

'Come, I will show you myself,' he said with unexpected enthusiasm, leading Nicolas by his arm to the library. 'We have a *Life of San Eusanio* dictated by the saint himself on his deathbed. There are copies, and you will read one, God bless your good fortune. And your brother Jacques, you say he is now an abbot? Then we will lend him a copy as a sign of our esteem. There is no man in the Holy Roman

Church whose soul will not be uplifted by a reading of the life and miracles of our San Eusanio . . .'

Once the tap was opened, words gushed like a mountain torrent, and Nicolas feared for a moment that he would be obliged to accompany Abbot Placido to the church of San Eusanio. But the thought of even such a short ride seemed to remind the abbot of his rheumatic pains. He gasped, gripped the small of his back with his palms, and quite forgot San Eusanio. A monk in the scriptorium took a copy of the *Life* of the saint from the single shelf, then escorted Nicolas from the library with unending apologies. It was with relief that Nicolas joined Briac in the courtyard below.

He paused outside the gate before mounting his horse, and leafed through the little book. He considered stopping somewhere on the way back to the house to study its contents. It was written in a good southern hand, with large and clear letters, in a Latin which Nicolas did not find difficult. But instinct told him that in this matter the expertise of Abbot Jacques as theologian and inquisitor was vital. The volume was carefully placed in a saddlebag on Briac's horse, and they left Santo Spritio amidst warm effusions of friendship and offers of hospitality. It was, Nicolas thought ironically, as if the abbot cherished a dream of the elevation of San Eusanio to the rank of the Fathers of the Church, and perceived Nicolas de Lirey as the means.

Beneath the abbey where the slope met the flat alluvial plain they stopped by a mill-race to water the horses. Nicolas stepped back from the rushing water, crossed the track and squatted against the bark of a pollarded poplar, leaving Briac with the horses. His back was tired from weeks in the saddle, and the moment's rest was welcome. The sun was warm on his body, and the total calm of the countryside belied the intense activity he knew to be nearby. The only sounds were the gentle chipping of hoes against flint as peasants worked in the fields by the river, and the quiet chirping of newly awakened crickets.

Thus he heard the horsemen before seeing them. A small party of three knights and their squires. He shifted his position to move into shade as they approached, thankful for the distance from the track. He watched as Briac saluted them, and was glad they did not halt. The knights kept their mounts at a steady trot, with the others doing their best to keep up. A fine cloud of dust settled on Nicolas, causing him to cough his lungs free and fan himself with his cap. He stood up, taking care to remain behind the trunk. But the movement was enough to attract the attention of one of the knights, who moved forward in his saddle to lift himself, and turned his gaze full on Nicolas from a lance's throw.

He would never know who received the greatest shock. For the knight was as familiar to him as he knew he was to the knight. They had ridden together under the colours of the King of France, jousted in Champagne as young gallants, and seen their fathers toast their loyalty and affection. Yet the Sire of Estissac was clearly as aware of the delicacy of his mission as Nicolas, and refrained from comment. It was a sign of breeding and diplomacy such as Abbot Jacques would never understand, Nicolas reflected. He glanced towards Briac, but the guard had seen nothing.

Thank the Lord, Nicolas whispered to himself. His shock could not have been greater: for he had heard that Gilbert de Estissac was now in the service of Lord Bernard. Yet he had not halted; neither had he uttered a single word. Either the rumours were false, or Bernard was playing a double hand, he thought bitterly. Perhaps Jacques was correct to distrust his own Superior. But in that case, who was it possible to trust completely? Only Jacques himself. He tried to push the questions from his mind

First Guillaume de Paris. Now Gilbert. Did that mean that Bernard de Caen himself was nearby? At first the thought was so absurd that Nicolas wanted to laugh: yet nothing seemed impossible any more. The very fact of his presence by this mill-race would have been absurd only a short time ago. And now the whole of Paris seemed to be here . . .

The name of the city sparked a new chain of thought: the last time he had seen Guillaume de Paris was outside the royal audience hall, deep in conversation with Lord Bernard. And they had known each other for decades, been in Italy together at the time of Pope Boniface. Though now, it was true, they were on opposite sides. Church and State. Was it possible that they could be conspiring together? Could there be something deeper that held them in mutual thrall? That led two such important men to make this long and uncomfortable journey? Yet again something prompted him to recall, as if they were spoken now, the words of Bernard de Caen that he had once overheard. Could it be?

'You know,' he spoke softly to himself in wonder as if it were a revelation, 'in this morass of loyalty and disloyalty, the best man is Abbot Jacques Fournier. He's as close as any man to the truth now,

255

albeit decoy to the hare. And he's straight as a rod. He would never nurture such ambition.'

'What was that, sire?' The guard had joined him by the poplar.

'Nothing, Briac.' Nicolas shook his head vigorously to bring himself back to reality, and took the reins which the guard proffered. He stepped across Briac's elongated shadow, and looked west to the declining sun. 'Let us join Abbot Jacques before sunset.'

Jacques watched Nicolas and Briac return across the fields as the sun pinked the snow-capped mountain peaks to the north. Then their heads disappeared as their horses picked a path down to the brook. Flat rays of orange sunshine swept across the fields behind them, like soldiers in pursuit. The fierce horizontal light threw newly appeared shoots of green into shadow while illuminating the burnt earth beneath them.

When the familiar heads reappeared they were within hailing distance. Within moments they were dismounting in the square before the house. 'A sour lot up there,' Briac grumbled, pointing towards the monastery. 'They didn't want us to come near their precious monastery.' He stretched legs and back as he spoke the last words.

Jacques smiled as he recalled his own visit with Nicolas. 'But did they admit you eventually?'

'Eventually's the right word, Lord Abbot. When we mentioned San Eusanio. They'd've made us wait all day . . .'

'Thank you Briac. I'll explain what happened.' Nicolas de Lirey spoke softly, but the habit of command was in his voice. He passed the reins of his horse to a guard and joined Jacques, genuinely pleased to see him.

Briac scowled.

'Yes indeed. Thank you, Briac. You've done a good job,' Jacques tried to encourage him. 'There's good broth on the fire against a chill night like this.' Then he addressed Nicolas. 'Well?'

'It's as he said. You remember them. But they relented after a while, and the abbot was most curious to know why we'd returned. He invited us to stay there.' He longed to speak openly, but the time had not yet come. He must be sure about Guillaume de Paris' purpose, and the whereabouts of Bernard de Caen, before he committed himself to Jacques.

Jacques smiled. 'That's an invitation I'd rather decline.'

'I think you're right. Anyway, I questioned them as best I could without arousing their suspicions, and I'm certain they know nothing of the Templars. Nor even of Guillaume de Paris.'

'That's as I expected. And the other matter?'

'That was no problem. It was the only information they were willing to give. An entire book! They hold our friend San Eusanio in great regard. Here!' He consigned the thin, roughly bound volume to Jacques.

'Thank you,' Jacques said, suddenly overwhelmed with exhaustion in spite of his eagerness to read the little volume. 'You've both done a good job.' Even as he spoke Jacques realized that he had sounded patronizing, and that would do nothing to increase Nicolas' trust in him. 'Good night,' He clasped the book to his breast as he spoke.

'Good night,' Nicolas said quickly. Then he retired to the sleeping platform. It was obvious that the inquisitor wished to read alone, and he was not displeased. The prose had looked turgid when he riffled through the volume, and Jacques would soon tell him if there was anything important. He wanted to sleep long and deep, for the next days might offer little time for rest.

The following morning he would find Gilbert and discover the truth. Then he would be able to declare himself to the abbot.

Jacques pulled an oil lamp close to his mattress and began to read the fine Beneventan script. Excitement battled with fatigue. At first he tried to push his eyelids back with his fingers, but it was to no avail. Reluctantly, he blew out the lamp. The book would have to wait. He pushed it deep into the pocket inside his habit, patted it as if to wish it goodnight, and rested his head against the soft straw.

257

39

An eerie stillness enveloped the house when darkness fell completely. There was little wind, so that every sound in the valley carried to Jacques' ears with unusual precision. The horses shuffled uneasily in the sheepfold, and the guards' voices rang as clear as mountain water. He lay on his mattress, but did not sleep. The presence of Guillaume de Paris had disturbed him more than he had liked to admit to Nicolas. He had chased the Templars from Paris at breakneck speed, believing that his party would be the first to reach Ocre, but they had arrived in Italy to find not only the Templars ahead of them at Milan, but also Guillaume already at Aquila. What route had *he* taken? Had *he* been advised by Bernard de Caen? The questions reverberated through Jacques' sleepless mind.

A screech-owl barked in the fields outside. He shivered in his bed and remembered how his father had told him that this owl tricked other birds to fall into the snares set by hunters, as Satan tricks humanity. Was he, the hunter, himself becoming the prey? But as soon as the question posed itself he smiled in the darkness as he realized how silly he was being, falling into the same superstitious beliefs as Rollanz – and King Philip. The owl was probably nesting in the sedge, and had been disturbed by the guards. Jacques leaned on his elbow to gaze through the narrow window. The moon was a sliver arching over the distant mountain peaks. There was a strange tension in the night air, as if the mountains themselves were pressing down upon the house. Hours seemed to pass as he reviewed the situation and attempted to make decisions for the following day. Sometimes it seemed obvious what he must do, and he nearly fell asleep; then he would turn, shake himself awake, and certainty vanished into the cool night air. He could not escape an inexplicable but mounting feeling that something odd was happening.

Yet as the night went on he began to drowse . . .

A sucking sound aroused Jacques first, like the bellows at Mirepoix, he thought. Then he sat up sharply, knowing that his slumbering memory had chosen the right simile. It was a fire, and the forage they had gathered was already blazing outside the door.

Jacques leapt from the mattress directly onto the ground, and bellowed to awake the others. Patches of brilliant flame where torches had landed blinded him so that he could see nothing and no one; he tried to cover his eyes, but it made no difference. He began to move cautiously to the corner where Nicolas was sleeping, but was blocked by a fiery torch which grazed his chest and fell onto the mattress behind him. Immediately it flared, caught dried herbs and straw which had been used to cover the floor and shot across the room like a thunderbolt. Jacques was about to run when a terrifying scream stopped him dead. A figure like the doomed in a painting of hell came towards him, engulfed in flames from trousers and tunic, with the mouth wide open as if the skull were about to burst with pain. There seemed to be no end to the scream, the lungs having been granted an infinite supply of air to fuel it.

Jacques stepped aside as the heat from this monstrous being began to burn his face, praying that it would not be Nicolas de Lirey. An unbearable stench filled his nostrils and brought vomit to his throat as flames licked and devoured the face. Then the scream stopped, abruptly, as all life was sucked out of the human frame. The body crumbled momentarily, like a man at rest; then, as the flames won over, it became a horrifying ball of fire. He could see nothing, but imagined the lips being burned back as had Jacques de Molay's. Tears of suffering mingled with those of smoke. But at the same time he realized that the figure had been too short for Nicolas. Again he looked towards the corner, which was now a single sheet of flame.

The sleeves of his own tunic were smouldering, and he began to choke. The room was now full of acrid smoke and an attempt to inhale caused a strange burning sensation in his chest. He knew that he could not remain any longer without endangering his own life. He prayed quickly for the blazing ball of man, then ran through the room and leapt through a bundle of flaming forage into the open air.

The night was illuminated by the burning roof of the house, while torches which had been thrown short seemed to blaze everywhere on the square. Horses screamed in terror, adding to the inferno-like vision. Jacques brushed smouldering flames from his chest, ripped off a bit of singed tunic and looked around quickly.

Beyond the scree wall he could see armed men moving towards him. Some of the nearer ones still brandished burning torches ready to throw. Fortunately both Briac and Renaud were well and whole, heading resistance to the arsonists as they tried to enter the compound. Beside and behind them the guards had fanned out into a protective semicircle with their backs to the house. They were engaged in fierce combat with swords and daggers. Terror gripped Jacques as he watched: his body shuddered as he realized what he had escaped, and his bowels loosened at the thought of what was to come. He watched with apprehension as Renaud drove one of the attackers back into the trough with a vicious sweep of his sword. He looked at his own empty hands, brushing bits of burnt cloth from his cuffs. Rarely had he felt so useless. He decided there and then that until the end of this mission he would carry a weapon.

One of the assailants moved towards him, but barely had enough time to take an initial stab before the ferocious, swirling mass of Briac was upon him. Jacques watched amazed as Briac's sword slashed through the man's chain-mail and fighting arm as if they had been paper. His victim screamed horribly as his lower arm fell away. Briac allowed him to retreat, then turned quickly. 'Get back to the wall!' he shouted to Jacques. 'They'll be no trouble for us.'

As Jacques moved backwards what seemed to be a blazing human torch rushed out of the house. The doorway and marble lintel were lit up like a vision.

Jacques wanted to scream as never before, but was struck dumb by the realization that it was his companion. Nicolas swatted helplessly against the flames which shot vertically from his tunic to his head, screaming like a wounded boar as he ran back and forth unwittingly fanning the flames. He coughed as if he wanted to bring up his entrails and tried desperately to tear his tunic off. Jacques was frozen with terror, and stood watching for what felt like an eternity while his companion burned in front of him.

Briac arrived as if by miracle. Jacques stared aghast as the guard floored Nicolas with what appeared to him a violent upper-cut, as if to burn wasn't punishment enough.

Then he understood as Briac began to kick earth over the unconscious body. 'If he'd run for the water-trough it would've been head or tails whether he died of fire or the sword,' the guard shouted as he worked. Jacques joined him, disregarding the pain in his sandalled feet as he dug deep into the earthen square. When the worst of the flames had subsided he bent forwards and grabbed the loose earth with his hands. There was a pungent odour like burning horn or nail issuing from the blackened object at their feet. He tried his best to push the image of Nicolas from his mind. Together Jacques and Briac managed to cover the body beneath them; then the guard ripped the sleeves of his tunic, and used them to douse the remaining flames.

Behind them the entire house was now ablaze, and lit the fields around as if it were day. Briac's men now held the wall around the compound. Beyond them, like scarecrows isolated in the knee-high wheat, their assailants were in full flight towards the safety of darkness.

'It's over,' Briac said simply, as if it had been but an exercise. He seemed untouched by the flames, probably because he had already been outside when they began.

Abbot Jacques sat, exhausted, while Renaud cleaned the earth from the human mound in front of them. Nicolas' clothes were reduced to a charred mess, and as they were lifted off the atrocious mixed stench of burnt wool and flesh came to Jacques' nose. Tears flooded to his eyes as his companion was carried into the house, writhing, screaming and gasping short breaths of smoke-free air as he came round. What a horrible death, Jacques reflected, thinking of the Grand Master of the Temple.

He looked around the battle scene: two of the mysterious enemy lay lifeless near the door, while one of Briac's guards appeared to be dead by the water-trough. Two men killed, and Nicolas severely burned: a harsh tally, Jacques thought almost abstractly. His own fear resurfaced, and he stood shaking by the door as if *he* had been the one to suffer the burns. A sense of shame then supplanted his belated fear, and he realized how lucky he had been. The fire-ravaged body of Nicolas could easily have been his. He thanked God for sparing his life, and vowed to seek repentance for his cowardice by finding the image they were all seeking – and were ready to kill for. He was about to go back into the house to see Nicolas when the guard's triumphant voice stopped him in his tracks.

'We got one! We got one!' he shouted. His expression of delight threatened to split his face in two.

'Well done,' Jacques said with sincerity, but he could not conceal his distress.

Briac understood. 'I'm sorry about Sire Nicolas . . .' He bowed his head like a man ashamed of his actions.

'You must not be sorry. You've done an excellent job. Don't let the prisoner out of your sight. I must tend to Nicolas first. Then we'll see what this rogue has to say for himself.' He entered the stone hut, which had been untouched by the blaze.

Nicolas had been wrapped in a blanket and laid on the only surviving mattress. The sight of him brought a lump to Jacques' throat. All the hair had been burned and singed from his head, and his once lean and white face was an appalling amalgam of soot and earth; he looked like a chimney sweep who'd lost brows and lashes to his eyes. He was almost unrecognizable. Even his disdain had been stripped away. Under the blanket his body writhed spasmodically. Renaud held a blistered hand firm as the injured man emptied his lungs against the agony. 'Have we got henbane, or opium?' he asked.

Jacques nodded his head. 'A little portion of henbane.'

The seneschal pursed his lips. 'Thankfully, it's not as bad as we thought,' he said. 'It was more dramatic than serious. He didn't burn much, thanks to the fact that he wasn't wearing hose. The extra flames would have destroyed his trunk.'

'May Heaven be praised,' Abbot Jacques said in genuine gratitude to his Lord. He addressed Nicolas in a weak attempt to make light of the injuries: 'I've had to dress up as a Dominican. Now you'll be forced to wear a Cistercian habit.' But even as he spoke he knew his words rang false.

In any case there was no reaction from the injured man.

'We'll give him henbane,' Renaud insisted. 'The pain must be intolerable. And we'll have to apply the cups later. He'll heal faster with less blood.'

'And then?'

'Then nothing, Lord Abbot. We must wait, and keep him well wrapped.'

Jacques knelt beside the mattress. 'We've got a prisoner, you know. We'll soon know who they were, although I could already make a fair guess.' He hesitated, but immediately wanted to kick himself for being churlish and ungenerous at such a time. 'They'll be Guillaume de Paris' men. I had a feeling something was going to happen, you know.'

Nicolas' eyes blinked as though they were trying to open. Jacques and Renaud watched as the man stretched out beneath them suppressed a scream with an astonishing feat of will. It occurred to Jacques that Pietro di Ocre was right when he pronounced his dirge for the passing of true knights. This was such a man.

Then they heard a faltering voice. It did not sound like Nicolas, but undeniably came from his dried lips. 'Jacques?'

The tremulous voice frightened Jacques more than the hairless face and burns. Was he requesting extreme unction? He looked at

Renaud, who appeared to understand these things. 'Will he survive?' he whispered.

'As sure as France is France. He'll be badly scarred when the wounds on his chest heal. But in a few days he'll be up and about, that I can assure you.'

Relieved, he turned back to Nicolas, moving closer to the mattress on his knees and leaning forward. 'I'm here, my friend. And my prayers are for you . . .'

The blackened face screwed up with pain, then relaxed. 'There's something I must tell you.'

'Later. When you are well.'

Nicolas grimaced in pain. 'I may die. There's no time.'

Jacques turned again to Renaud, who was shaking his head vigorously. 'Tell me then. But slowly.'

'Tonight has helped me decide . . . Ever since I was assigned to you I have been making reports to Lord Bernard. Everything you said and did. But tonight I looked death in the face.' Nicolas' eyes closed and he gasped for breath. Then, miraculously, he continued. 'I've been watching you closer than any man . . . and I hope you will forgive me for that . . .'

'Everything,' Jacques said with feeling. Was there the trace of a smile on his secular companion's face?

'Bernard never told me everything. But I do know that he wished you to arrive here late.'

'Why?' Jacques' mind reeled, even though he had suspected what Nicolas now said. That was why they'd been told the mountain passes were blocked, while Guillaume de Paris had taken that route.

'I told you, I don't know. Let me finish . . .' He paused and gasped for breath. Then his body arched through a series of convulsions which seemed to start in his legs and work upwards towards the head. This time he could not hold back his roar of pain.

Abbot Jacques closed his eyes and prayed. Disgusted that he had allowed himself to forget his companion's suffering. The fact that he was speaking at all was a rare feat of courage.

'This relic we are seeking is an object of immense power. It terrifies me. Lord Bernard is as determined as King Philip to obtain it . . .'

'Why would that be?'

'He always said you were the man who would find it . . .' Again the convulsions, and a scream like a dying horse which threatened to lift the roof off the house. When the words came, they were so faint that they seemed to be lost in the continuing echo of that scream: 'I think he's here in Ocre.'

'What? Where? Why do think that?' Jacques edged forward. Nothing could have shocked him more.

'Beatrice . . .' Nicolas replied. Now Jacques knew his secular companion must be dying. Had he a sister named Beatrice? A former mistress? He slipped to the role of confessor. 'Tell me . . .'

'The only person in whom our Lord Bernard ever confided totally was his sister . . .'

'Beatrice!' Now Jacques understood. It seemed to him incredible that such a man had been able to confide in a woman who had been recognized as a heretic. There must have been some very deep bond between them.

Jacques fancied there was a smile on Nicolas' face as he spoke. 'He would do anything for her . . . and in fact did so when he sent you to Caen.' He closed his eyes again. Jacques hoped that the drugs would not send him to sleep before he finished. 'For a long time I had been trying to understand our Lord Bernard's motives. There seemed to be a pattern in his actions, but a pattern established by his own reasoning processes rather than that imposed by Pope Clement. It was when we were sent to Aigues-Mortes that I began to suspect he had a grand plan. That was an ambiguous mission, something that he himself did not understand fully. Yet he knew that it was of vital importance, and I had an inkling of his purpose. Because, you see, Jacques, I had heard of this image before.'

'How, in the name of God?'

'From my mother's uncle, who had fought in these parts many years ago.'

'Geoffroi . . .?'

'. . . de Charny. Yes. You didn't need to lie to keep me away from Javiaux.'

For the first time, Jacques could share his companion's irony. 'So you knew?'

'Not really, since nobody knew the whole truth – except perhaps Pietro di Ocre.'

The sound of the name caused Jacques' eyes to drift up towards the castle, remote like an eagle's nest on the rocky bluff across the valley.

'Then, one day, by accident as I said, I overheard a conversation between Bernard and his sister. He needed her help in this matter for reasons we shall never understand now . . .'

'We could question her . . .'

'It won't matter now,' Nicolas said. 'Anyway, what I heard that day was quite unbelievable. In fact, I didn't believe it at the time. But I do now.'

'What, in the name of Heaven was it?' Jacques sat forward.

'Our Lord Bernard, Provincial of the Cistercian Order and Inquisitor-General for Provence, aspires to high places . . . higher than any man should dare . . .'

Again, Nicolas' voice faded. Jacques put his ear almost to Nicolas' lips, but in his heart he already knew the answer.

'To the Holy See.'

Abbot Jacques felt his jaw drop open, and stared at his burned companion, fearing this might be delirium. 'It's impossible.'

'Far from it. I believe he has King Philip's support now, as well.'

Jacques' mind reeled as it had done when he saw the image in the chapel. This meant that the real end of *Opus Christi* was to serve the Church's enemy. 'Since our last visit to Paris?'

'Even before that. Since the Emperor Henry died.'

'Henry?' Now Jacques simply stared open-mouthed.

'He was to take Rome as part of a pact with King Philip, and would then have been "removed", as they put it, so that our king could take his place. But Henry had his spies too, and found out.'

Jacques wondered how his companion summoned the energy and lucidity for his replies. It must be the work of God, he reasoned. But it wouldn't last for long. Soon the henbane would take him beyond the absence of pain to total rest. 'You mean Bernard . . .?'

'. . . was responsible for his death? It may well be. As you recall, it was rumoured that Henry was poisoned by a Dominican. But I have no proof . . . He may have believed that with the Emperor gone and the image in his own hands he could obtain what he desired from King Philip.'

Jacques' mind reeled. These shocks were more wearing than any journey or battle. 'Does he really believe it's possible?' he asked quietly, amazed that his own voice could even formulate such an incredible question.

'Yes. He believes the image will provide him with the power to realize his ambition. But I swear this secret will never leave my lips again as long as I live . . . if I live . . .' Nicolas' eyes closed from the immense effort of talking.

'I'll personally carry you to Avignon if necessary,' the inquisitor said, aware that Nicolas had slipped into profound sleep even as he spoke the words. For a moment Jacques stood embarrassed, not knowing what to do. Suffused with emotion, he left Nicolas in the hands of Renaud, and, going outside, called Briac and ordered him to send a man to Santo Spirito for more henbane and salves. When that was done an overwhelming desire for silence and solitude drove him to walk along the brook away from the hut. He wished profoundly that he could be back in Mirepoix, but made do with a clearing in the sedge.

He had come to Ocre for answers, but seemed only to be getting new questions. Was it possible that Bernard de Caen was here himself, or had Nicolas in his delirium meant Guillaume de Paris? Could the two of them be in league? Once again, Jacques was acutely aware of his own ignorance. He must be careful not to overestimate his own understanding and knowledge, for these men were always a stage ahead of him. Just as he thought he understood them, they moved into new convolutions of reason. At moments like this he doubted that he would ever understand fully the nature of power. It was extraordinary how the image they were seeking had such a hold over so many men.

Nicolas had come through to him just as he was beginning to feel he would never develop a personal liking for his aristocratic companion. There might be something in Pietro's nostalgic sermon after all, Jacques mused. The resistance to pain demonstrated by Nicolas reflected inherited reserves of courage. He must learn from men like Pietro and Nicolas, and then turn his knowledge against the Philips and Bernards of the world.

Then he remembered that there was a prisoner to question. Perhaps *he* would be able to supply some answers.

40

Briac spat on the floor of the roofless house as Abbot Jacques entered.
'I know this scum. I've seen him in Paris. At the barracks.'

'Yes,' Renaud Essart added thoughtfully, 'I've seen him before too.'
He walked around the prisoner, studying him from every angle like a
farmer judging livestock at market.

Jacques looked at the young man, who was short and stocky with
the broad open face of the countryside. There was no rope available,
so he was pinned to the wall by diagonal staves which two guards
had rammed into the earth and now pushed against him. Even as
he watched, Briac stepped forward and punched the prisoner in the
abdomen. His entire body weight went into the punch. The prisoner
gasped, and would have bent double but for the staves.

'That's enough. I'll tell you . . .' Jacques began.

'Scum!' Briac spat on him again. Then he stood back to size up
the man. 'The courage of a lamb and the belly of a woman, by the
wounds of St Sebastian.'

The prisoner cowered. It appeared that the punch had served its
purpose after all and, in spite of himself, Jacques was pleased that
Briac had delivered it. Some of his own anger had been discharged
by that violence, as after sex with Ida. It had also softened up
their man. 'Well, young man,' he began, 'who was it who sent you
here?'

Briac clenched his fist to reinforce the question.

'To Ocre? King Philip the Fair of France.' The words came
proudly from his lips. Briac drew back his arm.

'No, Briac!' The order was quiet but firm. The man's eyes were
wide open with fear, and he might not need further prompting. 'With
Guillaume de Paris?'

'Yes.'

Jacques took a torch and held it near the prisoner's face until
it seemed the flesh would burst into flames. He thought of the
devastated face of Nicolas de Lirey. For a moment he desired to
thrust the burning torch into the young man's hair; but he desisted,
surprised at the violence of his own reaction, and replaced the torch

in its holder. 'It was he who sent you on this mission of arson this evening?'

The man hesitated. But a glance from Briac was sufficient. 'Yes,' he replied nervously.

'What was its purpose?'

'I don't know.' His eyes burned with hatred, but he was little more than a boy.

Jacques sensed he was telling the truth. He decided to change tack. 'How long have you been here?'

'Three days.'

'Doing what?'

'Searching . . .'

'For what?'

'I don't know.' Briac menaced him. 'I swear I don't know, sire.' Now he cowered, and would have turned away but for the staves.

'Then, young man, how would you have known when you found what you were looking for?'

'I wouldn't, I wasn't looking, believe me. My Lord Inquisitor-General gave orders. We obeyed. Opening walls, ransacking buildings. Then he searched afterwards alone.'

'In camp you must have discussed between yourselves what you were doing. I can't believe you know nothing at all.'

'There were rumours, sire, there always are; and strange too . . .' He seemed reluctant to continue.

'Go on!'

The prisoner fell silent.

Briac drew out his dagger, a curved oriental piece with perfectly honed blade. He had once explained that it was a personal relic which his father had brought back from St Louis' crusade. Briac polished it each night with the devotion nuns accord to a rosary. He now drew it mockingly across his own throat, and leaned forward to the prisoner. 'Speak, scum! By St Sebastian, speak!'

The prisoner glanced nervously towards Jacques, as if pleading for help. None was forthcoming. He needed no further prompting.

'I've sworn to . . .' he began hesitantly. Then Briac glared again, and he quickly continued as though he had weighed instant suffering against future punishment. 'Men said there was a relic here, a famous picture of our Lord Jesus Christ . . . mind you, it was only a story. I don't believe it myself . . . but that's what we were searching for – thought God only knows why it should be here.'

In spite of the knife, this sudden garrulity struck Jacques as suspect. 'Where did you search?' he snapped.

'The castle of Ocre . . . mind you, it's little more than a ruin now . . .'

'And then?' Jacques persisted.

'The castle, then a monastery, the monastery of Santo Spirito . . . that's all.'

'In three days?'

'The castle is big, sire, and the monastery too.'

'Very well.' Jacques turned to the guard. 'Take him away.'

'What shall we do with him, sire?'

'As you think fit.'

Briac looked at Jacques, surprised. But then, as if he remembered the prison at Saint Germain, he smiled. 'There's one other thing –' he said, 'one of my men seems to have disappeared.'

'When?' Bad news was accumulating fast: and no good news was forthcoming.

'After the fire.'

'Where do you think he's gone?'

'I've no idea. Perhaps he was scared. He wasn't much good; thought too much of himself.'

'Well, if he's gone, he's gone,' Jacques replied with resignation. There were other more pressing problems. 'If you would leave me alone . . .' he said softly.

First light rimmed the mountains to the east as he spoke.

Briac retreated gracefully. 'I'll see if I can find out something about that renegade.' Then he turned to his men. 'Get that scum out of here this minute!' he roared.

Then he was gone.

269

41

Fatigue crept through Jacques' body in synchrony with the rising sun. He leaned heavily against the door-frame. Then his body slithered to earth of its own volition. He inspected it with strange detachment, as if it belonged to someone else: his arms were bruised and grazed, and now he noticed that he too had suffered minor burns to his hands. But the tiny blisters were nothing to the burns he had seen. He yearned for a quiet hour to ponder events and pray. But there was little time for thought. Guillaume de Paris had already began his search, ransacking both castle and monastery in vain. At least that eliminated two potential hiding-places, for Jacques was certain that Guillaume's search would have been thorough.

It also meant, however, that the Inquisitor-General must have left Paris several days earlier than their party. To have taken the mountain route was not enough. He began to sense that Guillaume had not been present on the royal balcony at the Templar burning. Just as he had substituted Pietro di Ocre, so they could have simulated Guillaume's presence. No one would have noticed from such a distance.

Now it was really no holds barred.

The first thing was to put themselves out of reach of further attacks. Without Guillaume or the Templars breathing down his neck it would be easier to concentrate on the task of discovery. 'Briac!' he called, with a force that surprised even himself, as soon as he had made his decision. 'We must leave as soon as possible. Make the horses ready.'

Then he went to visit Nicolas.

Freshly gathered mint and rosemary scented the room, with all traces of burning cancelled. Nicolas lay silently in his bed. Beside him sat the infirmary friar from Santo Spirito, who held a large sponge with which he dabbed the sick man's wounds. 'Henbane?' Jacques asked.

The friar nodded. 'With opium and mandrake.'

Jacques noticed a bunch of freshly bloomed yellow henbane flowers with their distinctive purple streaks, placed on a bench together with bags of other herbs and a jar of unguent. Nicolas' body was bare to the waist, revealing a patchwork of broken blisters. All body hair had been singed away. The lower part of his face was still black from the fire, while the upper part was bright red and swollen, with all signs of identity burned away and thin black lines where eyebrows and eyelashes had been – like the lines a child might draw on a picture of a ghost. But he was conscious. A thin smile appeared on his face as Jacques approached. 'Can he come with us?' Jacques asked the friar.

'He ought not to be able to,' the friar answered with a sense of wonder, 'but he is a man of remarkable will. Even this potion has not put him to sleep, although it is soothing his pain.' He lifted the sponge for the abbot to see, then vacated the stool he was sitting on. 'He can ride with you, but don't expect him to manage a sword.'

Shortly afterwards, Jacques led the small party surreptitiously along the stream towards the main river. He now had double reason to avoid Santo Spirito, since Guillaume would surely have arranged for it to be watched. They made camp by a deserted farmhouse hidden by a copse of beeches from the main road to the castle of Ocre. First he helped to ease Nicolas from his saddle and found him a comfortable sloping willow trunk to rest against. Then he stretched himself by the river to sleep in the shade of the same tree, watched over by Briac. He knew that he would soon require all his energy.

When he awoke, the sun was high above them. Nicolas was asleep against the willow. He sat up sharply, and saw Briac stretched out with his feet in the river. His men were positioned in and around them, as taut as the strings of a psaltery. The sense of danger and defeat which had followed the arson and battle of the night before had been supplanted by a fresh sense of urgency. Nervousness had led to increased alertness. 'At least we won't be taken by surprise again,' Renaud joked when he saw the inquisitor.

Jacques went to sit near him. Sleep had restored him, and now he enjoyed the company of his men. Furthermore, he rationalized, he was in much better condition than Nicolas. Yet the tension in the camp made relaxation impossible. He was conscious of guards looking askance at him, whispering in groups by the river, watching but waiting for him, rather than the enemy. The responsibilities of power outweighed the pleasures, he found himself thinking: minutes of Ida against months of danger. Fontfroide was an eternity away from here. Now *he* must take the initiative, before others regained it: the problem was, where was he to start?

From his sitting position, Jacques could see the Castle of the Madonna. He recalled his visit there, and the attack on them afterwards, but more than anything else, he realized, it made him think of the village and church of San Eusanio which he knew to be beyond the hill.

That strange church had a special place in the affections of the Ocre family, and as he sat there Jacques' vanity suggested to him that Guillaume de Paris did not realize this. His thoughts meandered like the river below: if Cardinal Tommaso had hidden the image anew, then he would have reasoned like the othe members of his family. For such a superstitious and traditional man the choice would be narrowed to a single building: San Eusanio. Jacques sat up quickly, startled at the simplicity of it all. If his line of reasoning were correct, the answer was simple: the relic was inside the church.

Yet ransacking the entire church would be as time-consuming as Guillaume's random searches had proved to be.

It was then that he felt a weight on his thigh. He touched his habit, smiled, and drew out the slender volume Nicolas had brought from Santo Spirito. How could he have forgotten? It was entitled *Passio S. Eusanii Confessoris*, and he saw from the preface that the author claimed to have copied it in the Year of Our Lord 1198. That meant that it was probably commissioned by the young Berardo of Ocre, Pietro's grandfather, who later built Santo Spirito. He settled down to read the *Passio*, fascinated to discover who the saint had been – and what he represented to the Ocre family.

The script was at first strange to Jacques, but urgency aided concentration and soon the problem letters became familiar. Once he had turned the first page, it seemed he had been reading this hand all his life.

He learned that Eusanio was made Bishop of Siponto in Apulia in the year 293, after bringing back to life the dead son of a local noblewoman. After that the bishop had wandered for many years performing miracles, and was noted for his practice of singing the psalms of David as he walked: those that began 'Blessed is the man who walks not in the counsel of the wicked' and 'Answer me when I call, O God of my right' were apparently his favourites. Eusanio often cured possessed women, and the *Passio* contained detailed descriptions of these events. On one occasion, the devil was reported to have replied picturesquely, 'Alas, I am forced to leave and cannot stay, and don't know where to go', after which Eusanio had been rewarded by a vision of St Peter and St Paul. The bishop had gone to Rome and to Tivoli, and then finally came to the village that now bore his name, then known as Forcona, where he cured the sick and baptized the pagan population.

So far there was nothing remarkable: the saint's life was similar to the life of many an early martyr and saint. Yet something nagged at Jacques' mind.

He read on.

The Roman governor of Forcona was a man called Prisco, who arrested Eusanio and had him beaten. But Eusanio claimed that to suffer for Christ was the thing that made him most happy, so Prisco imprisoned him in chains. Whilst in prison, Eusanio had a vision of an angel who unchained him and led him out of it. Prisco was supposed to have said: *'Heu me, victi fumus per Eusanium sacrilegum'*, 'Alas, we have been beaten by Eusanio the magician'. More interesting still was the fact that Eusanio was captured again and forced to worship an image of Jupiter. Eusanio refused point-blank, was stoned by Prisco's soldiers and thrown back into prison.

The next morning he was heard reciting one of his favourite psalms, 'Answer me . . .', when an extraordinary event took place. First a burning ball of fire appeared over the mountain of Ocre behind Forcona, and seemed to form itself into an immense image of Christ. Then four ministers of Hell, in human form but with wings, appeared from the mountains and carried Prisco away in front of the whole population. His wife Trisonia, with her son Quirillo and daughter Eleuteria, immediately went to Eusanio in his cell and pleaded forgiveness for their sins. He baptized them that very morning, and then the entire population of the valley. The image of Jupiter was destroyed together with all the other pagan images in Forcona. A cross was planted where the great fireball and image of Christ had appeared.

Jacques wanted to scream his joy to the world.

The next verse of the psalm which Eusanio had been reciting came to his mind with miraculous clarity, as if the words were being spoken by David himself: 'O that we might see some good! Lift up the light of thy countenance upon us, O Lord!'

That was it! Eusanio had appealed to the image of Christ to defeat the Roman governor. That was why the Counts of Ocre revered him so and rebuilt his church – which must stand on the site of the original cross; that was why Berardo had the *Life* written; that was why the temple was in the crypt with his body. San Eusanio was a magus and had the power to evoke visions and images. The problem was solved: there must indeed be only one place where a member of the family of the counts of Ocre would hide the relic.

Inside the altar of the crypt of San Eusanio, where the saint's bones were preserved.

Jacques turned to Nicolas, whose eyes were now open, and smiled warmly. 'Come, sir knight, I believe our journey is near its end. Are you strong enough?'

'I wouldn't miss it for all the relics in Christendom,' Nicolas replied as Briac drew him to his feet.

Together, Jacques and Briac helped him into the saddle. Once there, to Jacques' astonishment, he sat as rigid and firm as a knight on his first appearance in the jousts.

42

There was no mystery in the fortifications of the church now, Jacques thought when he and his party entered the village of San Eusanio.

As they approached the church, he fancied that he knew how thieves felt when entering a house with evil intent. 'Smash the door down,' he ordered Briac reluctantly. The guard grunted, and walked off to borrow a poleaxe from one of his men. Then the abbot turned to Essart. 'Renaud, will you arrange guards for the entrances to this square?' There was no time to waste.

Essart nodded. Within seconds it was done.

Jacques and Nicolas followed Briac through the breach he had created. The clandestine nature of this visit at first prompted Jacques to tiptoe across the stone flags, but the confident booted steps of Nicolas and Briac reassured him. He paused before the high altar, hastily made the sign of the cross, and beckoned them to follow him. 'Now we may go with a clear conscience,' he remarked. At the same time he was pleased to see that there were no signs of a previous search. The door to the crypt was unlocked, so they quickly descended the narrow staircase after carefully shutting the door behind them.

Squatting behind the altar in the crypt, Jacques easily found the catch which allowed the door behind it to swing open. Gently, he lifted the casket containing the relics of San Eusanio. 'Put it on the altar!' His voice was soft, but there was no questioning its tone of command. Briac complied with another grunt.

Then Jacques dropped to his knees, conscious of the incongruity of kneeling on the wrong side of an altar as he groped about inside it. There was nothing. The space was bare. 'But it *must* be here,' he muttered to himself angrily.

Nicolas was beside him now, knocking the stone with bandaged knuckles. 'This is solid stone,' he said.

Then Briac came forward, as if galvanized by Jacques' wrath. 'With respect, sire Nicolas,' he said, 'allow me to look inside.'

Jacques watched as Nicolas nodded, pleased that his companion was aware of his physical limits and recognized the justice of the guard's proposal. If there was anything to be discovered here, then strength would be necessary. He indicated an ancient broken capital near the altar, and Nicolas sat down.

Seering pain shot through his chest as he did so. It seemed to work outwards, first up to the neck and then along his limbs. He tried to make himself comfortable, but each time he leaned back against the wall the pain was almost too much to bear. He wished the infirmary friar was there to apply his salves, and knew that he must return to the friar's care as soon as this last search was over. He flexed his hands within their cloth bandages and willed himself to watch Jacques and Briac.

Meanwhile Briac had unbuckled his sealskin belt and his scabbard. At first he was going to lay them on the altar, but then he faltered – as though even for him it would have been tantamount to sacrilege to place them beside the relics. Placing them carefully on the stone floor within arm's length, he took Jacques' place behind the altar. He forced the simple door back on its hinges, and thrust his shoulders inside. Jacques watched curiously as a hand emerged and drew a dagger from its sheath on the belt. Then Briac began to strike the haft against the sides and floor of the interior of the altar. It gave off a full echo: thud . . . thud . . . thud . . . Then, against his wildest hopes, Jacques thought he heard a sudden change of tone. 'Wait! There!' he shouted excitedly. 'Do it again there!'

Briac hit the floor again in the same place, and exactly the same hollow sound issued forth. 'It isn't solid stone after all,' he shouted, 'it's a slate top.'

'Smash it!' There was no hesitation in Jacques' voice.

Briac stared at him. 'Are you sure?' This time his question was pregnant with doubt. Tough though he was, Briac was not one to desecrate a martyr's altar.

'Smash it!' Jacques repeated with vehemence. But as soon as he had uttered the command, he felt a qualm of conscience. He was pleased to recognize good in his chief guard. 'I will absolve you personally. You will be justly rewarded.'

No more encouragement was needed. Briac found another stone capital in a corner of the crypt. Only a man of his strength could have carried it with such ease to the altar. 'Be careful. We don't want to smash what is inside,' Jacques warned him. He kneeled anxiously as Briac lifted the capital into the altar chamber. When it was resting safely on the slate slab, Briac stood up for a moment, breathed deeply, and flexed his arms. Then he bent again to the door and grasped the capital firmly.

The third time he let it fall, the slate began to splinter. Now sweating, Briac dropped the capital onto the cracks that were forming. Eventually, he lifted it out of the altar altogether and threw it carelessly aside as if it were made of paper. Then he began to pick out the broken pieces of slate.

Jacques could see nothing but black space through the hole that now appeared. He began to fear that his instinct had been wrong, and that he himself was guilty of unnecessary sacrilege.

As this fear of error was becoming intolerable, Briac shouted eagerly: 'There's something here. A box!' He was pulling at the darkness, removing further pieces of slate. With what seemed to Jacques interminable slowness he gradually drew the box he had unearthed from its hiding-place. Then, with a triumphant grin on his face, he turned towards the inquisitor with the box in his grimy hands. 'This it?'

Jacques stared in awe. It was square, flat and about two palms square, the dark wooden frame covered with a silver grille just as Pietro had said. He felt the presence of Nicolas behind him as he spoke. 'Yes, this is it.' His hands trembled as he placed it on the altar. 'Give me your dagger.'

Disappointment coursed through his veins when he peered into the grille. He had expected to see a clear picture, but the only contents seemed to be a whitish cloth. He pushed a finger through the silver frets, but touched no hard object within. Could this object be the prey of so many hunters? Had they all been tricked by the Counts of Ocre?

He stared at the box, deluded. The diagonal silver trellis-work together with dust from Briac's slate-breaking made it difficult to see anything inside. Slipping his fingers under the catch, he tried to open the box, but it was firmly locked. Then he noticed that one side had four miniature hinges, so he turned it away from him and began to pry the catch open. There was no direct light in the chapel, but the whitewashed walls reflected and enhanced what little filtered through. Slowly, the lid began to give as he worked at the catch. Age and humidity had sealed the lid, but with the help of Briac's dagger he managed to get a good grip and prise it open.

As he finished, sunlight burst into the chapel through its tiny rose window. Jacques drew the white cloth out, holding it so that this spiralling shaft of sunlight shone through it. Now, in the chill of the crypt, he could feel Nicolas' warm breath on his neck.

Then he too began to understand. He stood up slowly and with some difficulty, aware that his legs were trembling as he gazed in disbelief. He recalled how he had laughed within at Pietro di Ocre's description of the same moment. 'May God forgive me my doubt,' he murmured.

'No one could have imagined this,' Nicolas said quietly as if to comfort him.

Before them, like a miraculous vision from over a thousand years before, was the face of Our Lord Jesus Christ firmly imprinted on a faded white cloth. It was a face he knew from a hundred paintings, but which, in this case, seemed to shimmer with a new freshness – as if it were alive. The prominent temples and high crown of the head made Christ appear noble as he had never seen before, while the eyes seemed to gaze out lovingly from eternity. The face was placid, gentle but strong, as the gospels described it. Jacques was struck rigid by its beauty and immediacy.

'My God, forgive me my presumption, and forgive me for doubting your infinite wisdom,' he muttered apprehensively. He felt that at any moment the Lord might strike him dead with a thunderbolt.

He drew the cloth further out.

To his utter astonishment, it was folded so that as he lifted it new planes became visible. 'Do you think I should?' he asked nervously.

Nicolas was so close that his voice seemed to come from within Jacques' own skull. 'Did we ride so far just to see a box?' he asked. All pain had vanished as he stood entranced beside the inquisitor. It was true that he had heard of this cloth, but nothing prepared him for the beauty of the face he could now see imprinted on it.

A dull thudding sound penetrated the silence of the crypt. Jacques looked away from the box towards the beginning of the staircase. 'What's that?' he asked.

'Horses!' Nicolas snapped. 'Somebody passing, or some of Briac's men.' Then it faded away. 'Go on! Take it out!' he insisted impatiently.

Caution prevailed. 'Briac, will you go to the door of the church and see who's there?' Nervously, when the guard had gone, he slowly drew the cloth from its box. Next appeared the shoulders, heavy with the drama of the crucifixion, and then the entire bust. Jacques' breast throbbed with ecstasy. In the third fold he saw the hands of Christ

278

reposing gently on his abdomen. And in the centre of each hand was a dark spot where the nails had pierced them as he was nailed to the cross. He drew the cloth to its full height, and was intrigued to see the same feature repeated in the feet: with one exception that riveted his interest. While the hands were crossed after the event, and the marks bore no relation to one another, it was clear that the feet had been nailed together by a single nail. Jacques was reminded of the curious painting he had seen in Santa Maria del Ponte under the southern gate of Aquila, and knew then that it had been painted by a man who had seen this cloth. Otherwise he would surely have followed the tradition. That was the final, conclusive proof. 'Nicolas,' Jacques said weakly, 'do you realize what we're looking at?'

The knight simply stared at the cloth, speechlessly.

Jacques went on: 'I believe that this is the authentic burial shroud of Jesus Christ: not just a face, but the entire body of the Crucified Lord.'

'So *that* was Pietro's secret. It's incredible . . .'

'And goes some way towards explaining King Philip's belief in its power.' Jacques noticed that his knuckles were as white as chalk as he spoke, and he imagined his face would be too. The power emanating from the image was quite unbearable. After carefully folding the cloth back into its box and closing the lid, he placed it on the altar.

Jacques leaned against the wall, all strength drained from his body. His calves were aching as if he had walked day and night for a week. The problem had indeed been solved in Ocre, but beyond his wildest expectations. His body slithered to the ground of its own accord, independent of his will.

Then he felt the presence of Nicolas close to him, and was ashamed of his weakness. 'So now you've seen it too,' the young knight said.

'I would never have believe it,' Jacques replied quietly.

'That's not all,' Nicolas went on. 'While you were busy with altar and cloth I had a chance to look round the crypt. Look!' He came round the altar to join Jacques, then pointed at the two columns nearest to them.

Jacques' eyes followed the aristocratic forefinger.

'You see? Two faces: of Christ and of the Devil.'

There could be no doubt. The shaft of sunlight entering the crypt illuminated the sculpted images Jacques had seen before while the remainder of the column was in shadow. It was a subtle effect, but there could be no doubt that it was carefully planned.

'Now look along the line of columns,' Nicolas said. 'They are perfectly aligned into three channels. This one leads straight forward, while the other two lead off at forty-five degrees.'

'So?' It was quite simple geometry.

'You can't see it?' Nicolas asked with a note of triumph in his voice. 'The two channels at forty-five degrees lead directly to Santo Spirito on the left, and to the Castle of the Madonna on the right. This one must run in a straight line through the New Jerusalem, Aquila. Almost as I guessed last time we were here.'

Jacques stared. If his companion was right about this and territorial magic, the man who stood here, with the image of Christ in his hands, would control everything that stood before him within the range of these lines.

Then Jacques recalled the words that Pietro had used. They had seemed incomprehensible at the time, but now made awesome sense: 'The New Jerusalem was founded as its custodian, and the Image of Our Lord shone over the valley. Where it shone was in the Light of God. With it we could have had the Church, the World . . .'

He was loth to allow his imagination to be overwhelmed with the 'magical' powers of the image he had seen, yet he began to understand how men like the counts of Ocre would believe they had the key to power with such a relic in their hands. Above all he could see how it spurred in them a desire for crusade. But he also knew that the idea of crusade was now anachronistic: the Church must move forwards with the age and become strong in Europe again. There was no more need for the knights of the Temple and their like. Furthermore, he began slowly to realize that inside the chapel behind him he had the means to destroy the old heresies forever and begin again. It was time to forge a new, stronger identity for the Church, so that it would again hold unchallenged spiritual sway over the temporal powers of such men as King Philip the Fair.

At that moment, the door which led to the crypt creaked as if someone had pushed it open. Jacques and Nicolas watched together as a shaft of light fell across the flags at the end of the crypt and listened to the shuffling of slippered feet and clatter of arms as men descended the stairs.

Jacques stiffened; with difficulty, Nicolas raised himself to his full height.

The familiar chubby face of Bernard de Caen appeared, followed by Briac. Jacques pursed his lips as he realized that Nicolas had been right, but he felt no surprise at his Superior's appearance. He would have to think fast now. 'Lord Bernard,' he said slowly, with a bow considerably less servile than those he had been wont to perform in Avignon.

'I am pleased to see you, Abbot Jacques. What news?' Close up, Bernard was red-faced and sweating with fatigue, yet his voice was matter-of-fact, as if his presence in San Eusanio were routine. His retinue of guards and inquisitors now followed him into the crypt.

'My lord,' Jacques replied. His mind was racing. He was considering his next words so carefully that he did not notice at first that Briac was waving to him. He stared ahead, still feeling at a loss, and followed Briac's pointing finger.

Then he understood. Amidst the men who accompanied Bernard de Caen was the missing guard from Briac's detachment. Perhaps he had been too trusting of the guards, allowing his suspicions of Nicolas to blind him to other potential spies; there was still much to learn.

Now, however, there was little left to be done. The power of decision had been removed from him. Jacques felt at first a great sense of relief that he would not be responsible for transporting the image to France, but even as he stood staring at his Superior the relief was replaced by a sense of disappointment, for he would be deprived of his moment of glory. Yet his immediate duty and his loyalty were undoubtedly due to this man, whatever his private schemes of power. 'We have the image, my lord, here behind me.'

'Have you seen it?'

'Not well. I deemed it wiser to join our escort and leave the area first.' Jacques spoke with confidence now, for at least part of the success would be his. Furthermore, he would need Bernard de Caen to recommend any promotion forthcoming from Pope Clement. 'Guillaume de Paris is in Aquila,' he added as an afterthought.

'I know.' Bernard's sarcasm was ill-concealed. 'Well? Where is it?' he added impatiently.

Jacques took the box from the altar and passed it over.

'This?' Bernard exclaimed. He clutched it with the jerky enthusiasm of a child grasping a new toy, vacillating between certainty and doubt that it was what he desired. His chubby fingers fondled the silver trellis-work.

A terrific crash from above froze them all to their places. This time the sound of horses and armed men was unmistakable through the opened door. Briac pushed brusquely through Lord Bernard's retinue and ran up the stairs.

Within seconds he was back, with half a dozen men following him. 'It's Guillaume de Paris, my lord, and his guards. I saw the bastard who wounded me in Burgundy there in the church. I'll have his guts this time, by St Sebastian I will. What's more, would you believe, Hugues de Pairaud is with them, and two other brothers in full battle regalia. And I'll bet them with the Templars are local men . . . those *shepherds* last time, remember? Shepherds, indeed!'

Jacques marvelled that Briac should find the time to talk. 'Do we have a chance?'

Briac laughed. 'Now you just take care of that there picture. See if you can't hide behind the altar there with Sire Nicolas . . . No, my good knight, you're in no shape to fight,' he added as Nicolas made to join him near the stairs. 'Renaud is upstairs in the nave, and we'll deal with such of them that gets down here.'

Jacques and Nicolas retreated behind the altar as instructed. It was then that the abbot noticed Bernard de Caen's face, as white as a winding-sheet as he sought refuge with his precious burden. At first Jacques did not understand, but then he saw with amazement that Bernard too was shocked by Guillaume de Paris' untimely arrival at San Eusanio. He had taken a sword from one of his escorts and stood with his back to the wall of the crypt as if ready to fight, clutching the box to his chest. With the shock and fear of a man who has been double-crossed, Jacques understood, a flash of sympathy passing through him as he saw that Bernard de Caen had been used by the Inquisitor-General for Paris and King Philip just as he himself had been used by Bernard. Now it was every man for himself. The relic was discovered, and the battle for possession of it would be fought in its hiding-place. Jacques was glad that Renaud and Briac were with him.

He watched in disbelief as knights clad in hauberk and mail-hose leggings, each and every one wearing a visored basinet, rushed into the crypt with all respect for the church thrown to the wind. He hoped that did not mean Renaud was already dead or captured, and was pleased to hear the sound of violent fighting above in the church. This strange attack, dodging columns and stone altars, was led, he now saw, by Templar knights armed with swords and ostentatiously wearing their white mantles with the red cross stitched on their shoulders. Behind that vanguard came Guillaume de Paris and a few of his soldiers, some armed with swords and some with maces, such as Jacques had never seen, each wearing hardened-leather greaves and arm protection and each a different-coloured tunic over his mail coat. He guessed that they were local knights from the Kingdom of Naples, recruited as mercenaries.

Jacques prayed with all his conviction for Pope Clement and the Holy Roman Church as they set about Briac and his guards.

Then, to his utter amazement, he saw Lord Bernard himself preparing to do battle: it was astonishing that such an obese man, who seemed to have difficulty merely staying firm in the saddle, should even contemplate fighting against the knights. Shame gnawed at him. For a moment, he considered leaving Nicolas and joining the men beyond the altar. He glanced at Nicolas, who shook his head vehemently as if understanding the inquisitor's thoughts. In fact such a reaction would not only be foolish but irresponsible. Thus, Bernard de Caen went into ungainly action against the knights of the man he had supposed to be his ally. Jacques felt for him, and could not but admire his courage.

The knights fought fiercely with swords and maces, but in their armour they were at a disadvantage in such a restricted space against the lightly armed guards of Briac and Bernard. Their seemingly unassailable superiority was reduced to inequality as their numbers decreased rapidly.

Briac was, as ever, in his element. While there was little space for horizontal sword blows, he wielded a poleaxe with terrifying ferocity in great swings which fell on unsuspecting helmets or sliced through sword-arms trying to attack him from beneath. At one point he had seen Guillaume de Paris against the wall near the foot of the stairs, and rushed towards him with the poleaxe swinging down, aiming at the Inquisitor-General with such force and momentum that Jacques closed his eyes in anticipation of the hideous mess such a blow would make of Guillaume's unprotected head.

When he opened his eyes, Guillaume had disappeared. 'As quick as a hare,' Nicolas shouted above the resounding clatter of steel against stone. 'Straight up the stairs with the box like a wounded hare into its lair!' Where his scalp might have been a gaping hole had appeared in the wall.

Two of the Templar knights now lay on the flags, while the other was engaged in a violent show of sword and dagger skill with one of Briac's men. There hardly seemed to be a man without injury of some kind, except Briac – who now fought back to back with another of his guards, and seemed to be pushing the knights away from the altar towards the stairs. The third Templar fell beneath his horrendous blows, and was then finished off with a dagger to the throat. The last survivors of Guillaume de Paris' escort hastened backwards for the stairs, then turned and disappeared from the crypt. They appeared to have lost all heart as soon as their master had left them. Briac held his own surviving men back, ordering them to care for their two fallen comrades. The battle for the crypt was won. As suddenly as the assailants had come, they were gone, but they had wrought havoc and left half their number for carrion. The walls and floor of the crypt were splattered with blood and plaster from columns which had been assaulted as though they themselves were human.

Just then Jacques' eye was drawn to one in particular on the other side of the crypt. He shifted so that he could see more clearly the chubby familiar face of Bernard de Caen beside it. The prelate's face was contrite, as if pulled taut by his arching backbone; all confidence was gone, and in its place was an expression of flabby uncertainty. Yet something of the old authority, and respect for his position, induced Jacques to kneel in the midst of carnage and pray for the man he could see but could not touch in life any longer.

Revulsion soon replaced respect. For this was the man who had created *Opus Christi* to protect the Church, and then subverted it to serve his own immense ambition; who had learned from the Counts of Ocre and sought to imitate their strategy. Jacques rose slowly to his feet as he recalled his first meeting with Bernard and Nicolas: the power, the opulence, the nobility of purpose, the urgency, were all reduced before him to a flabby corpse.

Other corpses were heaped into the far corner of the crypt. Jacques noted the white mantles of the three Templar knights, and recognized four of Briac's men. Briac himself was wearing a makeshift sling on his left arm: Jacques noticed with horror that his hand had been sliced off at the wrist, while his face was wet with the blood of lesser wounds. He walked on the arm of one of his men, yet, in spite of his pain, he was happy. 'We did it, Sire Inquisitor,' he said proudly as he arrived, 'and do you know, I got the bastard! That'll teach him to wound me.' He was laughing about his enemy as he was taken away.

Now there would be no more immediate danger, but it would be impossible to depart immediately with so many corpses to be buried. Jacques surveyed the carnage beneath him sadly, wondering why so many brave men should die for the object in that simple rectangular box, an image which, after all their efforts, had fallen into the possession of Philip of France, whose powers would now become unassailable, as a result of his treacherous attack.

He walked across to see whether he recognized the Templar knights; but they were unknown faces. He was about to turn away when he noticed the hole Briac's poleaxe had cracked into the wall. It was evident that he had in fact split the plaster concealing a bricked-up doorway, and the force of his blow had caused the implosion of an area of brickwork. Jacques peered into the hole revealed by the blow. At first he saw nothing in the gloom; then, as his eyes adjusted as the thin stream of light from a high window seemed miraculously to illumine the chamber, he began to make out strange forms scattered about the room. His curiosity was heightened, and he looked more carefully.

First the general outline of the room became visible. It was a long, narrow vaulted chamber with walls of large bricks but no decoration or columns evident. The far wall was covered by what looked like large wooden cupboards; that to the right by shelves; and that to the left by a long work-bench. Near this, Jacques saw a set of foot-bellows, and automatically searched for a fireplace; there was none, and it was some time before he noticed a free-standing brazier near the work-bench. What sort of metalwork could be done with such a small fire, he asked himself, here in a church? Then the answer slowly dawned on him. Among the larger tools, such as what appeared to be a tin-worker's small lathe and big copper pots, he began to see transparent receptacles: bottles, alembics, tubes and dishes ranged along the work-bench – and a goldsmith's balance. He shivered with excitement as he screwed his eyes and tried to push his face further into Briac's hole. Cobwebs as thick as fishermen's nets bespoke decades of disuse. But there could be no doubt: it was the laboratory of an alchemist. Who was it for, he wondered? Gualtiero or Tommaso? For it could belong to no other.

His eyes travelled down to the earthen floor. Jacques stiffened, and all casual questions were catapulted from his mind. There, almost within reach of his hand, was a corpse. Stretched out on its back, in perfect condition. Yet the room had been shut up for years. Jacques shook his head to dispel disbelief, then peered down again.

He smiled at his own foolishness, and the effect this crypt was having on him. It was a sepulchral relief sculpture ready to be placed on top of a tomb, but cast aside as if the dead person no longer warranted an effigy. A tall bearded man, with a face as serene as that on the capital, and his arms folded across his abdomen. Instinctively, Jacques began to pray silently for the man's soul – only stopping with a gasp as he pronounced the word 'Christ'. This place would never cease to produce surprises, like a conjurer at the Toulouse Fair. It was a relief of Christ that lay on the floor of the alchemist's chamber! It seemed strangely out of place: yet a nagging sense that there was something familiar about it plagued Jacques as he stepped away and cleared his throat of the dust. 'That's enough. Now we must make haste,' he said sharply.

He turned to Nicolas to share his amazement. But the knight had now slipped to the floor. At first Jacques was alarmed, thinking that his companion too was dead. But as he drew closer he heard heavy breathing and knew that Nicolas was fast sleep, his face bearing the peaceful and painless smile of a man who knows that his journey is over.

The box was lost, but they were alive.

43

Outside, fresh air revived Abbot Jacques' sense of urgency. The village people had come out to see the carnage. Veiled women crossed the arms of corpses strewn in the square across their chests like effigies on a sarcophagus. Barefooted children hunted for trophies, while adolescents went swiftly through pockets and purses. The men simply stood and watched, wordless. Weapons, abandoned at random, lay like children's toys left on the ground when greater excitement promises elsewhere. Great battle-chargers munched like country mules at tufts of grass growing between stone blocks; others drank from the fountain. The sweet odour of fresh death pervaded the still air.

In the middle of the square Renaud Essart was trying to alleviate the pain of the injured. Jacques walked towards him, accompanied by Briac, praying silently for the dead.

'You all right, Renaud?' Briac shouted.

'As right as any man after battle,' the veteran replied.

Then Jacques saw the box at the seneschal's feet. 'How did you get that?' he asked in wonder.

'Killed the man as carried it, Lord Abbot.' Renaud was blithely unaware of the immense significance of his actions.

'Guillaume de Paris?'

'No, my lord, his escort.'

So the Inquisitor-General had escaped, even though he went empty-handed. With Briac's help Jacques stowed the flat box across his mount, behind the saddle, covering it with a blanket. The shape could not be completely hidden, but the blanket would keep ordinary eyes from prying. While Renaud continued his work, he took his palfrey and rode up the slope to the chapel of the Castle of the Madonna. Briac followed at a distance.

Jacques uncovered the box and carried it into the chapel, feeling a profound, sceptical disgust that so many intelligent men had conspired and fought for it, and that so many dead bodies now lay below him in the valley for the same cause. He would open it now at his leisure and see if it was worth carrying it back to Avignon.

He placed it on a trestle-table just inside the chapel door. Then he opened it again and gazed on his prize. But in the absence of direct sunlight there was no image. He stared at the blank cloth, perplexed.

A strange and disturbing thought which had been forming in his mind since that morning in the crypt suddenly crystallized with stunning force: he had seen this image twice before. Once, on the capital facing San Eusanio's altar, which was hardly surprising since the possessor would doubtless wish to copy it in his private chapel; but more astonishing was his recognition that the same face could be seen on the relief sculpture in the nearby laboratory. If so, then the image that would decide the fate of Christendom was man-made.

This was an even more disturbing thought, given the obsessive desire of so many men to possess it. If it were false, why had it been so convincing? Again, Jacques realized with a clarity which unnerved him, the answer was simplicity itself. He had been searching, dreaming, digging, travelling for months to find the image, preparing himself to receive the impact the sight of it had previously had on so many powerful men. They believed, and were stunned; he had believed, and had been stunned. Nothing was more natural.

The realization of its powers brought warmth to Jacques' heart. He was neither ashamed nor shocked by the deception, for he had always doubted the authenticity of relics. He could perceive the burial shroud just as had done the fingers of John the Baptist months ago with Nicolas in St Jean de Maurienne. Now, as then, it did not matter whether *he* believed. It was the belief of the others which mattered. Now Pietro di Ocre was dead he was sure that he was the only man to know the true secret of Ocre. Somehow, through God knows what alchemical practice, Thomas Berard had managed to transfer the image on the relief to the burial cloth. Perhaps he had heated the relief, coated it with some diabolical concoction, and laid the cloth over it. There could be no other explanation – though even this was unsatisfactory to Jacques' mind. He decided, as soon as he realized this appalling truth, that he would tell no one, not even Nicolas de Lirey. Laboratory and relief must be destroyed at once. No one else would ever know and the secret of Ocre would be his own secret. 'Briac!' he called.

The guard rode quickly to him. 'Sire?'

'There is one last job before you obtain your just reward.'

'My lord?'

'Destroy that secret room and all its contents,' Jacques ordered.

As Briac rode away an odd notion began to gnaw at Abbot Jacques: that the journey begun in Avignon was not near its end, as he had believed only a short while before, but rather at the beginning.

44

Abbot Jacques stepped outside the church with Nicolas. The fields below were now brilliant green with newly sprouted wheat, sprinkled here and there with the yellow of dandelions like sugar thrown onto a cake. The earth had opened with the joy of a new season. Bushes and trees were ripe with fresh green buds. Below them, a solitary almond tree was in gorgeous pink flower. The air was still; no sound broke their concentration. It was as if the events of the past months were part of a bad dream. Nicolas propped himself against the outside wall of the chapel. Jacques sat nearby, beside a finely scented clump of thyme. 'We have it,' he said simply.

'Not bad for a baker's son,' Nicolas commented.

Jacques laughed, for this time there was no contempt in that voice, which had softened so that the same words became a quiet joke between friends. There was admiration and love in Nicolas' words. 'Our task is completed, and we must make haste for Avignon,' Jacques remarked.

'*Your* task is completed. I have yet to restore my family lands.' Nicolas' face screwed up with pain as he spoke, and he shifted himself against the chapel wall. 'But there's not much I can do now, save rest,' he complained.

'Sleep,' Jacques commanded with a gentle voice that reminded him of his own mother. 'Your time will come'. He made the sign of the cross, and touched Nicolas' feverish forehead as the young knight's eyelids began to drop again.

Jacques stared across the valley. He was overwhelmed with remorse for the violence he had used in his quest. The world he had been looking into from the outside with the eyes of Pietro di Ocre was a strange and anachronistic world, but he had been part of it too for some weeks now. He regretted leaving Pietro to die in the prison of Saint Germain, and even felt the same remorse for the three Templar knights who had ridden here in an attempt to save their Order. They had been true knights like Pietro and his uncle, but too weakened through years of inactivity and imprisonment to be a match for Briac and the papal guards. He remembered hearing once about

290

the ritual involved in the interment of Templar knights. They were buried in threes, their bodies forming a tau cross and their heads meeting at the point of the cross. He resolved to order that these three be buried thus, with their cross pointing towards the castle of Ocre. It was the least he could do, and they deserved recognition as much as, if not more than, Bernard de Caen.

Jacques quivered with apprehension as full consciousness came of the fact that he now possessed the secret key to power: that he could aspire to the same heights as Bernard. This recognition stunned him as much as anything he had heard or seen, but it was true. The image was his: no one other than Briac, Renaud and Nicolas knew the whole truth, and they had not seen it; only Nicolas and Briac knew of the laboratory, and the latter could be easily paid off with rewards and honours. Nicolas he trusted totally. With their connivance, there was no limit to what he could do. He had already thwarted King Philip's scheme; he would be able to ensure that the Templars would not rise again, and even to restore confidence in Pope Clement. There was simply no limit. All these people believed in the relic as if it were magical; he too had succumbed when he had seen it, but now he knew that it was a simple piece of cloth, no more sacred than many of the 'relics' in the Sainte Chapelle. The true miracle was that it was so convincing. He recalled how he had laughed at the three fingers of John Baptist on his first journey to Ocre, and how foolish King Philip had appeared to him with his fetish for collecting holy relics. How right he'd been, beyond his wildest imagination.

Yet, he thought with an ironic chuckle, they all believed fervently and were likely to continue to do so. For this image would give them everything; but *he* possessed it. And while they continued to believe, he would be able to do what he liked. The only feasible restraint on his power was that marked by the limits of their credulity, and they seemed infinite. Just as he recognized that all this would have been impossible without the acumen and long-sightedness of his Superior, he now realized that the future would have been even more difficult if Bernard had survived the battle. 'No,' he said aloud to himself, 'now there is no limit.' Nicolas stirred, but did not awake.

In the valley below he saw the dust cloud of horsemen galloping towards San Eusanio. The whole world has been there today, he thought, little caring who these new intruders might be. The battle was won, and he was the victor.

291

Jacques eased himself to the grass near the sleeping figure of Nicolas de Lirey, and watched the distant horsemen. Relaxed for the first time in months, recalling moments of youth on the hillside above Saverdun, he absorbed the surroundings as if in prayer: a lizard transfixed to a rock by late afternoon sunshine; a fluttering white butterfly; fresh bluebells and forget-me-nots; the mountains pinkish; a faint scent of manure on the breeze. And the chimes of vespers echoing across the valley.

EPILOGUE

When Abbot Fournier returned to Avignon in midsummer, he learned that Pope Clement had died while he was in Ocre. The conclave was long and contentious, and Fournier's name was often put forward as a possible candidate. But he realised that he was still young for the Holy See. He stepped aside when a compromise decision was made to elevate the aged Jacques d'Euse, who became Pope John XXII on 7th August 1316. Fournier believed his turn would come soon, and was rewarded when one of Pope John's first actions promoted him to the Bishopric of Pamiers.

Meanwhile, in November 1314, six months after the discovery of the Shroud, Philip the Fair died, a disappointed and broken man, whose dearest project had failed.

Throughout his pontificate, the superstitious John XXII used the services of Bishop Fournier as his closest advisor. The surviving supporters of the Counts of Ocre and Celestine V were declared to be heretical and excommunicated with the Bull *Sancta romana atque universalis Ecclesia*, promulgated on 30 December 1317.

On 20 December 1334, Jacques Fournier was elevated to the Throne of St. Peter as Benedict XII. All traces of the Ocre heresy were removed from official records. Thus Pietro di Ocre ceased to exist. One of the stated objectives of Benedict's pontificate was to move the papacy back to Rome. He did not succeed as a result of the objections of King Philip VI of France, who was thus the instrument of his father's revenge. Shortly before dying, in April 1342, Pope Benedict sent the Image in his possession to the only man who knew its story and could be entrusted with it: Nicolas de Lirey.

Nicolas himself died the following year, and left the case containing the Image of our Lord to his cousin, Godfrey de Charny, a knight in the service of the King of France. When the pious Godfrey discovered the contents of the case, he built a collegiate church to house the Image in his native village of Lirey, a few miles south of Troyes. For two centuries the Shroud remained in the possession of the Lirey–Charny family until it passed into the hands of the Dukes of Savoy. It was housed in the Savoy capital Chambéry until, in 1578, Duke Emmanuel Philibert of Savoy moved it to the cathedral of Turin, where it remains to this day.

HISTORICAL NOTES

1. The Turin Shroud

The facts about the so-called Turin Shroud are now simple. Three independent analyses, using radio-carbon dating, by laboratories in Tucson, Oxford and Zurich, have recently established that it was faked in the Middle Ages. It seems likely that it was made by some process which involved the laying of a cloth over a bas-relief figure in the supposed position of Jesus Christ in his tomb. Like many other good quality stuffs of the time, the material used may well have come from the Holy Land (Tyre or Damascus), thus explaining the presence of eastern pollens discovered in an earlier scientific analysis. The three-dimensional aspect discovered by the photographer Secondo Pia in 1898, and brought out by computer enhancement at NASA, was presumably accidental.

The shroud made its first appearance in history in the possession of Geoffroi de Charny at the tiny village of Lirey, which nestles invisible from nearby roads in a quiet fold in low hills twelve miles south of Troyes, just off the N77 after Bouilly. To house it, de Charny built in that village a wooden collegiate church – now replaced by a simple stone chapel – from 1353 to 1356, the year of his own death. It was first put on public show in Lirey by de Charny or his widow some time between 1356 and 1370. From that moment its history is well-documented: as stated in the epilogue, it remained in the possession of the Lirey-Charny family until it passed into the hands of the Dukes of Savoy, in 1453. It was then housed in Chambéry until 1578, when it was moved to the cathedral of Turin.

However, as early as 1389 Bishop Pierre d'Arcis of Troyes declared it to be a fake in a memorandum written to Pope Clement VII, preserved in the Bibliothèque Nationale in Paris. He described it as 'cunningly painted ... by a clever sleight of hand' and refers to belief in it as 'a delusion and abominable superstition'. On 13 October 1988 his judgement was confirmed when Cardinal Anastasio Ballestrero of Turin formally announced, with papal approval, that radio-carbon dating had shown the cloth on which the image of Christ seems to appear was manufactured between 1260 and 1390.

Thus only three real, and related, problems remain: who made it, where, and in exactly which year?

294

2 (a). Ocre: people

As Pietro di Ocre claims, his family and its power were of very ancient origins: the Berardi family who became Counts of the Marsica and of Ocre were in fact indirect descendents of Charlemagne (742–814) and his grandson, Pippin the Younger, and became feudal lords of the area in around 850. In 860 a Berardo was described as King of Italy and 1st 'Gran Conte dei Marsi'. The family is then mentioned in the *Chronicon Farfense* of 936, and a document of 947 lists their possessions. Berardo, Conte d'Albe (the area near the Roman city of Alba, just south of L'Aquila) seems to have moved to Ocre some time before the 1198 rebuilding of San Eusanio, starting a cadet branch of the family.

Berardo's son Gualtiero (Walter) – father to Pietro di Ocre in the novel – was an extremely interesting and important man. Already in 1220 he was *nelle grazie* of the Emperor Frederick II. Between 1236 and 1244 as Imperial Secretary he made several visits to the court of King Henry III of England at Winchester. His role can be deduced from mentions in Henry's official correspondence: in *Rerum Britannicarum Medii Aevi Scriptores: Royal and other Historical Letters Illustrative of the Reign of Henry III* (London, 1866), e.g. in Vol. I, pp.8–10, pp.467–9, pp.474–5; and in *Diplomatic Documents Preserved in the Public Record Office* (London, 1964), e.g in Vol. I, p.41, p.91, pp.202–3. It was he who negotiated the marriage of Henry's sister Isabelle to Frederick, as we learn in a letter from Woodstock, dated 6 July 1237, in which he is described as 'Magistro Gautero nunciis' (*Treaty Rolls Preserved in the Public Record Office*, London, 1955, p.22), and who gave the order to the Sheriff of Kent to provide 'a good ship to carry the money that the king is sending to the emperor' with Giles Bertaud and Master Walter (5 July 1237: in *Calendar of the Liberate Rolls preserved in the Public Record Office: Henry III* Vol I, London, 1916). He was also responsible for the remarkable letter from Henry III to 'Angelus prior de Aquila' (c.1256/7) offering assistance and money for the building of the new city (in *Diplomatic Documents*, pp.202–3). In 1245 he represented Frederick at the Council of Lyons, two years later became Archbishop of Capua, and from 1249 was 'Gran Cancelliere' to the Emperor until the latter's death a year later. He fulfilled the same role for Frederick's successors Conrad and Manfredi. He died in circa 1262, and his life is given in a small volume by G. Rossi called *Memoriale storico del Gran Cancelliere Gualtiero da Ocra* (Naples, 1829).

The identity of Thomas Berard, the Templar Master of England, and Grand Master of the order (1256–73), has long been mysterious.

But documentary evidence has been provided by Marie Luise Bulst-Thiele in her *Sacrae Domus Militiae Templi Hierosolymitani Magistri: Untersuchungen zur Geschichte des Templerordens 1118/9–1314* (Göttingen, pp.232–3, 1974), and there is no doubt that the Grand Master came from the family of the Counts of Ocre.

His nephew and Gualtiero's son, Pietro di Ocre, whose full name was Francesco Pietro, is referred to as 'magnus Templariorum Magister' in V. Perrot's *Collection historique des Ordres de Chevalerie* (Paris, 1820). Francesco Pietro's brother Tommaso was an early supporter of Pope Celestine, and was named cardinal during the latter's brief pontificate; his life is given by C. Telera in *Histoire Sagre degli huomini illustri per santità della Congregazione de' Celestini dell' Ordine di San Benedetto* (Bologna, 1648).

2 (b). Ocre: places

The sites mentioned in the Abruzzi area connected with the Counts of Ocre may still be seen today. Each of them has a curious history, as strange as that of the family itself. The village of San Eusanio lies about ten miles south-east of L'Aquila, on a minor road which leads under the great shadow of the rock of Ocre. The church of San Eusanio was originally known as St Peter, but in 1198 was reconsecrated by Bishop Odorisio of nearby Forcona – in the words of the document – 'Ad honorem D.N.I.C & sanctae vivificae Crucis, & SS. Apostolorum Petri, & Pauli, & omnium Sanctorum, & ad titulum, & Subjectionem Beati Eusanii', that is, to San Eusanio. At this time the church was in the fief of the Counts of Ocre, and in all likelihood the present facade was added to the ancient church in about 1220. A fragment of facing stone, placed upside down in the left part of the facade, bears the inscription: 'T.Ocratius.SA.D.D.S.F.C.Idem'.

As stated in the text, Pope Innocent IV issued a letter against Gualtiero di Ocre in 1247 in which he is described as 'indignum' or unworthy to hold the living. Sometime in the early fourteenth century the crypt was bricked up, and only reopened in the eighteenth century, when Father Coppola discovered it. He published his findings, together with the text of the *Passio Sancti Eusanii Confessoris* (discovered in 1664) in his volume *Lo Scoprimento del corpo di San Eusanio* (L'Aquila, 1749). Today the interior is disappointingly eighteenth century and uninteresting, although, as I write, restoration is under way. But the facade still retains its mystery and great age; the crypt also still retains its mystery; a strange, damp and slightly unnerving place with the bones of San Eusanio under the altar and the bricked-up doorway to the right. On the outside of the Romanesque apse there are some interesting magical symbols. A modern fountain stands in front of the church where Brother Jacques sees the shepherds.

Standing at the door of San Eusanio and looking right at forty-five degrees, just as Jacques did, one can see the Castle of the Madonna on its hill. The castle is now in worse repair, but the small chapel is still kept clean and used for the annual procession in June, when a statue of the Madonna kept in San Eusanio is carried up on the shoulders of local men. Since the fourteenth century the River Aterno has changed its course – as several now almost-disused bridges testify – and the stream beneath the hill runs in a small ditch.

To the left, one can imagine Jacques' view – now spoiled by a later building – of the monastery of Santo Spirito. The modern road up to the monastery, recently asphalted, follows the track used by Brother Jacques and Nicolas de Lirey. The monastery was founded in 1222 by Count Berardo for a hermit, Beato Placido, then living in a cave in the rocks under the castle. It later passed to the Cistercians, and was in fact under the rule of the now ruined monastery of Casanova on the slopes of the Gran Sasso d'Italia until 1310. It was closed and deconsecrated by a bull of Pope Innocent X, promulgated on 15 October 1652, as the result of unspecified heretical practices. For centuries it was left to decay. In the early 1980s a curious external room contained the remains of skeletons presumed burned by the Inquisition. Until four years ago it was the object of pilgrimage for local occultists: tombs were broken into (it was used as a cemetery until the Second World War) for corpses, and signs of black magic practices were frequent (the altar was smashed up for pieces to use elsewhere for altars, and fresh chicken's blood used in ceremonies). There is a curious fresco which can be seen as a representation of the Assumption of the Virgin or as the Devil, according to the angle of vision. Still today an aura of strangeness persists, and local people speak of the monastery with awe. Recently it has been restored, and was intended to become a school for restorers; but nothing has yet come of it.

The spectacular ruins of the Castle of Ocre still dominate the valley of the River Aterno. It stands on the site of an ancient necropolis belonging to the ancient city of Aveia, down in the valley, which in Roman times became known as Forcona and was ruled by the governor Prisco who imprisoned San Eusanio. Originally a double enceinte castle, 'cassari castrum', only half the original building remains, and with a single wall. It is worth the climb for marvellous views across the valley to the Gran Sasso mountain range, which reaches 10,000 feet in height. The castle is privately owned; visitors and occultists breaking in have been the bane of the owners for years. But the quarters of the Counts of Ocre were razed to the ground in 1280 by the people of the new city of L'Aquila. The fourteenth-century chronicler Buccio di Ranallo, who wrote a rhyming chronicle of the history of L'Aquila from 1254 to 1362 at the end of that period, noted:

'Multe castella strussero, non se porria cuntare:
Ocra et Castelluni fecero derupare;
Nulla grande fortelleza ce volsero lassare'

in *Cronaca Aquilana rimata di Buccio di Ranallo*, edited by V. di Bartholomaeis (Rome, 1907, p.20). Half the castle was rebuilt in 1448–9, and continued to be used until the early seventeenth century. It contained very fine thirteenth-century frescoes, some of which have lately been removed and installed in the Museo Nazionale in the sixteenth-century Spanish castle in L'Aquila. Their high quality is eloquent testimony to the power of the owners of the castle.

The construction of the city of L'Aquila itself was begun in 1254, when Nicolas de Sinizzo – an ex-monk at Santo Spirito and later bishop of the new city – persuaded Pope Alexander IV to ask the Emperor Conrad to found the city. It became a bishopric in 1257, the same year as Henry III of England's letter. In 1259 it was destroyed by Conrad's successor, Manfredi, as a result of the city's sympathy towards Henry III – who had been promised the Kingdom of Sicily in return for his support, thus becoming an enemy of Manfredi. In 1265 rebuilding started, supervised by Sinizzo, who was bishop from 1267 to 1294. In 1294 Celestine V was crowned inside the magnificent basilica of Santa Maria di Collemaggio (founded by him and financed by the Counts of Ocre) where his tomb may still be seen. The most interesting of many histories of L'Aquila from this point of view are Carlo Franchi's *Difesa per la Fedelissima Città dell'Aquila* (Naples, 1752); and G. Equizi's *Storia dell'Aquila e della sua diocesi* (Turin, 1957).